THE
GOOD SPY

JEFFREY
LAYTON

PINNACLE BOOKS
Kensington Publishing Corp.
www.kensingtonbooks.com

PINNACLE BOOKS are published by

Kensington Publishing Corp.
119 West 40th Street
New York, NY 10018

All Kensington titles, imprints, and distributed lines are available at special quantity discounts for bulk purchases for sales promotions, premiums, fund-raising, educational, or institutional use. Special book excerpts or customized printings can also be created to fit specific needs. For details, write or phone the office of the Kensington sales manager: Kensington Publishing Corp., 119 West 40th Street, New York, NY 10018, attn: Sales Department; phone 1-800-221-2647.

ISBN-13: 978-0-7860-3713-1
ISBN-10: 0-7860-3713-X

First printing: March 2016

10 9 8 7 6 5 4 3 2 1

Printed in the United States of America

First electronic edition: March 2016

ISBN-13: 978-0-7860-3714-8
ISBN-10: 0-7860-3714-8

To my wife, Meta

CHAPTER 1

DAY 2—TUESDAY

Kirov plowed into the gloom. The firestorm deep inside his right shoulder raged but he hung on. He'd lost all sensation below the left knee—it was just dead meat. If the unfeeling crept into his other limbs he was doomed for sure.

He focused on the captain's orders: "Get to shore. Call for help and then coordinate the rescue. Don't get caught!"

He was the crew's only hope. If he failed, they would all perish.

The diver propulsion vehicle surged against the aggressive tidal current. As he gripped the DPV's control handles with both gloved hands, his body trailed prone on the sea surface. Hours earlier he'd exhausted the mixed gas supply, which forced him topside where he used a snorkel to breathe.

The chilled seawater defeated his synthetic rubber armor. His teeth chattered against the snorkel's mouthpiece. He clamped his jaws to maintain the watertight seal.

Shore lights shimmered through his face mask but he remained miles from his destination. The DPV's battery gauge kissed the warning range. When it eventually petered out, he would have to transit the passage on his own, somehow swimming the expanse in the dark while combating the current.

Two grueling hours passed. He abandoned the spent DPV, opening the flood valve and allowing it to sink. He butted the tidal flow until it turned. The flooding current carried him northward.

He swam facedown while still breathing through the snorkel. As he pumped his lower limbs, his good leg overpowered its anesthetized twin, forcing him off course. He soon learned to compensate with his left arm, synchronizing its strokes with his right leg.

The joint pain expanded to include both shoulders and elbows. The frigid sea sapped his vigor to near exhaustion.

While staring downward into the pitch-black abyss, he tried not to dwell on his injuries or his weariness— or the absolute isolation, knowing he could do nothing to mitigate them. Instead, his thoughts converged on the mission. *They're counting on me. Don't give up. I can do this; just keep moving.*

He continued swimming, monitoring his course with the compass strapped to his right wrist. An evolving mantle of fog doused the shore lights he'd been using as a homing beacon. For all he knew, the current could be shoving him into deeper waters.

Maybe at dawn he would be able to get his bearings. Until then, he would plod along.

I wonder where the blackfish are now.

During a rest with fins down and a fresh bubble of

air in his buoyancy compensator, he heard dozens of watery eruptions breach the night air as a pod of *Orcinus orcas* made its approach. Sounding like a chorus of steam engines, the mammals cleared blowholes and sucked air into their mammoth lungs. The sea beasts ghosted by at ten knots. Their slick coal-black hulls spotted with white smears passed just a few meters away from his stationary position.

The killer whales ignored him. They had a mission of their own: pursuing the plump inbound silver and chum salmon that loitered near the tip of the approaching peninsula. At first light, the orcas would gorge themselves.

There was no time to be afraid; instead, he marveled at the close encounter. Oddly, the whales' brief presence calmed him. He was not alone in these alien waters after all.

Time for another check.

He stopped kicking and raised his head. He peered forward.

Dammit!

Still no lights and the fog bank oozed even closer.

Where is it?

He allowed his legs to sink as he mulled his options. His right fin struck something.

He swam ahead for half a minute and repeated the sounding.

I made it!

CHAPTER 2

Laura Newman sat on the tile floor with her long chocolate legs bent sharply at the knees and her spine propped against a cabinet. She wore only a plain white T-shirt.

Laura cradled her abdomen with both hands; her stomach broiled. "Oh Lord," she moaned. "What's wrong with me?"

It was 6:18 A.M. Jolted awake, she'd just made it to the bathroom before the first purge.

Ten minutes elapsed. Feeling better, Laura stood and walked back into the bedroom. She slipped on a bathrobe. Knowing further sleep would be impossible, she decided to brew a cup of tea. If her stomach settled down, she'd jog along the beach after sunup.

This was the third morning her unsettled tummy had roused her. She suspected stress. The demands from work never ceased, but she'd learned to live with it.

Laura opened the bedroom door and walked down the second-floor hallway of the rented beach house. She flipped on a light switch, illuminating the stairway. When she reached the base of the stairs, her bare feet stepped into a pool of water that covered oak flooring. *What*'s *this?* Laura wondered.

She took a few more steps on her way to the kitchen.

Laura stood opposite a doorway that opened onto a concrete walkway; it led to the beach. Although the side door remained closed, the door frame's splintered molding by the lock had not been that way when she went to bed.

Laura's muscles locked; her heart galloped.

Oh God, no! He's found me already.

Laura recovered enough to sidestep her dread. *I've got to get out of here.*

Laura was reaching for the side door's handle, when she heard movement from behind. She started to turn when a damp, gloved hand clutched her mouth. An arm ensnared her waist.

Laura shrieked but her muffled cries went nowhere.

CHAPTER 3

"Stop struggling or I'll cut you!"

Pinned by the intruder's bulk on the hardwood flooring, Laura complied when she felt the knife tip on her throat.

He sensed her capitulation and withdrew the blade. He rolled off Laura onto his knees but kept his eyes on her. He stood. The blade remained in his right hand.

"Get up," he ordered, offering his free hand as an assist.

Sunlight poured through the waterside windows. Laura sat in the dining room chair, still wearing the bathrobe. Gray duct tape anchored her wrists and ankles to the chair. The intruder was in the adjoining living room. He'd just built a fire in the stone fireplace. The cedar kindling crackled to life.

Laura observed her captor. Standing at least an inch over six feet, he had a muscular build, slate-gray eyes, and dense jet-black hair cut short. His angular face sprouted several days' worth of black stubble. She guessed his age around her own—early thirties.

Laura watched as he shed the diving apparel. He piled the gear onto the hardwood floor next to a window. He wore cobalt-blue coveralls under his neoprene dry suit.

Obviously injured, he favored his left leg as he moved about. He hobbled into the dining room.

That's when Laura decided to confront him.

"What do you want?" she demanded.

"Just stay quiet."

"Who are you?"

"No one."

"Where did you come from?"

"Stop asking questions."

"Why were you in diving gear?"

More tape secured a dishcloth he'd stuffed inside Laura's mouth. It encircled her head in two orbits, restraining her shoulder-length auburn hair. If she turned too far, hair at the nape of her neck pulled viciously. She had to sit statue-stiff, peering at a blank wall.

But she could still see him—out of the corner of her left eye.

Laura's captor was about twenty feet away on the sofa by the fireplace. After a thirty-minute catnap, he sat upright and stretched his arms. He picked up her smartphone from the coffee table. He must have discovered it on the nightstand in her bedroom. There were no other working telephones in the rental.

He keyed the phone, studying the screen. Laura

guessed he was running a search. A couple of minutes later, he dialed.

"I'd like to speak with the security officer," he said.

There was a trace accent but Laura couldn't place it.

He was mute for a minute before responding, "Yes, I want to report an accident."

The call lasted ten minutes. None of what he said made any sense to Laura. Some doctor had been in an automobile accident and was in a Seattle hospital. And he'd asked for a "security officer." What was that about?

The intruder nodded off again, his head slumping forward.

What is this jerk up to?

It was almost noon. Laura's spine ached and her limbs cramped, but her bladder demanded relief. She couldn't hold it much longer.

"Heyyyy!" she blurted in spite of the gag.

His eyes blinked open.

She called out again, louder.

He stood and shuffled toward her.

"What is it?" he asked. Now his accent sounded Eastern European.

Laura mumbled.

He leaned forward and pulled down a section of tape covering her mouth.

She spat out the dishcloth and met his eyes. "Please—I need to use the bathroom." Her frail voice transmitted a palpable quaver.

"Bathroom?"

She gestured with her head, ripping half a dozen strands of hair anchored by tape.

He spotted the open door near the base of the stairs. "Oh, you need to use the toilet."

"Yes, please."

He replaced the gag and then limped to the bathroom. After inspecting its interior, he returned to Laura where he withdrew his dive knife from a scabbard lying on the nearby coffee table. He sliced the tape that anchored her arms and legs to the chair. She stood as quickly as her cramped muscles would allow.

With the knife still in his right hand he said, "You can use it but the door stays open. And don't touch the window."

Laura nodded her understanding and made a beeline for the bathroom. He followed.

She walked inside, immune to the embarrassment. Laura was thankful to be alive.

CHAPTER 4

"Aloha," he said, speaking into the cell phone. "I'd like Laura Newman's room.

"That's right, Laura Newman. From Redmond . . . Washington State.

"Hmm, she's not registered . . . you know, she might be using her maiden name, Laura Lynn Wilson. Could you check that for me?"

Half a minute passed. "No luck there, either. Well, I guess I got some bum info. Thanks."

Ken Newman had already called fourteen hotel and condominium resorts on Kauai, and as on his last call, he'd failed. There were nearly twenty more to go.

He'd searched the Web for an hour, compiling a list of candidates. He concentrated on four- and five-star establishments; he knew his wife's preferences. He would check the remaining resorts but didn't expect the effort to yield anything.

Ken called from his Spartan studio apartment in Bellevue, sitting at the kitchen table. Dirty dishes overfilled the sink, sports magazines and newspapers littered the coffee table, and a two-foot-high pile of soiled clothing occupied a corner by the window. They'd been living apart for four months. The previous morning a King County sheriff's deputy had served him with the breakup papers and a temporary restraining order.

But Ken wasn't done.

Laura had changed cell phones so he'd called her secretary this morning, ignoring the no contact order. Ken learned that Laura had flown to Kauai for a two-week vacation. He had no reason to doubt the secretary's storyline but remained suspicious.

Ken retrieved a coffee mug from the table. As he sipped, he planned.

Tonight he would drive to Sea-Tac and cruise the huge parking garage's aisles. If Laura had parked her silver BMW 7 Series at the airport, he'd know that she'd fled. If he didn't find it, she might still be around.

"Why are you doing this to me?" Laura asked.

"Just cooperate and you'll be fine."

Laura again sat in the dining room chair, her wrists and ankles re-taped to the chair's mahogany armrests and legs. An eight-place black marble table occupied the room. The view of the beach and the water's edge— just steps away—was dazzling.

Sweat beaded across Laura's brow. Her captor stood at her side, a half-full water glass in hand. She leaned forward and took another gulp, draining the glass.

Her thirst satisfied, she said, "Thank you."

He was about to reseal her mouth when Laura turned her head to the side. "Please, don't gag me. My stomach's bothering me; I might vomit."

"All right, for now I won't but keep quiet. I need to rest."

"I will—I promise."

Laura watched as he made his way back to the connecting living room; his limp had worsened. He lay down on the sofa facing the fireplace. Searing heat radiated from the fresh charge of fuel.

He'd turned up the home's gas furnace to maximum, too, roasting Laura.

What's wrong with him?

He hobbled onto the timber deck, dragging his useless lower left leg. The mid-afternoon sky was cloudless, allowing the sun to bathe his body; it had been weeks since he'd last felt its touch.

Water lapped at the rock revetment fronting the home. In the distance, a mammoth ship steamed northward, its decks overflowing with hundreds of shipping containers.

Although no longer chilled to his marrow, he remained unpleasantly cool. A wool blanket from a bedroom encased his shoulders and upper torso. He also shed the jumpsuit, replacing it with the civilian clothing he'd carried during the ascent. The waterproof bag leaked, soaking the blue jeans, black long sleeve shirt, running shoes, and other gear. He discovered the home's laundry room, where he washed and dried the garments.

He unconsciously shook his head, still amazed that he had survived. It could have been much worse. The bends could have just as easily killed him, or he could have succumbed to hypothermia.

Why had God spared him?

His mother had sparked his early belief, but her guidance ceased after his twelfth birthday and his faith withered. Nevertheless, his impermeable armor of disregard now had a couple of chinks in it. Surviving the sinking came first. His solo escape followed.

He again wondered why he was alive when so many others were not.

His thoughts dissolved as something caught his eye far in the distance. The floatplane cruised northward up the inland sea, about two hundred meters above the water. He couldn't help but think that it probably passed right over the *Neva*.

Seven nautical miles to the southeast and over seven hundred feet below the surface, the *Neva*'s crew was oblivious to the Kenmore Air charter. The beat of the Beaver's propeller penetrated the water but never reached the stranded submarine.

Underwater sounds rarely travel in a straight line. Instead, they refract or bend due to varying temperature, salinity, and pressure. On this afternoon, the only sounds that the *Neva*'s passive sonar sensors registered were biologics.

The thirty-four-year-old slightly balding and fleshy engineering officer left the central command post and entered the sonar room. Catapulted to acting-captain status nearly forty hours earlier, he hoped for good news.

"Anything new?" he asked the sole inhabitant of the compartment. Packed with electronic gear from the deck to the overhead, the space contained three consoles.

"No, Captain," said the technician, a man in his early twenties sitting in the center console.

They spoke in their native tongue—Russian.

The tech removed his earphones and flipped a switch on his console, activating a bulkhead speaker. The sound of bacon sizzling on a grill broadcast throughout the compartment. "Still the same biologic we've had all day long—fornicating shrimp."

"Anything else?"

"I did pick up a ship's propeller. Merchantmen most likely headed to Vancouver."

"How about small vessels?"

"No, sir, nothing like that. In our degraded condition, they would need to be close by for our remaining sensors to register."

The commanding officer nodded. He'd anticipated something more encouraging. The diver should have made it to the shore by now. Still, it was early.

"Captain, how's the scrubber repair going?"

"It's working again. CO-two is stabilized."

"Good . . . that's good." The sonar tech scratched the stubble on his chin. "And the reactors?"

"We're still bailing out muck. We might be able to test a heat exchanger in a few hours. Once circulation is reestablished, we should be able to restart Unit Two."

"That will help a lot."

"Yes, it will."

Neither man wanted to ask the ultimate "what if" question: What if they couldn't restart the reactor?

Programmed to prevent a core meltdown, the computer controlling the reactor would automatically squash the chain reaction if the coolant system were not adequate. Without the heat generated by the fission process, there would be no steam. Without steam, the generator would not turn. Without the generator, there would be no electrical current to run the ship's oxygen maker. And without fresh oxygen, they would all die.

CHAPTER 5

Laura and her captor sat at the kitchen table, facing each other. They sipped tea from mugs, having just finished dinner—scrambled eggs and fried potatoes that he'd prepared.

Although Laura's hands were free, her ankles remained bound. But she no longer sweltered; he had dialed back the furnace and the fireplace.

Laura had read somewhere that establishing a personal relationship with a captor helped in hostage situations. She decided to test the theory.

"My name is Laura. May I ask yours?"

He took a sip of tea. "John."

"Your leg, it looks like you really injured it. Do you need help with it?"

"It's fine."

"I live in Redmond; I'm just renting this place."

No response.

Laura racked her brain to formulate another question that would not alienate him. Her demands during their initial encounter had resulted in the gag.

"I'm a software engineer," she offered.

"You write programs?"

"Sometimes, but others in my company write most of the code. My job is to coordinate and assemble the software we develop."

"John" leaned back in his chair and said, "You're a manager?"

"I am."

"How many do you supervise?"

"There are about six hundred programmers and engineers in my division."

He returned his chair to its normal position and cocked his head to the side. "You own this company?"

"I'm one of four principals. We have just over two thousand employees."

"What software do you write?"

"Mostly business applications with some science-based work."

He said, "You must make a lot of money."

"I do well."

"Were you raised in Seattle?"

"No. The Bay Area."

His brow wrinkled.

"You know, San Francisco Bay."

"Oh, yes."

"I grew up east of the bay in a city called Castro Valley."

"Ah, you're a California girl."

"I was."

"Tell me about your parents."

Laura expected the inquiry. It always came up with someone new. "I was adopted as an infant. My birth mother was Caucasian; my birth father was African American. I've never met them."

"Your parents—who adopted you—white or black?"

"Caucasian."

"What was it like for you growing up, with your father's blood?"

He was direct, if anything.

"Great. No real problems."

Laura skirted the truth, not wanting to revisit past hurts.

"Where did you receive your university education?"

"Caltech—California Institute of Technology."

"Oh, I know that school." He shifted position in his chair. "How did you end up in the software business?"

"Well, assembling computer code is like solving a puzzle. I've always enjoyed working on things that make you think. You know, like chess and math games and . . ."

Laura and John continued their dialogue. She had just mentioned her soon-to-be ex.

"You came here to get away from him?"

"Yes, my attorney served him with the divorce papers on Monday."

"He doesn't know you are here?"

"Absolutely not. Even my office doesn't know I'm here."

Laura regretted her last statement, knowing she'd revealed too much. "My attorney knows where I am; we've been communicating daily." True to a point. She'd received one e-mail from her Seattle lawyer verifying Ken had received the court filings.

Laura folded back the bathrobe from her right shoulder and pulled up the sleeve of her T-shirt, revealing a nasty bruise. "He's vicious when he drinks. He hit me a couple of weeks ago. But never again."

"The man is a pig. He should be in jail."

"I just want him out of my life."

Laura sat on the couch in the living room, her wrists tied in front and her ankles still bound.

Laura's captor worked at the dining room table; "John" had been at it for over an hour. Electronic parts harvested from a living room AM /FM stereo receiver covered the tabletop. A stainless steel pressure cooker and a telephone handset completed the parts collection, both taken from a locked cabinet in the pantry that he had pried open with his knife. The cabinet contained personal items of the homeowner.

Laura had been tempted to ask what he was doing but refrained, believing the less she knew the better off she'd be.

Since their initial encounter with the knife, there had been no additional threats and he hadn't touched her, except for the restraints. Even so, Laura remained wary. He could turn on her.

Still she had hope, sparked by their dinner conversation. His interest in her background came across as genuine. He asked additional questions about her birth parents, but Laura simply repeated that she'd never met them—truthful yet evasive. She had a complete file on her birth parents.

Just remain calm, Laura self-ordered. *I can get through this. He's going to slip up sometime and I'll escape.*

Captain Lieutenant Yuri Kirov looked up from the worktable to check his prisoner. She remained on the sofa about twenty feet away. He had used rope from the garage to bind her this evening. He'd exhausted most of the roll of duct tape that he'd discovered earlier in a kitchen drawer.

Yuri watched as she leaned against the sofa cushion, eyes shut.

Despite her tousled hair, lack of makeup, and the unpretentious bathrobe, Yuri found Laura Newman alluring—an exotic blend of Scandinavia and equatorial Africa.

Laura had inherited her Nordic birth mother's high cheekbones, full ripe lips, azure eyes, and russet hair. Her father's tall willowy frame, broad nose, and cocoa skin, all linked to his distant Bantu ancestors, complimented her mother's genes.

Yuri wondered what it was like for Laura growing up chocolate in a black and white world. In Russia, biracial children often had a tough life. Maybe it was easier in the USA.

He considered asking more questions about her family but thought better of it. He could not afford personal involvement. Laura represented a liability that he might be forced to eliminate for the sake of his submates.

Yuri turned back to the table and picked up one of the speakers. He inserted the woofer inside the pressure cooker and ran the connecting wire from the speaker through the relief valve opening in the lid. He set the lid on the pan and rotated it, engaging the rack-and-pinion lock mechanism.

Perfect!

CHAPTER 6

DAY 3—WEDNESDAY

The nearly full moon illuminated the vast inland waterway for miles, its surface silky smooth this early morning.

Yuri Kirov sat at the aft end of an aluminum skiff, guiding it southward. He had swiped the boat and its trailer from the yard of a neighboring beach house. It was early November and the owner, like those of most of the other homes along the seashore, had departed for the season.

Before locking out from the *Neva*, he'd memorized the bottom coordinates from the sub's inertial navigation system. Using the GPS unit in Laura's iPhone, he retraced his path. Yuri glanced at the digital display of the smartphone. He cut the outboard engine.

Yuri lowered the device into the water. It was an odd creation consisting of a kitchen pressure cooker filled with stereo radio components connected to an extension cord.

Yuri submerged the contraption just three meters. Any deeper and the seals he'd fashioned might fail. If the gadget flooded, his efforts would have been for nothing.

It took five minutes to connect the additional gear. He used the battery from Laura's BMW to energize the system. He'd discovered the sedan in the garage.

Yuri checked his wristwatch: 12:59 A.M. It was time. They should be listening. But what if it didn't work? What then?

He ignored his doubts and pressed the Transmit switch on the makeshift microphone—a hybrid constructed from the telephone handset he'd found. He spoke in English, using a pre-arranged code: "Alpha to Bravo, testing, one two three."

The hydrophone broadcast into the deep. His voice propagated downward at over fifteen hundred meters per second. He repeated the call eight times at fifteen-second intervals.

Four minutes after the first transmission, a black one-meter-diameter globe surged to the surface in a flurry of bubbles.

Laura peeked through the curtains, searching for movement on the dimly lit beach below.

Her captor left two hours earlier. Instead of binding her to a dining room chair, he'd used an upholstered chair in the upstairs master bedroom. He lashed her wrists and ankles to the chair's frame with rope.

She could move just enough to maintain circulation in her limbs but not enough to loosen the bounds. For the present, she'd given up trying to escape.

John hadn't bothered with a gag. Instead, a single layer

of duct tape sealed her lips. She could grunt muted words but nothing coherent. Even if she could have screamed full throttle, no one was around to hear. He'd made that point to her more than once.

Before heading downstairs, he'd informed Laura that he would be gone for several hours. She had no choice but to wait for his return.

From her second-story perch, Laura could see the moonlit beach through a narrow gap in the draperies. She'd watched him struggle to drag the twelve-foot skiff onto the beach; the man had only one good leg. He launched the runabout and motored into the darkness.

Laura wondered what he was up to, and why was he doing it in the middle of the night?

As Laura sat, occasionally peering through the window, she thought of her husband. He was up to something, too. *But what?*

Laura feared Ken as much as she feared her captor, maybe more. Just two weeks earlier, he had shown up at Laura's house unannounced. Reeking of whiskey, Ken knocked Laura to the floor and attacked her with his size 11 Florsheims. He fled before the cops arrived.

Laura vowed that he would never touch her again.

As she peeked through the curtain, Laura again wondered about her captor.

Where did he go?

"Can you hear me?" asked Yuri Kirov.

"Yes, your signal is five-by-five."

"Five-by-five here, too."

Yuri grinned. Direct voice communication had been

his goal. He'd just accomplished that task—speaking with the submarine's acting commanding officer, Captain Third Rank Stephan Borodin.

The *Neva* bristled with high-tech communication devices, but to use them required the submarine to be under way, not marooned on the bottom.

After signaling with his makeshift hydrophone, requesting deployment of the very low frequency radio antenna buoy, Yuri connected with his shipmates. He accomplished that task by coupling a pair of wires he'd harvested from the stereo set to the buoy's cable; he cut through the armored outer sheath and spliced the wires to an internal VLF radio receiving circuit. He attached the other end of the stereo wires to the telephone handset—now disconnected from the hydrophone. After the *Neva*'s communication officer energized the cable, Yuri could speak with Borodin. It was a crude arrangement but it worked.

"Are the reactors still offline?" Yuri asked.

"Yes. We're still fighting that damn muck. It's as if we sucked in half of the bottom."

"What about the batteries?"

"Bad. We've got everything powered down, except the radio compartment."

Yuri knew what that meant: no lights, no heat, and foul air.

Borodin continued, "We've got enough battery power left for a restart. But if that fails, we'll be *profukat'*." Down the toilet.

"You're still working on the seawater intakes, right?"

"Of course. Dima and his boys are mining that crud as we speak. Unit One is hopeless. But if we can unplug a condenser, we'll be able to fire up Unit Two."

"Okay, I understand." Yuri chose his next words with care. "I'm working on getting us help, but it's going to take a little time."

He included himself by using the word *us*, even though he'd escaped from the underwater tomb.

"What kind of help?"

"I've made contact with our embassy in Washington."

"They can't do anything. Or won't, once they know what happened."

"I won't reveal everything. Only what they need to know."

"I don't know about that. According to our orders we're supposed to be dead."

"That's only if we were caught, but the Americans and Canadians are in the dark."

"What can the embassy do anyway?"

"I don't have any answers for you yet. It's going to take awhile to sort out."

Yuri refrained from informing Borodin that he'd yet to talk with anyone that could offer help. His cryptic call to the embassy represented a first step in a convoluted and risky process of informing his superiors of the *Neva*'s fate.

As a military intelligence officer, Yuri had been schooled in the "dos and don'ts" of operating in North America. Use of the telephone was discouraged. The FBI routinely monitored phone calls to and from the Russian embassy and its consulates. The Royal Canadian Mounted Police scrutinized Russian Federation facilities in Canada. The RCMP was meticulous about that.

When he'd called the embassy, he masqueraded as a U.S. citizen and deliberately spoke in English. An

American who used Russian would draw the FBI's instant attention.

"Why are you even bothering with the embassy?" Borodin asked. "I thought you were going to make contact with Petro first."

"The satphone didn't survive the ascent and I can't risk an unsecure call to the base. The Americans could intercept it."

"Govnó!" Shit.

The U.S. National Security Agency monitored virtually every telephone call, fax, e-mail, text, and tweet into or out of the Russian Federation. Trafficking of fissile materials from Russia's not so secure nuclear installations petrified the White House. An audit earlier in the year revealed that fifty-five kilograms of weapons-grade uranium had vanished from a nuclear weapons storage facility at Snezhinsk. Al Qaida, the Islamic State, and other terrorists had standing offers of millions for any loose nukes.

That's why Yuri had to be so careful. Just one slipup could forever condemn his surviving shipmates to the deep.

"What about a surface escape if we run out of time?" Captain Borodin asked.

"You're too deep. I barely made it with my own equipment."

Yuri did not mention his bout with decompression sickness and his paralyzed leg. It would only make matters worse. Because of his extended bottom time, it had taken longer than planned to make his rise—but it hadn't been long enough to purge all of the helium from his body.

Trained in deep-diving techniques, Yuri had employed a heliox rebreather system to install and monitor seafloor-based espionage equipment—and to escape. Only Yuri and one other member of the crew had access to the equipment.

"So the Hydro Suits are still out," Borodin said.

"I'm sorry—a decompression stop is an absolute must at the *Neva*'s depth."

Like all military submarines, the *Neva* was equipped with individual dive gear that would allow the crew to escape in an emergency. The *Neva* relied on the recently deployed Hydro Suit, which would rocket a sailor to the surface inside a bubble of compressed air.

Borodin said, "If we can't swim out on our own, you remain our only hope."

"I'm afraid so."

"Well then, my friend, please hurry. We're running out of time down here."

Laura used her upper-body mass to rock the chair from side to side while at the same time leaning forward against the restraints. She was halfway across the bedroom. Her goal was the mirror on the vanity. She'd smash it and use a glass shard to slice away her bounds.

Laura managed to track another foot when she shifted her torso a little too much. The chair teetered on two legs before tipping onto its left side. Laura's head slammed onto the floor.

In spite of the carpet, the impact sent her reeling.

Laura recovered her senses after several minutes and tried righting the heavy chair. She managed to spin in place.

Now what do I do?

Laura's stomach flip-flopped.

Acknowledging defeat, she felt tears well up and nausea caught in her throat. Now he would know that she'd tried to escape.

She closed her eyes and swallowed the bile. With her mouth sealed by tape she feared what might happen if her queasy stomach erupted.

CHAPTER 7

Two men met on the top floor of a mammoth building in Moscow's Arbatskaya Square. It was mid-afternoon. They sat facing each other in an office that could have accommodated an infantry platoon at full parade rest. The tall, silver-haired man behind the enormous desk had in fact started his distinguished military career as an infantry junior lieutenant in the Red Army. Some forty years later, he had ascended to its highest rank, Marshall of the Russian Federation. Appointed minister of defense eight months earlier, Ivan Volkov now commanded all Russian military forces.

Minister Volkov's guest served as the chief of the Main Intelligence Directorate of the General Staff of the Armed Forces of the Russian Federation. Cue ball bald and portly, General Rybin ruled over Russia's military intelligence service, the *Glavnoye Razvedovatel'noye Upravlenie*, aka the GRU.

Both men drank coffee imported from the USA. The pleasantries were over.

"What's so urgent?" asked the minister as he set his

mug back on the desktop. He retained his flat belly despite the years. "Is it about this *Deep Blue* business?"

Deep Blue was an American Japanese naval war game under way in the western Pacific offshore of Russia's Southern Kuril Islands. Two U.S. Navy carrier strike groups were in play.

"No, sir," the GRU general said, "it's not Deep Blue—something else, a troubling puzzle."

Minister Volkov tilted his head to the side.

"It started yesterday . . . originated from Washington Station's security office. Apparently, the embassy received a rather peculiar phone call from . . ."

General Rybin spent the next few minutes summarizing the coded cable traffic sent to the GRU's Fifth Directorate. He got to the real news.

"The accident victim's connection to this so-called Vega Institute in Saint Petersburg was what first raised Washington Station's interest."

Volkov shifted in his chair. The reference to Vega had his complete attention, too. *Vega* was a code word for a Russian espionage operation designed to collect intelligence on the perceived plan of the United States to neutralize Russia as a military rival. Russia's bullying of Ukraine and other neighbors had chilled relations with the West, especially the United States.

Rybin continued. "When we ran the embassy's request through our data banks, that's when the real mystery developed. We entered the crucial word groups from the cable—Tomich, Gromeko, Kirov—and then let the computers chew on it for a while."

The GRU general removed a document from a file folder he held in his lap. "This is what the computer spat out." He handed the report to his boss.

Minster Volkov scanned the three-page document. When finished he said, "This can't be right—it must be a coincidence."

"That was my first reaction as well but I had my staff analyze it. They tell me it's possible."

Volkov uttered a curse while reaching for the phone.

Eleven time zones away, Yuri Kirov stood in the doorway of the master bedroom. It was a few minutes past three in the morning. Laura Newman lay on the floor, still lashed to the sideway chair. Her gag remained intact. Exhausted, she slept.

Yuri stepped inside and knelt by the chair. Laura woke, her eyes seemingly expanding to the size of saucers.

With one hand gripping the top of the chair back and the other cupping Laura's shoulder, he rotated the chair until it was upright.

Yuri spent a minute checking her bindings and then left, closing the door.

Too wired to sleep, Yuri retreated to the kitchen where he enjoyed a cup of tea.

Standing by a window that overlooked the still dark beach, he sipped from a mug while considering his tactical situation.

She had tried to free herself.

If she escaped, it wouldn't be long before the authorities captured him. That would mean the end for his shipmates.

One thrust from his dive knife would end the threat.

No, he wasn't ready for that—at least not yet.

* * *

Defense Minister Volkov and GRU Chief Rybin re-convened their meeting in the minister's office, now late afternoon. The Navy's top officer joined them.

"What do you make of this, Pavel?" asked Volkov.

Admiral of the Fleet Mayakovsky looked up from the GRU report. "Sir, this is most unusual. I'm at a loss for an explanation."

"But could there be something to it? The report says the names fit the Anaconda profile. It can't be coincidence." *Anaconda* was a code name.

The sixty-two-year-old naval officer fidgeted in his chair. Tallest of the three, he was plagued by residual pain from a lumbar injury aboard a ship two decades earlier. "Pacific Fleet headquarters briefed me after you called. We've had no direct communication with the submarine for over ten days. That's a concern but it's not unusual, especially for the type of mission it's on. Sometimes they'll go ten, twelve days without checking in."

"So what is Anaconda?" asked Minister Volkov.

"Retrieval and surveillance mission for the Fleet Intelligence Directorate. The boat assigned to this duty is home-ported at Petropavlovsk-Kamchatskiy." Although Anaconda was a GRU mission, operational control of the submarine remained with the Pacific Fleet.

"Retrieval of what?"

"The *Neva*'s primary mission was to recover the acoustic recording units and replace them with new ones."

"For that missile sub base they have . . . what's it called?"

"Bangor. It's near Seattle. The recorders are located in the waterway that their subs pass through to and from the base."

"But it shouldn't take them a week to do that," General Rybin said. "You've had submarines in there before."

"Yes. Under normal protocols, they would have been in and out in no more than four days. But the *Neva* had a second mission."

"To do what?" asked Volkov.

"It was optional for Anaconda, at the discretion of the captain. If the conditions warranted, he was to attempt installation of sensors near a Canadian torpedo testing station."

"Where?"

"North of Vancouver. The Nanoose Bay Torpedo Test Range. The Americans and Canadians jointly run the base. The U.S. Navy has been testing its newest torpedo up there. Apparently, it's a radical design; we need to find out just how radical it really is."

"So what does all this mean?"

"Sir, I think it's likely that the *Neva* hasn't checked in yet because it's busy planting the probes. And if I were the captain, I wouldn't risk any transmission within those confined waterways—I'd wait until I was back in the Pacific."

"Why?" asked the GRU chief.

"The American satellites might pick them up, even a microburst. They wouldn't be able to read the signals, but they'd know something was up in their backyard."

"Okay," Minister Volkov said, "let's assume they're still operating on radio silence. What about these names?" He pointed at the briefing paper on his desk. "How do you explain that?"

Admiral Mayakovsky picked up the document and

stared at the first page. "That's what is most troubling to me. The reported accident victim, Anatolii Tomich, is, in fact, the same name of *Neva*'s captain, just like this says."

"The other names—Tomich's so-called uncle in Petropavlovsk . . . Gromeko."

"According to the roster, there is a Mikhail Gromeko aboard. He's the executive officer."

"And the physician in Seattle supposedly treating Tomich, what about him?"

"There's also a Yuri Kirov aboard; he's the intelligence officer. This doesn't say but he's probably in charge of the probe operation."

"He is," confirmed GRU Chief Rybin.

Minister Volkov sighed heavily. "How could anyone outside of this Ministry know the names of three key officers on one of our most secret missions? The person that started all of this phoned the Washington embassy yesterday and used all of these names—like a code. Something's wrong."

"Could the Americans be behind this?" asked General Rybin. "With all that crap they're dumping on us in the Kurils, could they also be screwing with us about the *Neva*? If they somehow found out about its mission . . ."

"How about that, Pavel?" Volkov asked.

"I don't know. None of this makes any sense to me."

"Well, I think you'd better find out just what's going on. I don't like the smell of this."

"I understand, sir. This will be my highest priority."

CHAPTER 8

"How long have you worked for this company?" Yuri asked. He rested on the sofa by the fireplace; it broadcast an amalgam of snaps, crackles, and pops from a fresh bundle of cedar kindling.

"Just over ten years." Laura Newman sat at the nearby dining room table. "I was hired out of college—the sixth employee."

"And now there are two thousand."

"Yes. We've done well."

It was early afternoon at the beach house. After freeing Laura from the bedroom chair, he let her shower and change clothes; she wore a pair of jeans and a long-sleeved blouse. He let her eat lunch. After the meal, she'd asked permission to work. A collection of documents covered the tabletop along with a laptop. He'd left her hands untied but bound both ankles together.

"What are you working on currently?"

"I'm reviewing the marketing plan for a new product that we'll be launching in the spring."

"What kind of product?"

"It's an update of an existing software system that uses seismic data to map subsea oil and gas formations."

"You work for oil companies?"

"About one-third of our business is related to hydro-carbon exploration."

"So you must have training in geology," he said, looking back at Laura.

"No, but there are around a hundred geologists and geophysicists that work in my division; about half are PhDs. Their work generates unbelievable volumes of data, which is where my computer skills come into play."

"Interesting."

The oil business, Yuri reflected. *No wonder she's rich.*

He remained on the sofa by the fireplace. The radiant heat helped. Nevertheless, his misery persisted. Most of his joints throbbed and the numbness in his lower left leg endured.

The bends' relentless assault continued.

Laura worked at the dining room table. Before allowing her access to the Dell, he'd disabled the wireless broadband port. He also tucked Laura's cell phone in his pants pocket.

He pulled out her 4G smartphone and called up the search engine. The website appeared in a flash. He navigated through the site, keying the About Us icon.

There she is! He studied the color headshot of Laura Newman, a serious professional portrait that also accentuated her natural beauty. Her company title was Vice President of Operations.

Yuri devoured the rest of the website's contents, im-

pressed with the company and in awe of Laura Newman. *Wow, she's really something.*

Yuri set the phone aside and peered out a living room
window, taking in the expansive seascape. He thought
of his maritime home—mired in abyssal ooze about
twelve kilometers to the southeast.

Yuri had been a member of the *Neva*'s crew for sixteen months. They were his family and he missed them
all, especially Senior Warrant Officer Viktor Skirski.

Viktor had perished along with fifty-three others.
He made the first dive after the accident to inspect the
fouled seawater intakes. He never returned.

Guilt consumed Yuri: He should have stayed aboard.
Why should he be the only one to escape? No one else
had a chance of making the ascent. He knew that yet it
still stung.

And there was the issue that really tore at Yuri's
heart.

*I should never have moved the deep-water gear to
the torpedo room. If they were still by the aft escape
trunk, some of the crew might be able to make it to the
surface.*

To Yuri's relief, Borodin had not revisited his blun-
der during their early-morning talk. Nevertheless, an
earlier accusation from one of the other surviving officers still festered.

It didn't matter to Yuri that Captain Tomich had approved his request to relocate the ten obsolete IDA59
rebreathers and companion bulky immersion suits to the
now flooded first compartment to make room for Yuri's
special spy gear. Nor did it matter that there were not
enough IDA59s aboard for everyone or that they required

specialized training at depths greater than fifty meters, which most of the crew had never received. Still, that fateful decision haunted Yuri.

I have to get them help soon or they'll perish.

The environmental conditions aboard the *Neva* were deteriorating. Foul air, near freezing temperatures, and leaks plagued the crew.

If they can get a reactor online, that'll buy time.

Survival of his submates required a reactor restart, which continued to elude the crew. A source of electricity would mean heat, oxygen generation, and energy to drive the bilge pumps.

And what about Moscow? Yuri wondered. They had to know by now.

All morning Yuri grew anxious waiting for a callback from the Russian embassy in D.C.

They had to send help. But would they?

The *Neva*'s mission—spying deep inside U.S. and Canadian waters—was an act of war. The *Neva*'s orders had been explicit: If detected, exit unfriendly waters immediately. Under no circumstances could the *Neva* or any of its crew be captured. Should capture be imminent, the submarine and its crew were to self-destruct.

And that would mean the death of Yuri's family.

Yuri had no thoughts of his parents. They had evaporated long ago.

His mother died almost eighteen years earlier. Ovarian cancer took her over ten miserable months. During most of her suffering, Yuri's Army officer father had served in the field. Major Ivan Kirov could have requested a hardship assignment to Moscow, but he elected to avoid home.

Yuri had no siblings and the aunt that helped raised him—his father's older sister—had been about as warm and loving to him as the Barents Sea in mid-January.

The one bright spot in Yuri's early life had been his maternal grandfather, retired Vice Admiral Semyon Nikolayevich Fedorov. During summer vacations, Yuri traveled by train from Moscow to St. Petersburg and stayed with Grandfather Semyon.

A widower, Fedorov had lived in a well-appointed apartment that overlooked the Neva River. The three consecutive summers Yuri spent with Grandfather Semyon were the best times of his life. They hiked in the country, day-sailed on Lake Ladoga, visited St. Petersburg's plentiful museums and monuments, spending countless hours in the Hermitage, and took in dozens of performances at the Mariinsky Theatre, the Ballet Theatre, and the Pushkin Drama Theatre.

Yuri enjoyed their visits to Semyon's previous command the most. The St. Petersburg Naval Base was one of Russia's largest naval facilities. Grandfather Semyon's office had been located in the Admiralty building; its landmark gold-coated spire towered over the lower Neva.

Yuri's visits to the naval base and Semyon's stories of Cold War skirmishes with NATO—he had commanded a submarine—inspired Yuri to follow in his grandfather's wake.

Yuri retrieved the smartphone and typed in the Web address, one that he had memorized long ago. He smiled when the image appeared. Admiral Fedorov's official portrait reflected his tough no-nonsense warrior pose, but Yuri still adored it. The private website, owned and maintained by retired Russian naval officers, honored their beloved brethren. Grandfather Semyon was among the most honored.

For a fleeting moment, Yuri was tempted to send the e-mail—a quick message to one of his comrades back in Petro, informing the officer of the *Neva*'s fate. It would be so easy to do with Laura's phone. But he soon dismissed the thought, knowing the risk was not worth it. He would continue to follow protocol and work through the embassy.

Thanks to Grandfather Semyon's influence, Yuri attended the Nakhimov secondary school in St. Petersburg. He then entered the Higher Naval Submarine School located on the St. Petersburg Naval Base campus for five years of officer training.

Those were marvelous times for Yuri. He embraced military life, excelling in his studies and bonding with his future brother officers. Semyon died during Yuri's fourth year, passing in his sleep.

Over three thousand attended Admiral Fedorov's memorial service in St. Petersburg's Naval Cathedral at the Church of St. Nicholas. Although invited, Yuri's father had been a no-show.

After the funeral and in the privacy of his grandfather's apartment, Yuri wept, mourning the loss of his mentor and best friend.

The Russian Navy was now Yuri's only family. The officers and men of the *Neva* were his brothers.

CHAPTER 9

"That's weird."

"What?"

"I've got an anomaly on one of our sensors in the South Georgia Straits area."

"What's the problem?"

The twenty-four-year-old University of British Columbia research assistant looked up from his laptop's screen to face his boss. They were inside a conference room in the Fisheries Centre of the Vancouver campus; it was mid-afternoon. Stacks of files and reports covered the table where they sat. "It looks like some kind of underwater outburst, a pretty big one. Take a look."

He flipped the Apple around and slid it across the table. The attractive thirty-two-year-old assistant professor of marine zoology leaned over and eyed the LCD monitor. "That is odd. When did this happen?"

"Monday, one thirteen a.m."

"Hmm."

"I wonder if it's one of those geophysical companies testing equipment again."

"No way," the professor said. "That pressure spike and its duration are way beyond any normal equipment testing levels."

For the past three years, she had been studying the effect of manmade underwater sounds on marine life, orcas in particular. The Greenpeace grant had allowed her to install eight hydrophones along the length of the 150-mile-long Strait of Georgia.

"Maybe it's the military—some kind of new sonar test," offered the RA.

"Yes, that could be it. Can you pinpoint the source?"

"No, just that it originated south of Vancouver, probably in deep water."

"What about *Venus*?"

"I checked earlier this morning; it's still down and there's no estimate of when it might be online again. Apparently, they don't have a clue as to what's wrong."

Venus, a cabled undersea research laboratory system, transmitted video, acoustic, and real-time oceanographic data from seafloor instruments via fiber-optic cables to the University of Victoria. One of its arrays was located on the bottom of the Strait of Georgia near Vancouver.

"Too bad," the professor said, again eyeing the acoustic output on the Apple. "Whatever this event was, it occurred right in their backyard."

"I know," he said.

The professor keyed the laptop, initiating a search. The webpage downloaded. She flipped the laptop around, displaying a newspaper article titled "U.S. Navy's Sonar Lethal to Sea Life."

"Americans?" the RA asked.

"Could be, especially in the middle of the night."

"Trying to hide what they're doing?"

"Yes."

"So, what would you like me to do?"

"Cross-check everything first and prepare me a summary."

"You going to blow the whistle on this one?"

"Damn right. The U.S. Navy is not supposed to be doing any sonar testing near the Gulf Islands. It's bad enough that we let them operate at Nanoose Bay." She shook her head. "The arrogance of those Pentagon bastards—thinking we wouldn't find out."

CHAPTER 10

Ignoring the no contact court order, Ken Newman searched for his wife. He staked out her office, the house, and even her attorney's office. He'd also made two trips to Sea-Tac International, on the lookout for Laura's BMW. Ken even considered checking the private parking lots that surrounded the airport but abandoned that idea; there were too many. Ken tried hacking into her banking and e-mail accounts—he knew Laura's Social Security number—but ran into cyber brick walls.

No solid leads, until now.

"I wonder if you could help me," Ken Newman said, addressing the receptionist. He'd just walked into the lobby of a property management agency in downtown Kirkland at 3:25 P.M.

"I'll try, sir."

"I'm tracking down some unauthorized charges on my wife's credit card. One of them was made by your firm." Ken held up a billing statement.

"Let me see if I can get you some help."

"Okay."

Desperate to find Laura, the previous evening Ken

drove to their Redmond residence. He couldn't get in because she'd changed the door locks. But Laura forgot about the locking mailbox by the driveway. Ken still had a key. Luckily, it contained a Visa card statement along with the usual junk mail. He didn't think twice about stealing the statement.

Ken sat at a table in the conference room staring at a wall, when the office manager entered.

"I'm so sorry to keep you waiting, Mr. Newman. It took awhile to download the files." Holding up a stack of hard copies in her right hand, she seated herself across from Ken. "I don't think you have anything to worry about, at least for this charge. Your wife did pay for the rental."

"How can you be sure of that? Some punk snatched her purse and used her credit cards. Laura couldn't have made that charge. I would've known about it."

The manager heaved a sigh. "The rental agreement and credit card authorization form were e-mailed to your wife last week. She signed both and then e-mailed them back."

"I don't understand," Ken said, lying.

"Sir, we have concrete proof that the charge was legitimate. The property owner required Mrs. Newman to sign the rental agreement." She held up a collection of papers in her left hand, then removed a credit card receipt clipped to the papers and handed it to Ken. "As you can see, your wife authorized the charge."

The manager laid the pdf copy of the contract on the tabletop but did not offer it to him.

Ken examined the Visa card e-receipt but used it as a diversion. As a commercial real estate agent he'd become adept at reading contracts upside down while explaining deal points to his clients. He used that skill to scan the first page of the contract.

Ken handed the receipt back. "I'd like a copy of that please, and a copy of the rental contract, too."

"I'm sorry but I can't do that. The account is in your wife's name only."

Ken frowned. "Could you at least tell me where the rental is located?" He'd already memorized the address but the more information he could glean, the better.

"All I can say is that it is in Washington State."

"Is it a condo, house, or what?"

"It's a beach house."

"Oh, Laura," Ken whispered, just loud enough for the manager to hear, "what are you up to?"

The manager froze in place, not offering anything else.

Ken grimaced, pushed away from the table, and stood. "I'm sorry to have bothered you. I didn't know about this."

"No trouble at all."

By the time Ken climbed into his Corvette, his hang-dog pout had transformed into a broad grin. He'd pulled it off.

Point Roberts, Ken wondered as he started the engine. *Where the hell is that?*

CHAPTER 11

Yuri waited all afternoon for a callback from the embassy. Finally, at 4:04 P.M., Laura's cell phone rang. He answered on the second ring.

"Hello," Yuri said in English.

"John Kirkwood?"

"Yes." Yuri had selected his alias from a phonebook he'd found in the kitchen.

"I'm from the embassy. We talked yesterday."

The caller worked for the SVR—*Sluzhba Vneshney Razvedki*. As the successor to the former First Chief Directorate of the KGB, the SVR served as Russia's CIA. The intelligence officer was in a safe house in Arlington, Virginia. He took extreme measures to insure that he did not pick up a tail and he used a new cell phone.

"I've been waiting for you," Yuri said.

"Sorry, but it's taken us awhile to check things out."

Encrypted signals between Moscow and the embassy in Washington repeatedly bounced off Russian communication satellites all day. The minister of defense had ordered an immediate full-scale investigation.

The SVR officer continued, "As you requested, I've been checking on that individual you called about, the accident victim, Professor Tomich." He vacillated. "How is he?"

"Poorly. They're going to have to operate soon or he won't make it."

"Well, I have some information on his background that might be helpful to the doctors. However, I need to verify something first."

"What?"

"Did Dr. Tomich happen to mention what he was working on at the Vega Institute in Saint Petersburg?"

This was the final test, the decisive moment. Moscow remained skeptical, suspecting a trap.

Yuri smiled, knowing they'd solved his puzzle. "Yes," he replied, "I believe he said it was called Anaconda."

Knowledge of Anaconda had been limited to ten senior defense ministry officers in Moscow, Vladivostok, and Petropavlovsk. Aboard the *Neva*, just Captain Tomich, executive officer Gromeko, and Yuri knew.

"Okay, thank you. It turns out that we happen to have a specialist in thoracic trauma who is visiting California this week, San Francisco. Dr. Nicolai Seliskov. He's agreed to consult on the Tomich case. We've already e-mailed him Tomich's medical records. He can fly to Seattle tomorrow morning."

Yuri considered the caller's carefully constructed report: They were sending someone from San Francisco, probably the Consulate. That made sense.

"Tell him to fly to Vancouver, not Seattle."

"What?"

"I'll explain when he gets here."

"Okay, Vancouver—British Columbia, correct?"

"Yes."

"Can you meet him at the airport?"

"No."

"What do you suggest?"

"Have him call this number when he arrives. I'll tell him what to do."

"All right."

The call ended. As Yuri slipped the cell phone back into his pants pocket, he speculated on who controlled Seliskov.

He hoped for GRU but expected SVR.

Laura Newman had never been so cold. Half-soaked, her legs vibrated uncontrollably and her teeth chattered. Her stomach roiled, too.

She'd been in the aluminum runabout for about an hour. It was 10:28 P.M. She sat on the center bench, her back to the bow. John squatted next to the outboard engine a few feet away. His right hand gripped the tiller. The boat headed north, back to the beach house.

Earlier in the evening, he'd informed Laura of the excursion. He needed help with the boat. She looked forward to it—anything to be rid of the bindings and maybe get a chance to escape.

They had struggled to launch the skiff through the churning waves. Both waded to above their knees and hauled themselves into the boat in between the two-foot-high wave crests. He barely made it, his injured leg deadweight.

Not once did he explain where they were going or why. After clearing the breakers, now soaking wet, freezing, and furious, she'd demanded answers.

He had peered at the oncoming seas, ignoring her.

Half an hour later, the boat slowed. How he found the buoy, black like the sea, mystified Laura. She could barely see it from ten feet away. She helped him moor the runabout to the buoy.

And then the strangest thing of all occurred. He retrieved a wire from the buoy's cable, hooked it up to a telephone, and spoke into the handset.

Between the wind and sea sounds, she couldn't hear much. From what she did hear, she knew he did not speak English.

He spoke for about ten minutes and then disconnected. A couple of minutes later the boat began the return trip.

Laura turned to the side, peering over the bow. The shore approached fast. She would soon be drenched again; landing the boat would be even trickier than launching. But that didn't worry her. Instead, her thoughts focused on a single question: Who was he talking to out there?

CHAPTER 12

DAY 4—THURSDAY

Aleksi Zhilkin had just turned eighteen when he was drafted. Seven months earlier, thousands of others from the Volgograd Oblast had joined him during one of Russia's semiannual roundups. All males between eighteen and twenty-seven were subject to conscription. Draftees made up about one-third of the non-officer military. Volunteers accounted for the balance, lured by flashy ads on television and YouTube rebroadcasts that promised adventure, travel, and girls.

Aleksi had been an exceptional student, but that didn't matter to the civilian administrator responsible for assigning draftees to the fleet. Submarines needed cooks.

No cooking occurred aboard the *Neva* now. The ship's galley and mess had flooded, along with almost everything else in Compartments One and Two. When the *Neva* bottomed out, Aleksi had been fortunate to be off duty. Otherwise, he would be a soggy corpse, like the rest of the galley watch.

Over ninety percent of the boat's foodstuffs had been stored in Compartment Two but they might as well be on Mars. The remaining supplies were in Compartment

Eight. Those cases of canned meat, vegetables, and fruits sustained the remaining crew. A stash of English tea in a central command post locker supplemented the canned provisions.

Aleksi and one other surviving galley rat had busied themselves with feeding the crew. They doled out measured rations of cold fare into paper cups and whatever containers they could find. For tea, the only hot concession allowed, a blowtorch from engineering fired the kettle.

Now off duty, Aleksi lay on his bunk in Compartment Seven. He occupied the middle berth of a three-high unit. He'd closed the curtain partition of the coffin-size unit when he'd climbed in ten minutes earlier. The black fabric provided the only privacy he or the other sailors had aboard the *Neva*. A feeble reading light just above his head illuminated the space. He stared at the pine boards that supported the upper berth.

Even with the wool blanket and his winter coat, he still shivered. With the continuing power problem, the temperature inside the hull had plummeted to near ambient conditions—just a few degrees above freezing.

The headache had been building for the past hour. He'd swallowed a couple of aspirin earlier but they had no effect.

Miserable, Aleksi reached up and flipped off the light switch. In the darkness, he rehashed the scuttlebutt from his last watch.

Engineering had restarted the reactor but the plugged seawater cooling lines limited its output, forcing the electrical generating unit to operate at a bare minimum level. The ship still leaked more seawater than it could pump out. The one officer who'd managed to escape had yet to offer any real hope of rescue.

Dread gripped Aleksi's core. *We're all going to die down here.*

It was half past nine in the morning. Yuri and Laura were inside the BMW. The sheaved dive knife tucked in the waistband of Yuri's trousers ensured her cooperation. She drove while he sat in the passenger seat. Spent from their late-evening excursion, Laura would have slept until noon if he hadn't intervened.

Point Roberts, U.S.A., was not much in area, only about five square miles, but politically it was unlike anything Yuri had ever encountered.

After driving north on South Beach Drive, Laura turned onto Benson and headed west. About two minutes later, she made a right turn onto Tyee Drive.

"This is the main road into and out of Point Roberts," Laura said, continuing her rundown on the American enclave.

"The only way you can drive here from America is to go through Canada?"

"That's right. I came through the border at Blaine, then drove around the lower mainland of British Columbia, and passed through a second border crossing."

"It has its own border, too?"

"Yeah, the U.S. and Canada both have customs and immigration people at the end of this road. The U.S. checks everyone who comes into Point Roberts and the Canadians check everyone who departs."

Dismayed by Laura's revelation, Yuri felt a chill

flash down his spine. The border meant U.S. federal agents were nearby.

They bypassed the American border station and drove along a portion of the 49th parallel. The contrast between the two sides was stark. Expensive, modern homes occupied the north side of the borderline; sparse development characterized the opposite side.

Yuri soon discovered that most of Point Roberts was rural. The town center offered a smattering of retail stores and restaurants, a grocery store and bank, and several gas stations. About fifteen hundred full-time residents called the Point home, but during the summer, the population swelled to nearly five thousand. The beaches were the attraction.

Unlike most of Point Roberts's interior, its water perimeter was developed. Hundreds of cabins, beach houses, and McMansions lined its three coastlines. Many of the homes were vacation getaways owned by Canadians from nearby Vancouver. About a dozen eateries and drinking establishments also occupied the Point's waterfront.

After exploring the western shore of Point Roberts, including the golf course and Lighthouse Park, they now drove along the south shore. Heading east on Edwards Drive, Yuri noticed the masts first.

"What are those?" he asked, pointing with his right hand at the approaching forest of fiberglass and aluminum sailboat masts projecting above the land in the distance.

"It's the marina," Laura said. "A big one, and very nice."

Laura turned onto Marina Drive and proceeded northward along the edge of the small craft harbor. Located near the center of the peninsula's south shore, and just a couple hundred meters west of Laura's rental house, the dredged backshore boat basin provided sheltered moorage for hundreds of vessels ranging from runabouts to megayachts. This morning the tide was out, so the boats were riding low in the water; most of their hulls could not be seen from the roadway.

Yuri's outlook rebounded as Laura drove past the marina. The skiff he'd been using to visit the *Neva* was marginal at best. With such a magnificent harbor close by, surely he could find a more appropriate vessel to commandeer.

Later, when he and Laura returned to the beach cabin, the revelation hit.

During Yuri's first day at the beach house he had pried open a locked storage closet in the pantry that contained the homeowner's personal property. Besides household items, he discovered a key chain hanging on a hook. Linked to the chain were an electronic keycard, a couple of metal keys, and a round plastic orange ball about two inches in diameter; Yuri originally dismissed the finding but now reconsidered. The ball could be a float, designed to prevent the key chain from sinking if dropped into water. And maybe—just maybe—the owner of the beach house also had a boat in the marina. Tonight he would find out.

The passenger peered through the viewport. He sat on the left side of the cabin, forward of the wing. The clear skies resulted in exceptional visibility. Two hours earlier, when he'd departed San Francisco International at 11:25 A.M., the Bay Area had been foggy with drizzle.

The northbound Airbus 320 just passed over Anacortes, Washington. It had been in a slow descent for the past twenty minutes.

The passenger glanced down at the map in his lap; the consulate had supplied it. He verified another landmark. It wouldn't be long now.

He worked for the SVR, a sixteen-year veteran. The consulate's SVR *resident* had ordered him to identify the mystery person who'd called the embassy and find out what he really wanted.

Nicolai Mironovich Orlov craned his head to the side, trying to peer farther ahead through the window. It took a moment for the seascape to register. He checked the map and returned to the window.

Officially listed as the consulate's technical services director, Major Orlov's real job was to recruit agents—spies. He targeted the high-tech engineers and scientists of nearby Silicon Valley. His hunting grounds included the bars, clubs, gyms, and other Bay Area establishments that attract computer techs in their off hours.

Recruited by the SVR's Foreign Intelligence Service just after completing his university studies, Orlov rarely spent time in Russia. His last duty assignment had been in London, before that Paris, and before that Tehran. Single with no strong family ties to the homeland, he found that his itinerate lifestyle suited him.

The Airbus descended to five thousand feet. It sped past the San Juan Islands and cruised over a huge inland sea. The Strait of Georgia, the north arm of the Salish Sea, and massive Vancouver Island filled Orlov's viewport. Several points left of the aircraft's heading, a long narrow peninsula jutted several miles into the strait. Beyond the peninsula lay a vast metropolis bracketed by jagged snowcapped peaks.

Captain Lieutenant Yuri Kirov ignored the drone of the jetliner as it passed to the east. He stood on the deck fronting the living room, gazing at the seascape. Sipping from a steaming mug of tea, he considered what he'd discovered earlier in the morning. The American border station continued to vex him. The presence of federal police so close was an oversight on his part. It was something he had not planned for or anticipated but should have if he had planned his mission thoroughly.

Yuri checked his watch: half past one. The contact would be calling soon. He walked back into the living room and headed up the stairs. He needed to check Laura's bindings.

He'd sensed something odd about her behavior today. After the tour, Laura had inquired about his family and asked if his injured leg was any better, as if she really cared.

Another caution flag went up.

Despite the crowds, she eyed the visitor when he walked out of the arrival terminal for U.S. flights at Vancouver International. His handsome facial features and trim black hair matched the pdf color ID photograph she held. His build also matched the physical report e-mailed from Moscow: 188 centimeters and 83 kilograms.

"Dr. Seliskov . . . over here, please," she called out in English, using his cover name. She extended an arm, signaling.

Nicolai Orlov made eye contact and walked toward the young woman. He'd already passed through the Canada Border Services and Immigration holding area with just a glance at his expertly fabricated Canadian passport that displayed his alias: Nicolai Seliskov, MD.

"Ms. Krestyanova, I presume," he announced as he approached the striking blonde.

"Yes, and please, just call me Elena."

"Sure, Elena, and it's Nick for me." He smiled and she returned her best.

"Okay, Nick. Did you check your baggage?"

"No. Just this." He raised an overnight bag suspended from his right hand.

"Good. Let's go to my car."

Five minutes later, they approached a late-model jet-black Mercedes-Benz sedan. Both climbed into the vehicle, she behind the wheel and he in the front passenger seat. With her skirt hiked up to mid-thigh level, her long perfect legs presented a stirring sight.

"Our Trade Mission must be doing very well up here," Orlov offered in Russian as he settled into the luxurious leather seat.

"We do a lot of entertaining. This helps."

He smirked. "Back at the consulate all I get to drive are pool cars—Chevys and Fords."

After crossing the North Arm of the Fraser River and turning north on Granville Street, Elena said, "The caller John Kirkwood, what can you tell me about him?" She'd only received a cursory briefing on the new case.

"He's one of ours. Voice analysis of his calls with

the embassy indicates a ninety-two percent probable match with the test recording in the file."

Orlov reached into his coat pocket and removed a four-by-six color print of a young male in civilian dress. He held up the photograph. "His real name is Kirov—Yuri Ivanovich. He's a captain lieutenant."

She stole a quick look. "A military officer?"

"Navy—submarines. He's done well for being so young; only twenty-nine."

"What else do you have?"

Orlov cited Kirov's stellar education, secondary and academy levels, and his fluency in English. He continued with the rundown. "After earning his commission, Kirov received a year of postgraduate training in electronics and communications at a technical institute in Moscow. Then spent sixteen weeks training with a naval dive unit based out of Sevastopol on the Black Sea."

"He's a diver?"

"Apparently he's some kind of underwater Intel expert. He's assigned to a sub from Petro."

"GRU?"

"He's a naval officer assigned to the GRU's Pacific Fleet Intelligence Directorate."

Traffic was building, almost stop and go. Elena braked and turned toward Orlov. "What's his personal background? Married, family?"

"He's single. No siblings. Mother's deceased; his father is retired Army—a light colonel. Lives in Moscow."

Orlov continued to rubberneck, amazed at the approaching vista. Ultra-modern glass and steel spires jutted into the crystalline sky, back-dropped by the emerald waters of the False Creek inlet.

Vancouver was an exquisite city. Elena ignored the cityscape. As an eight-month resident, she had become immune to the metropolis's charms. Instead, she focused on processing Orlov's verbal report. A few minutes away from their destination, she asked the question that had been gnawing at her. "Major, if he's with submarines, what in the world is he doing here?"

"He's supposed to be aboard a sub right now."

"There's something wrong here," Elena offered.

"I agree."

CHAPTER 13

Captain Borodin's orders called for at least one officer to stand watch in the central command post
every hour of the day, even with the boat glued to the
bottom. This watch was no exception; the *Neva*'s lowest ranking officer staffed the CCP alone. During past
watches, at least two sailors would staff the control
center with an officer. This afternoon, however, the
rest of the crew rested in their bunks—captain's orders. Exhausted from cleaning the clogged seawater
intakes, the men had earned a respite.

The twenty-three-year-old sat in the captain's leather-
lined chair near the center of the compartment. He
scanned the control panel displays, readouts, and gauges
that still functioned inside the sub's nerve center.

The junior lieutenant turned abruptly to his right; a
new blinking red light caught his eye. He leaned forward, focusing on the escape trunk display. The readout indicated that the aft escape chamber was open to
the sea and flooding. He reached to pick up a microphone and call the captain—normal watch protocol.
But his hand froze in mid-air. Borodin had retired to

his cabin at the beginning of the watch; he'd been awake for fifty hours straight. The lieutenant's supervisor had warned him not to bother the captain unless there was a real emergency. *"Nyet fignjá!"*—no bullshit—he'd ordered.

He tapped the light with his right forefinger. Its intensity remained unchanged. He checked other displays, looking for anything that might offer an explanation. Nothing.

The officer leaned back in the chair, convinced that the wiring in the escape trunk panel had a fault; scores of other displays had malfunctioned because of the accident. He took a full minute to look over the other monitors and readouts. When he finished, he peered back at the suspect panel. The ruby eye winked back. *Govnó!*

Seawater blasted into the chamber with the force of a fire hydrant. Already it had reached seaman-cook Aleksi Zhilkin's knees. He backed off the manual flood valve, trimming the flow. It inched upward toward his thighs.

Aleksi inhaled and exhaled at an accelerated rate, the result of near blinding fear and the rising pressure inside the steel cylinder. The rapid breathing helped equalize the pressure in his ears; otherwise, he would blow out his eardrums.

He wore two layers of everything under his standard issue blue jumpsuit: pants, shirts, underwear, and socks. The Hydro Suit covered his clothing, isolating him from the four-degrees-Celsius water. The combination dive suit, breathing apparatus, and lifeboat had a maximum operating depth of 180 meters—600 feet. The *Neva* was 220 meters deep, just over 720 feet.

The water level had just reached his waist. His breath fogged the plastic viewport of the emergency escape suit, but he could see well enough. The submerged battle lantern on the opposite side of the chamber broadcast a silky jade.

Aleksi floated when the water reached his abdomen, buoyed by the air-inflated suit.

Thirty seconds later, as he bobbed inside the cocoon, his upper spine slammed into an unseen metal fitting. The sting of the collision annoyed him, but the prospect of puncturing the suit's rubber lining supercharged his already racing heart.

He grasped the rungs of the ladder with his hands as the rising water engulfed his torso. When the water surged past his head he shouted, "Thank you, God."

No leaks.

The junior officer ignored the indicator light as he kept watch, but his thoughts leapfrogged.

No one would be using the escape trunk—we're too deep . . . there must be a short in the wiring . . . maybe I should call the chief and ask him . . . no, he'll just chew on my ass.

Forget it; it's probably nothing.

Eerily quiet now; the roar of the incoming water had ceased when the chamber reached ambient pressure. Completely submerged, Aleksi remained anchored to the ladder with his hands and feet. The battle lantern continued to illuminate the escape trunk. The steel tube was about four feet in diameter and seven feet high.

Aleksi panted, almost hyperventilating. A tendril of vomit surged upward but did not quite erupt. He swallowed hard; the residual sourness burned his throat.

What should he do?

It all came back in a flurry: Charge the suit one more time; trigger the manual hatch release. Wait for the air trapped under the hatch to purge. Hang on to the ladder until clear of the . . .

Aleksi had learned how to work the escape chamber from a friend. The nineteen-year-old from Kazan assisted the two Russian intelligence officers who used the aft escape trunk for their seabed excursions. Modified for lockout work, the chamber could be operated by the divers independent of the controls located inside the pressure casing.

Aleksi rotated his head back and peered upward. He could see the circular opening of the outer hatch. The gray steel had just rotated upward, leaving a ring of blackness. Once through the opening, he would water-rocket to the surface.

Fear of what might lie outside consumed him: How would he see? Was it even daylight on the surface? He didn't know where he was; they said America but where in America? Would he be imprisoned? Would they return him to Russia? Was he a traitor?

He could shut the hatch and drain the chamber. No one would know.

For nearly two minutes, Aleksi clung to the ladder debating. Finally, a soothing calmness engulfed him, like a warm bath. He had to continue; it was the only way.

The junior lieutenant's eyes remained fastened on the escape trunk console. Another red light blinked on. The aft outer hatch was open to the sea. He started to make the call but again remembered his orders not to disturb Captain Borodin.

Was it an emergency? Maybe someone was using the trunk for something else. But what?

Aleksi rechecked his equipment and charged the escape suit with another blast of compressed air from a hose connected to a valve in the escape trunk. He'd been exposed to the full pressure of the depth for almost five minutes.

Aleksi summoned the courage to release his grip on the ladder and enter the void.

He'd just managed to pass into the outer hatchway when a fresh wave of nausea hit. He stopped, weaving his left ankle through the next to the last ladder rung as an anchor. The buoyancy of the air trapped inside the escape suit was ready to blast him out of the hatch. He took another deep breath, trying to clear his head.

Aleksi's skin smoldered. Several seconds later, his vision narrowed as if peering through a keyhole. And then he blacked out.

A few seconds passed before he convulsed. The seizure lasted about thirty seconds, triggered by oxygen toxicity brought about by breathing air compressed over twenty times normal.

A quarter of a minute went by before another full body quake hit—this one a 9.0.

With his ankle trapped, Aleksi's torso and arms flailed inside the hatchway. His teeth clamped down, ripping his tongue. His eyes rolled back into their sockets. His forehead slammed into the steel handle of a nearby valve fitting.

A stream of bubbles burst from the escape suit. Within a minute, the suit flooded and Aleksi inhaled a lungful of seawater.

"What?" asked Captain Borodin, answering his cabin intercom.

"Sir, the control panel indicates that the outer hatch on escape trunk two is open to the sea."

The CCP watch officer braced himself for the captain's wrath.

"How the hell can that be?"

"I don't know, Captain."

"Send someone to check."

"Yes, sir."

CHAPTER 14

"You're sure this cell is clean?" asked Nick Orlov.

"Yes," Elena Krestyanova said. She sat at her desk with Orlov on the opposite side. "It's prepaid—never been used."

"Good, then let's call him."

"Okay."

It was mid-afternoon. The SVR officers were inside Elena's office in the Russian Trade Mission. Located in downtown Vancouver, the mission's primary goal was to promote trade between western Canada and Russia.

Orlov engaged the speakerphone option of the cell and punched in the number.

Four rings. "Hello."

"Mister Kirkwood?" asked Orlov, speaking English.

"Who is this?"

"I'm your contact . . . from San Francisco."

"Where are you?"

"Vancouver, but I'm ready to meet with you at your convenience."

"You come to me."

"Okay, but where?"

"I'm in Point Roberts. I'll meet you at a restaurant called the Georgia Straits . . . in the bar, an hour from now."

Nick looked at Elena with a puzzled expression and mouthed *Point Roberts*?

She whispered, "It's close by."

Nick continued, "The Georgia Straits . . . how will I find this place?"

"It's near the marina. Just ask around. Someone will tell you."

"Okay but what about our injured friend. How's he doing?"

"Be here in an hour and then you'll know."

The line went dead.

Orlov turned to face Elena. "He's being careful—saying nothing more than needed."

"I agree."

Orlov stood. "What is this Point Roberts place?"

"I've never been there but heard about it. It's south of Vancouver, about thirty minutes away." She paused. "Point Roberts is part of the U.S. but it's isolated from the mainland. You have to drive through Canada to get to it."

"Really—what do you think he's doing there?"

"I have no idea."

"Do you know what he was talking about—the Georgia Straits place?"

"No, but let's see what we can find out; should be easy."

Elena turned to her desktop computer and initiated a Bing search. Within half a minute she'd found the restaurant's website. "Here it is, the Georgia Straits. It has a bar called the Pod Room."

"Good, let's go."

The Russian intelligence officers occupied an idling Chevrolet Suburban. Elena sat behind the wheel. She turned to face Nick and said, "The best way to deal with this is to not say anything unless you're asked."

"Got it."

Elena had traded the Mercedes sedan for the SUV. The big Chevy provided plenty of room for Orlov to crouch down when they drove out of the parking garage, just in case the RCMP monitored the mission. The Mounties, however, were busy elsewhere.

The Suburban inched forward in the holding lane. There were six automobiles ahead.

Orlov could see the U.S. border station in the near distance. A single lane was open. The Customs and Border Protection officer staffing the check-in station interrogated every driver who entered Point Roberts this afternoon. Just beyond the station, Orlov spotted a Toyota Camry parked in a turnout. The vehicle's driver and two passengers—all of East Asian descent—stood by as two uniformed CBP officers searched the car.

Five minutes later, Elena handed their passports to the federal officer. Like Nick, she also carried a manufactured Canadian passport using an alias. It simplified access between Canada and the United States. Use of their real passports would be problematic.

To minimize detection further, the Suburban and Elena's Mercedes were both registered to a Canadian shell corporation instead of the Trade Mission.

"Where are you heading today?" asked the female CBP officer as she accepted the passports.

"Ah, we've never been here before. We thought we'd drive around and maybe have dinner some place."

The officer eyed Elena and checked the passport photo. She repeated the process with Nick and handed the passports back.

"Enjoy your visit."

"Thank you."

Three cars behind Elena's Suburban, a sleek Chevrolet Corvette idled while Metallica pulsed from the surround sound system.

The "arrest me red" Corvette pulled forward into the holding lane next to the check-in station. The CBP officer typed in the license number on her computer. Ten seconds later, the registered owner's driver license photo and ID data appeared on her monitor: Kenneth Lawrence Newman, Washington State resident, age thirty-four, Caucasian, five-foot-ten, 185 pounds, blue eyes, blond hair, organ donor.

She turned away from the screen and said, "Your travel documents, sir?"

"What?"

"Turn your radio off," she ordered with a raised voice.

Instant silence.

"I need to see your passport."

"Oh." Ken reached into his shirt pocket, removed his U.S. passport, and handed it over.

The officer swiped the ID through the scanner on her computer. She read the output data and then turned back to face Ken. "How long have you been in Canada, Mr. Newman?"

That took Ken by surprise. "Gee . . . I guess half an hour or so. I just drove from Blaine."

"What's your business at Point Roberts?"

"Ah . . . ah looking for . . ." Ken was taken aback by the question. He'd almost blurted out "looking for my wife." He corrected himself. "I'm just looking around, nothing in particular."

Not at ease with Mr. Newman, the officer leaned forward and examined the interior of the two-seater.

"Sir, drive forward and park by those officers."

"What for?"

"Just drive forward and wait."

"All right."

Yuri noticed them as soon as they passed through the entryway into the Pod Room: A tall, well-built male in his late thirties and a curvaceous woman with a golden mane in her early thirties. While the other bar patrons wore casual garb, the new arrivals could have stepped out of a Fortune 500 company board meeting.

Yuri had spotted the Georgia Straits earlier in the day while touring Point Roberts with Laura. He selected the restaurant because of the water view.

He watched as the couple searched for him. Eventually, the male walked toward Yuri's booth, located in a quiet corner with no nearby patrons. The woman followed.

"Mr. Kirkwood?" asked Major Orlov, using English.

Yuri gestured to the vacant half of the booth. "Sit down, please."

The female slid across the vinyl bench seat, followed by Orlov.

Orlov started to speak, when Yuri held up his right hand. Switching to Russian and in a hushed voice he said, "Before we go any further, identify yourselves."

"I'm Nicolai Orlov, from the San Francisco Consulate."

"And I'm Elena Krestyanova. I work in Vancouver at the Trade Mission."

"Who sent you?"

"The Washington embassy," answered Orlov. "We're here to help you with Dr. Tomich."

"What did they tell you?"

"Dr. Tomich, he's from the Vega Institute in Saint Petersburg. He was in some kind of automobile accident, a severe chest injury."

Yuri leaned forward. "So who am I?"

Elena responded, "You're Captain Lieutenant Yuri Ivanovich Kirov, a naval intelligence officer."

Nick finished, "You're based out of the Rybachiy Naval Base at Petropavlovsk-Kamchatskiy. At this moment you're supposed to be aboard a submarine engaged in a highly classified mission. So, what's going on?"

Yuri leaned back a few degrees. "Welcome to Point Roberts, comrades."

CHAPTER 15

"That sucks!" Ken Newman mumbled as he accelerated away from the Point Roberts border station.

He'd waited for half an hour while the CBP officers searched his Corvette. They found nothing significant, just a pocketknife, a pencil, and several wrappers from Snickers candy bars.

Little did Ken know he happened to fit the profile, just more rotten luck.

The FBI had developed a catalog of likely personality profiles of criminal types. In Ken's case, what sent the border agent's "bad guy" meter ringing had been his obvious nervousness—the bungled response about his reason for visiting Point Roberts. His body language didn't help, either. He'd radiated deception and the CBP officer had picked it up.

Ken shifted into third as he headed south on Tyee Drive. Huge stands of evergreens lined the asphalt roadway, but in the distance he spotted a smidgen of blue. He checked the dashboard GPS display. His destination was just a couple of miles away.

*   *   *

"You mean it's stranded on the bottom . . . out there?" Nicolai Orlov gestured with his right hand at the adjacent window in the Pod Room. The Strait of Georgia was about thirty feet away.

"Yes, but south of here," Yuri answered. They now spoke English but in muted tones.

"How far down is it?" asked Elena Krestyanova.

"Over two hundred meters."

"That's deep," Nick said, astonished at Yuri's tale.

Yuri continued, "The crew was able to restart one of the reactors yesterday but they're still fighting the fouled seawater intakes so it's throttled way back."

"What fouling are you talking about?" Nick asked.

"The ship's seawater cooling system for the reactors and electrical generators. The inlets are located on the bottom of the hull and buried in mud. The suction from the pumps pulls in bottom sediments along with the water. That gunk plugs everything up."

Nick shifted position in the booth, slumping to one side. "So they don't have much power."

"Yes. There's just enough to run life support and to power the bilge pumps. Nothing for the heating system. It's like living inside a refrigerator down there."

"How long have they been marooned?" Elena asked.

"This is the fourth day. I left on the second."

She mulled over that tidbit. "If you made it, why can't the others do the same?"

"It's too deep to try without a rebreather. Plus you have to be trained to use it." Yuri took a sip from his glass. They all had ordered vodka martinis. Russian-style vodka, chilled and neat, would have been too obvious. "Even with my experience, I barely made it. And we also lost another diver."

"What happened?" Nick asked.

"Viktor Skirski, a warrant officer . . ." Yuri's forehead wrinkled. "He volunteered to try. Viktor had more deep-diving experience than I do so it made sense."

Yuri took another sip. "He made it through the escape chamber but after that I don't know what happened."

"Maybe he did make it up and ended someplace else." Elena pointed seaward. "There are countless islands out there. He could be anywhere."

Yuri stared at the inland sea.

His assistant . . . No, Viktor had been more than that. His friend and companion of nearly two years most likely drowned. Or maybe he threw an embolism and had a heart attack or a brain attack. Or maybe his rebreather malfunctioned and he sucked in a lethal dose of oxygen. There were just too many ways to die at that depth.

Orlov straightened his shoulders. "Captain Lieutenant Kirov, you have presented us with a difficult problem. Just what is it that you want us to tell our superiors?"

Yuri turned back, eyes blazing. "They've got to get them out. There are thirty-seven men down there—still alive!"

The GPS unit guided Ken straight to the rental house. He parked in the driveway and climbed out of his Corvette. He carried a colorful garland of freshly cut flowers, purchased from the local grocery store.

The two-story beach house appeared new. Expecting Laura's BMW, he found no vehicles in the driveway but did note the attached double stall garage. As Ken approached the home's entryway, he peeked through a window panel on one of the garage doors. No Bimmer.

Ken knocked on the front door. Receiving no response, he walked along the narrow alleyway on the west side of the house toward the placid waters of the Strait of Georgia. He peered through several sets of windows into the living room: nothing, no one inside.

Five minutes later, Ken returned to the Corvette where he rechecked the address. He had the right place, but where could Laura be? He considered checking with the occupants of neighboring residences but then thought better of it. They might tip her off to his presence.

Ken's plan to win Laura back would only work if he could surprise her. He knew that, given advance warning, she'd flee.

Ken loathed what he'd done. Laura embodied the best part of his life and he'd ruined everything, his alcohol addiction the root cause.

His last blowup remained a blur but its aftermath still rocked him. Although he couldn't recall much of that night, the affidavit that Laura had signed and attached to the restraining order set the record. How could he have hurt her like that—using Laura as a soccer ball, and calling her all of those ugly things?

Ken feared that he'd lost Laura for good this time.

He hadn't had a drink in three days—a new milestone.

Ken would make it this time . . . if Laura would just give him one more chance.

* * *

Nick and Elena followed in the Suburban, careful to remain out of Yuri's sight. They watched as he drove around the marina's east side and disappeared.

"What now?" Nick asked.

"Let's wait a couple of minutes for him to park. Then we'll check." Laura pulled off the road onto the shoulder. She opened her purse and removed the tracker.

Nick eyed the device. It was the size of a cell phone. "How does it work?"

"It's a transceiver. Has a range of around two hundred meters."

Embedded within the logo of Elena's business card she'd given Yuri was a minuscule radio frequency identification chip. When energized by a unique RF signal emitted by the transceiver, the nanotech RFID tag broadcast its location.

Laura remained a prisoner in the master bedroom. Twenty minutes earlier, she'd heard the knock at the front door but could not respond. Before leaving, her captor had anchored her to the bed on her back with arms and legs moored to each corner of the frame with rope. Tape once more sealed her lips.

Laura shifted her torso, trying to get comfortable. She turned her head toward the nightstand and checked the clock: quarter past four. A couple of hours had passed since "John" left.

Laura took several deep inhalations, trying to relax. It didn't help. The pressure in her bladder was increasing but she'd just have to hold it until he returned.

Perhaps tonight she would get her chance.

Laura was waiting for the right circumstances. But they had not yet occurred. She remained patient. He would eventually slip up and she'd escape.

Laura wouldn't bother with the local deputy sheriff. She planned to head straight for the U.S. border station, running if she had to; it was only a couple of miles away.

They would have FBI agents here in no time at all.

CHAPTER 16

Captain Borodin entered the *Neva*'s engineering compartment. "Has there been any improvement?" he asked.

"No, Captain," the reactor officer said. "Unit Two's barely maintaining itself. If the efficiency drops much more, it'll automatically shut down."

Restarted the day before, the starboard nuclear reactor's heat output remained a fraction of normal. Just enough seawater streamed into the *Neva*'s cooling system to keep the reactor from redlining. If the flow increased, more bottom sediment would be ingested, further plugging the condensing units. The cooling system efficiency would deteriorate, initiating an automatic shutdown. Without heat from the reactor, the steam-powered generating plant would stop producing electricity—the ship's lifeblood.

"How are the batteries?" Borodin asked, referring to the reserves in Compartment Five; the mains had fried, shorted out by seawater when the first two compartments flooded.

"They're about fifty percent recharged so far, but I

don't trust 'em. They were due for replacement last year."

"I know."

Deferred maintenance was the norm for the *Neva*. Within three years, the nuclear cores for both reactors would be spent but they would not be refueled. The ship would be retired soon. Held in reserve for eight years after commissioning due to military funding limitations, the *Neva* had been in active service for nearly two decades. It had performed well above the standard for its class thanks to an advanced propeller design secretly purchased from the West and to several acoustic-quieting upgrades to its running gear. Because of its superior stealth, the *Neva* had become an ideal platform to conduct covert reconnaissance. Nearly half of the submarine's patrols during the past eight years involved espionage.

As Borodin headed aft, continuing his once every two hours tour of the boat, the reactor officer asked, "Sir, the man that tried to escape, what happened to him?"

"Drowned. Somehow he punctured his suit and it flooded."

"What was he thinking—we're too deep to try that."

"I know. Scared I assume. Can't really blame him, but he was doomed from the moment he flooded the chamber."

The officer said, "Any updates from Yuri Ivanovich?"

"I'm expecting to hear from him soon."

"Yuri's a good man, sir. He'll get us help."

"Yes, he will."

* * *

Nicolai Orlov was in the Vancouver Trade Mission. He occupied the code room alone; Elena Krestyanova had relocated to her office. It was early evening.

Orlov sat at a computer console. He'd been composing the report for half an hour, addressing it to the SVR *rezident* at the San Francisco Consulate. But Orlov really wanted to talk directly with Moscow. Vancouver Station had that capability thanks to the parabolic dish on the building's roof. When aimed at a Russian military satellite in a geostationary orbit over the North Pacific, it could transmit and receive encrypted voice signals to and from SVR headquarters.

As much as he'd like to short-circuit the process, Orlov followed standard operating orders. In the next few minutes, he would send the report to his boss with a copy to Moscow.

Orlov leaned back in his chair and rubbed his eyes. They were blurry from staring at the screen. He leaned forward and typed out the final lines.

Based upon Captain Lieutenant Kirov's assessment of the Neva's current condition, he estimates that the crew can survive for approximately ten days from the date of this transmission. That assumes that the one running reactor remains functional. Accordingly, he requests that the Pacific Fleet launch a rescue mission immediately. He is ready to coordinate from his present location. Please advise me on Moscow's decision as soon as possible. Orlov.

Orlov e-mailed his report to the San Francisco Consulate and the SVR's main directorate in Moscow. The algorithm used to encrypt the message was based on the latest efforts of the Russian Federal Security Service—*Federal'naya Sluzhba Bezopasnosti*. The FSB served as Russia's FBI and then some.

He attached an encrypted snapshot of Kirov to the report. Nick had used his cell phone to photograph Yuri while in the Pod Room. He also included a second attachment, a photo of a beach house located by the RFID tracker.

Yuri had not volunteered his hiding place, only acknowledging that he'd found shelter in a vacant house. And he'd said nothing about Laura.

About twenty miles south of downtown Vancouver, Ken Newman watched television from his hotel room bed. He had planned to stay overnight at Point Roberts but discovered the Point lacked public accommodations. No motels or hotels, and the handful of bed-and-breakfasts were already booked.

Forced to drive back into Canada, he found the hotel near the north end of town. Although Tsawwassen bordered sleepy Point Roberts, you'd never know it. The town of twenty thousand thrived as a bedroom community to Vancouver.

"Dammit!" Ken mumbled as a thought flashed. He would have to stop again at the U.S. border station tomorrow. He hoped the witch that had detained him would be off duty.

Ken turned away from the TV screen and eyed the mini-bar, the longing always at hand—especially in the evenings. But he was okay, even proud of himself. Earlier, after having dinner in the hotel's restaurant, he noticed the neon signs across the street. A new nightclub had just opened up. He had resisted temptation and returned to his room.

"I'm sorry to have to do this but I have to leave again."

"How long?" asked Laura. She lay on the bed. John hovered over her, reattaching the lashings.

"A couple of hours."

He returned at sunset. After removing her restraints, he allowed her to use the bathroom and then he fed her sausages and more fried potatoes.

"Please, not too tight on that wrist."

He adjusted the knot. "Better?"

"Yes, thank you."

Flat on her back with each limb reattached to the bed frame's corners, Laura heard John drive off in her BMW five minutes earlier. He left a table light on next to the bed. She stared at the ceiling, a fresh strip of duct tape resealing her mouth.

Laura sensed John did not relish his role as captor. On his return, he carefully removed the tape that had sealed her mouth. It would have been easier to rip it off. He also allowed Laura to apply hand cream to her wrists and ankles before he reapplied the rope bindings.

Besides his thoughtfulness, something else caught Laura's eye—something that ran counter to her common sense. She found him attractive.

Laura also recognized that she must have presented a ghastly appearance in her current condition: no makeup, stringy hair, and frumpy clothing—a pair of tattered blue jeans and a wrinkled long-sleeved shirt.

Realizing it was silly to worry about her personal appearance, Laura again focused on her captor.

What is he up to now?

Yuri piloted the thirty-one-foot powerboat southward in the marina channel. The offshore breakwater was just ahead.

The key chain discovered in the pantry led him straight to the Sea Ray. The dock and slip numbers were hand-printed in black ink on the key chain's float. The electronic card opened the parking gate and dock gate. The other keys opened the cabin door and turned the ignition.

He considered the finding a godsend.

Yuri guided the boat around the southwest tip of the breakwater and goosed the throttle. The boat accelerated to thirty knots.

Twenty-five minutes later, Yuri reestablished communications with the *Neva*. Using the buoy-com line, he just briefed Captain Borodin on his meeting with Major Orlov. There wasn't much to report. Nevertheless, Borodin's spirits rebounded.

"Yuri Ivanovich, there's no way we can ever thank you for what you have done. When Orlov makes his report, Moscow will certainly send *Kaliningrad*. If we can just hold out, we'll be okay."

"Right," Yuri replied. "I'll help pilot her right to you and we'll use the mini to make the transfer—the Americans will never know."

"And then we can all celebrate back in Petro!"

"It will be a great party!"

Yuri did not share his colleague's optimism but never let on. The rescue sub was iffy. The Pacific Fleet's sole rescue submarine was a former missile boat recently converted to carry a hybrid *Priz-Mir* class submersible. Home-ported at the Vladivostok Naval Base, the *Kaliningrad* was designed for rescue in Russian coastal waters, not a covert operation over a hundred miles behind enemy lines. Yuri doubted Moscow would authorize its use. Nevertheless, if he were in Borodin's position, he, too, would have expected the *Kaliningrad*'s immediate deployment.

After Borodin briefed Yuri on the *Neva*'s ongoing battle with the fouled seawater intake system and the efforts to keep the reactor online, he lowered his voice and said, "Please, Yuri, tell them to hurry. Some of the men are clawing at the bulkheads. We even had an escape attempt today; drowned before he could exit the aft trunk."

"Who?"

"One of the cooks, a conscript."

"Aleksi?"

"Yes."

"Oh no . . . he was good man." Yuri taught chess to Aleksi and two other crew members.

"Yuri, we can't stay down here much longer, functioning reactor or not."

"I know. I'm going to get everyone out."

After returning the Sea Ray to its marina slip, Yuri sat inside the cabin sipping a beer. He found the six-pack of Heineken inside a locker in the galley.

He took a long pull from the bottle as he recalled the events of the day. His meeting with Orlov and

Krestyanova dominated. He was leery of the pair. They were SVR—not military. Because their actions might not be in the best interests of the *Neva*'s crew, Yuri decided he would not reveal the submarine's exact location and depth. It was to ensure he would remain involved in the rescue and not rushed back to Russia.

CHAPTER 17

DAY 5—FRIDAY

"This is incredible—how could it have happened?" asked Minister of Defense Volkov, addressing the guest who had just arrived in his mammoth Moscow office.

"Sir, we don't know anything other than what the case officer from the San Francisco Consulate reported."

Nick Orlov's report on the *Neva*'s mishap had rocketed up the Russian military chain of command.

"What's this place called—Point what?"

"Point Roberts." The chief of the Russian Navy reached into his briefcase and removed a document. He unfolded the U.S. government navigation chart that his staff downloaded gratis from a National Oceanic and Atmospheric Administration website. He continued, "Point Roberts is a tiny peninsula, connected to Canada, very close to Vancouver. It's about—"

"But it's American territory?"

"Yes." Admiral Mayakovsky pointed to the upper center of NOAA chart 18421. "See it here?"

"Where did it sink?"

"We don't know the exact location, only that it is south of Point Roberts in two hundred plus meters of water."

"Can't they use escape equipment?"

"According to the report, they're too deep for the gear aboard."

"What about the rescue capsule?"

"It's not equipped with one—it's an older boat. Only our newer boats have them."

Minister Volkov sank back into his chair. "How many alive?"

"Thirty-seven on board plus the one who managed to escape."

"How'd he get out—if the others can't?"

"He's a diver and an intelligence officer. The boat is equipped with lockout diving gear, part of his mission equipment but just for him."

For the next twenty seconds the defense minister pondered what he'd learned. He then reengaged. "I don't understand . . . didn't the mission orders call for self-destruction?"

"Yes, sir. If the *Neva* were detected and trapped by the Americans or Canadians."

"So why didn't they fulfill their duty?"

"The Americans and the Canadians know nothing about this incident. The *Neva* has not been detected, or trapped. It's actually marooned. There's a difference."

Volkov reluctantly nodded. He said, "So what can we do about this?"

"I have a plan, sir. It's rough at this point but I think it might . . ."

* * *

Volkov sat alone in his office. He had approved Admiral Mayakovsky's action plan. Later in the afternoon, he would brief the president on the Asian crisis. He speculated on how his boss would react to the new wrinkle the *Neva* represented.

The United States and Japan continued to taunt Russia with Deep Blue, now in its fifth day. Just the hint of a possible invasion of the Southern Kuril Islands had traumatized the Kremlin. Thinly deployed in the Far East, Russia's military forces would be crushed if the Americans decided to repossess Japan's Northern Territories.

Russia had grabbed the Japanese islands in the final weeks of World War II. Japan claimed that it never ceded sovereignty. The dispute simmered until recent offshore exploration hinted of a petroleum bonanza in the island chain. Japan wanted the islands back more than ever. The United States supported Japan's claim for return of the Southern Kurils.

As long as the oil and gas flowed, Russia's energy-based economy would get by. But should the hydrocarbon prices once again decline or production falter, the Russian economy would tank. After having crawled out of the poverty pit, Kremlin leaders were horrified by the specter of the Russian populace forced back into the sludge.

Russia had about ten years to prepare. By investing carefully, reducing corruption where it could, and gradually cutting back on public subsidies, the financial performance models predicted a stable economy. But paramount to that success was *increased* petroleum production.

The new discovery in the Southern Kurils represented a potential godsend. If it proved to be a mega-elephant field, the recovered hydrocarbons would be readily accessible to conventional offshore drilling and production equipment. The infrastructure needed to bring the oil and gas to market already existed on Russia's nearby oil-rich Sakhalin Island. The Southern Kurils could bolster Russia's economy—or maybe not.

Japan, aided and abetted by the United States, had again upped its rhetoric, demanding return of its Northern Territories. It, too, needed the Kurils' natural riches. Japan continued to suffer from the aftermath of another killer earthquake and tsunami that had ravaged Honshu's east coast from Tokyo to Kobe.

Volkov pulled up the hidden keyboard to his PC and clicked on a shortcut. The desktop screen flashed to current world energy market prices. "Good," he said, relieved. Crude oil continued to climb out of the pit that hamstrung Russia's economy.

The minister knew his boss monitored the price of oil. Up $1.10 from the previous day, it was likely the president would be in a good mood for their upcoming meeting. That portended well for the *Neva*'s crew.

CHAPTER 18

"How many times has he done this?" asked Yuri.

"Too many," Laura said.

"The man is a vermin, hitting you like that."

"He's sick—alcohol is a poison to him. He can really be a nice guy when he's not drinking."

"Still, that's no excuse. You should have left him a long time ago."

"I know."

Yuri and Laura were in the living room, sipping coffee after lunch. Yuri found he enjoyed his daily dialogue with Laura. She had just detailed her failed marriage.

"The divorce—how long will that take?"

"My attorney says it could take over a year to finalize."

"Why so long?"

"Ken will be out to get as much as he can from me."

"Money?"

"Yes, most likely he'll be after my stock in the company. Most of it I earned before we were married, but that won't stop him. He knows the potential. We've had several unsolicited offers to be purchased—offers beyond my wildest dreams."

"So you would be rich."

"Very comfortable."

"Hmm."

Yuri and Laura remained in the living room as Laura revealed more about her family and past. She told Yuri that her adoptive father had succumbed to a heart attack in her junior year of high school; it happened at her soccer game. William Wilson, MD, collapsed on the sidelines just after Laura scored a goal. He died in the ER.

"I'm sorry for your loss," Yuri said.

"Thank you."

"Does your mother still live in California?"

"Yes, she moved to Santa Barbara. My brother and his family live there. They have three daughters—they're wonderful."

Ten years older than Laura, the Wilson's biological son Thomas followed his father's profession; he was a neurosurgeon.

"Wow, three girls. Your brother and his wife must have their hands full."

"They are blessed."

"Yes, they are."

"Do you have siblings?" Laura asked.

"No."

"Do you see your parents?"

"Not really. My mother passed away when I was very young."

"I'm sorry to hear that."

"It was a long time ago."

"Do you see your father?"

"Rarely. We're not close."

* * *

Yuri leaned against the deck railing gazing seaward. To ward off the afternoon chill he wore a jacket commandeered from the Sea Ray. Laura napped in the living room a few steps away. He allowed her to sit on the sofa by the fireplace, ankles hobbled.

Admiring Laura's intellect, Yuri remained mystified as to her choice in men. How could she have ever married an idiot like that?

Touched by Laura's adversity and recognizing her goodness, Yuri regretted involving her in his affairs. Nevertheless, she remained his prisoner. All of his training told him he couldn't trust her. Or could he?

Racked with decompression sickness and on the verge of passing out, he'd overtly threatened her only once with his dive knife. Following that crude warning, just the presence of the knife perpetuated the threat.

Meanness was not in Yuri's nature, and during the past several days he showed compassion where he could. Laura responded with obedience and recently expressed interest in his welfare, especially his injured leg.

Yet, he remained cautious.

Again, he wondered if he could trust her.

She was an American citizen and therefore his enemy.

What should he do?

With lives of the crew at risk, he would eliminate the threat Laura represented if it came to that. His instincts, however, conveyed another message: If motivated, she could be useful.

Now that Orlov and Krestyanova were working on the problem, real help would be on the way. Or would it? Yuri recognized that the *Neva*'s fate eventually would be determined at the highest levels of the Russian government.

If Moscow approved, a rescue team would be mobilizing soon. But lingering doubts remained. Because of those misgivings, he could not afford to dismiss any option.

As Yuri shuffled back into the living room, he made a decision. If Moscow wavered, he would start working on Laura.

"Who the hell is that?" Ken Newman muttered to himself.

He hid behind the sidewall of a vacant beach house just east of Laura's rental.

An hour earlier, he'd spotted Laura's BMW in the driveway. After parking on the shoulder of the road, he walked to the home's entry, a fresh bundle of flowers in hand. He almost knocked on the door, when he heard muffled voices: Laura talking with someone inside—a male.

From his hideout, Ken had just watched the stranger step back inside the house. Despite the limp, he saw enough to set off alarms. Tall, lean, and fit with a good-looking face, the man contrasted sharply with Ken's developing beer gut, double chin, and receding hairline.

His imagination shifted into overdrive: "She's cheating on me!"

CHAPTER 19

A steady drizzle blanketed the dark and chilly Point Roberts peninsula. Ken Newman shrugged off the wetness from his parka as he walked along the water's edge. He would have been shivering if he hadn't traded his nylon windbreaker for the down-filled water-repellent REI jacket he kept in the Corvette.

Ken approached the west side of the beach house. The lower floor blazed with light. He cautiously climbed over the collection of slime-coated logs and jagged rock riprap that fronted the house.

On his hands and knees, Ken crawled across the drenched lawn. Within seconds, the knees and lower halves of his Levis were soaked. But Ken remained focused: *Who's that son of a bitch with my wife?*

Ken reached the side of the house, just below a living room window. He could hear an exchange between two people. Although muted by the window glazing, he recognized one of the voices. He stood up. Despite the glare from the interior lighting, he could see enough.

"Ah shit, I knew it," he muttered under his breath.

* * *

Laura kneeled as she faced Yuri. He sat on the couch half-naked, having removed his trousers; a towel covered his groin. Laura worked her right hand up and down his lower left leg while applying a white cream squeezed from a plastic tube.

"Do you feel anything yet?" she asked.

"No—nothing."

"It may take awhile for this work. It helped me when my legs bothered me."

"We'll see."

Laura stood and rubbed her hands together. Already the Deep Heating sizzled in her palms. She turned and walked into the kitchen, where she washed her hands.

Laura returned to the living room. She sat in a chair by his side. "Anything?" she asked.

"Nothing."

"Well, I guess my idea isn't going to work." Laura frowned. "Just what did you do to yourself, anyway?" She'd asked this before.

"It's nerve damage."

This was a new admission. "But how?"

"Don't worry about it."

"John, if you don't level with me, there's nothing I can do to help you."

"I'll be all right." Yuri leaned forward and pulled up his trousers. He stood and took a step. His left leg buckled; he collapsed back onto the sofa.

"It's getting worse, isn't it?"

A reluctant, "Yes."

Laura offered her right hand. "Let me help you up."

He grasped her hand and launched himself off the couch.

*   *   *

Ken watched as his wife helped the stranger shamble across the living room, her right arm grasping his waist. They disappeared around a corner.

Ken slid down from the window and squatted on the ground next to the house. The drizzle streamed off his nose in a tiny rivulet, but he was too stunned to notice.

CHAPTER 20

The Russian submarine *Barrakuda* patrolled along the northern California coastline at 2143 hours local time when the extremely long frequency radio wave engulfed the hull. The three-hundred-meter cable streaming behind the vessel intercepted the signal.

Five minutes later, the communications officer entered the central command post—the sub's nerve center. He approached the commanding officer, who sat in a pedestal chair near the center of the compartment. A dozen men sat at electronic consoles on either side of the CO.

"Captain, we just had Flash traffic on the ELF circuit."

"What've you got?"

The comms officer handed over the message. It read:

ECHO ONE ABLE.

Echo represented the mission call sign for the *Barrakuda*; *One Able* was a directive from the squadron commander at the Rybachiy Naval Base in Petropavlovsk.

"I guess we'd better find out what the boss wants."

"Yes, sir. I'll get the VLF buoy ready."

The *Barrakuda* ascended to a depth of one hundred meters. The ELF cable was reeled into the stern pod and the very low frequency cable deployed. The buoy at the trailing end of the cable bobbed five meters below the ocean surface.

The encrypted data stream from the VLF transmitter on Russia's Kamchatka peninsula broadcast continuously. It took the sub's commanding officer two minutes to decrypt the message, using a laptop computer in his cabin. He sat at a compact desk and reread the message, astonished at its content.

"Rescue mission," he mumbled. "How do they expect me to do that?"

CHAPTER 21

"Good night," Laura said. She leaned across the bed and switched the light off.

Yuri didn't reply. He rested on the carpet near the base of the bed. A blanket covered his body. A thought struck him, his knife—he'd left it downstairs.

Before removing his trousers for the leg massage earlier in the evening, he'd slipped the dive knife with its scabbard into the folds of the sofa. He needed to retrieve it. But he didn't have the energy, especially for the stairs. It would have to wait until the morning.

He should have tied Laura up, too. But he also reasoned that away, confident that he'd hear her if she tried to escape.

Yuri rubbed his right foot against his left shin; it remained inert. If the deterioration continued, he would have to fabricate a crutch to get around.

He had planned to head out to the *Neva* this evening, but his leg would not coöperate. Besides, he told Borodin the previous night he might not be able to make contact every night. Still, he carried the guilt.

Having to rely on others annoyed Yuri. He'd waited all day for a callback from Major Orlov—nothing. He'd called Orlov's cell several times but only got voice mail. He tried texting but received no reply. Finally, at a quarter past seven the SVR officer phoned. Nick reported that he'd not yet received new orders and that he would check in with Yuri in the morning.

Yuri tried to relax but remained anxious. Everything took too long. More than ever, he feared for the welfare of his shipmates.

His thoughts shifted to Laura. Grateful for her help tonight, Yuri was comforted to know he could call on her for additional assistance should his leg worsen.

But could he really trust her?

They occupied a table in a downtown Vancouver hotel bar. The nearest patrons, another couple, were three tables away and by the sound of their chatter, giddy from drink.

Elena Krestyanova and Nicolai Orlov, on the other hand, had been drinking vodka most of the evening yet both remained nearly sober. Their Russian blood had long ago pickled, resulting in astonishing levels of tolerance.

The SVR operatives spent the afternoon at the Trade Mission waiting for new orders. But nothing happened. There had been no reply to Orlov's status report of the previous day from either the Washington embassy or the San Francisco consulate.

Nick and Elena eventually left the mission at seven thirty. She treated him to dinner at a waterfront restaurant on Coal Harbour and they visited a packed jazz bar. After driving back to his hotel, Nick invited Elena in for a nightcap.

They both slugged down another round of Beluga—chilled and neat, and Elena said, "I still can't believe what Kirov told us."

"I know . . . it's a wild story."

"If it's true, what do you think Moscow will do?"

Orlov shrugged. "I don't think there's much they can do."

Although they could talk freely, they spoke intimately and in English, adhering to their spy schooling.

"You don't think they'll just leave them there, do you?"

Nick gestured with his hands, signaling his frustration. "What can they do? Or for that matter, what can we do? A rescue operation would take enormous resources; it'd be impossible to hide."

"There's no easy way out of this."

"No, I'm afraid not."

Ten minutes passed. Elena pried out a personal disclosure from Nick.

"You live on a houseboat!" she said.

"Yeah, I rent a small one in Sausalito; that's just across the bay from downtown. I commute on a ferry."

"Wow. Living on the water . . . that must be a fun lifestyle."

"It is—I love it there."

Elena considered her options. Attracted to Nick, she wondered if he might have mutual interest. There had been no overt signals so far. He'd remained aloof. More spy training camouflage or could it be that he's seeing someone else? Maybe, but so far he had not mentioned it. That encouraged Elena.

"Tell me, Nicolai Mironovich," she said, flashing a bewitching smile, "where did you grow up?"

"Nizhny."

She toyed with a strand of hair, twirling a finger. "How many siblings?"

"Two older sisters."

"Ah, you were the baby of the family."

"Captain, I'm worried. Some of the men are in trouble."

Stephan Borodin looked up from the cramped desk of his former CO's quarters, facing the *Neva*'s senior warrant officer. "What do you mean?"

"They're terrified, sir. They're convinced the boat is doomed."

"How many?"

"Just a few right now. But it'll spread—I'm certain of it." He paused. "Once it starts, I won't be able to control them. Anything could happen."

"Are you thinking mutiny?"

"Yes!"

Of the remaining thirty-six survivors, two-thirds were just eighteen- to twenty-year-olds with at best the equivalent of a high school education. Too few officers had survived to maintain control. If the crew mutinied, Borodin and the others would be overwhelmed.

With the officers eliminated, the mutineers could release the emergency buoy.

Although Captain Tomich had padlocked the buoy's

release mechanism when the *Neva* entered hostile waters, a bolt cutter could easily sever the lock.

Once on the surface and still tethered to the *Neva*, the buoy would broadcast an SOS. The U.S. Navy would be on top of them in a matter of hours.

"So what do you suggest?" asked Borodin.

"Maybe you could address the crew again—another report on Yuri's progress."

"But I don't have anything new to report. He may not even come out here for another day."

"I know, sir. But maybe we could go into the radio room and raise the antenna buoy, like we have a new report from Yuri. We'll make up something, anything to give them hope."

Borodin reluctantly gave in. Dima's suggestion grated him; nevertheless, he understood its utility. "If Yuri doesn't show up at the usual time, we'll try it."

"Very good, sir."

The Tsawwassen nightclub was a madhouse this late in the evening, thanks to a dozen girls in the lineup. The first few had already paraded their silicone-enhanced wares in front of the rowdy booze-guzzling crowd.

Ken Newman sat two tables back from the stage, a glass of premium Canadian whiskey in his right hand. The drink had cost twenty bucks U.S., the price of the T & A show.

"Son of a bitch!" Ken mumbled as he again thought of Laura and the man at the beach house. Her betrayal gutted him. He seethed at the thought of her in bed with another.

He flushed those images as a new dancer strutted out on the runway: a nineteen-year-old brunette, 34-D cup. The raucous music ramped up and she worked the pole. Kenny swigged down the remaining Crown Royal and held the glass up. The barmaid homed in on him with the precision of a cruise missile.

CHAPTER 22

DAY 6—SATURDAY

Laura's bladder woke her at 4:40 A.M. She drank three full cups of water before bed, counting on the consequences. Yuri remained on the floor. She listened for the next few minutes, his breathing slow and steady.

She'd been waiting for this opportunity. It was time.

Laura slipped out of the bed and retrieved her jeans, blouse, and deck shoes, all stacked neatly on the dresser top. She walked gingerly toward the door, skirting Yuri's inert form.

In the dining room, she packed her laptop and filled her briefcase with the work papers that had been scattered across the table.

She already retrieved her purse from the floor next to her briefcase and was almost ready to leave. *Where's the key?*

Laura walked into the living room. A single table lamp emitted just enough light to see. No SmartKey for her BMW.

She stepped back into the kitchen. The light fixture over the stairway flashed on. She looked up; Yuri stood at the top of the stairs.

Laura froze.

"Laura, I'm sorry to have involved you in my troubles. I had no right to keep you here. You're a good person."

Yuri's words did not yet register. Laura remained dazed. Her ploy had been discovered. He was perched near the top of the stairway, hands fixed to the railings.

As Laura stared upward, all she could comprehend was a singular thought: *Where's the knife?*

Yuri continued, "The key to your automobile is in my coat pocket." He gestured with his right hand toward the closet by the front door. With one hand on a rail, he wobbled on his feet—his lower left leg still useless. "I'm not going to stop you." He inched his way closer to the staircase. "But please, Laura, know this: If you report me to the authorities you'll be condemning three dozen men to their deaths."

Yuri stepped down onto the first stairway tread. His left leg buckled. Caught off guard, he fell forward. The right side of his head clipped the wall-mounted handrail, tearing his scalp. Stunned, he tobogganed down the stairs on his belly. He landed in a heap on the oak floor at the base of the stairway. Blood gushed from the head wound.

Laura headed north on Tyee Drive. The U.S. border station was just a minute away. She didn't bother with her suitcase or anything else in the upstairs bedroom. She'd grabbed the laptop, recovered her electronic car key, and dashed through the front door.

She'd ignored him as she exited. Yuri lay on the

foyer, moaning. Blood from his head wound pooled on the oak flooring.

But now, five minutes later, Laura had calmed down enough to consider what had happened.

He let me go—why?

What did he mean I would be condemning men to their deaths if I reported him?

CHAPTER 23

Elena Krestyanova stood by the hotel room's balcony door. Except for an oversized long-sleeved shirt that she wore—his shirt—she was naked. Elena peered around an edge of the curtain. A mini-monsoon ravished Vancouver this early morning.

She turned around and took in the other view. Nicolai's tapered torso and broad shoulders remained on full display as he lay facedown on the queen-size bed.

Elena was tempted to climb back and arouse him to wakefulness, one of her specialties. Maybe later, she thought as she walked into the bathroom.

Ken Newman lay faceup on his Tsawwassen hotel bed. A pillow covered his head. Tears pooled in his eyes.

Nursing his hangover from the four whiskies he'd downed at the nightclub, Ken relived the all too familiar low points of his life: the beatings by his father that had spawned self-doubt, which seeped into everything he touched; his early addiction to alcohol that continued to plague him; his dream career in the U.S. Navy that had sunk when he washed out of the special training program, forcing him to finish his enlistment as an ordinary seaman; his less than stellar academic performance, including his failure to complete his university degree; his boyhood dreams of grandeur quashed, replaced with mediocrity.

Now the one positive element of his life—his passport to Easy Street—was in jeopardy.

Laura had a lover! How long had she been sleeping with him? Was he the reason for the divorce?

Ken tossed the pillow aside, the green-eyed monster taking form.

Energized and dry-eyed, Ken schemed.

Half a mile south of Ken's hotel, Laura occupied a booth in a café just off Fifty-sixth Street. Her right hand trembled as she sipped from the coffee mug; she reran the events of the last hour.

When Laura approached the U.S. border station, she hesitated for half a minute before driving into the bypass lane. The Canadian border agent granted her passage into British Columbia.

She could go back right now and tell them everything. Then again, Yuri's warning remained up front and center.

How could Laura be responsible for the deaths of thirty-six people?

There'd been no time for explanations nor had Yuri

been in any position to offer one. Blood gushed from his head wound. Laura hadn't tried to assist him, not even offering a towel to help stem the flow.

She couldn't ignore what had happened.

But what could she do?

CHAPTER 24

"You need stitches," Laura said.

"No. I'll be all right."

"You could start bleeding again."

"I'm okay."

"I don't know about that." Yuri rested on a sofa in the living room. It was sunrise but the beach remained in the dark.

Laura used a pillowcase to bandage his head. With the white fabric knotted to the side and blood soaked, he looked like a pirate.

Laura sat in a chair facing Yuri. She made eye contact, took a deep breath, and said, "So, just who are you?"

"My name is Yuri Kirov. I'm an officer in the Russian Navy."

"You're Russian?"

"Yes."

"What are you doing here—in Point Roberts?"

"I was aboard a submarine that was on patrol when there was an accident. It sank. I'm the only one that made

it out so far. The rest of the survivors—thirty-six men—
are still aboard."

"They're on a submarine—a Russian submarine?"

"Yes, it's called the *Neva*."

Laura felt bewildered. "Where is it . . . where did it
sink?"

He gestured toward the windows and the sea beyond.
"It's on the bottom south of here." Yuri explained how
he'd escaped and ended up in her beach house.

Laura connected the dots: the offshore boat trips,
the stereo speaker in the pressure cooker, his mysteri-
ous calls on her cell phone.

"What were you doing here . . . in your submarine?"

"We were on a reconnaissance mission."

Laura countered, "You were spying on us, weren't
you?"

"No, not America—Canada."

"Canada?"

"Yes, a torpedo testing station near Nanaimo in
Nanoose Bay."

Laura cocked her head to one side.

"We were careful to stay out of American waters,"
Yuri continued, improvising.

"Why?"

"The U.S. Navy has too many sensors for us to risk
it—the submarine base at Bangor."

"The one on Hood Canal?"

"Yes."

"So just to be clear, you were not spying on the United
States and you stayed in Canadian waters the whole way
here?"

"Yes."

"Where exactly is your submarine right now?"

Yuri reached up with his left hand and adjusted the head bandage. "During the accident, we lost navigational control and drifted with the current. We bottomed out in Canadian waters but close to the border with America."

"How close?"

"About two hundred meters."

Laura cupped her forehead with both hands and stared at the floor.

Yuri left the living room to use the bathroom. Laura stood by a window. Whitecaps dotted the seascape and gray-black clouds boiled across the post-dawn sky.

If not rescued soon, Yuri's submates would perish. But how could he hope to save them? He could barely walk.

And what were they really doing in that sub? Yuri and his shipmates were spies. He said they were checking on a Canadian naval base. What else were they up to?

And the part that distressed Laura the most: Yuri had asked for her assistance with the Sea Ray later in the evening.

What should she do?

Yuri lay stretched out on the sofa in the living room. Laura sat at the dining room table, working. He'd built a fire and welcomed its therapeutic warmth. His head still ached but new pain radiated from his shoulders and lower back. His tumble down the stairs had levied a new tax on his already beat-up body.

Thankful that Laura had agreed to help him with the boat tonight, he thought ahead to the mission. *What am I going to tell Stephan?* Yuri called Nick Orlov but the SVR officer had nothing new to report regarding any rescue effort.

Everything's taking too long. They don't have much time left. What should I do?

Yuri regretted the lies and half truths he'd told Laura. She was innocent. He wished he didn't have to involve her in his business.

Nevertheless, he needed her help.

It was late morning. Laura sat at the dining room table staring at her laptop's screen. Yuri dozed on the sofa by the fireplace.

She tried concentrating on the marketing memo but her mind wandered, still stunned by Yuri's tale. Laura looked up and peered seaward again. The wind howled out of the southeast. Waves exploded on the seawall, spilling spray onto the lawn.

They're out there, she thought, reflecting on the Russian sailors—entombed on the bottom under hundreds of feet of water with no hope except for Yuri.

But what can he do?

And what can I do? Besides, it's not my concern. I should just go home.

Laura couldn't do that. She'd already agreed to help Yuri—just tonight. He clearly needed aid. His limp had worsened.

It would be a rough voyage. Laura rubbed her belly; it ached—again. She stretched out her arms, inhaled, and ordered herself back to work.

Laura typed several more paragraphs, when a knock at the front door broke her focus. She looked toward the entry. Another knock, louder this time. She'd had no visitors since arriving—except for Yuri.

Laura glanced at the sofa where Yuri slept. She stood up and walked to the foyer. She unlatched the dead bolt and opened the door.

Her husband stood in the entryway.

"Hello, Laura," Ken said.

Laura's right hand raced to her mouth. *"What are you doing here?"*

"We need to talk."

Laura smelled alcohol on his breath.

"You can't be near me—the restraining order prohibits any contact." Her voice quavered; her hands trembled.

"I'm sorry about what I did. I don't know how it happened. It won't—"

She cut him off. "Leave now or I'm going to call the police."

"Can I come in?"

"No. Go away."

She pushed the door shut, but he thrust his right foot into the doorjamb. He wore sneakers and the door pinched his foot.

"Ahhhhh!" he roared. He shoved the door open, propelling Laura backward.

She tripped and tumbled onto the hardwood floor.

"Oh damn, I didn't mean to do that," Ken said as he stood over Laura.

She curled into the fetal position, raising her arms to guard her head, just as she'd done the last time Ken had kicked her.

Ken bent down to offer a helping hand, when a blur rushed his way. The attacker slammed into Ken's left side.

Ken staggered backward through the open doorway onto the concrete walkway. Before he could mount a defense, a fist knifed into his gut. He doubled over and sank to his knees.

As Ken fought to regain his breath, he looked up. His assailant towered over him, his face flush, teeth clenched, and fists poised for a second round. The bloodstained bandage encircling the man's head completed the menacing image.

Ken raised his left hand in surrender. "This is all a mistake. I didn't mean to—"

"You get out of here now!" Yuri ordered. "And don't ever come back."

"Okay, okay. Just leave me alone."

"Are you all right?" Yuri asked.

"Yes, I think so."

Yuri wasn't so sure. Laura's hands continued to tremble and perspiration beaded on her brow. They stood in the foyer; the front door was closed. The screech of burning rubber on asphalt marked Ken Newman's hasty retreat.

Despite his impaired leg and new injuries, Yuri had mustered every ounce of reserve strength during his brief but fierce confrontation with Ken. Within minutes, his body would revert to its former bruised and battered state as the adrenaline rush faded.

"I don't understand how he found me so quickly," Laura said. "My office doesn't even know where I am."

She shook her head. "I don't trust him. He's vicious when he drinks."

"What do you want to do about him?"

"My attorney told me that if he ever confronted me to call the police and then call him."

Yuri handed her cell phone back to Laura. "Here's your phone. But give me ten minutes to collect my gear before making your calls."

"Why?"

"I must leave—I can't be here when the authorities arrive. I have no papers."

Laura considered. "I think you scared him away."

"I wouldn't count on it." Yuri hobbled toward the stairway to the upper floor.

"Wait. You don't need to go . . . I'm not going to call the police."

He turned around. "You're not safe here. He will come back."

"But if you're here, he won't dare bother me." She smiled weakly. "I'm more frightened of Ken than I've ever been of you."

Laura walked to Yuri and clasped his right hand. Looking up to meet his eyes she said, "Thank you for protecting me. I'm truly grateful."

CHAPTER 25

Ken Newman sat in his parked Corvette at a water-front park near the southwest tip of Point Roberts. Like the turbulent seascape he faced, his thoughts roiled.

He didn't mean for Laura to fall; it was an accident.

The ferocity of the attack remained fresh. *That prick blindsided me; if I'd seen him coming, I would've cleaned his clock. I had no choice but to back off.*

He has no idea who he's dealing with.

The incident ripped open a long festering wound, taking him back to Coronado; he'd just turned twenty.

For two grueling weeks, Ken had endured the challenges: four-mile-long timed runs along the California beach, exhausting obstacle courses that never got easier, swimming a couple miles in the freezing Pacific every other day, and carrying that damn rubber boat on top of his head—and those of the other six members of his boat crew—just about everywhere.

He watched others DOR—drop on request. They dropped their helmet liners next to a pole with a ship's bell mounted to it and rang the bell three times, signaling their surrender.

But Ken was determined. He would make it.

Aptly named Hell Week, the third week of Basic Underwater Demolition/SEAL (BUD/S) training was five and a half days of nonstop exertion with just a total of four hours of sleep.

Ken lasted fifty-six hours and then rang the bell.

He flushed those hurtful thoughts with a long swig from the beer bottle. He would have just one to help calm down before driving home. He could handle it. He knew his limits.

Ken refocused on Laura's protector. All doubt had evaporated.

That bastard is screwing my wife.

So what's so great about him?

Ken took a long gulp, draining the bottle.

He's a gimp for God's sake! What does she see in 'im, anyway?

Ken tossed the empty aside. He rearmed, removed the cap, and took another bolt.

Laura rested on the bed.

How did he find me? she wondered.

They met nearly three years earlier at a dinner party hosted by one of Laura's girlfriends. Ken Newman drew in Laura with his warm smile, teal eyes, and shock of blond hair. Outgoing and upbeat, the real estate professional had represented a welcome diversion to the typical men she'd dated, geeky tech-heads.

During the six-month courtship, Ken had lavished attention on Laura like no other suitor.

The first hitch occurred in the spring following their marriage. Ken lost the listing on a Bellevue office park to a rival. Already drunk from an afternoon bender at a local bar, he'd slapped Laura around at home, tearing a lip and bruising an arm.

When he sobered up, Ken pleaded ignorance and begged forgiveness. Eager to save her marriage and optimistic that she could turn Ken around, Laura conceded.

Ken ran straight and true for about a year but went off course, again—a hot stock tip turned toxic and he lost forty grand overnight. After bingeing, he took it out on Laura. She worked from her home office for a week until the black eye healed.

Ashamed, Ken voluntarily sought treatment and joined AA.

Laura loved Ken. If she just gave him time, he would change.

All went well until earlier in the current year when an office building deal Ken had shepherded went south. He'd been counting on the fat commission; he hadn't scored in months.

Laura again took the brunt of Ken's bad luck after another whiskey spree. She called 911 that time and Ken spent the night in the King County jail, booked for domestic violence.

Laura banned Ken from their home but declined to pursue prosecution. He again committed himself to an alcohol treatment clinic. Laura's insurance paid for the rehab.

Once detoxed, Ken eagerly attended joint sessions with their marriage counselor. Heartened with his progress, Laura prayed that Ken had passed a milestone and their marriage could be saved. They even talked about having a child. But then he lost it again.

Ticketed for speeding in his sports car, his third time in a year, Ken drowned his hard luck in bourbon. Later that evening—just a few weeks earlier—he used Laura for soccer practice.

That's when Laura finally realized she'd been living with Dr. Jekyll and Mr. Hyde.

Laura thought of Yuri.

He's a good man.

All he's trying to do is save his shipmates.

And he protected me from Ken!

CHAPTER 26

Nick Orlov watched the daily NFL briefing on cable TV while stretched out on his hotel bed. He'd become an ardent 49ers fan after attending a home game while wooing a prospective agent. The Google engineer rejected his pitch but Nick ended up hooked. He now held season tickets. The 49ers were ten and one. Tonight's tube chatter hinted the team might be on its way to another Super Bowl.

Nick's cell buzzed. He muted the television and picked up the phone. The SVR officer was calling from a pay phone in the lobby of a downtown San Francisco hotel.

"So what's going on?" Nick asked, speaking in English.

"A marketing plan is being prepared."

Both men spoke in code, designed to avoid NSA and FBI interest.

"But what am I supposed to do?"

"Wait for further instructions."

"That's all I've been doing up here—waiting."

"Same for me. Headquarters is in a frenzy over something happening in the Tokyo office. They're consumed with it. We're on the backburner."

"Chërt voz'mí!"—Dammit—Nick said, violating his own security protocol.

"I know but try to relax; Vancouver's a great town."

Nick did not reply.

Nick's colleague switched gears. "You've got to tell me: Is she as good as she looks?"

"What?"

"Elena. I saw her file today. *Klássnyy!*" Classy.

"She's okay."

"Just okay? I'd be sniffing around that every chance I had."

Nick ignored the innuendo. "Do you have anything else for me?"

"No, I'll call you in the morning with an update."

"All right, good night."

Nick couldn't fault his coworker's desire for Elena Krestyanova, aka Nastasia Vasileva. He, too, read her file before heading north. Recruited for both her beauty and her smarts, she worked exclusively undercover.

Elena's assignment called for her to assist the chief of mission with promoting Russian fisheries and mineral exports to Canada. Her real orders originated from the SVR.

Directorate X in Moscow selected Elena's target. The fifty-seven-year-old headed an electronics company based in Vancouver. The corporation had over fifteen thousand employees with manufacturing plants located throughout North America. It provided satellite communication systems to the U.S. Department of Defense and other NATO countries.

Elena met her target at a party arranged by a Canadian accomplice affiliated with the Trade Mission. As planned, the CEO took the bait. He had a stale thirty-three-year marriage and was starving. Elena knew exactly how to satisfy that craving.

They had sex twice, both times at Elena's apartment. Each liaison was videoed. Her SVR handler wanted one more encounter before confronting the target.

The handler would make the tender up front and to the CEO's face: Provide access to his company's secrets, or else.

The "else" would be the transfer of the videos to a hundred plus digital videodiscs. The DVDs would be mailed anonymously to the CEO's wife, his four grown children, his firm's board of directors, his fellow church elders, and every member of his Rotary club.

The honey trap was an old espionage tactic but one that still produced results.

Nick slipped off the bed and headed to the shower. Elena had arranged another working meeting this evening: "Dinner for two at the Four Seasons and then we'll see."

Even though cheating went against his grain, Nick couldn't resist the temptation.

Svetlana Petrova would be returning to the consulate in early December. The previous week, she flew back to Moscow for a month of training; she worked in the consulate's cryptographic section. Nick had been sleeping with her for nearly half a year.

"If you make that shot I'll kiss your ass."

While leaning against the pool table, Ken Newman

turned to his right and peered over his shoulder. He grinned at the tall Canadian lumberjack standing behind him. Ken turned and lined up the cue stick. With a flick of the wrist, he hammered it into the ball. The ivory sphere blasted across the table, rebounded from the opposite side, and raced past a cluster of his opponent's balls. It kissed his target. The eight ball dribbled into the corner pocket.

"Son of a bitch!" the loser called out in unbelief. The crowd of spectators surrounding the table erupted in laughter.

Ken bent to the side, aiming his right buttock toward the loser. He patted it with his hand and while grinning said, "Pucker up, man!"

"No way!"

Ken broke the pose and stood. "Just buy me another beer, Clive, and we'll be good."

"My kind of Yank!"

Ken was in a watering hole located along the western shore of Point Roberts. It was half past eight in the evening. There were about sixty patrons, mostly Canadians.

On his way home earlier, he drove past the Tides, a tavern and eatery that had been constructed the previous year. Its parking lot was packed, typical for a Saturday afternoon. Although Ken had already killed a six-pack while sitting in his Vette, he decided to have one more for the road.

After downing a beer and playing several rounds of video games Ken began playing pool, the one game he excelled at. All thoughts of Laura and her lover had dissolved, replaced by an all too familiar buzz.

Ken took a long pull on a fresh bottle. He belched loudly and called out, "Who's next?"

A tall redhead with stunning jade eyes, fire engine red lips, and blue jeans glued to her exquisite butt strolled up to the table. "My turn, love," she said, her "down under" accent clearly marking her.

She appeared to be in her early forties. Crow's feet around the eyes were the only distractions to her otherwise pleasing face.

She stood by his side, cue stick in her right hand. "What are we playing?"

"Eight ball, you break 'em."

"Okay, sounds good." She offered her right hand. "Hi, I'm Emma."

"Ken," he muttered, shaking her hand.

"Nice to meet you, Ken."

"Same here."

"You live here—at the Point?" she asked, rubbing the end of the cue with a chalk block.

"Nahh. I'm from the Seattle area, up here looking around. How about you?"

"Just across the border, Ladner."

Ken leaned against the table.

Emma unbuttoned the top two buttons of her blouse and slipped her right hand inside. She removed a folded U.S. fifty-dollar bill and unfolded it with her long, manicured fingers. Ken's eyes tracked her every movement.

She placed the bill on the edge of the table and said, "Kenny, love, what do you say we make our game a little more interesting?"

He met her eyes and again looked down at the fifty. "Okay, I'm game."

Ken placed two twenties and a ten on top of her bill.

Emma set up the rack and leaned forward, lining up for the break. Ken's heart almost skipped a beat. Her blouse remained partially unbuttoned, and cleavage oozed from the opening.

She made a clean break and as Ken took up position for his first shot, she walked over to his side and whispered into his left ear. "Kenny, if you beat me two out of three games, you can take me home, too."

Holy shit!

CHAPTER 27

Laura had been seasick once before, during a sailboat excursion on San Francisco Bay while in high school. But what she endured this evening dwarfed that experience.

For the past fifteen minutes, she'd locked herself inside the head—the Sea Ray's lavatory. Both arms embraced the bowl as she dry-heaved. Laura had already emptied her stomach and flushed the contents.

Laura took a deep breath, her nose and mouth seared by vomit. "Oh Lord," she moaned, "I think I'm going to die!"

Yuri avoided motion sickness but he worried over Laura's welfare. The storm's four-foot waves bore down on the thirty-one-foot fiberglass cruiser out of the southeast, the course he steered. With the engine throttled back, they'd been plowing into the oncoming seas for almost half an hour but had another twenty minutes to go.

Yuri slipped off the captain's chair, transferring most of his weight onto his right leg. With his right hand on the wheel and his good leg braced against the instrument panel, he leaned forward, ducking his head into the open companionway that led into the main cabin. The door to the head remained shut.

"Laura, are you all right?" he yelled.

The door flew open and Laura poked her head out, still on her hands and knees.

"No, I think I'm—" But before she could finish another spasm racked her stomach and she turned around. The boat rolled and the door slammed shut.

Yuri returned to the helm. He thought about turning about and running with the waves. It would be a more comfortable ride. But he dismissed the idea. They had to tough it out, no matter how sick she got. His crewmates were counting on him.

Ken Newman didn't have a chance. Emma fleeced him two games straight, collecting one hundred dollars. He later met a couple of Tides regulars, both Americans living at the Point. That's when Ken learned that to their collective knowledge she'd never lost a game.

Ken decided to call it a night at half past one. Too wasted to drive home, Ken wanted only to get back to the hotel in Tsawwassen and crash.

He was halfway down Gulf Road when a Whatcom County deputy sheriff pulled him over. His Corvette had strayed across the centerline but not because of the wind and rain.

As the deputy approached, the headlights from the cruiser flooded the interior of the sports car. Ken sensed peril. "Oh shit," he muttered.

The *Barrakuda* crossed into the territorial waters of Canada at 0147 hours local time. The submarine cruised northeasterly one hundred meters below the surface at a stealthy five knots. It closed on a deep-water channel that skirted the southern boundary of the Swiftsure Bank.

To ensure quiet conditions, crew members not on essential duty occupied their bunks. The galley and mess had been shut down.

Captain Second Rank Oleg Antipov stood beside the chart table in the central post. The tallest man aboard at six-foot-six, he had thick blond hair that brushed the undersides of the cables and piping suspended from the overhead. During his twenty-year career in submarines, he'd developed a sixth sense about ducking to avoid obstacles.

The ship's navigator was at Antipov's side; they both studied the Canadian Hydrographic Service chart. It depicted the southwestern coast of British Columbia's Vancouver Island and the northern shoreline of the United States. In between lay the Strait of Juan de Fuca. The *Barrakuda* would enter the shared waterway in a few minutes.

"Once we reach the one hundred and thirty meter contour, turn east and head in on Backdoor," Antipov ordered.

"Yes, sir," the navigator replied.

Antipov picked up a microphone. "Sonar, control. What's your status?"

"No change, Captain. We're still tracking five primary targets, two inbound and three outbound—all classified as merchantmen. There are three secondary contacts. All are consistent with commercial fishing craft or recreational boats."

"Very well."

Antipov again studied the chart. Although top quality, as were the multitude of other Canadian and U.S. charts stored in the flat files under the table, it didn't measure up.

Once the *Barrakuda* reached the 130-meter bottom contour, the navigator would switch to a computerized chart system. The digital underwater roadmap had an accuracy of one meter vertically and two meters horizontally.

Such precision was crucial. To avoid the U.S. Navy's acoustic arrays positioned along the length and breadth of the Strait of Juan de Fuca, the *Barrakuda* would take a serpentine route.

Predecessors of the *Barrakuda* had mapped the way, nine separate probes in total with each new survey built on the work of the previous excursions. Code-named *Backdoor*, the underwater path represented one of the most decisive espionage operations ever conducted by Russia. It extended to the very doorstep of the U.S. Navy's most potent weapon system.

A squadron of *Ohio*-class ballistic missile submarines home-ported at Naval Base Kitsap-Bangor located on Hood Canal. Armed with twenty-four Trident intercontinental ballistic missiles with each missile carrying up to eight nuclear warheads, just one *Ohio* boat could inflict a near deathblow to the Russian Federation's strategic forces.

The prime mission for the *Barrakuda* and its sister subs was to make certain that never happened. But it now had a new mission, one never anticipated or planned for in the Russian Navy.

CHAPTER 28

By the time the Sea Ray arrived over the *Neva,* the waves had subsided enough to allow Yuri with Laura's help to link up with the VLF buoy and reestablish comms. Sunrise remained hours away.

Still queasy, Laura stood beside Yuri in the cockpit as he spoke with Captain Borodin over the closed circuit phone line. Although she could not understand their conversation because of the language barrier, the strain in Borodin's voice was obvious.

After just five minutes, Yuri signed off.

"How are they?" asked Laura.

"Not well. More equipment problems and the lack of heat are wearing all of them down. Some are starting to get sick."

That all sounded ominous to Laura. "How about oxygen, is that still functioning?"

"Thankfully, yes."

"That's good."

"One less thing to worry about, but they need to be rescued now."

"That's in progress—right?"

"I hope so."

But Yuri had no assurance that was the case. He had not yet heard back from Orlov or Krestyanova.

Yuri hobbled toward the stern. "Please help me disconnect from the buoy. It's time for us to return to the marina."

"Let me take care of that."

Laura climbed over the rear seat cushions and lowered herself onto the swim step. Her running shoes and the calves of her jeans were soaked again as residual wave action washed over the cantilevered platform.

Laura disconnected the telephone handset cable from the VLF cable and handed the free end to Yuri. With her left hand gripping the hull, she leaned seaward and used her right hand to free the mooring line from the buoy.

"Okay, we're free now," she called out.

Yuri offered a hand as she climbed back into the cockpit.

Once aboard, Yuri said, "Thank you, Laura. I could have never done this tonight without your help."

"You're welcome."

A jackhammer worked overtime inside Ken Newman's skull. He sat on the edge of the mattress, elbows resting on his knees, hands clasping his head.

He'd had hangovers before, but this one achieved a new level of misery. "Ahhhh," he muttered, "this is bad."

Ken tried to stand, when the queasiness struck. He collapsed back onto the bed, rolled onto his side, and gagged.

"Don't puke on the floor."

"Whaaaat?" moaned Ken, clutching his stomach.

"I said don't spill your guts on the floor. Use the bucket." The middle-aged man sitting on the twin to Ken's bunk, six feet away, kicked the plastic bucket. It skidded across the floor and slammed into the metal frame of Ken's bed.

Ken lay still until the spasm passed. "Where are we?" he asked.

"You're in jail, you moron."

"Jail—oh God!"

Ken surveyed his surroundings. The holding cell was about twelve feet square. It had no windows, just a single steel door with a tiny glass window at eye level. A bank of fluorescent lights lined the ceiling. A toilet and a sink claimed one corner.

Ken faced his cellmate. The heavyset stranger with shoulder-length black hair reclined on the bare mattress, his back propped up by a pillow jammed against the bed frame.

"What time is it?" Ken asked, noticing for the first time his missing wristwatch.

"Damned if I know. Pricks always take your watch." Tats littered the man's exposed forearms.

Ken turned away, trying to think despite his pounding brain. *What the hell did I do?*

It came back in a rush: The fight with Laura's lover; the six-pack in the Vette; more beer and shooting pool at the Tides; Emma's boobs, her hustle and even more beer; and then he couldn't remember. What happened to his right wrist? Like his head, it throbbed, too.

"Are we in Point Roberts?"

His cellmate laughed. "At least you got that right."

Ken walked to the door. He pounded it with his uninjured hand. No response. "Open the door," he yelled. "I want to call my attorney."

His companion let out another belly laugh.

"What are you laughing at?" Ken snapped, turning around.

"Ain't going to do you no good banging on that door. No one's home right now."

"What do you mean?"

"Hey, man, this is Point Roberts. There's just one full-time deputy up here plus another on weekends and holidays. They're probably having breakfast."

"I can't stay here—I've got things to do."

"You ain't going nowhere fast, that much I can tell you."

"Why?"

"You get picked up for drunk driving?"

Ken peered down at the floor as fragments of his arrest coalesced. "Yeah," he answered.

"So why'd you take a swing at one of the deputies?"

"What?" Ken said, looking up.

"I heard 'em talking when they brought you in. You clobbered one of 'em; he was bitching about his sore jaw."

"Oh no."

"That's assault, man. They're going to throw the book at you."

Ken glowered, disgusted with his behavior. He'd had a few bar tussles over the years, and he'd used Laura as a punching bag—only when drunk. But hitting a cop? Another low for Ken.

"What are they going to do with me?"

"Nothing here. You're headed to jail to be arraigned. Then you can post bail."

"Where?"

"Bellingham, but don't be surprised if it takes a couple days before you get there."

"What? It's just an hour's drive away."

"Sure, but that means you've got to drive through BC. The Canucks won't let the cops transport U.S. prisoners on their soil."

"So how do we get there?"

"Usually by boat. But the sheriff's office don't like making the crossing to Blaine unless it's a millpond—something about safety requirements. So, if it's still snotty out there, we've both got a wait ahead of us."

Kenny collapsed back on the bed. "How come you know so much about this place?"

"Been there, done that."

Both rested from their early-morning rendezvous with the *Neva*, Yuri and Laura sat side-by-side on the leather sofa in the living room. Crackling flames in the fireplace helped ward off the afternoon chill.

Yuri stared into the stone fireplace. He reached up with his right hand and caressed his scalp. The wound throbbed. Just before leaving for the boat trip, Laura smeared Neosporin onto a thread and a sewing needle from her cosmetics case and stitched the inch-long tear. His hair partially concealed the injury.

"Is it still bothering you?" Laura asked.

"It's a little sore."

"Maybe I should check it."

He lowered his hand. "It's okay."

Yuri shifted position on the sofa and said, "Laura, I

think it would be best if you just went home. I'm sorry to have involved you in my problems."

"But what about your submates? How will you help them? You can barely walk."

"I'll manage, and with help from the Trade Mission we'll find a way to make the rescue."

Laura's instincts told her that she should leave. The *Neva*'s plight was not her responsibility. Instead, she responded, "I could get help for your crew."

"What do you mean?"

"I could call our Navy and they'd mount a rescue."

Yuri frowned. "Remember what I told you earlier, if the *Neva* is detected by your nation or the Canadians, the crew will self-destruct."

Laura looked away, her eyes dropping downward.

Aboard the *Neva*, the hull temperature was a few degrees above freezing. Every surface dripped with condensation. Bone-chilled in their damp clothing and bedding, the crew languished with spirits bordering on bankruptcy.

Several men had pneumonia. The boat's medic was treating them with antibiotics and bed rest.

Those that could work tackled the fouled seawater cooling system. Pump equipment, filters, valves, and piping not designed for disassembly while submerged had to be first isolated and then each part bypassed to maintain the flow of seawater that cooled the turbo generator. The workers extracted the gunk from inside the isolated parts and reassembled the equipment.

All work had to be done by hand, employing block

and tackle to suspend and move the bone-crunching heavy hardware. With hundreds of feet of pipe and numerous appurtenances, it was a Herculean task.

The crew had managed a diminutive improvement. The electrical power output increased from 11 percent to 15 percent, not enough to make a real difference but moving in the right direction.

The bilge pumps continued to match the leakage. That boosted the crew's morale.

Unfortunately, the one remaining head malfunctioned. The pump that jettisoned the contents of the toilet's holding tank seized up. A two-man crew worked the problem but no joy yet.

With the holding tank filled to the brim, the crew used buckets, pails, and any available container. The stench spread throughout the pressure casing. It was like living inside of a septic tank.

Despite the awful living conditions, the *Neva*'s crew still had hope. Yuri promised them all that he would bring help. With that spark of optimism, they endured.

CHAPTER 29

DAY 8—MONDAY

The *Barrakuda* was ten nautical miles south of Victoria, Vancouver Island's largest city and the provincial capital of British Columbia. For the past twenty-four hours, the sub had followed the pre-surveyed route code-named Backdoor, creeping just above the bottom.

Captain Antipov remained at the conn during the transit of the Strait of Juan de Fuca. He successfully skirted the U.S. Navy's acoustic sensors planted along the seabed, their GPS coordinates provided by a paid turncoat in the Department of Defense. But a perpetual threat remained. American hunter-killers—*Los Angeles-*, *Virginia-*, and *Seawolf*-class submarines—inhabited these waters at times. They were designed to destroy submarines like the *Barrakuda*. Antipov took extreme care not to rouse one of those steel sharks.

The *Barrakuda* would soon depart from the Backdoor route. Instead of turning southward toward Admiralty Inlet and Hood Canal beyond, it would head northward into Haro Strait—uncharted waters.

The approaching waterway was narrow and torturous in places, and likely laced with acoustic monitors. Antipov would need to maneuver with maximum stealth and acute care. That meant running slow and staying deep.

Nicolai Orlov and Elena Krestyanova arrived early. They picked a booth in the back, away from the main dining area, and ordered coffee. There weren't many patrons in the Point Roberts restaurant this late morning, but that would change in about an hour. Hungry regulars from both sides of the border eagerly sought Fat Billie's cheeseburgers. The restaurant was a remake of Fat Willie's, the Point's legendary eatery from the 1980s.

"Why did he choose this place?" asked Elena. "The other one we met at has a water view." She peered at a nearby window. "Here, just a field."

"I don't know. Maybe he likes—" Orlov stopped speaking as he craned his neck in the direction of the front door, some thirty feet away. "There he is!" He stood and raised his right arm.

Yuri Kirov walked toward the couple, his limp pronounced, but he made it without stumbling. He sat down in the booth next to Elena.

"Good morning," offered Orlov in their native tongue, speaking softly.

"Please," Yuri said, "English only here. I don't want to draw any more attention to myself than I already have."

"Your leg?" asked Nick.

"Yes, I try to blend in but I still stand out with this limp."

Elena smiled and said, "How are you managing . . . is it any better?"

"A little." He lied.

A waitress approached Yuri. "Care for coffee?" she asked.

"No, thank you, but I'd like a chocolate milk shake and a double cheeseburger."

"With fries?"

That threw Yuri for a temporary loop and then he remembered: french-fried potatoes. "Yes, please, lots of those. And ketchup, too."

Yuri remembered something else. "And give him the bill for my lunch."

"Got it." She faced Nick and Elena. "What can I get for you folks?"

"Just some more coffee for me," Elena said. Nick echoed her request and flashed a friendly grin, wondering how Yuri had learned to pass on the bill so quickly.

After filling the cups, the server moved to another customer.

Nick asked, "How's the crew?"

"The men are getting sick. Lack of heat, stress, bad air, poor sanitation. I'm extremely worried." Yuri set both elbows on the table and interlaced his fingers. "We must initiate rescue."

"I thought you said they could last a week or so."

"Borodin told me the crew's morale is shot—they're giving up hope. There was even one escape attempt, completely unauthorized. The man drowned."

"Did he get out?" Nick said.

"No."

"Where's his body?"

"Recovered from the escape chamber."

"Good."

"The chamber is now guarded. It won't happen again—unless there's no hope."

"What do you mean?" Elena asked.

"If we can't get them out, their only chance will be to risk a free ascent." Yuri dropped his hands while shifting position on the bench. "Maybe a few will survive, but most won't. Anyway, that would be a quicker way to go than rotting away inside that stinking *sortir*."

Elena reacted silently to Yuri's admission: If dead Russian sailors started washing up on the shore, the Americans and Canadians would never stop looking for the source.

Major Orlov was more direct. "You know they can't do such a thing. It's against all protocols. If they can't be rescued they'll have to do their duty."

"Self-destruct? *Ni khrená!*" Nothing of the kind. "The codes to trigger the scuttling charges were known only to the captain and the executive officer—and they're both dead."

"But surely, they could figure out some way to do it."

"*Nyet!* All of the extra explosives are in the torpedo room. It's flooded; there's no access."

Yuri spiked his responses with the occasional Russian epithet to elicit sympathy from the SVR officers. He also lied. *Neva* had three scuttling charges, each bomb containing one hundred kilograms of semtex and molded into unobtrusive shapes in the bilge piping. The first charge was in the torpedo room, flooded and inaccessible, the second under the CCP, and the last in the engine compartment. Borodin could easily rig manual detonators to the two accessible charges.

Although Yuri had used the self-destruct threat to motivate Laura and confuse Orlov, he never broached the subject with Stephan Borodin—something he could not do. Still, his colleague had to be considering the role he would be expected to fulfill. The order would be direct: *"Captain Borodin, for the good of the Motherland, you must do your duty."*

Moscow had to be thinking about it, too, perhaps just at the contingency level. A shattered hulk, its fragments swallowed up by the bottom muck, and the entire crew shredded into fish-food chunks would solve all of the Kremlin's problems. The official decree from fleet headquarters would acknowledge that the *Neva* had failed to return to its homeport due to unknown causes and that the submarine and its ninety-two men were lost.

Yuri addressed Orlov "Enough of this self-destruction *chush' sobách'ya*." Bullshit. "We must rescue the crew. They're our brothers, our comrades."

Nick and Elena acknowledged their agreement.

Yuri leaned forward, meeting both sets of eyes. "When can I expect some help?"

"We should have something for you tomorrow," Nick said.

"Good, what's Moscow planning?"

"I don't have any details. All I was told last night is that a rescue plan is being prepared."

"How? Where?"

"We have no details yet."

"When you drive back to Vancouver, call your superiors and tell them to hurry. I'm worried about what might happen to the officers if we wait too long."

"What do you mean?" Elena said.

"Captain Borodin is just one man. If the crew panics"—Yuri scowled—"hysteria can spread like a wildfire. If the crew wanted, they could overpower Borodin and the other officers. They could release the emergency buoy and signal the Americans and Canadians. Can you imagine the *govnó* that would create back in Moscow?"

Nicolai and Elena departed; Nick left a U.S. twenty-dollar bill. Yuri was wolfing his way through the burger when Laura walked into the restaurant. She slipped into the booth, opposite Yuri.

Still chewing, he pushed his plate with a mound of fries to her side. "Have some."

"You must really like this place." Laura declined, not hungry and her stomach queasy—again.

"Ummm," Yuri said, devouring the last of the sandwich. "That was delicious. There's nothing like this back home." He took a long draw on a straw, sucking in the thick creamy shake. He'd visited a McDonald's in Moscow just once, not wanting to return.

Laura smiled at Yuri's fondness for such common fare. Yesterday he had his first all-American combo, also at Fat Billie's. Tired of eating at the beach house, Laura convinced him to lunch out—her treat.

"So what did they say?" Laura asked. She could have been halfway to Bellingham by now. Yet, she didn't leave.

Yuri swallowed another slug of the milk shake before answering. "They claim there's an operation under way but have no details. They're supposed to have more information tomorrow."

"Do you believe that?"

"I expect what they told me was what they'd been told to say."

"What can they do, I mean, how will they help?"

"With the right kind of equipment, I can get them all out."

"What would you need?"

"A large workboat outfitted with a rescue diving bell and hoist system. The bell can be lowered down and . . ."

When Yuri finished, Laura asked, "Where can you find such equipment?"

"The American offshore oil industry. They're pioneers in deep diving."

"I don't think there are any oil companies around here."

"You're right. They're mostly in the Gulf of Mexico and some in California and Alaska."

"But those places are thousands of miles away. How could you ever get it here?"

"Easy. Find the bell and rent it, or buy it. Put it on an air freighter and fly it to Seattle. Mount it on a workboat and sail it to Point Roberts. It can all be done in a couple of days."

"But you certainly can't do all of that."

"Of course, but we have resources here that can do it."

"You mean spies?"

"Call it what you like, but we have the capability to accomplish the task, with your help."

Laura's already tender stomach flip-flopped. She recalled the Russian spy ring that had made national head-lines a few years earlier. The FBI rounded up nearly twenty sleeper agents scattered across the United States.

What am I doing here? Laura wondered to herself.

If I help them directly—the Russian Navy, even if they are in Canada, I could go to jail!

If I tell the government, the Neva*'s crew will blow themselves up.*

If they're not rescued, they'll all die.

That was Laura's paradox.

Finally, she considered Yuri; he had stood up to Ken, protecting her.

Just one more day, and then I'll go home.

"Captain, I need a few minutes of your time."

"Come in."

The U.S. Navy lieutenant commander walked into her boss's office. The commanding officer of Naval Undersea Warfare Center Division, Keyport, Washington, sat behind his desk.

"What's up?" asked the CO as the naval base's environmental officer took a seat.

"Sir, I had a phone call this morning from a senior scientist with NOAA in Seattle. We've had another complaint."

The captain frowned. "Those fish people again?"

"Yes, National Marine Fisheries Service. But they're not the ones making the stink. Turns out a professor from the University of British Columbia contacted them. She's accusing us of making unauthorized sonar tests in the south end of the Strait of Georgia."

"That's nuts. We don't operate anywhere there."

"I know, and I relayed that to NMFS."

The officer opened a file folder and removed a ten-page document. She handed it to the captain. "NMFS e-mailed the complaint. It's quite detailed and I can understand the professor's concern."

The CO glanced through the document, stopping at a graphical plot. "What's this about?"

"It appears the BC researchers picked up some kind of underwater anomaly. The pressure spike in that plot is way above background levels."

"When did this happen?"

"A week ago."

"Hmm, well that's certainly not anything from us."

"Yes, sir."

"Let's have our technical group look at it. Maybe they can figure out what happened."

"Very good, sir. I will notify Dr. Markley."

CHAPTER 30

The *Barrakuda* crept into Boundary Pass at 1304 hours local time, hugging the bottom. Captain Antipov would have preferred tackling the channel at night when his submarine could run on the surface. But they were late and every minute counted.

Low-power sonar searched the waterway ahead. Anything more powerful might alert the Americans or the Canadians or both. The lack of precision bathymetry further complicated the passage. Unlike the Strait of Juan de Fuca, where Antipov had detailed Soviet Navy and more recently Russian Federation bottom charts, no such charts yet existed for the channels and waterways that led to the Strait of Georgia. That was the *Neva*'s assignment.

Relying on surface charts to make a deep submerged passage created additional risk to an already perilous mission. Antipov had no choice but to trust the NOAA chart spread out on the navigator's plotting table.

"Sonar, conn. Report," Antipov said, using the intercom.

"It's quiet, sir. No major surface traffic, just one small craft, outboard motor."

"Where?"

"Bearing one seven five. Range thirty-four hundred meters, heading away at fifteen knots."

"Very well; stand by."

"Aye, sir."

Antipov turned toward his executive officer, who was a head shorter. Both stood next to the plotting table. "Leniod, I want a confirmed fix on this buoy before we make the final turn." He pointed to the U.S. chart. "It's tight ahead—I want to see the passage with my own eyes."

"I understand, Captain."

The XO turned to the chief of the watch. "Bring the boat to periscope depth."

The *Ava Jane* made eight knots bottom speed. She ran before the northeasterly breeze on a splendid, sunny afternoon with the main full out to the port and the flying spinnaker to the starboard. The forty-two-foot-sloop ghosted through the water; two-foot-high following seas hissed as their waveforms passed under the hull.

Tim Mackay, the forty-five-year-old captain and owner, had the helm; four other men accompanied him in the cockpit. They sipped soft drinks and munched on sandwiches.

Running before the wind required constant helm control, forcing Mackay to concentrate. His crew, however, relaxed. They had a winner. *Ava Jane* sliced through the water with ease.

Custom manufactured in Vancouver, the brand-new fiberglass yacht was on her maiden voyage, bound for her new homeport at the Seattle Yacht Club's Elliott Bay Marina Outstation. With a series of winter races coming up in Puget Sound, Mackay couldn't wait to flaunt her speed and agility.

Mackay made his fortune in the building industry, constructing warehouse and office buildings through-out the Pacific Northwest. An Annapolis graduate and six-year active-duty veteran as a U.S. Navy surface war-fare officer, he'd served on frigates and destroyers. He remained in the reserve at the current rank of lieutenant commander.

Mackay had been focusing on the compass binnacle when one of his crew made the sighting.

"What's that?" the man shouted out.

"What?" asked Mackay, now looking up.

The crewman pointed.

"What the . . ." Mackay muttered.

In the near distance, a black tube broke the sea sur-face; a churning wake marked its presence. All five men aboard peered at the slender tube just a boat length away. A few seconds later, it slipped under the surface.

"Tvoyú mat'!" Son of a bitch.

"What's wrong, Captain?" asked the XO.

"Down scope, down scope now!" Antipov yelled.

The chief petty officer of the watch triggered a switch, and the search periscope retracted into its housing.

Antipov's face reddened; he could barely contain his rage. "Sonar," he roared into an intercom mike, "there's a damn sailboat up there. We almost hit it."

"But, Captain, we heard nothing—and there's nothing now."

Antipov tossed the microphone aside, furious.

"Did they see us, Captain?" asked the executive officer.

Antipov surveyed the CCP. Eleven pairs of eyes watched his every move.

"They saw the tube, no doubt about it. I could see their eyeballs."

"What do we do?"

Antipov issued new orders.

"Skipper, was that really a periscope?" asked *Ava Jane*'s navigator.

"Absolutely. I've seen lots of 'em. No question about it." Mackay still had the helm. The sailboat heeled to the starboard and headed diagonally into the wind, the chute replaced with a Genoa jib. All eyes searched the waters ahead as Mackay guided *Ava Jane* back toward the sighting.

"Isn't that dangerous, making a run through these waters submerged?"

"It can be."

"Could that have been one of those Trident subs?" another crewman asked.

"No way," answered the navigator. "They're too big; besides, they only operate in the Strait of Juan de Fuca, not up here. Right, skipper?"

"Yes."

"Then what could it be?" asked a new voice.

"Maybe it's a Canuck sub," offered another.

"Yeah, that's probably what it was all right," Tim

Mackay said. Still, he had doubts. He turned to the first mate. "Billy, take the helm for me." He then addressed the crew: "You guys keep your eyes peeled for that scope, and if you see it again let me know pronto!"

"What's up?" asked the first mate as he made his way to the wheel.

"I need to check something."

"I can barely hear it now, Captain," reported the chief of the sonar watch. "The surface clutter is high but I've managed to isolate its signature."

"The sailboat. You're certain?"

"Yes, sir. It's zigzagging, heading east, following us. I'm picking up hardware noises and wave impact on the hull. It's about half a kilometer away."

Antipov cursed.

Tim Mackay stood at the chart table inside the cabin. He'd just dialed his cell phone.

"Base Commander's office, Petty Officer Owens speaking."

"This is Commander Mackay. I need to speak with Captain Harrison."

"I'm sorry, sir, he's in a staff meeting. He'll probably be finished in the next hour or so."

"This can't wait, Owens. It's urgent. Go find Captain Harrison and tell him I need him on the line right now."

"Aye, aye, sir."

Within a minute, the commanding officer of Naval Air Station Whidbey Island was on the other end of the open circuit. He and Harrison had been classmates at the Naval Academy. "Tim, what's going on?" he asked.

"Sorry to interrupt, Chuck, but I've got a bizarre situation here." He cleared his throat. "We're bringing the new boat down to Seattle today from Vancouver and right now we're in Boundary Pass, west of Waldron Island. About five minutes ago the oddest thing happened."

Mackay told his story.

CHAPTER 31

DAY 9—TUESDAY

"Hi there," Laura announced as she walked into the kitchen.

"Good morning," Yuri replied. He sat at the kitchen table holding Laura's cell phone.

Laura walked to the coffeepot and poured herself a cup. Having just showered, she wrapped her wet hair in a towel turban-style and slipped on a knee-length bathrobe. She had no idea how lovely she looked from Yuri's perspective.

Laura pulled up a chair next to Yuri and sat down. That's when she noticed the phone. "What's up?"

"My Vancouver contact finally called back. He doesn't know anything. He said the Trade Mission hasn't received anything from home about the *Neva* for the past forty-eight hours."

"Why doesn't he call them?"

"It doesn't work that way. Every message is in code. He sent another one yesterday afternoon but there's been no reply yet."

"Don't they know time is running out?"

"They know."

"They've got to help. They're your fellow countrymen."

"The SVR's handling this—not the Navy. There's a big difference."

Laura chewed on that. "You mean they might not help."

He did not respond.

"Can you still proceed with a rescue without the help you were expecting?"

"I'm not sure."

"There must be something that we can do together to help your friends."

Yuri reached out to clasp her free hand. "You're a kind person, Laura Newman. But it's too dangerous for you to help me any more."

Laura savored his touch; the warmth tingled along the length of her forearm. "But what about your crewmates?"

"Moscow is leaving me few options and none of them are good. That's why you must remove yourself from me and this situation." He released her hand. "You should leave today; go back to your home as you planned."

"What are you going to do?"

"I don't know."

"Save your men, Yuri—whatever it takes."

"I don't think I can save them now."

"Yes, you can. And I'll help."

"No, you must go. It's not safe."

"But I want to help."

"You've done too much for me already."

Laura cupped Yuri's right wrist with her hands. She met his eyes and said, "Don't give up. You can do it."

"Captain, I was thinking about the intake problem some more."

Stephan Borodin looked up from his desk. The *Neva*'s assistant engineer stood in the doorway to his cabin holding a thick roll of drawings. "Yes, Yakov."

"If we could elevate the Kingston valve above the bottom muck, the reactor could run without limitation. We'd then have plenty of power."

"Of course, but we're mired in the bottom. We have no reserve buoyancy left."

"I know the tanks are blown dry, but that's not where I'm going."

Borodin tilted his head to the side. "What are you getting at?"

"We still have a fair amount of compressed gas available."

"Yes."

"If we could route some of that gas through bypass piping using the HVAC venting system, and let it discharge directly into the overhead of Compartment Two, maybe we could get enough displacement of seawater out of the rupture to make us a little more positive."

"Hmm, blowing out several cubic meters of seawater would certainly lighten us."

"Right, we'd still be on the bottom, but maybe the intake would be out of the muck. That might allow us to go to full power on the generator."

"That's a terrific idea—using Compartment Two as a semi-ballast tank. We'd have to make sure we don't set up a backflow, but that can be handled with valves."

"That's right, sir, and I think I know how to do it." The engineer opened up the roll of drawings that he'd been holding. He pointed to the first sheet, a schematic of the *Neva*'s heating and ventilation system. "If we tap into this pipe right about . . ."

Clad in orange coveralls, Ken Newman sat shackled to a chair inside a holding cell at the Whatcom County Courthouse.

After waiting in the Point Roberts holding cell all day Sunday, Ken and his tattooed cellmate were transported Monday afternoon by a U.S. Coast Guard launch to Blaine and then by a sheriff's van to Bellingham. The two prisoners separated upon arrival at the Whatcom County jail. Ken had not seen the man since.

Ken's mid-morning bail hearing just finished. Had his case been a simple DUI, he would have been able to post bail with the cash he had on hand. But the judge did not take kindly to the battery charge, especially since the victim with the fractured jaw wore a deputy sheriff's badge.

The judge set the bail at one hundred thousand dollars with the trial in three weeks.

A bail bondsman would charge a 10 percent premium upfront plus Ken would have to provide collateral for the balance of the bond. Without Laura's income, he barely kept his head above water. It had been a tough year for commercial real estate.

How would he ever make bail? And how would he ever get back to Bellevue in time? He had a must-attend luncheon with his boss and a new client the following day.

It had been a dicey thirty-two hours for the *Barrakuda*. Both aircraft and surface vessels prowled the Strait of Juan de Fuca. The submarine eluded the pursuers by following the reverse course of Backdoor.

Well beyond American and Canadian territorial waters, the *Barrakuda* crossed the continental shelf. The deep waters of the North Pacific lay ahead.

Captain Antipov had no alternative but to retreat. An hour after the *Ava Jane*'s crew sighted the periscope, the *Barrakuda*'s sonar unit detected the drone of a low-flying aircraft circling overhead. Suspecting a P-3C Orion from nearby NAS Whidbey, Antipov took evasive action. Confirmation came ten minutes later when sonar detected the telltale entry splash of the first of ten sonobuoys. The underwater microphones could listen for submarines and radio their findings back to the aircraft for analysis.

Moscow's orders were clear: If detected, abort the rescue mission and exit hostile waters.

The *Barrakuda* would head west for two hundred kilometers. Antipov would then send a burst radio transmission to Petropavlovsk reporting the incident and requesting new orders.

CHAPTER 32

DAY 10—WEDNESDAY

"That's fantastic news, Stephan," Yuri said, speaking into the telephone handset. "Thank Yakov for me. What an excellent idea."

"I will."

Yuri sat in the captain's chair of the Sea Ray, which was moored to the *Neva*'s VLF buoy. Laura stood at his side. It was a few minutes before one o'clock in the morning.

Engineer Yakov's hybrid plumbing worked. The extra flotation elevated the hull a few inches within the muck that gripped the outer casing. In that critical boundary layer near the starboard reactor's main seawater intake, uncontaminated water flowed into the heat exchangers. Already, power output had increased by 20 percent and heat finally returned to the interior. To the crew, it was near miraculous.

"Can you pump some more air into number two?" Yuri asked, winking at Laura in the process.

"We tried that but there was no change."

"Must be surging through the opening."

"That's our conclusion, too."

"What are your compressed air reserves like?"

"We still have about forty percent."

"I wouldn't release any more gas. You're going to need it later."

"I concur."

"You know," Yuri said, "if we could somehow seal up Compartment Two, we might be able to evacuate it."

"But we have no access."

"I know, but if it's just an open bulkhead door, maybe we could figure out how to secure it."

By a process of elimination, Borodin and Kirov had speculated that the most probable route for the flooding of Compartment Two was either a rupture in the bulkhead that separated the first and second compartments or an open bulkhead door.

Borodin replied, "For all we know the door could have been blown off its hinges."

"Yes, that's probably what happened." Still, Yuri had doubts.

"What's the latest on the rescue?"

"I have no details yet."

"What's taking so long?"

"I expect Moscow is having trouble moving equipment and personnel into the area. This place I'm at—Point Roberts—it has its own border station. There are American federal agents just a couple of kilometers from where I'm hiding."

"Chyort!" Damn. Borodin said, "What about Vancouver?"

"I either talk with them on the phone, but that's limited because of security issues, or they come here and we meet."

"When are you supposed to hear from them?"

"I'll call Major Orlov later this morning. I should have more information for you tomorrow."

"Yuri, even with the improved power situation we're still critical here. We've got to get our men off this boat—soon!"

"I understand. I won't let you down."

The Sea Ray headed back to Point Roberts. Yuri had the helm; Laura remained at his side. He told her the news. "They used a heating vent to pump compressed air into the second compartment. It expanded a leftover gas bubble, which made the boat slightly more buoyant."

"And that raised the intake out of the mud?"

"Yes, it wasn't much, just ten to twenty centimeters, but that was enough to improve flow to the heat exchangers."

"That's fantastic!"

"Yes, it helps. They can now power up the ship's heating system; they've been freezing. And with the extra power, they can make oxygen and water, too."

"That must be a huge relief," Laura said.

"It is but it's not enough."

"What do you mean?"

"The improved life support systems will help, but the men are still depressed. They're slowly going crazy."

"What can you do to help?"

"Without equipment and support, I can't do anything."

Laura glanced through the windscreen. The distant blinking red light marked the marina's breakwater. She faced Yuri. "Just what kind of equipment do you need?"

"To help the crew?"

"Yes."

"Right now, I'd just settle for some remotely operated gear that would allow me to check over the damaged area of the hull."

"Be more specific, exactly what type of equipment?"

He spent the next two minutes being specific.

"Where would one find that kind of system?" Laura asked as she peered forward, monitoring the approaching marking light.

"Gulf of Mexico for sure."

"How about the Northwest, Seattle, maybe even Vancouver?"

"I don't know—I suppose it's possible."

"Who would we need to call to find out?"

Yuri turned to his left. Just enough reflected light from the instrument panel revealed the gleam in her eyes. "Laura, what do you have in mind?"

Nick Orlov and Elena Krestyanova sat at the conference table inside the Trade Mission's code room. It was mid-morning. With white walls, no windows, and just one steel door with rubber seals on all edges, the room presented a sterile surgical environment. Embedded within the walls, floor and ceiling, were grids of copper. When electrified the mesh defeated eavesdropping devices. The speakerphone centered on the tabletop linked the operatives via secure military satellite to their boss.

"I want you to bring him out now," ordered the chief of the SVR from his Moscow office. His flat monotone voice resulted from the encryption system used to make the secure satellite phone call.

"But, sir, I don't think he'll come." Orlov paused. "He's fiercely loyal to his crewmates."

"I don't care. It's far too dangerous for him to remain there any longer. If he's picked up by the Americans, who knows what he might reveal?"

"Sir," Elena said, "I agree with Major Orlov. Kirov will not leave voluntarily. He's expecting help from the Navy and has made it quite clear to us that until his men are rescued, he's staying put."

The chief of foreign intelligence operations replied, "There will be no help from the Navy or from any other source."

"I don't understand," Nick said. "We were told that there had been a change in plans but that a rescue mission was still under way and I so informed Kirov when we last talked."

"I can't give you the details, but the rescue mission has been terminated."

"But what about the survivors?" Elena asked.

"The decision has been made at the highest level that the crew is expendable."

Nicolai and Elena sat in stunned silence.

Nick finally said, "Sir, what are we supposed to do if Kirov refuses to leave?"

"That's your problem. I want him out of there immediately. Do you understand?"

Elena and Nick met each other's eyes and collectively answered, "Yes, sir."

"Good."

A squelch of static erupted from the speaker. Elena reached forward and switched it off.

Nick muttered, *"Duráks."* Fools.

"There must be something else going on," Elena offered.

Nick continued his rant. "They're just a pile of *"kakáshkas."* Turds.

The SVR chief had similar thoughts to those of Orlov and Krestyanova. Yet, like his two field officers in Vancouver, he had to follow orders, as disgusting as they were.

The decision came from the top. The president and the prime minister were too preoccupied with the crisis in the Southern Kurils to worry about the *Neva*'s crew.

The Project Vega analysts speculated that if the United States discovered another Russian spy submarine deep inside its territorial waters after having just chased out the *Barrakuda*, it would provide the excuse for the Americans to transform the Deep Blue war game into a full-scale invasion of the Southern Kurils.

The executive decision process had excluded input from the Navy. Failure of the *Barrakuda*'s mission provided the excuse for Russia's intelligence services to reinstate control of the "rescue" mission. The Pacific Fleet received orders to stand down. Operatives within the FSB's military spy group kept close tabs on the Navy to make sure it complied.

CHAPTER 33

"How difficult is it to operate?" asked Laura. This was her fifth call. The lead came from Craigslist.com.

"That's right," Laura continued. "The depth is around seven hundred feet.

"I'm not sure, hang on a minute." Laura looked at Yuri. "They want to know the maximum current it will have to operate in."

Yuri sat at the opposite end of the kitchen table. "Three knots."

Laura spoke into her cell, "Max of three knots.

"Good, so how do I rent one?"

Laura listened for half a minute and said, "You mean we have to have your people operate the system?"

Yuri shook his head. Laura signaled her understanding.

"No, we can't do that. But what if we came to your office and hired you to certify us for its use, would that work?"

As Laura listened to the reply, she pursed her lips.

"Okay, I see where you're coming from. Because of the nature of our project we just can't do that."

Yuri slumped back in his chair, staring at the ceiling. Another dead end!

"So if we can't rent it for solo use, how much if we buy it?"

That captured Yuri's attention. She had not asked that question before.

"That's right, the whole system, cable, monitor, controls—the works.

"Hmm, that is expensive." She ran a hand through her hair while thinking ahead. "You're sure it's available right now, not sitting on some dock in Hong Kong?

"Yes, that's right; we'd come down and pick it up."

Yuri now stood, waving his arms, trying to get Laura's attention. She ignored him.

"Okay, for that price I'm definitely interested, providing you give us personal instruction on its use.

"In the water? Yes, of course.

"That's right; we won't buy it unless you show us how it works. You pick somewhere down there but it has to be realistic.

"Electronic transfer of the funds, yes, I can do that.

"Okay, I'll be there tomorrow morning by one. So just how do I get there?"

Laura ended the call and addressed Yuri: "Great news! They have a small one. It's used but reconditioned. They used it to inspect underwater pipelines. Has a maximum operating depth of a thousand feet. They won't rent it but they will sell it. Forty thousand for everything: the unit itself, fifteen hundred feet of cable on a reel, plus a video monitor and a recorder."

"It's in Seattle?"

"Yeah, some place on the Duwamish River." She glanced down at her notes. "South of downtown. It shouldn't be too hard to find."

"How do we get it?"

"You don't, I do—unless you want to risk the border crossings."

"But how will I learn to use it? This equipment is complicated, even a small one."

"I'll learn. Part of the deal. The owner's going to take the unit out on a boat and provide me with half a day of instructions. Then I'll teach you."

"But the price!" Yuri clenched his jaw. "It's such an enormous amount—how will you do that?"

Laura grinned. "Don't worry, I've got it covered."

Yuri moved to her side of the table, dragging his left leg. He steadied himself and dropped onto his knees.

Laura's forehead wrinkled. "Yuri, what are you —"

He embraced her right hand with his own hands and said, "Laura Newman, you are truly an amazing person. On behalf of the crew of the *Neva* and myself, I thank you from the bottom of my heart."

He kissed the back of her hand.

CHAPTER 34

Elena Krestyanova and Nicolai Orlov sat inside the Suburban. They were parked in a lot on the western shore of the marina in Point Roberts.

"Where is Yuri?" Elena asked in Russian. She occupied the driver's seat. "It's been half an hour."

"This is where he said to meet."

"Something's wrong. Call him again."

Nick was reaching for his cell phone when another vehicle pulled next to the Suburban on his side and stopped. Its driver was an eye-catching young woman.

He spotted Kirov in the front passenger seat. "It's him," he announced.

Yuri extracted himself from the sedan. The BMW backed up and exited the parking lot.

Nick rolled down his window and said, *"Dobryj den'!"* Good afternoon.

"Privet!"

"Who was that?" Nick asked, continuing in Russian.

"A local I met; she gave me a ride." He opened the right rear passenger door and hauled himself inside the SUV. The interior reeked of cigarette smoke.

Elena and Nick turned in their seats to face him.

"We were wondering if you'd ever show up," Nick commented.

"I had some business to take care of."

Nick frowned. "Where do you want to go for coffee?"

"I don't. Let's just talk here."

"Fine."

"Is your leg any better?" Elena asked.

"About the same," Yuri said. "So, are we going to get any help or not?"

"Moscow continues to work on the problem." Nick followed the script that he and Elena had crafted. "Apparently, they're in the process of mobilizing the equipment and personnel that you requested. However, we have not yet been provided any time frames."

"This is taking too long. A team should be here already."

"I agree but you know how our system works. I can hardly scratch my butt here without getting permission from home."

Yuri did know. The Kremlin loved "red tape." He slumped back into the seat.

"How's the crew?" Elena asked.

"Better. They were able to adjust ballast and free up one of the intakes. They have more power now. That allows use of the heaters plus the oxygen and water generators."

"That's great news!"

"Yes, but they're still not going anywhere."

Nick said, "With the improved life support systems, how long can they last?"

"A week or so, if the reactor remains online and the

intake doesn't plug up again. But that all could change in minutes."

"How?" Elena said.

"If the bilge pumps stop working, the boat will fill up with seawater from the leaks. If a bulkhead door seal goes, it'll be over in seconds." Yuri scowled. "And a fire—I don't want to even think about that."

Elena was about to ask another question when Nick preempted her. "Your friend, the woman we just saw, how much does she know about what's going on?"

"Nothing; she thinks I'm a treasure hunter, looking for a wreck offshore of Point Roberts."

"That's a good cover."

Elena reengaged, "What about security? We can't have her involved with this."

"She's involved, so just accept it. If she hadn't helped, I would never have made it this far."

"But she's an American. One call to the border station here and we've had it!"

"Don't worry. She doesn't have any idea what we're really doing."

Elena turned away, briefly eyeing Nick. She suspected Yuri was sleeping with the woman, and guessed that Nick thought the same.

"Where did she go?" asked Nick.

By now, Yuri expected that Laura had passed through the Canadian checkpoint at Point Roberts and was on her way back to the U.S. border crossing at Blaine. "She went to the town next to this place. I don't remember the name."

"Tsawwassen," Elena offered.

"Yes, that's it."

"What's she doing there?" Nick said.

"She's shopping for me—clothes. I'm tired of these rags."

"You should have said something; we can get whatever you need."

"I'm okay."

That provided a new opening for Nick. "Why don't you come back with us to Vancouver? We can get your leg checked out by a doctor."

"Plus the restaurants there are fantastic," added Elena.

"I can't leave here. The border."

"No problem." Nick reached into a coat pocket and handed Yuri a Canadian passport.

Yuri flipped it open. His photograph stared back, a copy from his military personnel file. The forger had deleted his uniform jacket, replacing it with a blue blazer. He had a new name: Peter Kirkinski—a Ukrainian immigrant to Canada.

"Nice work, don't you think?" Nick said.

"It appears authentic."

"It was created from a real blank, not a fake. Elena and I use the same type. You'll be able to come and go at will."

Yuri continued to thumb through the document.

Nick leaned farther toward Yuri. "So, why don't you come back with us to get your leg checked out. We'll bring you back here later tonight."

The offer tempted Yuri. His leg remained numb. Perhaps a drug prescribed by a physician could help restore feeling. But he remembered just whom he was dealing with.

"No, I'm not going anywhere. I won't leave here until I know the crew is safe."

"Okay," Nick said, "suit yourself."

"What's the next step?"

"We wait for an update from Moscow. Maybe we'll hear something tonight."

"Phone me."

"I will, but you know I won't be able to divulge any details over the telephone."

"Then we'll have to meet here again."

"All right."

Yuri opened the door as Elena spoke, "Can we drive you back?"

"Thanks, but I'll walk. The exercise helps my leg."

"Okay," Nick said. "We'll call you when we hear something."

"I'll be waiting."

CHAPTER 35

Yuri sat upright in the reclining chair in the darkened living room. It was eerily quiet this early evening. The hushed "tick tick" of the wall-mounted battery-powered clock dominated.

For over a week there had been no feeling in his injured left leg. But twenty minutes earlier, his calf began to wake up: First, the skin smoldered like sunburn; then it had morphed into a sizzle. Over the past several minutes, he'd repeatedly reached down with his left hand to test himself, worried that his brain had invented the sensation as a weird derivative of the bends.

He felt the bite when he pinched the skin with his thumb and forefinger.

Maybe that miserable walk really helped after all!

Yuri launched himself from the chair and took a couple of steps toward the kitchen. The limp remained unchanged but the calf pain persisted.

Yuri poured himself a tall glass of water from the sink faucet and walked out onto the deck. He peered southward into the darkness. *They're still out there . . . on the bottom . . . waiting for me!*

He had never been more alone. His crewmates remained stranded, his homeland floundered in its attempt to rescue them, and he missed Laura.

He carried her cell phone in a trouser pocket; Laura had left it for his use. She'd promised to call when she arrived in Redmond.

Laura represented Yuri's one remaining hope. Although she faced a daunting task, Yuri had confidence that she could do it—with a little luck.

There was a downside to his optimism: Maybe Laura would come to her senses and stay away. He'd told her to do that very thing the previous day. But she wouldn't think of that now.

Or would she?

Laura made it to her home in the late afternoon. Weary from the long drive, she soaked for forty minutes in the bathtub and then made dinner: macaroni and cheese from a premixed package. She sat at the kitchen table sipping merlot while sorting her mail.

There were the usual bills and a pile of junk mail along with a couple of magazines. But the correspondence from her divorce attorney caught her eye. She read the letter. The court had set the first hearing for early January.

Good, Laura thought, anxious for closure. She made a mental note to call her attorney and advise him about Ken's latest antics. He had made no additional trouble and left Point Roberts without further contact.

Laura leaned back in the chair and thought of Yuri. She remained grateful for how he had stood up to Ken.

Laura also remained conflicted about her own actions.

He really needs my help or his shipmates might not make it.

Laura reassured herself with another taste of wine. *Besides, it's stuck on the bottom in Canada, not the U.S., so I should be okay.*

The Sea Ray arrived over the *Neva* after a calm late-evening voyage.

Over the VLF buoy comms line, Yuri reported the news about the remotely operated vehicle—ROV—to the *Neva*'s CO.

"I should have it tomorrow."

"Where's it coming from?" asked Captain Borodin. He was in his cabin alone.

"Seattle."

Yuri decided not to mention Laura's role in procuring the underwater robotic craft, alluding to his SVR contacts as the source.

"What good do you think that's going to do?"

"I'm hoping to get an assessment of the damage. That way we'll be able to work on a repair."

"There's too much damage to repair—two flooded compartments. This boat isn't going anywhere."

"I understand, but remember I looked the area over when I locked out. The only damage I could see was tube five. The muzzle door and bow cap were missing but that's it. The tube itself looked undamaged, as much as I could see inside."

And that wasn't much. Rushed for time and forced to use a glow stick when his dive light flooded, Yuri had only been able to examine a couple meters of the torpedo tube's interior.

"Why do you want to look at it again?" Borodin said. "With the muzzle door gone the tube's open to the sea. Either the breech was blown off or the tube itself was holed. No way can we fix that."

"If we can find out what happened we might figure out a way to repair it from the outside."

Yuri described his plan while Borodin listened without enthusiasm. "I suppose it's worth a try, but what we really need is a rescue chamber."

"I know and I'm working on that. I just need more time to set it up."

"Dammit to hell! We don't have much time left. The increased power helps and the boat's warmer, but we're barely keeping up with the leaks. We've been maxing out the pumps for days now. If we lose just one more . . ."

Yuri knew the rest. The leaks would fill the boat, sinking it farther into the muck. The reactor would overheat and shut down. As incoming seawater steadily increased pressure, it would be a race between hypothermia and oxygen toxicity as to which would kill the crew first.

Borodin continued his rant. "The men are barely holding it together. Many are convinced that our government has left us here to rot. And I agree with them."

"But we just need more time."

"Yuri, I know you're trying but that's not going to wash with the crew."

"Tell them that the ROV is the first phase of the rescue. Anything to boost their spirits."

His heart racing, Yuri waited.

Finally, Borodin responded. "All right, Yuri. I will try that, but neither of us has much goodwill left."

"I'll figure it out. Don't give up on me—please."

CHAPTER 36

"Good morning," Nicolai Orlov said. He stood in the open door of Elena Krestyanova's office at the Vancouver Trade Mission.

Located on the four-story building's most desirable perimeter wall, the window had a lovely view of a nearby park. The furniture was upscale, fitting for Elena's role as an envoy. The display shelf next to her desk contained assorted decorations—a crystal figurine of a ballet dancer the most prominent—but not one photograph of family, friends, or loved ones.

Elena looked up from her laptop. "Hi, Nick. Come on in."

She gestured to the teapot on a nearby table.

"No, thanks. I'm fine." He sat in one of two chairs that fronted her desk.

"Sleep well?" she asked.

"Great."

They slept in separate beds last night—Nick's doing; he'd complained of being tired and in need of a good night's sleep. Elena had not been sympathetic.

"I got your message," Nick said. "What's up?"

"All I know is that we're supposed to be in the code room at ten for a conference call."

"The chief?"

"Who else?"

Nick checked his watch. "He's working late again. What do you think he wants?"

"I expect that he's going to want a progress report on Kirov."

"Yeah, probably." Nick cracked his knuckles. "He's going to be pissed that we haven't been able to get him out of there."

"I know."

The SVR officers discussed how best to respond to their boss's expected demands, and Nick departed for another unoccupied office to call the consulate.

Elena returned to the laptop and clicked on another link. A two-month-old article from the *Vancouver Sun* flashed onto her screen.

"Incredible—right in our own backyard," she muttered as she raced through the story.

Nick and Elena sat at a conference table in the code room alone. The tabletop speakerphone linked the operatives via secure military satellite to their boss.

After camping out at his office over a week monitoring Deep Blue, SVR director Borya Smirnov had retreated to his *dacha* in a guarded forest compound on the outskirts of Moscow. The American and Japanese naval war game offshore of the Southern Kuril Islands had concluded. The carrier strike groups dispersed. If an invasion were to occur, it would have happened by now. All remained quiet on the East Asian front.

Still, the other annoying problem demanded his attention.

After listening to Nick's briefing, the SVR general responded, "Major, I don't care how you do it, but you are to get him to the mission today."

"He won't come voluntarily."

"I wanted him brought in yesterday!"

"I know, but he wouldn't come. We had a passport for him and doctor lined up, but he wasn't interested."

"I'm not going to say this again. I.want him out of Point Roberts today. He's too much of a liability. Involving that woman and stealing boats, he could be picked up at any time."

"I'm not so sure about that, General," added Elena. "Kirov's careful and cunning."

Nick rejoined, "Sir, Kirov's American friend is actually helping him. She believes he's searching for sunken treasure offshore of Point Roberts."

"Are they lovers?"

"Probably. She's quite attractive."

"Then it's even more important that we bring him in, plus the woman, too."

"And if we can't coax them to come?"

"You both know what has to be done."

"Sir?" Nick responded.

"Dispose of them."

Elena and Nicolai were silent as the director's words sank in.

"Do I make myself clear?"

"Yes, sir," echoed Elena and Nicolai.

"Report back to me as soon as you've completed your mission."

The circuit disconnected and the speakerphone broadcast static.

Nick muttered, "*Kakógo chërta?*" What the hell?

Elena rolled her eyes.

Nick leaned back in his chair. He said, "So what are we supposed to do now? I've never been involved in an assassination before."

Elena had but did not let on; part of her undercover training included "wet affairs."

"I don't think we'll have to resort to such extremes," Elena offered.

"Why?"

Reaching into a file folder, she pulled out a hard copy of a downloaded newspaper article and handed it to Nick. He read the headline from the *Vancouver Sun*: "Local Company Sets Record Dive."

"*Fantastíčeskij!*" Fantastic.

Ken Newman eyed the check for ten thousand dollars. "This is really generous, Mom. Thanks very much."

"If the attorney needs more, let me know."

"Okay."

Ken Newman and his mother sat inside her Lexus four-door in the parking lot of Ken's employer. It was a few minutes before noon. Deborah was in her early sixties with luscious shoulder-length jet-black hair, a dark tan complexion with sparse facial wrinkles, and a slim curvy figure. A widow for three years, she had a flock of suitors, attracted to her fine looks—and her money. Deborah's husband, Ken's late father, owned a chain of furniture stores, which she continued to manage.

With no one else to turn to, Ken had called home. Deborah Newman paid his bail in Bellingham earlier in the morning, pledging a CD for security. After stopping at Ken's apartment for a change of clothing, she drove him to his workplace.

"Let me know if you need a ride to pick up your car."

"Sure, thanks."

The Corvette remained in Point Roberts, towed to an impound lot. He told Deborah he was on business in Vancouver and decided to visit the Point out of curiosity. He had yet to mention the divorce papers.

"How is Laura?"

"Good."

"Are you making progress?"

"Slowly."

"I know it's hard, honey, but keep trying—she's really worth it."

"I will."

Ken climbed out the car and Deborah headed back to her Mercer Island home.

As he walked toward the building entrance, his thoughts raced.

It's all Laura's fault! She's the cheat. And who's the cripple she's sleeping with? What's so great about him?

And what about the company stock?

Laura had already received hefty stock bonuses and would be in line for huge future payouts—potentially tens of millions.

Ken wasn't about to walk away from his share of that gold mine.

Yuri stood beside a pay phone at the marina's fuel dock; his lower left leg throbbed. He'd just called Nick Orlov's cell.

"I'll get you another phone," Nick said. "Don't worry about it."

When he was docking the Sea Ray after the late evening's contact with Borodin, Laura's smartphone had slipped out of his coat pocket when he'd reached over the side for a mooring line. It plopped into the water.

Nick said, "Anyway, I'm just glad you called. I've been trying to reach you all afternoon."

"The rescue—it's on?"

"I don't have news on that but I wanted to let you know that we found something real interesting right here in Vancouver."

"What?"

"There's a deep-water diving company based in North Vancouver. It has all kinds of equipment and works all over the world." He named the company.

Nick continued, "I just talked to them. I think they have everything you could want: diving bell, recompression chamber, and a one-atmosphere suit—whatever that is. They even have access to U.S. and NATO military submarine rescue equipment. Apparently, some of it is manufactured right here in the Vancouver area."

"What do they know of our needs?" Yuri said with a raised voice while turning away from the main dock and pressing the handset hard onto his right ear. After fueling, a fifty-eight-foot-long commercial fishing boat had just started its diesel; the purse seiner needed a new muffler.

"Nothing other than I told them we had possible salvage work at a depth of two hundred plus meters. They think I'm after some valuable sunken cargo."

"It'll only work if we have our own people operate it. It can't be a charter with outsiders."

"That's what I told them. They said they'd consider it as long as we're creditworthy."

"What's that?"

"That we have the money to pay them and that we can guarantee return of the equipment."

"I see. It's all about money."

"Da!"

"Do we have enough?"

"Absolutely!"

"Then let's proceed."

"I don't know what to get. I was hoping you could help."

"Of course, how?"

"They said they'd meet with us this afternoon in their yard. If you'll come, you can look over their stuff and if it'll work, we'll make a deal."

"You want me in Vancouver?"

"I know you don't want to leave, but it's the only way to get what you really need."

"Yes, but the border . . . I'll have to cross it—twice. I can't be detained."

"You have the passport we gave you yesterday, don't you?"

"Yes."

"That should be all you need. You can come and go at will."

"I guess so," Yuri said, but not convinced.

"I suppose I could try to broker this deal over the phone, but I don't . . ."

"No, no, you're right. I must be there. We have little time left."

"Klassno." Cool. Nick continued, "Can you have your friend drive you to Vancouver? We could meet at Elena's office and then all of us drive to the yard. It's only twenty minutes away."

"She's not here and won't be back for several hours."

"I have some business to take care of but Elena could pick you up within an hour. I'll meet you both at the diving company."

"Yes, please have her come."

Yuri hung up the phone, energized.

This could be the answer to everything.

The plump balding middle-aged man stared at the sedan parked on the pier next to the *Hercules*, his ninety-six-foot workboat and home. Captain Dan Miller turned to face Laura. "Mrs. Newman, I don't think we're going to be able to get the gear into that fancy car of yours."

"I see the problem," she replied, peering at her BMW.

The underwater probe might fit in the trunk with the lid left open. But the steel reel with its fifteen hundred feet of cable wouldn't come close. Then there was the control station with its joystick, a video monitor, and a DVD recorder.

Miller continued, "If you want, we can crate it up and get UPS or a local freight forwarder to ship it up to you. But that could take awhile."

Laura looked away from her automobile. Although

the *Hercules* was neat and orderly, Miller's boatyard was anything but. Scattered over the property were assorted piles of metal debris and rock riprap, stacks of salvaged lumber including barnacle-encrusted creosote-treated timber piles, and half a dozen pieces of rusted heavy construction equipment that appeared to have taken root in the ground.

Everything took longer than Laura anticipated. She had stopped at her office, intending only to check her snail mail but ending up sidetracked for nearly two hours putting out fires. Later she bought a new phone and visited her banks, making sizable cash withdrawals.

Laura arrived at the marine construction company's South Seattle office a few minutes before two o'clock. The complete system had already been loaded aboard the *Hercules*. Using her new smartphone, Laura logged onto to her e-bank account. She let Captain Miller verify the funds but was not yet ready to execute the transfer. They headed off to Elliott Bay for a two-hour tutorial.

The workboat hovered over a sunken barge near the north shore of the bay. The windless afternoon and slack tide created ideal conditions for the test dive. The remotely operated vehicle deployed and Captain Miller "flew" it down to the wreck to demonstrate its capabilities.

About the size of a shopping cart, the ROV contained two high-pressure air cylinders that served as buoyancy chambers, a stainless steel control box, and four electrically powered propellers with ducts to control water flow. An underwater TV camera with a pair of lights completed the package.

With simple adjustments to the joystick, the ROV,

nicknamed "*Little Mack*," soared like an underwater eagle.

For over an hour, Laura maneuvered *Mack* in and around the wreck. She took care not to foul the trailing four hundred feet of yellow tether that supplied electrical power and transmitted signals to and from *Mack*. The monitor displayed color video images along with readouts of water depth, compass heading, and camera angle.

At 4:15 P.M., Captain Miller reeled *Little Mack* aboard and the *Hercules* headed home. Before reaching the dock, Laura completed the funds transfer.

With *Little Mack*'s former owner still at her side, Laura again considered her predicament: She told Yuri that she'd bring it back today. But how?

Laura glanced back at her BMW and then to the ROV and its appurtenances. No way would everything fit. And even if it could, what would happen at the border crossings?

Laura was just about to have the ROV shipped when a new idea hatched. "Captain, how much would you charge me to deliver *Little Mack* to Point Roberts?"

"I'd have to call UPS for a quote and we'd have to mark it up."

"No, I mean like right now—on your boat."

"You mean charter the *Herc*, to go to Point Roberts?"

"Yes, leave tonight and get there tomorrow morning."

"Hmm, she's not scheduled for anything for a couple of weeks, but my deckhand is going elk hunting tomorrow. With such short notice, I'll have to call around for a replacement."

"I'll pay double-time for a deckhand, if you get under way within the next hour."

"Double-time, you say."

"That's right plus your normal charter fee, all in cash if you like. So how much?"

"You'll pay the deckhand separate, so I don't have to put 'im on my books, and no receipts for the charter?"

"Fine, not a problem."

"You pay for the diesel?"

"Yeah."

"Okay, let me see here . . ."

The transaction closed two minutes later when Laura doled out fifty bills, one hundred dollars each.

Nicolai Orlov sat in the Suburban for almost forty minutes before Elena and Yuri finally pulled alongside and stopped.

All three got out of the vehicles. They peered through the six-foot-high chain-link fencing that encircled the industrial waterfront site in North Vancouver. The yard lights provided enough illumination; the sun had set earlier. The two-acre yard contained several huge steel shipping containers, a portable office building, and an odd collection of heavy equipment. The equipment captured Yuri's interest.

"That's a deck decompression chamber right there," he said, pointing at a twenty-foot-long by six-foot-diameter steel cylinder parked next to one of the shipping containers. Painted white with both ends capped with steel hemispherical covers, the tube looked like an oversized fuel tank.

"Are those air tanks?" asked Elena, gesturing at the bank of steel cylinders neatly racked next to the DDC.

"Mixed gases—helium and oxygen I expect."

"Why helium?" Nick said.

"This rig is set up for saturation diving—deepwater work. Sat-divers use helium instead of nitrogen to counter the narcotic effect of breathing nitrogen under pressure."

"Got it." Nick had a rudimentary understanding of diving physics from a scuba course he had taken at a beach resort several years earlier.

"What about the bell?" Yuri asked. "We still need the diving bell."

"They have one here someplace. They assured me of that."

Yuri scanned the yard. "I don't see it."

"Maybe it's in one of those shipping containers," offered Elena.

Yuri's eyes narrowed. "Maybe."

Nick checked his watch: 5:52 P.M. "There's nothing more that we can do here until tomorrow morning. How about we head back to downtown for dinner and get you a hotel room?"

"I have to get back to Point Roberts."

"But what about the equipment here? Don't you want to come back tomorrow to check it?"

"No, I must return tonight. I've seen enough so you can make the arrangements; I'll help you over the telephone."

Nick scowled.

Elena said, "Yuri, for the next hour or so traffic's going to be just as miserable going back to Point Roberts as it was getting here. Let's all go to my apartment; we can have a glass of wine and relax for a while. Then I'll drive you back."

"All right," he conceded.

Yuri walked to Elena's Mercedes and opened the passenger door.

Elena stood on the opposite side of the sedan. She waited until Yuri climbed inside. She glanced toward Nick and winked. He flashed a smile and slipped into the Suburban.

CHAPTER 37

"What do we do now?" asked Elena.

"Let him sleep." Nick leaned back into the sofa and yawned. "I'm beat, too."

The Russians relaxed in the living room of Elena's high-rise condominium apartment.

"What do we do when he wakes up?" Elena sat in a chair across the coffee table from Nick. She sipped wine.

"Reason with him. I think he'll come around—eventually." He yawned again.

"I'm not sure about that. He's stubborn and incredibly loyal to his shipmates."

Nick's eyelids flickered and closed. His head slumped to the side.

"Nicolai!" Elena called out.

No response.

She tried again—nothing. The three glasses of merlot had taken their toll.

Elena swallowed the last of her wine. She walked to the guest bedroom and cracked the door. Yuri Kirov remained on top of the bed fully clothed and snoring.

The sedative worked. She'd spiked his wine with

the drug. He would sleep for at least eight hours; it had been a desperate measure.

The mandate handed down by the SVR chief had been explicit: Remove Kirov from Point Roberts—whatever it took. Elena and Nick had carried out their orders.

The deep-diving equipment had been nothing more than bait. Nick had solicited the basic information from the Canadian diving company over the phone. He learned enough to entice Yuri. There would be no meeting with the company in the morning. The diving bell Nick had promised currently operated from an oil exploration platform in the North Sea.

When Yuri eventually awakened from his chemically induced rest, he'd be livid that his compatriots had duped him.

Elena closed the bedroom door. As she walked back into the living room, she wondered what to do with Yuri. Two options came to mind. First, convince him to return to Russia to receive treatment for his injuries.

Should Yuri refuse to cooperate, the second option would come into play. If Nick balked, Elena would take care of it herself. But she fretted over another quandary: the American woman that Yuri had entrusted. How would Elena deal with her?

Elena toyed with driving to the Point and taking care of the loose end. But she dismissed it; that business could wait until tomorrow. She had something else on her mind.

Elena returned to the living room where she cozied up to Nick's inert form, stretched out on the sofa. She slipped a hand inside his trousers and whispered into an ear, "Come on, lover, time for fun."

CHAPTER 38

The two men rarely spoke directly to each other. Both were powerful in their own directorates; each considered the other a rival. This afternoon they had united in their common cause. The order came from the president himself.

The subject matter called for a face-to-face, yet neither budged, each demanding the other visit their respective office. The Military Counterintelligence Directorate occupied a floor in the mammoth headquarters of the FSB at Lubyanka Square. The SVR—foreign intelligence—had its own palace at Yaseenevo on the Moscow Ring Road.

They settled for the private club. Both had memberships—perks of their positions. There on the banks of the Moskva, they met in an elegantly appointed private room with a riverfront view. Their personal aides stood by outside the door. Undercover security forces occupied the lobby and patrolled the grounds. Just prior to meeting, the room was swept for listening devices.

Both men sipped tea. With the pleasantries concluded, it was time for business.

"What do you propose we do with this mess?" asked FSB Colonel General Ivan Golitsin. Pushing sixty with thinning blond hair, Golitsin wore an off-the-rack black business suit that did little for his portly physique.

The SVR chief tossed the hot potato back. "You tell me. This is certainly not my mess." In his early fifties, Borya Smirnov wore a Savile Row navy herringbone classic fit suit. The custom tailor ensemble complimented his trim six-foot build.

"Nor is it my doing, need I remind you," countered Golitsin. "The Navy is to blame here. It is *their* submarine that sank and it is *their* captain lieutenant who's running around loose on American soil."

"But he's assigned to you."

"Doesn't matter, he's still Navy."

Smirnov looked away. The river's banks froze overnight, but the main channel remained ice-free. A workboat towing a barge pushed upstream.

Golitsin said, "So I ask you again Borya, what should we do?"

The SVR director turned back. "I directed my case officers in Vancouver to conclude the matter with Captain Lieutenant Kirov. By today's end he will be either on a plane back to Moscow or terminated."

"Otlíčno!" Excellent.

Smirnov reached for a glass of water. "Still, that leaves the problem with the submarine itself. My people can't deal with that. That's a military matter."

"Operation Eagle is under way. A team is being mobilized but it will be at least twenty-four hours before they will be on scene."

Smirnov took a sip. "They must have deep-diving experience?"

"No—they're not divers."

The FSB general explained the mission of his special operations team.

With his left elbow planted on the tabletop and his arm and hand supporting his chin, Smirnov pondered his military counterpart's latest disclosure. "Won't the Navy be suspicious when this equipment is shipped out?"

"We already have it; we've been experimenting with it for cable taps. Works well from what I've been told."

"Good, this just might work." Yet, something still nagged at him. "What have they been told about the *Neva?*"

"That the crew is dead but the hull remains intact and pressurized. Because of its location the hull has to be neutralized to keep critical components out of American hands."

"How will that be accomplished?"

"Shaped charges inserted onto the exterior surface of the pressure casing. They don't have to be huge. Just crack the shell and two hundred meters of seawater will do the rest." General Golitsin anticipated the next question. "They'll go quick, Borya. In an eye blink."

"But what if the *Neva*'s crew tries to alert the team? What then?"

"They've been told it is impossible to rescue any remaining crew—too deep."

Smirnov commented, "The Navy can never learn of this. They can't go after the president or prime minister, but you can be certain they'll crucify both of us."

"I'm well aware of that. Right now only you and I know where all the pieces are and how they fit together."

"And we need to keep it that way."

"We will."

CHAPTER 39

Yuri switched on the lamp by the bed and checked his wristwatch: 5:48 A.M. He glanced out the window at the cityscape. Vancouver remained asleep.

Searing pain in his lower leg made sleep impossible. He swung his legs over the side of the bed and still fully clothed sat upright. The back of his calf throbbed. A new ache in his forehead announced its presence.

How could he be hungover from one glass of wine?

He opened the bedroom door and stepped into the hallway. He had no recollection of when or how he ended up in the bed, but he did remember the bathroom at the end of the hall.

Yuri shuffled past a partially open door to the master bedroom. He would have ignored it except for the trail of clothing that led to the bed: a pair of briefs, black socks, a shirt, and trousers. He peered inside. No lights on but the huge window next to the queen-size bed broadcast residual city light.

Elena occupied the center of the queen bed under a quilted bedspread. One bare arm projected out from under the cover along with a clump of flaxen hair. Nicolai lay prone on the carpet along the right side of the bed, his head resting on a pillow. A down comforter covered his body.

Yuri shook his head as he continued down the hall.

Five minutes later, he returned to the bedroom. He was about to lie down when he remembered: *Laura!*

"Nicolai, wake up!"

Elena squatted next to Nick; a bathrobe covered her nude body. He remained wrapped mummy-style inside the down comforter.

She tugged on his shoulder. "Nicolai! Come on— get up."

Orlov turned toward Elena. His eyelids fluttered open; he coughed once and sat up. "What's going on?" he asked.

"He's gone!"

"What?"

"Kirov—he took off! He's not in his room and the keys to my Mercedes are gone."

"But how could . . . ?" Nick's brain misfired. "He was supposed to be unconscious until noon."

"I don't know, but that doesn't matter. He's gone and we've got to deal with this."

Nick stood draped with the comforter. "When did he leave?"

"I have no idea. He was out cold when we went to bed."

Their lovemaking lasted half an hour. Somehow, they ended up on the carpet and Nick, too sated and too tired to move, stayed put. Elena had retreated to her bed.

Nick rubbed his throbbing temples. He was not used to wine. "What time is it?"

She gestured to the clock on the nearby nightstand: The readout announced 7:06 A.M.

"Chërt voz'mi!" Dammit.

Elena said, "He could have taken off hours ago."

"I knew this was too easy." Nick admonished himself for not binding Kirov to the bed; he'd trusted Elena.

"But why would he take off like that?"

"It must be the woman that's been helping him."

"Then he's gone back to Point Roberts!"

"That's my guess."

"Should I call the mission and get some help?"

Both operatives recalled the orders from their boss.

"No way. Nobody else is to know about this screwup. We're going to take care of it ourselves."

"Okay."

Nick paced across the carpet, thinking. He turned back toward Elena. "Do you still have the RFID scanner that we used the other day—to follow him to the beach house?"

"Yeah, it's in the Suburban but its range is limited."

"I know but it could be useful if he still has your business card." A new thought sparked. "How about a weapon, do you have one?"

"Not here. There's one at the mission, a nine-millimeter Beretta—with a suppressor, if needed."

"We may need it."

CHAPTER 40

The sun had just risen yet it remained bleak this morning. The crew watched from the wheelhouse of the ninety-six-foot steel hull as it came upon the beam of a fishing boat. The thirty-foot aluminum gill-netter bucked its way into the oncoming waves and wind.

"That's a pretty small boat to be out here in this kind of weather," Laura Newman offered.

"Those tribal fishermen are tough—they'll be okay," said Captain Dan Miller.

The *Hercules*'s owner sat in a pedestal-mounted chair behind the helm, his right hand resting on the oak wheel. The instrument panel fronting the wheel contained a digital compass, knot meter, various engine and fuel gauges, autopilot controls, multiple depth finders, two radar displays, GPS unit, and VHF and single sideband radios.

Laura stepped up to a radar display and peered at the screen. Dan had given her a tutorial on radar navigation. With her computer skills, its operation was straightforward.

The screen refreshed as the radar dome mounted on

top of the pilothouse made another orbit. Laura identified the approaching peninsula eight miles away. She glanced through the windscreen; the wipers cycled at maximum as a new torrent cut loose. She spotted a brown-gray smudge on the horizon.

"Looks like Point Roberts is straight ahead," she said.

"Right, we'll be there in about an hour."

Laura chartered the *Hercules* with Miller as skipper. Unable to find a deckhand on short notice, Laura volunteered, paying Miller five hundred cash for his tutelage.

Miller instructed Laura in the basics of helm and engine control. Always a quick study, she ate it up. It didn't hurt that she'd been around boats before. One of her Caltech professors owned a forty-foot racing sloop. She'd spent numerous weekends crewing.

Laura reached into her coat pocket and removed her new cell. She hit the Speed Dial.

Dammit!

Her worry festered. During the fourteen-hour run north, she called at the top and bottom of every hour. Each time the voice mail greeting of her company phone answered.

Laura again checked the radar display. She peered through the windscreen with binoculars. The approaching coastline remained a blur, but she could see a few structures. She carefully searched for familiar features.

Finally, she spotted the house.

She called again; still no answer.

Where is he?

* * *

Yuri drove into the driveway of Laura's rental house at 7:16 A.M. He'd found Elena's Mercedes in the condominium's garage. The onboard GPS navigator guided him straight to the Point.

Laura should have the ROV by now. Despite the lure of the North Van deep-diving equipment, the underwater robot offered another avenue that could be the *Neva*'s salvation. He wanted desperately to examine it.

Yuri stepped out of the sedan. His lower left leg throbbed but he ignored it. Laura's BMW was not in the driveway. He walked to the garage and looked through a door window.

Where is she?

Hammering rain and howling wind continued to assault the southern shore of Point Roberts, but the *Hercules* had moored to a channel-side end-tie deep inside the basin. Before entering the marina, Captain Miller called the harbormaster for a temporary slip assignment.

Miller and First Mate Laura secured the workboat to the floating concrete pier. She went ashore alone.

It took Laura twelve minutes to walk to the beach house. She found a Mercedes-Benz with BC plates parked in the driveway. At first, she thought it might belong to a new renter but dismissed that notion. The previous day she'd extended the rent on the beach house for another week. The sedan must belong to one of Yuri's Russian colleagues.

Laura stood at the front door. She turned the unlocked doorknob.

"Hello!" she called out as she stepped inside.

No reply.

She walked toward the kitchen and again called out but still no response. She snapped an ear toward the nearby stairway, detecting a weak but familiar cadence.

Laura bounded up the stairs, heart racing. She entered the master bedroom.

Stretched out on top of the bed, Yuri snored steadily.

CHAPTER 41

"Yuri!—Yuri, please wake up!"

He did.

"Are you okay?" Laura asked, stroking the side of his cheek.

He didn't reply. Instead, he sat up and wrapped his arms around her.

They embraced for half a minute and he kissed her, for the first time ever—a passionate kiss that electrified Yuri.

He slipped a hand under her blouse and cupped a breast. She moaned.

Laura started to pull her jeans off when Yuri finally sensed trouble. Part of him wasn't responding.

The desire, the heat, the want—everything had been tracking; yet those precursors were not enough.

The nerves that controlled his lower left leg had been slowly returning to life, but another part of his body remained inert. Only then did he understand another dreadful consequence of decompression sickness.

"Something's wrong with me. I'm sorry but I can't . . ." He couldn't say it.

They hastily redressed. He couldn't wait to exit the bedroom.

CHAPTER 42

Nick came out of the beach house's garage. "It's not in there!" Nick announced as he climbed back into the passenger side of the Suburban.

Expecting to find her Mercedes at Yuri's hideout, Elena's angst doubled. "If he didn't come here, where the hell did he go?"

"Who knows?"

"Try the tracker."

Nick reached into a coat pocket and removed the RFID transceiver. He turned it on and waited for a response. Ten seconds later he reported, "No hits."

"We've got to find him!"

"I know that!"

Both sat silent for half a minute until Elena turned to face Nick. "I know he's here someplace."

"That's possible but he could just as well be stuck somewhere back in Vancouver."

Elena said, "So what do we do now?"

"We wait for him to show up."

"Here? He knows this vehicle. If he sees it, he could run."

"Where's he going to go, and who is going to help him? Remember, he still thinks that we have that dive company on board. I'm sure he doesn't suspect that we tried to trap him. For all he knows, he just fell asleep last night."

"Hmm . . . I see your point."

"We should stay here and let him come to us."

"Maybe."

"Maybe what?"

"Maybe we should drive around here and see if we can spot the car."

Nick smiled. "You're worried about the Mercedes, aren't you?"

"It's one of the nicer perks for this assignment."

Nick laughed. "Remember, Elena, you don't own it. The SVR does."

"It's mine as long as I have this assignment."

"Well, unless we reel Kirov back in, you're going to have a lot more to worry about than that damn car."

"That goes for you, too!"

"All right then," Elena said, "let's assume he shows up. Just what do you have planned?"

"We talk."

"You know he won't come back."

"He might, if we reason with him."

Annoyed, Elena said, "Nick, we can't have him running loose down here."

"I know that but think about what he's been trying to do. Thirty some men are still alive, and he's their only hope."

"They're expendable; you know what the chief said."

"But we can't just walk away."

"Yes, we can."

Elena reached into a coat pocket and removed the nine-millimeter Beretta. From the other pocket, she produced a steel cylinder. She attached the sound suppressor to the pistol's muzzle. Holding the weapon by its barrel, she handed it to Nick.

He eyed the weapon. "We don't need that yet."

"Yes we do—take it!"

"Put it away."

"No. We're going to end this situation today, one way or the other."

Nick refused to accept the pistol.

Elena slipped the Beretta into her coat pocket. She opened the door and stepped out.

"Where are you're going?" Nick asked.

She looked back. "I'm going to search the house; he could be hiding in there. That woman could be with him, too."

Major Orlov scowled as he opened his door and joined her.

CHAPTER 43

"This is well constructed," Yuri said.

"I thought you might think so."

Yuri leaned over *Little Mack*, examining the remotely operated vehicle's television camera. Laura stood nearby. The ROV and its supporting equipment were set up on the *Hercules*'s spacious afterdeck.

Yuri examined one of the four ducted electric drive motors. "How much lift can it generate?"

"I'm not sure. When Captain Miller comes back, I'll check with him." Miller had just left for the harbormaster's office to pay the moorage fee.

Yuri continued to look over the underwater robot. At last, he had a tool that could make a real difference for his shipmates. His growing admiration for Laura also buoyed his spirits.

She had risked everything. No one except for Grandfather Semyon had ever done anything like that for Yuri.

Yuri remained standing next to the ROV, amazed at what Laura had accomplished. "We need to go out there tonight. I must contact the *Neva*."

It had been almost a day and a half since his last communication with the submarine.

"What about the weather?" Laura asked. "It's nasty out there."

"This vessel can take it."

Laura agreed. At a hundred and fifty tons, *Hercules* would be a stable platform for deploying *Little Mack* in the rough seas.

"What are we going to tell Captain Miller?" she asked.

"What does he know so far?"

"Only that we're searching for some lost cargo in deep water."

"Good, we'll keep it that way. But he must remain in the pilothouse at all times. He cannot see the video output from the robot."

"What about the buoy? If your crew deploys it, he'll see it for sure. And when you connect the phone, how will you explain that?"

Explaining the buoy would be easy: an acoustically triggered underwater release mechanism. But hooking up the phone, Yuri's only means of communicating with Borodin—that would be harder to cover up.

After exploring the beach house, Elena and Nick stood next to the Suburban.

Elena said, "With all of that female clothing up-stairs, Kirov's woman friend must still be around here."

Nick lit a Winston. He took a puff and responded, "She may not be coming back, but then again she could be late."

Elena reached into her purse for a cigarette, annoyed that Nick didn't offer one of his. She lit up and turned away from Nick.

Nick said, "Let's wait here a little longer, and then we'll drive around." He took another deep drag. "You know he loves that burger place up the road. Maybe we'll hang out there at lunchtime and see if he shows up."

"Normál'no." Okay.

CHAPTER 44

Laura Newman watched as the couple approached. She stood in the wheelhouse twelve feet above the water, sipping tea.

She'd spotted them a minute earlier as they walked along the floating pier. The woman, her long golden hair billowing in the wind, appeared out of place with an umbrella. The man, a trim six-footer wearing blue jeans and a windbreaker, fit the typical marina patron profile.

The pair walked alongside the *Hercules*. Laura made the connection. She stepped into the companionway that led down to the galley, headed forward to the crew quarters where Yuri was napping.

"Yuri, your Russian friends are outside on the dock."

"What?"

"It's the pair you met with at Fat Billie's."

Yuri sat up, swinging his legs over the side, using both hands to leverage the left limb into place. He stood and rubbed his eyes.

"What are they doing here?" Laura asked.

"I'm not surprised—I did take one of their vehicles."

"What are you going to do?"

"Talk to them."

Laura watched from an open door that led to the aft deck as Yuri and the two visitors caucused on the fantail. The ROV and its support gear remained on full display. She could hear their voices but couldn't make out one syllable.

"If you won't come back to Vancouver to meet with the diving company, what are you going to do?" Elena asked. She spotted her Mercedes in the marina parking lot and Nick used the RFID tracker to trace the tagged business card in Yuri's coat pocket.

"I've thought about all that," Yuri said. "They probably have the right gear but it's going to take too long to mobilize to Point Roberts—at least several days, maybe even a week if they have to get border clearances; and if we try to rush 'em, they'll be very suspicious.

"Plus we'll have a huge security problem with their crew." He gestured toward *Little Mack*, parked at their feet. "With this ROV and staging from this vessel I can be working on the *Neva* tonight. And we'll have only one person to be concerned with." He pointed toward the wheelhouse: Captain Miller's domain.

"What do you plan to do with him?" Elena asked.

"If we keep him confined to the bridge deck he won't know what we're doing back here. Laura's convinced him we're trying to salvage something valuable but illicit."

"If he suspects what's really happening, that could be a huge problem for all of us."

"Then he will be dealt with."

"I don't know. It sounds risky to me."

Nick commented, "Elena, his plan does make sense. It'll be much easier to maintain security with just one person."

Elena ignored Nick as she peered at *Little Mack*. "What good is this thing, anyway?"

"It'll allow me to assess the damage and design a repair."

"What kind of repair?"

"There's a breach between Compartments One and Two. I'm going to send the ROV down an open torpedo tube to see if we can find it. If it can be sealed, air will be pumped into Compartment Two. That may help pull the hull's seawater intakes farther out of the mud, allowing the reactor to run at full power. That will buy the crew a lot of time."

Nick squatted down next to *Little Mack*. "This looks pretty big. Can you really get it inside?"

"I'll probably have to remove part of the frame and then it should fit. But if debris is in the way that could be a problem."

Elena said, "Let's assume for the moment that this all works and you come up with a way to fix it. How are you going to implement the fix? Surely this thing can't do it."

"You're right. A diver will have to go down and apply a patch."

"Just where are we going to get a diver to do that?"

"You're looking at 'im."

"Oh, come on. You can't even walk right."

"True. But under water I'll be fine."

"But how will you make the dive?" Nick asked. "Don't you need special equipment?"

"I still have my gear stored back at the beach house. I do need a new dive light and some extra glow sticks. You should be able to get them for me at a dive shop."

"What's a glow stick?"

"A plastic packet filled with chemicals. Break it in half and the chemicals mix, producing light."

"Cool—what else do you need?"

"I need to recharge the tanks of my rebreather with helium and oxygen, plus I'll need extra oxygen and compressed air for decompression during ascent."

"Dive shops carry that stuff?"

"Probably compressed air only; you'll need to get the helium and oxygen from a specialty dive shop that services rebreathers. I'll also need more soda-lime for the scrubber."

"What's that?"

"Soda-lime—it's a mix of calcium oxide and sodium hydroxide. It's used to remove carbon dioxide, part of the rebreather."

"Where do we get that?"

"Specialty dive shop. A medical supply company should have it, too. Soda-lime is used to treat respiratory illnesses."

Nick's forehead scrunched up. "We'll try to get it all today but . . ."

"I don't need the gas or absorbent tonight but maybe tomorrow, the next day for sure."

"What do you need for tonight?"

"Nothing. We're just going to make a test run with the ROV."

"Okay."

Laura and Yuri were alone in the wheelhouse, standing next to the helm. Orlov and Krestyanova departed ten minutes earlier and Captain Miller just retired to his cabin.

Alarmed at the spies' unplanned visit, Laura let Yuri know her opinion of the pair.

"I don't trust them, especially the blonde."

"What's wrong with her?"

"When you were outside talking with the other one, I followed her up here with Captain Miller. He offered to show her the bridge controls."

"So?"

"It was disgusting. She cozied up to his side and continually praised him for his nautical skills."

Yuri's right eyebrow twitched up. "She was probably just trying to be friendly."

"That went way beyond friendly. It was as if she was trying to seduce him—and he loved it. I don't know what would have happened if I had not been there."

"That is a surprise. I don't know what to make of her behavior." Yuri inched closer to Laura. "Nick, however. I like him. He's clearly on board with the rescue."

"But she works with him." Laura turned away, staring down at the deck.

"Let me worry about her. I still need their help but I'll keep an eye on them both."

Yuri reached up with his left hand and caressed Laura's neck; her skin sizzled from his touch. A moment later, he kissed her on the forehead and whispered, "Laura, what you have done for me and for my crew—this wonderful boat, the ROV, the money you've spent—I'm indebted to you forever."

Laura didn't reply. Instead, she buried her face into his shoulder and pulled him closer.

Laura sat at the mess table in the galley. It was a couple minutes before noon. She just brewed a cup of tea. Yuri napped in the crew cabin while Captain Miller slept in his stateroom. She remained too wired to rest.

Laura sipped the green tea, using both hands to clasp the mug. The heat of the porcelain diffused into her fingers. Yuri's burning touch and his warm words of gratitude remained fresh, too.

And earlier in the morning, back at the beach house, the flames of passion that engulfed Laura were of blast furnace proportions. The fire had never been that intense—never.

Only now did she question that encounter, concluding Yuri's failure must have been a consequence of decompression sickness. And then a new shocker hit.

She'd buried the package of condoms somewhere in her suitcase. There hadn't been any thought of breaking that magical spell with Yuri for birth control.

A minute passed and that revelation evolved into a new panic.

Laura hadn't considered the timing until now, not with what had happened the past two weeks. Her menstrual cycle was steady and when she did the math, the numbers were a concern.

"I can't be," Laura said to herself.

Starved and needing release, she'd had sex one evening with Ken after a movie date—a couple of weeks before his last blowup.

Contraceptive pills gave Laura headaches and she did not trust implants, so they relied on condoms. And during their reconciliation, Ken hinted about wanting a baby. But Laura wasn't ready, her work too demanding. Besides, she remained leery of Ken's motives. With the pending divorce, Laura had been relieved that Ken could not leverage a child.

Or could he?

Laura gasped in revulsion as a new suspicion jelled. *He wouldn't dare!*

She made a mental note to examine the condoms for sabotage.

Thirty seconds passed. "I just can't be," she repeated to herself.

Laura then had another memory flash: Her stomach had been in a knot lately. She'd attributed the nausea to a bug of some kind. But doubt now put in an appearance.

Could it be morning sickness?

Laura's spells had started in the pre-dawn hours but now occurred randomly. She'd suffered another upset stomach the previous evening, almost vomiting while aboard the *Hercules*. She credited the nausea to motion sickness and downed a Dramamine tablet.

Laura sat quietly for the next couple of minutes, mulling over the facts.

She finally convinced herself to stop worrying, attributing her menstrual condition to stress. Plus she probably did pick up a bug of some kind.

Once Laura was home and rested, her cycle would return to normal.

CHAPTER 45

"Tom, how in the hell did that Russian boat manage to penetrate so far into the Sound?"

"We're still working on it, sir, but our preliminary assessment suggests that it snuck in by hugging the BC coast."

The two U.S. Navy officers spoke over an encrypted telephone circuit. The senior officer, a three-star admiral, initiated the call from his palatial waterfront office in Pearl Harbor, Hawaii. The junior officer, a one-star, sat at his desk in a drab World War II vintage building at the Bremerton Naval Shipyard in Washington State. It was early afternoon in his time zone.

"Even so, how could they evade the sensors in the Strait of Juan de Fuca?" the three-star asked. "They're on both sides of the boundary line." He sipped coffee from a "Top Gun" mug he earned nearly two decades earlier when he attended the U.S. Navy's Fighter Weapons School.

"We just don't know. NOPF's network should have heard it but none of the bottom hydrophones picked up anything, coming or going." He referenced the Naval Ocean Processing Facility located on the grounds of Naval Air Station Whidbey Island. As part of the U.S. Navy's Integrated Undersea Surveillance System, NOPF monitored Pacific Northwest waters for submarine activity along with other missions.

"What was it, then?"

"An Akula—Tier Two. Early in the incident, a P-three from Whidbey managed to get a solid recording for about twenty minutes before it lost the signal. Blade count and hull noise were a textbook match."

The senior officer leaned back in his chair. "This whole thing is bizarre. If that Russian boat got that far into our waters, what was it doing in the San Juans? If anything, it should have headed south, toward Bangor or maybe Everett." Earlier in his career as a naval aviator, the deputy commander of the U.S. Pacific Fleet had commanded a wing of F-18 Hornets attached to a carrier home-ported at Naval Station Everett.

"I agree, sir. It doesn't make any sense." Unlike his boss, the commanding officer of Navy Region Northwest was a surface warfare officer. He had commanded an Arleigh Burke class guided missile destroyer before his recent promotion to flag officer status. He currently was in charge of all U.S. Navy operations in the Pacific Northwest, which included Washington, Oregon, Alaska, and several other states.

"It must have been on a recon mission," the three-star offered. "Trying to see how far it could penetrate. God only knows how many times our own subs have done the same thing to them."

"That has crossed our minds, too. In fact, the analysts at Keyport are wondering if it could have been involved with that other incident that occurred earlier in the month."

"What are you talking about?"

"A researcher from the University of British Columbia has been monitoring killer whale activity in the Strait of Georgia; she installed several recording hydrophones. One of 'em picked up an unusual event in the south end of the Strait about two weeks ago." The one-star recounted the details.

"A rocket motor, what could that be about?" asked the senior officer.

"It's weird. Our acoustic people say the pressure spike in the recording is similar to a tube-launched Tomahawk but somehow muffled, possibly a misfire."

"Jesus, what does that mean?"

"We don't know; whatever the source was, it didn't last long—less than half a minute."

"What does the scientist in British Columbia know about that?"

"We've kept her in the dark; she thinks we were running some new tests."

"Is she part of the group that's bitching about your sonar testing program?"

"Not that we know of. She has legitimate concerns. She made her complaint through a contact with NOAA rather than using the press."

"Okay, that's good. I assume that you've also managed to keep a lid on the search efforts for the intruder."

"Yes, sir. Most searching was done at night. Routine for NAS Whidbey training operations."

"Let's keep it that way. I don't want to see this plastered over the *New York Times* or on *Sixty Minutes*. That boat should have never penetrated our defenses. If the periscope sighting hadn't been made, we would've never known it was there." He paused. "Dammit, Tom, it could have been doing just about anything, and with the Bangor base and its Trident subs just around the corner—that's just not acceptable."

"I understand, sir. We're running a top to bottom security review right now."

"All right, keep me posted. But until we figure out what happened and fix the damn problem, I'm deploying a six eighty-eight to patrol the Strait. COMSUBPAC will be sending one of his boats from San Diego. You'll be notified when it departs."

CHAPTER 46

Nicolai Orlov leaned against the railing as he stood on the *Hercules*'s starboard deck outside the wheelhouse. The workboat cleared the marina's breakwater and headed southbound at a leisurely six knots. The wicked weather had blown itself out; tonight the waters were smooth and the air ice-cold.

Nick lit up while eyeing the lights that blossomed on the distant shores.

He and Elena had returned to the *Hercules* late in the afternoon after working on Yuri's wish list. They purchased a dive light and ten glow sticks from a specialty dive shop in Vancouver and ten pounds of soda-lime absorbent from a pharmacy in Richmond.

Nick inhaled another lungful and exhaled. The nicotine helped but he remained on edge. He still reeled with his encounter with Elena.

Half an hour earlier, as the *Hercules* prepared to depart, Elena took a stand against him.

"I just talked with the Trade Mission," she'd reported in Russian as they stood on the pier next to the workboat.

"So what's new?"

"We've been ordered back to Vancouver. I couldn't get any details—the unsecured phone. Anyway, we need to leave."

"I can't do that."

"What do you mean?"

"I promised Kirov that I'd help him."

"You're going out on this boat—to the *Neva*?"

"That's right, and we could really use your help, too."

"To do what?"

"Keep Miller occupied. It's obvious that he likes you."

"So you want me to have sex with him?"

"Of course not. Just keep him company in the bridge so I can help Kirov with the ROV."

"What about the woman? Let her babysit Miller."

"She's the only one that knows how to run that underwater gear besides Miller, and we sure as hell can't let him do that."

"This whole thing is crazy. If the chief discovers what we've been doing . . ."

"Dammit, Elena, there are still thirty-six men trapped down there and we're their only hope. I can't walk away from that."

"Well, I can, and it's your duty to do so, too."

"That's not going to happen."

"I'm still returning to Vancouver. And if the chief asks me, I'm going to tell him everything."

"Just give us tonight. I'll call you in the morning and tell you what happened."

Elena never responded. Instead, she'd turned around and walked back to shore.

Nick stiffened as the chilled breeze penetrated his jacket. Elena's unyielding stance also smarted, which left him on edge.

Forty feet aft of Nick, Yuri and Laura stood on the fantail next to *Little Mack*. A rack of overhead flood-lights illuminated the deck. They kept their voices toned down.

"I still don't think you can trust her," Laura said. "Or even him."

"What choice do I have? I can't control them. Be-sides, we need their help."

"What do you think she's doing right now?"

Yuri raised his hands, frustrated. "I don't know, just that Nicolai said she had to return to Vancouver but that she'd be back in the morning."

"Too many people know what we're doing. If just one of them says something to those federal officers at the border . . ." Laura's voice trailed off.

"I understand."

Yuri watched as Laura leaned over to check the ROV's camera. He dreaded what he was about to do, knowing he had procrastinated as long as he could.

"Laura, there's something I need to tell you."

Laura stood up. "What?"

"I lied to you about the *Neva*'s location; it's really on the bottom in American waters, not Canada like I said." He looked down at the deck, ashamed. "I'm sorry. When I told you that, I was desperate for help. It was a mistake I truly regret."

Laura took several deep breaths as Yuri's bomb-shell registered. She had collaborated with Yuri on the thin veil of legitimacy that the rescue would take place inside Canada.

Laura turned away and stared seaward into the blackness.

Half a minute passed when Laura again faced Yuri. "It doesn't matter anymore where your submarine is located. To save your crew, we need to continue as planned."

"This is going to end soon, one way or the other."

"What do you mean?"

Yuri gestured toward *Little Mack*. "If this doesn't work tonight and Moscow continues to flounder, I may have no choice but to turn myself into the authorities and request that the American Navy rescue the *Neva*'s crew." He rubbed the back of his neck with his left hand. "I'll first try to convince Captain Borodin to give up. But no matter what happens, he will still scuttle the boat. There's no way he will let your government get our secrets."

Yuri's admission staggered Laura. "But you'll be arrested; I'll never see you again."

He evaded the obvious. "If it comes to that, I'll give you plenty of time to get out of here so that you're not implicated."

"I'm already implicated—up to my neck. I left a paper trail a mile long."

He grimaced, unsure of her jargon.

Laura glanced down at the ROV. "I paid for this thing with an electronic transfer; the FBI will trace it directly back to me. No way will they believe I wasn't involved."

"But I forced you!"

"I crossed over the line. Aiding and abetting espionage is a real problem."

Laura's revelation startled Yuri. "You would go to prison?"

"They'll throw the key away."

The color drained from his face.

Laura continued, "Don't worry about me. What counts is your crew. If there are no other options, you must ask for help."

"Then you will inform on me to the authorities. That will help you for sure!"

"No, I won't do that." Laura met Yuri's eyes. "If we have to, we'll turn ourselves in together."

CHAPTER 47

Elena sat at a computer in the code room. She was the only one in the Trade Mission this evening.

She just decoded the directive from Moscow. The men in charge of the SVR and FSB hatched Operation Eagle. It now steamrolled forward.

Elena had a choice to make. Either she embraced the plan or it would crush her. Elena's natural instinct for self-preservation prevailed.

SVR Director Smirnov ordered Nick and Elena to meet a special operations team that would be arriving at Vancouver International later in the evening. They were to provide whatever assistance the team might need to carry out Operation Eagle.

Accompanying the encrypted message from Yaseenevo were brief dossiers on the FSB operators, along with a status report on the shipment of their equipment.

She reread the directive and then leaned back in her chair, staring blankly at the ceiling tiles.

Nick is not going to like this at all.

*   *   *

Ken Newman typed in his credit card number and clicked the Purchase icon. The electronic ticket appeared on the laptop's screen. He pressed Print.

Ken sat at his apartment desk. He pulled the hard copy of his bus ticket from the printer. The Greyhound would depart from the Seattle terminal at noon the following day.

At first, he planned to fly. But security at Sea-Tac could be a problem. On the bus, no one would bother checking his carry-on bag during boarding, and probably not even at the Canadian border crossing.

Ken walked into the kitchen. He needed a nightcap, or maybe two.

Elena Krestyanova studied the pair as they walked out of the Canada Border Services and Immigration clearance gate and entered the public greeting area. Each carried a suitcase. The British Air 777 from London had landed thirty-five minutes earlier at Vancouver International.

He had an average build with short sandy hair and a plain but pleasant face.

She stood six-foot-three and weighed 233 pounds. Her muscle-based physique resulted from years of rigorous weight training and a steady diet of steroids.

She's an Amazon! Elena thought while making her way through the mob of passengers and visitors that crowded the lobby. She held up her right arm and called out, "Ms. Koloski, Mr. Marshall, over here, please!"

The FSB special operations team walked toward Elena.

She directed them to the nearby vacant area.

Elena lowered her voice and spoke in their common tongue, "Welcome, I'm Elena."

"Captain Dubova," the female officer said.

Dubova turned to face her charge. "This is Lieutenant Karpekov."

Elena smiled.

"Have you heard anything about our equipment?" asked Dubova.

"It should be arriving tomorrow morning."

"At the harbor?"

"Yes, in Bellingham."

The Ford van with the FSB team's gear left the Bay Area a few hours earlier. Flown into San Francisco International and delivered to the consulate the previous day under diplomatic seal, the secret equipment was then smuggled out of the consulate in a rental van. The drivers, both illegal agents under the control of the SVR's Directorate S, were instructed to obey strictly the speed limits and refrain from any drinking during their long haul north on Interstate 5.

The Illegal's destination was Squalicum Harbor in Bellingham. An SVR officer from the San Francisco consulate chartered a forty-two-foot Grand Banks trawler yacht sight-unseen. He posed as an experienced American yachtsman who wished to take a fall cruise through the San Juan Islands with his wife. Although an unusual request for this time of year, the charter company gladly accepted the spy's Visa card number.

"So how do we get to this place—Bellingham?" asked Dubova.

"I'll drive you in the morning; it's only about an hour away."

"How do we get through the U.S. border?"

"Your Canadian passports will work fine."

"Are we staying in Vancouver tonight?" asked the junior officer.

"Yes, I've reserved rooms for both of you at a downtown hotel."

"Good," announced Dubova. "We need sleep. We're still operating on Moscow time."

Elena and Dubova exchanged cell phone numbers and the trio headed toward parking.

Elena considered her options: *Maybe I should tell them about Kirov and tonight's mission. Perhaps they could help with the rescue. Nick would certainly go for that!*

All true, but then Elena remembered her orders. Kirov should have been neutralized by now, and the *Neva*'s crew had been ruled expendable.

Dubova and Karpekov were janitors, tasked with sanitizing the litter from a mission that had gone bad.

Just leave it alone, she decided.

CHAPTER 48

"Captain, it's not the same boat he's used before."

"You're certain?"

"Yes, sir. Much slower revolutions. Might be diesel powered."

Captain Lieutenant Stephan Borodin processed the sonar operator's report. "What's it doing?"

"Still circling at three knots, maybe centered a hundred meters or so to the south."

"Has it detected our hull?"

"Negative. It's low powered so our coating should handle it well enough."

The four-inch-thick rubberized anechoic tiles encasing the *Neva*'s outer hull absorbed a wide spectrum of mechanically generated sound waves, especially those produced by depth sounders.

"What about with the radio buoy hatches, they're open?"

"There might be some return echoes from the pressure casing. It's not coated inside."

"Give me your best estimate of the vessel type."

"It could be a fishing boat or some kind of work-boat."

"How about a patrol craft?"

"Maybe a small one, probably under thirty meters."

"Chyort!" Damn. "Who the hell's up there?"

Nick Orlov climbed up the interior companionway stairs and entered the wheelhouse.

"Are they ready yet?" asked Captain Miller. He sat on his pedestal chair in the pilothouse of the *Hercules*. His right hand rested on the helm.

"I think they're close," Orlov said.

"Well, I hope they're careful with *Little Mack*. It's deep out here and there's bound to be current, which could make it tough to control with so much tether."

"I see how that could be a problem all right."

"Are you set?" Laura asked Yuri. They stood on the main deck ten feet aft of the cabin superstructure. *Little Mack*, the remotely operated vehicle, was at their feet.

"Yes. You can go."

Laura headed to the wheelhouse.

Yuri removed his makeshift device from a plastic container parked next to the ROV. He stepped to the starboard bulwark and lowered the hybrid "woofer in a pressure cooker" hydrophone overboard, suspending it five feet below the hull with an extension cord. He triggered the broadcast switch three times, transmitting the "Here I Am" signal.

About a minute later, the *Neva*'s radio antenna bobbed twenty meters to the south.

Under Laura's direction, Captain Miller backed the workboat until the stern closed to within a meter of the buoy. Yuri captured it with a boat-hook and rigged up the telephone link. Captain Borodin waited on the other end of the cable. Yuri explained the mission and disconnected.

Yuri peered forward. Laura remained on the deck adjacent to the wheelhouse, monitoring the *Herc*'s position relative to the buoy. He shouted, "Pull ahead twenty meters and hold."

She raised her right arm and relayed the order to Miller.

Yuri used the boat's hydraulic crane to raise *Little Mack* from the deck; the ROV dangled over the starboard side, suspended three feet above the water by a wire rope.

Yuri backed off the crane's clutch and allowed *Little Mack* to reel into the water, stopping with the upper frame awash.

Laura rejoined Yuri. She sat in a plastic lawn chair beside *Little Mack*'s control unit; the fiberglass box was perched on a wood crate next to the deck crane. After running diagnostic tests, she turned and met Yuri's eyes. "All systems are go."

"Release the cable?" he asked.

"Yes."

Yuri triggered the remote cable lock, releasing the hydraulic clamp that connected the steel lifting cable to *Little Mack*. The ROV submerged a few feet and headed aft, running parallel to the *Hercules*. The yellow pencil diameter tether that supplied electrical power and communications to the ROV spooled off its deck-mounted reel.

Laura guided *Little Mack* toward the *Neva*'s radio buoy, still bobbing about sixty feet to the south. Yuri watched the glow of the underwater craft's dual search-lights.

"What are they doing?" asked Captain Miller. He stood on the starboard observation deck just outside the wheelhouse. He looked aft, over Nick Orlov's left shoulder.

Nick spun around. "Captain, please return to the wheelhouse. You know the rules."

"Where'd that buoy come from?"

Nick pushed Miller toward the open doorway. "Let's go back inside."

"Get your hands off me!"

Nick jerked his hands away. "Please, Captain, back inside."

Miller stepped into the pilothouse, Nick right behind.

Miller stood next to the helm but he ignored the wheel; the *Herc*'s GPS-linked autopilot headed the boat into the ebb current. The ship's engine spun the propeller with just enough thrust to match the tidal flow. The bow and stern thrusters also kicked in automatically when needed.

"Just what are you people up to?" Miller demanded.

"Captain, this is not your business. All we want you to do is drive the boat. Nothing else is your concern."

"Well, if I wrap the screw around that buoy cable, it'll become everyone's concern real damn quick."

"Those two know what they're doing; they won't let your propeller get fouled. That would mess up the whole plan for sure."

"Just what are you trying to recover down there anyway—can you at least tell me that?"

"Some lost cargo."

"That's what Laura said but all of this secrecy stuff just isn't right. What are you hiding?"

"Like we've told you before, we don't want to advertise what we're doing until we know for certain that we have the right target. That's why we're working at night."

"Well, this whole operation makes me nervous. I don't like working in a vacuum; it's not worth the risk to the *Herc*."

Nick homed in on Miller's anger. "Captain, we can't reveal what we're after until we know it's there for sure. If we manage a recovery, I'll see that you got a sizable bonus. But only if you continue to help and keep it confidential."

"What kind of bonus are we talking about?"

Bingo! He had him now. "Twenty thousand."

That took the wind out of Miller's sails. "That's in addition to the charter fee?"

"Of course."

"All I have to do is drive the *Herc*, no hanky-panky?"

Miller's idiom was unknown to Nick but he guessed its meaning. "That's right."

Captain Miller cocked his head to the side while

raising an eyebrow. "How can I trust you? I don't know you from Jack."

Nick knew he'd hooked Miller. "If we're successful tonight—that we've found what we're looking for, tomorrow I'll have a down payment of ten thousand wired to any account you want anywhere in the world."

"I want cash."

Nick said, "All right, we can swing that but it'll have to be in the late afternoon."

"Four o'clock. If you don't have it by then, the *Herc* sails back to Seattle."

"Okay."

Miller wasn't done. "Regardless of recovery, I want the balance on Sunday, no later than noon."

CHAPTER 49

Little Mack wasn't as easy to maneuver as Laura remembered. The ROV's sluggish response to her joystick adjustments compounded her queasiness. She would have attributed her upset stomach to seasickness but now suspected otherwise.

Yuri read her facial tension: beads of sweat on the brow and a clenched jaw.

"What's wrong?" he asked.

"It's hard to control—feels slow compared to the other day."

"Could it be fouled on the buoy cable?"

"No. I've stayed down current."

"Then it must be the current dragging on the tether."

Laura faced Yuri. "I think you're right."

"Can you do this?"

"The current keeps trying to push *Mack* away from the cable but if I can keep it in sight, we should be okay." She returned to the monitor.

Yuri leaned closer to the screen. The VLF radio cable remained centered, illuminated by *Little Mack*'s dual lights. He also noted the digital readouts on the upper portion of the display. He focused on the depth reading. "You've only got about fifty meters to go."

"Good."

Several minutes passed and Yuri issued a warning: "You're close, so get ready."

"I am."

Within seconds, the afterdeck of the *Neva* materialized in the video screen. The open buoy hatch doors, hinged on each side of the opening, loomed in the murk.

Laura stared at the display, dazzled at the image of the *Neva*'s hull. She glanced up at Yuri. "What should I do?"

"Head forward, toward the bow."

Little Mack scooted along the starboard hull and slowed to a crawl.

"Turn it to the left—that's it," Yuri said. "Hold it right there." He peered at the digital image of a circular opening.

"Is that the torpedo tube?" Laura asked.

"Yes."

"*Little Mack* will never fit in there."

"Not as configured, but if we remove the frame I think it'll pass."

"What's the diameter of the tube?"

"Six hundred fifty millimeters."

Laura made a quick conversion: about two feet. "Yeah, that might actually work."

"Bring it closer, I need to look down the bore to make sure it's clear."

"Okay."

Little Mack's forward protective frame pressed hard against the exterior surface of the torpedo tube. The lights mounted above the camera penetrated deep into the pipe-like interior.

Yuri stared at the video display. Confusing at first, the image registered. He cursed.

"What's wrong?" Laura asked.

"The tube's obstructed halfway in."

"What do we do?"

"Let me think."

"Okay—sorry."

Half a minute elapsed. "Just how much thrust can the ROV gencrate?" Yuri asked.

"Under full power, I'm not sure but I'd guess forty to fifty pounds of horizontal thrust. But what good will that do if the tube's blocked?"

"If we're lucky, maybe we can push it out of the way."

"Push what out of the way?"

"Viktor's body."

CHAPTER 50

At 3:25 A.M., Captain Dan Miller peered through the wheelhouse windshield into pea soup–thick fog. "Still can't see shit," he mumbled.

While Laura and her associates tinkered with *Little Mack* on the main deck, preparing for the second dive, Miller piloted the *Herc* in a slow orbit two miles east of the first dive location. Wary of the developing fog bank, Miller wanted plenty of separation from the nearby northbound shipping lanes. He worried about colliding with another vessel, especially one of the Asian behemoths calling on Vancouver.

Miller kept a close eye on the radar but he also had another thought that would improve safety.

Maybe I should turn AIS back on.

Before departing from the marina at Point Roberts, he had switched off the AIS transponder. The *Hercules* was equipped with a GPS-linked automatic identification system that provided the real time location of the vessel. AIS's main purpose is to avoid collisions. However, it also allows anyone on the Internet to track the vessel.

Miller made a decision. *No way. That sucker remains off. I don't want anyone monitoring what we're doing out here!*

If questioned over the VHF radio by the Coast Guard or the Vessel Traffic System, he would report a malfunction.

Miller checked the radar display again. *Good, all clear.*

He wondered about his passengers.

Miller's babysitter—Nick—had headed below thirty minutes earlier. At that time, Miller stepped outside onto the starboard bridge wing for a quick peek aft. Laura and the other guy had been crouched over *Little Mack*, removing parts. They were still at it, now assisted by the babysitter.

Why are they taking Mack apart?

"Yuri, I don't know if this is such a good idea," Laura said, kneeling next to the ROV.

"We don't have any choice. It will never penetrate the tube with the full frame intact." Yuri squatted on the opposite side of *Little Mack*, a socket wrench in his left hand. He was removing the fourth of six stainless steel bolts that connected the ROV's protective frame to a ballast tank.

"But the buoyancy chamber might not have sufficient support."

"I'll reinforce it—don't worry."

Nick stood behind Yuri, eyeing the transformation

of *Little Mack*. He knew nothing about the operation of the underwater machine but did share Laura's concerns. Yuri had stripped away most of the ROV's upper frame, exposing the camera and light systems. To Nick's eyes, it looked vulnerable to impact damage. But what did he know?

While Yuri worked on the next bolt, Laura stood up. She stretched her lower back and looked around. That's when she noticed. "Wow, it's even foggier now. I hope Captain Miller knows where we are."

Nick answered, "I don't think you need to worry about that—the radar cuts right through this stuff." To amuse himself while babysitting Miller he'd monitored the radar display.

Laura dropped back to her knees and adjusted the ballast tank. When complete, she caught Yuri's eyes. "You know, I think we should ask Captain Miller for some advice on how to check *Mack*'s center of gravity after we make these changes. If anyone knows, it should be him."

Yuri stopped working the wrench. "That's a good idea."

"You want me to go get him?" asked Nick.

"Yes," Yuri said.

Dan Miller eyed the remnants of *Little Mack*, appalled. "What the hell are you doing with the framework?" he said, addressing the trio standing beside him.

Yuri replied, "It's too bulky to make the penetration we need so I've removed the upper pipe frame and remounted the camera and lights on top of the buoyancy chambers."

"You try to send it down like that, and it'll be all over the frigging place. The center of gravity is screwed up royally."

"Captain," Laura said, joining the conversation, "we have no choice but to jury-rig *Little Mack*. What we'd like—and what I'd personally appreciate—is your advice. We know that we need to compensate for the changes we've made, and anything you can offer us now will save us a ton of trial and error adjustments later on." She chose her next words carefully. "I know how much you care for *Little Mack*, and believe me, I was not in favor of tinkering with the design, but it's just too big to do what we need."

Laura's flattery worked. "Well, I suppose there are a few things you could do."

"Great, please explain."

"In a moment." Miller challenged Nick. "I know that you've found your stuff so I still get my bonus, regardless of whether or not *Little Mack* gets the job done—right?"

Nick smiled. "That's right, Captain."

"Okay then." Miller squatted down beside the ROV's port side and pointed with his right index finger. "I'd remount the camera back in this area instead of . . ."

CHAPTER 51

"Where is it?" asked Captain Borodin.

"Amidships, port, sir," reported the sonar tech. "It's close in—a few meters at most."

Borodin took a deep breath and slowly let it out. He'd been on the edge for the last ten minutes.

Even in its degraded state, the *Neva*'s passive sonar detected the high-pitched whine of the ROV's thrusters as it struggled on its return voyage to the submarine. The flooding current taxed its propulsion system.

Borodin faced the sonar watch stander.

"Is it still heading toward the bow?"

"Yes, sir. Coming up on it right now."

"Xoróšij!" Good.

"Okay, what do you want me to do now?" asked Laura as she stared at the video display.

"Ascend three meters," Yuri said.

It was 6:37 A.M. The ROV redeployed twenty minutes earlier. During a previous attempt, after modifying *Little Mack*, the camera had broadcast static only. It took over an hour to locate the corroded cable connector.

"Three meters—ten feet, okay." Laura eased back on the joystick while keeping her eyes on the hazy video image of the underside of the *Neva*'s rounded bow.

"Better slow up," Yuri warned as the tip of the bow approached.

"Right." Laura backed off the control and *Little Mack* hovered.

"Can you bring it in a little closer?"

"I think so but the current's still a problem."

"You're almost there."

"I can see it."

Laura maneuvered the ROV opposite torpedo tube five.

"That's it, perfect!" Yuri said.

"I'm just about maxed out here with the current. I have to do it right now."

"Go ahead."

Laura rotated her right wrist and *Little Mack* crabbed into the current. Two seconds later, she backed off one thruster, letting the current swing the camera end of the ROV into alignment. She powered up all thrusters and *Little Mack* squirted into the torpedo tube.

"We're in!" Laura shouted while backing off the power.

Little Mack hovered inside the opening of the 25.5-inch-diameter cylinder. The outer bow cover or shutter had sheared away from its mount. The torpedo tube's muzzle door that normally would have sealed the tube from the sea had also disappeared.

Both Yuri and Laura stared at the video display. The camera and its supporting lights probed deep into the tube.

Laura commented, "I see him."

A pair of black fins and dry suit–encased lower legs filled the camera's view.

Yuri didn't respond. He'd had several hours to prepare but remained distressed. Warrant Officer Viktor Skirski had been his diving partner and friend.

Laura faced Yuri. "What should I do?"

"Let me do this."

Laura stood and stepped to the side, allowing Yuri to take her place.

"I want to see what happens if we push forward." His right hand rested on the joystick.

"Let me help you," Laura said. She placed her hand over his and rotated the joystick forward.

Little Mack crawled down the tube until the modified pipe frame guarding the camera lens was about a foot away from the right fin.

"I've got him," he said.

Laura took her hand away.

Yuri added thrust and the camera slipped past the fin, riding up onto the leg. The lights above the camera scraped against the metallic lining of the tube.

"Govnó!"

"What's wrong?" Laura asked.

"He's not moving. I was afraid of this."

"Afraid of what?"

"There must be debris in the tube. That's what Viktor got caught on."

Laura leaned closer to the screen.

"I don't know about that. I can see under the body a

ways and I don't see any damage." She paused. "Maybe something else happened now that the body is decomposing . . ."

"No. It's fouled on something."

"Try increasing the power."

Yuri did but Viktor's corpse still refused to yield.

Laura said, "I guess it's time for your backup plan."

"Yes, we have no choice."

"Okay, I'll bring it up."

Eighty minutes later, after returning to the surface for another modification, *Little Mack* reentered the torpedo tube. The grappling device that Yuri bolted to the upper frame extended about two feet beyond the camera.

"I'm ready," Laura announced.

"Okay, do it."

Laura gunned the thrusters and the ROV jetted down the tube. It slammed into the corpse, the barbed stinger pierced the dry suit and tore into the corpse's right thigh.

A plume of inky fluid clouded the camera's eye.

Yuri looked away, disgusted at the desecration.

The water cleared.

"Now?" Laura asked.

"Go ahead."

She applied reverse thrust.

Half power: The barb held but still no movement.

Three-quarters power: The corpse refused to budge.

"Here goes everything," Laura said, her eyes glued to the monitor.

Yuri turned back. *Little Mack* hadn't moved a centimeter. "It's no use," he said. "We'll have to think of something else."

Laura held up her left hand. "Hang on. I'm going to try something different." She adjusted one of the thrusters, forcing *Little Mack* to rotate in place.

Yuri watched as the camera's view angle changed. After reaching eighty degrees of arc, the TV screen blinked and the camera lost focus.

"What happened?" he asked.

"I think it moved." Laura shut down the thrusters. She continued to stare at the nearly blacked out video screen. "Something's jammed tight against the camera lens."

"Viktor's shifted position. Back up—slowly."

Laura applied power. The video image changed as several inches of space opened up between the lens and the obstruction.

"That's Viktor's rebreather," Yuri announced as he pointed to a black plastic boxlike object in the screen. One corner of the housing appeared bent.

"Could that have been what was jammed?"

"Maybe."

"See if he's really free," Yuri said.

"Okay." She reapplied reverse thrust.

Little Mack crept backward.

Nick Orlov and Captain Miller stood facing each other in the wheelhouse. Both were on edge.

"Remember, now, if I don't have my cash by four o'clock this afternoon, me and the *Herc* are sailing back to Seattle and you and your friends can go screw yourselves."

"You'll get your bonus, Captain."

"I'm not kidding around. You promised it and that's that."

With eyebrows tight and straight, Nick backed out of the wheelhouse, barely able to contain his anger.

Nick sucked on a Winston while leaning against the guardrail until his anger finally subsided. Captain Miller remained inside the pilothouse. The *Hercules* was bathed in welcome mid-morning sunshine. The workboat hovered in place about a hundred feet north of the VLF buoy.

In the distance, Nick could see the southern shoreline of Point Roberts. With the exception of a southbound containership in the adjacent shipping lanes, the *Hercules* had this stretch of the Strait of Georgia to itself.

Nick looked aft. Yuri stood next to the starboard railing, peering overboard.

The submarine officer and his American companion had been monitoring the ROV's video display for hours. Nick checked in with them several times but learned zilch.

Captain Miller, on the other hand, was a royal pest. Part of their latest clash was Nick's fault. He had forgotten that it was the weekend and offhandedly mentioned to Miller that he might need additional time to assemble the funds. Big mistake.

Having thought about the tactical situation, Nick made a critical decision. But before he could act, he needed help. He'd already called Elena's cell three times, each one connecting to her voice mail.

Nick flipped the spent butt overboard and was about to head back to the bridge, when he noticed that Laura and Yuri were leaning over the starboard bulwark. They reached for something in the water.

He headed aft, curious.

"Can you free him while still in the water?" Laura asked.

"I don't know, maybe."

Yuri hung on to the end of a boathook. Its hooked end had snagged onto *Little Mack*. The ROV surfaced.

"Say, Yuri," Nick Orlov said in Russian, approaching the pair, "I think it's time that we—"

He stopped in mid-sentence when he spotted the black-clad form next to the ROV.

"What's that?"

Yuri turned to face Nick. "It's one of the crew—a diver. He's dead. Come and help us."

After Yuri extracted Viktor's corpse from *Little Mack*'s stinger, a quick examination on the main deck revealed no hints as to the cause of death of his friend and colleague. Yuri next removed Viktor's backpack and salvaged the dive light still strapped to the left wrist.

Laura said a prayer just before Yuri and Nick gently eased Viktor's earthly remains back into the water. Still encased in the heavily weighted diving gear, the body promptly submerged, commencing its final descent.

CHAPTER 52

Elena Krestyanova drove south from Vancouver. Captain Dubova sat beside her. Lieutenant Grigori Karpekov occupied the backseat of the Mercedes.

Posing as Canadian tourists, they breezed through the U.S. border station at Blaine. Elena's stated reason for visiting the United States: shopping at the Bellis Fair Mall in Bellingham and then lunch.

Dubova yawned and said, "All you know is that the *Neva* is somewhere south of Point Roberts."

"Yes. We've been trying to obtain its precise location."

Unsure how much the FSB operators knew, Elena doled out the minimum. Yuri had never revealed the *Neva*'s exact location and Elena used it to her advantage.

"This boat your partner is using, it's roughly twice the size of the one you're taking us to."

"I suppose that's right."

"And it has a hydraulic crane?"

"Yes, but what's that—"

"I think we should use that vessel. The boat chartered for us is marginal at best."

"I don't think we can do that," Elena said, caught off guard.

"Why not?"

Elena invented an instant response. "The charter is up today."

"Can't we rent it for a few more days?"

Elena could not let the FSB operators anywhere near Yuri Kirov or his woman. They would blab back in Moscow and her boss would know that she and Nick hadn't followed orders.

"What's so great about the bigger boat?" Elena asked.

"The crane, ma'am," answered the backseater.

Elena looked at the rearview mirror.

Karpekov stretched out his arms. "The underwater robotic gear we need to deploy to set the charges is heavy, so the crane will really help there." He yawned. "And by the way, what kind of survey equipment is your partner using?"

"What?"

"You know, to search for the hull."

Elena was clueless, lost in her lies. "I don't know."

"Well, if it's standard side scan sonar they may never find it because the hull is covered with anechoic tiles. The side scan gear we have has been modified to account for the tiles."

"Side scan?" Elena said.

"Like underwater radar but uses sound waves rather than radio signals. We tow an instrument through the water—a fish. It sends out acoustic signals that reflect off objects on the bottom. The fish picks up the reflections and software turns the signals into images."

Dubova rejoined, "We'll probably have to use our search equipment to find the *Neva*. Having a large deck with the crane would be more efficient."

Elena scanned an approaching roadside sign. Bellingham was ten miles away. "I might be able to extend the charter but there's no way we can access the vessel today."

"How about tomorrow? If you could have the workboat meet us at the Bellingham harbor, we could load up there."

"Possible, but I don't want to do it at the harbor. Too many people around."

"Yes, I see your point."

"What do you suggest?" the junior officer asked.

"We could make the transfer offshore, out of sight of land."

"Yes, that could work if it's calm," Dubova said. "We'll load up our equipment on the trawler today and run a systems check to make sure it's all working. Tomorrow we'll rendezvous with the workboat and make the transfer."

"That could work. After I drop you off I'll return to the mission to set it up."

"Good."

Elena would be heading back to Vancouver but not to the Trade Mission. She had locked the Beretta and its suppressor inside the desk at her apartment. Later in the day, she would return to Point Roberts and confront Nick Orlov.

Yuri Kirov had to be stopped—now.

CHAPTER 53

"I don't see anything else in the way, do you?" asked Laura.

Yuri leaned closer to the screen. The brightness of the late-morning sun played havoc with the video image. "It looks clear but stay away from that guide, it could snag the ROV."

"Okay."

Little Mack was inside torpedo tube five, halfway into the forty-foot-long cylinder, next to the twisted remnant of a plastic rail guide. The four guides, equally spaced apart and extending the full length of the conduit, isolated a torpedo from direct contact with the tube's steel surface. The six-foot section of damaged rail guide had snagged Viktor's rebreather backpack. Whether he had expired after becoming ensnared or died first while exploring the tube and drifted into the tangle remained unknown.

"What now?" Laura asked. The ROV hovered near the end of the torpedo tube. Light from the camera system revealed an opening ahead.

"Move to the edge but don't enter the compartment. I want to look at the damage."

"Okay."

Laura inched *Little Mack* forward. The twin searchlights beamed inward.

"Oh dear Lord," she muttered.

Several intact bodies, and assorted body parts, were suspended mid-depth inside the flooded torpedo compartment.

"What happened to them?"

"It was a *Shkval*. A special kind of torpedo—rocket powered. We had a new heavyweight model aboard."

"Did it blow up?"

"No. But somehow its motor ignited while still inside the tube—without warning."

"How could that cause all of this?"

"It's designed to fire the rocket motor *after* being ejected from the tube."

Laura scrutinized the video feed. She looked beyond the human carnage. "Everything's been scorched."

None of the *Neva*'s survivors knew for sure what had happened that fateful morning almost two weeks earlier. But it was now obvious to Yuri. The terror of that day came back in a torrent. First, without warning, a horrendous roar engulfed the entire pressure casing. Then the deck unexpectedly tilted downward at a steep angle. When the *Neva* plowed into the bottom, Yuri and the other men in his compartment were tossed about pell-mell. The main lighting blinked off, but ten seconds later the emergency lights flickered to life.

Yuri had called the central command post using the intercom but received no reply. Five minutes later Stephan

Borodin's voice had broadcast over the submarine's master intercom. "This is Borodin. I have assumed temporary command. All compartments make your damage reports," he'd ordered.

By protocol, the watch officer for each compartment made the report, starting at the bow with Compartment One—the torpedo room—and working aft.

Borodin started the roll call. "Compartment One, report!"

An awkward ten seconds passed. Borodin repeated the command.

Again, no reply, so Borodin moved on. "Compartment Two, report!"

Silence.

A repeat plea, also not answered.

"Compartment Three, report!"

There would be a response here—Borodin called from three.

The CCP watch officer standing beside Borodin responded, "Compartment Three on emergency power. No flooding. Twelve crew. Three minor injuries."

"Compartment Four, report!" Borodin ordered.

"Compartment Four on emergency power. No flooding. Reactors are offline. Five crew. No injuries."

"Compartment Five, report!"

"Compartment Five on emergency power. No flooding. All turbines and turbo generators shut down. Seven crew. Two minor injuries."

"Compartment Six, report!"

Yuri had keyed his intercom microphone and said, "Compartment Six is on emergency power. No flooding. Six crew. No injuries."

"Compartment Seven, report!"

"Compartment Seven on emergency power. Minor flooding. Five crew. No injuries."

That report drew a command from Borodin. "Describe your flooding situation."

"Sir, a seam in a cooling water pipe opened up. We've banded it but it's still leaking."

"Flow rate?"

"About half a liter per minute."

"Very well, let me know if it increases."

"Aye, aye, sir."

Borodin continued the roll call, "Compartment Eight, report!"

"Compartment Eight on emergency power, sir. No flooding. Four crew. No injuries."

Borodin: "All compartments stand by as you are. We'll get back to you soon."

The intercom clicked off.

Yuri recalled how bewildered he and the others inside Compartment Six had been after the roll call. When he did the math, he'd discovered that fifty-three members of the ship's company were unaccountable. If both forward compartments had flooded, there would be no survivors.

The leak in Compartment Seven also alarmed Yuri. It was only a trickle at the time but a harbinger of more trouble ahead.

"Try moving forward a couple of meters," Yuri said.

"Okay."

Laura advanced the joystick and *Little Mack* swam into the torpedo room.

"That's good! Now turn the camera around. I want to check the tube's breach."

She executed the maneuver.

Yuri leaned forward, examining the screen with a hand over his eyes to block the sun. He muttered, *"Vot der'mó!"* Oh shit.

"What?" Laura asked.

"I was afraid of this." He pointed to the screen. "The breach door was blown off its hinges. See the door on the tube next to it?" He tapped his right index finger on the image. "This is what's supposed to be on the end of the tube."

"That's a huge hunk of metal. There must have been a titanic explosion to tear it apart."

"It didn't explode, not in the conventional sense. Instead, the rocket motor ignited while inside the tube; it was sealed at both ends."

Laura pictured the process. "I see—the motor fired inside the tube. The pressure built up from the exhaust and then the door was blown off."

"Yes!"

After an internal electrical short circuit ignited the rocket motor, the three-ton weapon blasted forward in the torpedo tube. The forward end of the torpedo, with its thick tempered steel super-cavitating disk mounted on its very tip, slammed into the tube's muzzle—the outer door.

Trapped by the muzzle door, the torpedo's rocket motor continued to burn fiercely. Weakened by the searing blast flames and overstressed by the mounting exhaust pressure in the tube, an existing microscopic crack in the breach door's rack-and-pinion locking ring elongated and then fractured. In just a millisecond, the

breach door ripped open while simultaneously shear-
ing from its hinge mounts.

The torpedo pumped thousands of cubic feet of toxic
white-hot gases into the submarine every second. With
a burn time of about a minute, the buildup of pressure
from the rocket gases could have burst the *Neva*'s internal bulkheads.

But that didn't happen. Instead, after burning for
just under half a minute, achieving maximum thrust,
the weapon tore open the outer door and blasted the
bow shutter from its mount. It launched itself into the
sea.

As it exited tube five, the torpedo's steel casing split
apart from remnants of the outer door. A torrent of
ripped metal spat from the tube, followed by the half-
spent rocket motor; it tumbled through the deep like a
Fourth of July fountain wheel.

Had the rocket motor continued to burn inside tube
five for a few more seconds, the assortment of torpe-
does and other arms stored in the adjacent weapons bay
would have cooked off. That would have been the end
of everything—like the *Kursk*'s fate in 2000.

Still, the rocket torpedo's exhaust wreaked may-
hem.

The weapon's crew died in seconds, their bodies
shredded and incinerated.

The sailors in Compartment Two might have lived
if there had been time to close the bulkhead door to the
torpedo room. While the blast flames didn't penetrate
the second compartment, the exhaust flooded the compartment's main accommodations section in just a few
breaths. With the full force of the rocket engine venting into the torpedo room, the pressure inside Com-

partment Two skyrocketed. Piercing ear pain from burst eardrums took the initial toll on victims.

The vile exhaust gases invaded everything, displacing nearly all breathable oxygen. Those few with ready access to emergency breathing apparatus had just moments to don their gear before the toxic fumes killed. Several men succeeded, including the *Neva*'s executive officer, Mikhail Gromeko. The XO had been on his way to the CCP when the *Shkval* erupted.

The final assault took place thirty-four seconds into the event. The instant the rocket torpedo blasted through the bow shutter, the excess internal pressure in the hull vented through the open torpedo tube—like air bleeding from a balloon. Seawater gushed into the tube.

The main storage batteries flooded under the deluge and shorted out, triggering a cascade of events that led to the shutdown of the reactors.

Without power, the propeller stopped rotating. As the *Neva* slowed, its forward diving planes lost lift, causing the bow to dip downward. The seawater pouring into the open torpedo tube tripled the downward track.

The CCP watch officer had ordered an emergency blow of the ballast tanks, hoping to surface the boat. But it was too little, too late.

The enormous weight of the flooded compartments caused the *Neva* to plunge bow first into the bottom; it plowed a thirty-meter-long furrow into the muddy bottom before coming to rest.

The XO and the three other survivors with EBAs evacuated to a partially flooded upper deck in Compartment Two. With no lights and the intercom shorted out, they sat in the darkness, freezing. They lasted twenty minutes before succumbing to oxygen toxicity induced by breathing air compressed over twenty times atmospheric pressure.

Laura studied the live video images of the torpedo room until Yuri said, "It's time that we move to Compartment Two."

"Okay. How do I get *Mack* there?"

"Stay to the right and head aft."

Laura checked the screen as she manipulated the ROV's joystick. The opening revealed a narrow hallway. Mechanical debris, mainly piping and electrical cables, hung from the overhead—impact damage when the *Neva* collided with the bottom.

"Mind the debris," Yuri warned. "The tether could get hung up."

"Okay."

About an hour after the sinking, acting Captain Borodin had summoned all compartment heads to the central command post. That's when Yuri learned the nature of their situation.

The *Neva* lay mired in muck under 220 meters of enemy waters. Captain Tomich, XO Gromeko, and fifty-one of the crew were dead.

With the nuclear reactors offline and the main batteries fried, the backup batteries in Compartment Five served as the *Neva*'s only source of power; but they provided just a quarter of the main's amperage.

The forward 30 percent of the pressure casing had flooded, which in addition to the torpedo room included most of the crew's quarters, the boat's galley and mess areas, and much of the food.

Yuri remembered his thoughts at the end of Borodin's briefing. *We're all dead men. No one's getting off this thing.*

As *Little Mack* swam aft through the passageway, Yuri scrutinized the video display. His heart rate accelerated in anticipation of what lay ahead. He spotted it in the merged beam of the dual floodlights. *Thank God!*

"That's the door just ahead," Yuri said, tapping a finger on the display.

Laura stared at the screen. The ROV hovered about twenty feet away from a bulkhead. Near the center of the steel wall just above the deck, she spotted a circular penetration. "It's open like you thought it might be. That's good, isn't it?"

"Yes, very good."

The passageway to the second compartment was about three feet in diameter. Had the side-mounted steel bulkhead door next to the opening been shut, the buildup of pressure would have ruptured the bulkhead. Repairing a burst bulkhead underwater would be virtually impossible. But closing the door would be no simple matter, either.

Although hidden from the camera's view, a latch locked the open door in place.

"What should I do?" Laura asked.

Yuri refreshed his memory. This particular latch had a simple spring-loaded mechanism. Once released, the three-hundred-pound door would pivot into the closed position with a gentle shove. But one needed a hand to trigger the release. *Little Mack*, unfortunately, had no means to accomplish such a task.

"Try coming alongside the door and giving it a little push."

"You want me to see if I can move it?"

"Yes."

"Okay."

Yuri watched as the ROV moved closer to the door. Twelve feet away it stopped advancing. He leaned toward Laura. "What's wrong?"

"It's not responding. I'm applying maximum thrust, but it just stopped."

"Try moving it up half a meter."

"Okay, but I don't think that'll help."

Laura adjusted the control and the video image responded. *Little Mack* moved upward a foot but remained the same distance from the door.

"I still have vertical control but why won't it—" Laura stopped as she made the connection. "Oh no! The tether must be caught on something!"

"I think you're right. You'd better turn it around and take a look."

Laura backed off the thrust and rotated *Little Mack* in place. The neutrally buoyant tube snaked into the forward section of the torpedo room.

She saw the problem—a coil in the tether looped itself around a valve stem.

Laura worked the snag for ten minutes. Near tears, she said, "Yuri, I'm sorry but I just can't seem to free it!"

"Take a break—this was bound to happen. It's not your fault."

Laura slumped back in her chair.

Like a dog chained to a stake, *Mack* could move about twenty-five feet forward or aft from its anchor point but no farther.

Yuri considered the options: They could keep trying to fish the loop off the valve stem. Yet, he knew it would be an almost impossible task considering the severe limitations of the ROV.

They were so close—they couldn't give up!

After Laura made several more attempts to unravel the coil, Yuri surrendered. "Laura, we've done all that we can."

"What do you mean?"

"It's time we head back in."

"But why? We can keep trying."

"It's no use. We're not going to free *Little Mack* that way. I have another plan."

Laura stood. "What are you going to do?"

"*Little Mack* proved there's a clear path from the open torpedo tube all the way to the door between Compartments One and Two. That's great news because all that needs to be done is to seal the door. Then the crew can release compressed air into Compartment Two to displace the water. Like we talked about, that will significantly increase buoyancy."

"Which will break the hull's bond to the bottom," Laura added.

"Yes, with luck."

Laura furrowed her brow. "Just how do we seal the hatch if we abandon *Little Mack*?"

"I'm going to do it."

Laura canted her head to the side, aghast. "That's insane—it's so deep and you're still hurt. No way!"

"Once I'm in the water my leg will be fine."

"You'll have to swim down and come back up. The decompression time will be horrendous."

"I've done it before; I can do it again."

Laura's face tightened. "No, Yuri. You're in no condition to make a dive like that."

"There is no other way."

"Let me work with *Little Mack* some more!"

"No. We don't have the time."

"Another half hour—please!"

"We need to wrap this up. I have to brief the *Neva* and then we're going to return to the marina."

"What for?"

"We need to go to Vancouver—to that place that Nicolai found that has helium and oxygen. I've got to recharge my tanks before I can make the dive tonight."

"Tonight!"

"Yes. This has to be done at night. I can't allow the *Neva* to surface in the daylight."

CHAPTER 54

"*Privet,*" Elena announced as she stepped into the *Hercules*'s main cabin.

Nick sat at the galley table, scanning the Sports section of Saturday's *Seattle Times*. He looked up. Even in blue jeans and a windbreaker, Elena looked terrific. He smiled. "I wondered when you'd get here," he replied in their native tongue.

She slid onto the bench seat opposite Nick. "What have you been up to? The mission's in a frenzy—I was called in. The chief was there himself."

Nick shrugged and gestured toward the companionway that led up to the pilothouse. He continued in Russian: "Miller's been a total jerk. He won't cooperate anymore unless he gets his bonus, up front and in cash."

Elena had been at her apartment, preparing to return to Point Roberts when she took the call ordering her to the mission. She now served as the chief of mission's official cash delivery person. She also carried the Beretta and its suppressor in her handbag.

"Do you have it?" Nick asked.

Elena reached into her handbag and removed a small packet. She handed it over.

He peeled the cover away revealing a stack of U.S. hundred-dollar bills.

"Twenty thousand?" he asked.

"Yes."

Nick fanned through the bundle of bills. "This should take care of the *mudák*."

Elena eyed the cash. "How did you pull this off? The chief just gave me the money and told me to get it to you—nothing else."

"I called my boss from the boat and told him I needed twenty K in four hours."

"I bet that went over well."

"He was not happy." Nick grinned. "He was getting ready to head over to Golden Gate Park for an afternoon outing with his wife and daughter.

"Anyway, he called your boss. Apparently, the mission keeps a stash on hand for emergencies. I think I made a big dent in it."

"Are you going to give all of that to him now?"

"Just half—his down payment, the rest tomorrow. This vessel is critical so I have to keep him motivated."

"What did you do out there today?"

"Yuri and Laura got the robot inside the hull to survey the damage."

Her eyes widened. "They were inside the *Neva* with that underwater machine?"

"Yeah, she swam it through a torpedo tube—just amazing."

Elena slumped back in the seat, stunned.

Nick toyed with the wad of cash. "Yuri says they accomplished everything they could with the ROV.

He's going to make a dive later tonight and needs to replenish his air supply first."

"How's he going to do that?"

Nick checked his wristwatch. "He and Laura took off half an hour ago, heading back to that place we took him the other day."

"That diving company in North Van?"

"Yes."

"But it's closed. What does he expect to find there?"

"All I know is that he took some of his diving equipment."

"I don't like the thought of those two running around in Vancouver. If he's picked up . . ."

"I was in no position to interfere. He's in charge here."

"Why didn't you go with him, keep an eye on him?"

"Because I'm alone, Elena. Remember, you took off, wanted nothing to do with this operation!" He again glanced at the nearby stairwell. "I've got to watch over that jerk up there. He's the wild card."

Elena knew when she was checkmated. She said, "What's Kirov's plan?"

"He's going to swim inside a torpedo tube and close a door that separates the torpedo room from the next compartment. When it's closed, the *Neva*'s crew will pump the water out of the isolated compartment and then the hull's supposed to pop up to the surface."

"They could be rescued—tonight?!"

"Yeah, that's what he said."

Elena was stunned. "There's what, thirty of them?"

"Thirty-six now, I think."

"What are YOU going to do with 'em? I don't have anything set up."

"What about the warehouse you found near the air-port and that chartered jet? And the passports? You know, the exit plan!"

"There is no plan! Everything was canceled when Moscow called off the rescue." Elena raised her hands in frustration. "What were you thinking? When they pulled the plug on the operation, the entire exit process was shut down."

"I thought there might be something usable." Nick took a deep breath. "What do you expect me to do, now?"

"You've got to call it off."

"Impossible. When Yuri returns we're going back out. He's going down to the *Neva* and seal that door."

"But you know our orders. He's supposed to be on a plane back to Moscow by now or dead."

"Moscow has no comprehension of the tactical situation here. Yuri has a good chance of pulling it off."

"But what if he fails—then what do we do?"

"Try something else, I guess."

"You guess! Don't you remember what he told us when we first met him?"

"What?"

"As a last resort, the *Neva*'s captain will send up some kind of emergency beacon that will alert the Americans."

"But they'd only do that after destroying all of the critical codes and equipment."

"Maybe they could do that but the remains of the *Neva* would be right here, under their noses. What kind of intelligence coup do you think that would be for the American Navy, along with all the bad PR we'd get? I can see the headlines: 'Red Spy Sub Caught Red-Handed!' "

Elena did not add that she might also be captured and charged with espionage. Even with diplomatic immunity, her career would be over.

Nick's eyes narrowed. "Elena, that's not going to happen."

"It's too risky. You've got to stop this."

Nick was disgusted with Elena's shortsightedness. "We must do everything we can to help the crew—they're our own people. We can't let them die because of SVR protocols."

Elena said, "There's another complication to all this."

"What now?"

"Moscow dispatched a special team to secure the *Neva*."

Nick leaned forward; his stomach tightened.

Elena spelled out the basics and Nick responded, "Are they *spetsnaz*?"

"No, some kind of special FSB team." Elena divulged the details of Operation Eagle.

Nick reacted, "Their job is to secure the *Neva*—nothing about rescue?"

"They've been told that the crew died in the initial accident. They're supposed to survey the hull, plant scuttling charges, and then blow it up."

"By diving to the bottom?"

"No. They have some kind of robotic device they're going to use. The officer in charge said it's designed to detect and defuse underwater mines. It's launched from a surface vessel."

"Must be some kind of ROV."

"ROV?"

"Remotely operated vehicle—like what Kirov and his woman have been using."

"I guess so. It was still crated up when I left Bellingham."

"Do they know anything about Yuri?"

"No, nothing. They've been told there were no survivors."

Nick scowled. "What a screwup. Those *bolváns* in Moscow don't give a crap about the *Neva*."

"That's obvious."

"What's their schedule?"

"Tomorrow morning they start searching for the *Neva*—they still think we don't know its location. They have search gear, some kind of underwater radar."

"If we're still out there, they'll spot the *Hercules* for sure. Then what'll we do?"

Dan Miller sat in his captain's chair in the pilothouse sipping coffee. He gazed westward. It would soon be dark as the sun dipped behind the peaks of Vancouver Island. He had just returned from the galley, refreshing his mug and collecting his ten-thousand-dollar down payment. Nick the Prick and the sexy blonde remained seated below at the mess table.

The previous night's excursion had drained Miller yet he remained alert thanks to coffee. He'd had far more than his usual two to three cups a day. Since they would be heading out again this evening, he hadn't let up.

He did not trust the pair below.

Miller had to play hardball with Nick over the bonus.

And sometimes he heard them talking in low tones but not in English, like this afternoon—what was that about?

Miller spent several minutes recalling what had transpired over the past twenty-four hours. *What are they looking for on the bottom?*

He'd asked that question on several occasions to each of the four players. Yet, not one of them had revealed any details.

He suspected a wreck. Oddly, though, nothing had shown up on any of the three depth sounders when the *Hercules* repeatedly crossed over the target coordinates. Miller purposely kept a close eye on the main depth sounder display, waiting for a telltale bottom bump to reveal the wreck's presence. But he observed nothing concrete, just a slight blur now and then.

With no clear evidence of a wreck, Miller concluded that his charter customers were trying to recover something small dropped overboard from a ship. But what could be so important to go to all this trouble?

After running through several scenarios of likely possibilities, he'd narrowed it down to just one: Most of the vessels in the adjacent shipping lanes sailed from Asia; most of the world's heroin came from Asia; and Vancouver had a growing drug problem.

It took a few seconds before the full impact of Miller's revelation registered: He'd chartered the *Herc* to drug traffickers.

The forty-two-foot *Explorer* returned to its berth— an enclosed boathouse at the Squalicum Harbor in Bellingham.

Captain Duscha Dubova stood on the floating pier next to the boathouse, viewing the early-evening harbor lights. Her assistant, Lieutenant Grigori Karpekov, remained inside the yacht's salon running diagnostic checks on the survey electronics.

The test run in Bellingham Bay took about an hour once Karpekov worked out the bugs. Operation of the side scan system was black magic to Dubova; nevertheless, she endorsed its use. Trying to find the *Neva* without the sonar would be a near impossible task. They only had a general location of the sunken submarine.

Once Karpekov finished his tests, Dubova would take over and check the subsea explosives package. As a tech-head, Karpekov had never come closer to working with volatile materials than when he struck a match to light a cigarette.

Dubova, on the other hand, had ten years' experience with high explosives including a short tour in Chechnya. The team she led took out two mid-rise apartment buildings in Grozny, obliterating the rebel cells operating from those structures—along with the three dozen innocent families that also occupied the commandeered buildings.

CHAPTER 55

"How's the leak?" asked Borodin as he entered Compartment Eight.

"The bilge pump is able to keep up with it, Captain."

"Good."

Earlier, one of the two bilge pumps serving Compartments Seven and Eight burned out. The remaining pump controlled the persistent leak from the propeller shaft.

The officer in charge of Compartment Eight reported on the status of his men and critical systems. Satisfied, Borodin started to return to the CCP, when the officer asked a parting question.

"Sir, any word yet on when Captain Lieutenant Kirov will make his dive?"

"He should be in the water in a couple of hours."

"That's good to hear, sir. I know he can do it."

"Me too," Borodin offered with a friendly smile. Still, he had his doubts.

Even if Yuri managed to close the bulkhead door, the *Neva* might not rise to the surface.

When Compartment Two was relieved of seawater, buoyancy calculations confirmed that the submarine should float to the surface, even with the flooded torpedo room. But success of the operation hinged on two critical factors. First, to displace the flooded seawater in the second compartment there must be sufficient compressed air available. Additional math indicated that the assembly of high-pressure air flasks nested between the top of the pressure casing and the outer hull covering contained just enough volume to do the job. But it would be a onetime event. Once the reserve tanks had vented, there would be no additional compressed air for another attempt.

The *Neva* had the capacity to recharge the compressed air cylinders, but only when on the surface. Igniting the diesel-powered compressor while submerged would suck out the entire air volume of the hull within seconds.

The second critical factor was an unknown. With the *Neva* partially buried in the bottom, the suction power of the semi-fluid muck against the steel hull remained an elusive commodity. Even with the compartment dewatered and every ballast and trim tank blown dry, the submarine might stay glued to the seabed.

"Can you take me to Point Roberts?" Ken Newman stood next to a yellow cab outside of the Vancouver bus station at 5:15 P.M. The Greyhound from Seattle had arrived ten minutes earlier.

"Sure," the cabbie replied. "I can take you there but it'll cost you."

"How much?"

The cabbie quoted the price.

"Wow, why so much?"

"I heard from one of our other drivers that the Yanks have just one lane open tonight, some kind of staffing problem going on at the border. The lineup could take thirty to forty minutes to get through. The meter runs the whole time."

"Get me as close as you can and I'll walk across."

"That'll work. Climb in."

As Ken settled into the backseat of the taxi, his carry-on bag at his side, he rehearsed his storyline for the border station: He needed to pick up his car—he'd left it at Point Roberts a couple of days ago to go on a boat trip. The boat broke down near Port Angeles so he had returned for his vehicle.

Ken wanted his Corvette back, especially with his pending trial. If he was convicted of a DUI, Canada would deny him entry. But that didn't really motivate him. More than ever, he wanted payback. Laura was not going to dump him without a fight!

Captain Miller removed the .45-caliber Colt M1911 semiautomatic pistol from the ship's safe in his state-room. He had inherited his father's handgun, a souvenir from the Korean War.

Sitting at his desk, Miller inserted a seven-round magazine into the butt of the handgrip and slammed it home. He pulled the slide back, chambering a round. After setting the safety, he turned and pointed the barrel toward the port bulkhead. "Get the hell off my boat," he said, rehearsing.

Miller's conscience told him to take off, the specter

of incarceration the driver. But another worry plagued him: He dreaded the prospect of losing the *Hercules*. The workboat not only represented his livelihood but also served as his home. He'd read somewhere that the U.S. Drug Enforcement Administration could confiscate any vehicles involved in drug trafficking: cars, airplanes, and boats.

The *Hercules* would be a juicy target. He had just over two million invested, most of it in the form of a mortgage. The Feds could take the boat and sell it at auction, pocketing whatever cash it generated. He would end up owing the unpaid loan balance— a total screwing by Uncle Sam.

Miller's initial reaction was to evict Nick and Elena, both still in the galley; Laura and the other guy had not yet returned. Miller would then fire up the *Herc*'s engine and cast off the lines. But he backpedaled.

They hadn't told him a thing about what they were looking for. It could be anything! He was just a hired hand, an innocent party.

Miller considered *Little Mack*. He had never operated it while offshore of Point Roberts. Laura owned it. And he had a Bill of Sale to prove it.

Miller's initial panic mitigated. One more run with the *Herc* and he'd earn the balance of his bonus.

Another ten K—it's worth the risk!

Nevertheless, Captain Miller's guard remained up. At the first hint of trouble, he would order all ashore. The .45 would ensure compliance.

CHAPTER 56

Ken Newman reclaimed his Corvette in a lot near the border station. The gas tank was low.

"I need forty bucks of gas for pump three," he told the clerk of a Point Roberts gas station.

The kid punched in the transaction on the cash register and it computed the exchange. He said, "That'll be forty-eight fifty-five."

Ken removed two U.S. twenties from his wallet.

"Oh," the cashier said, eyeing the U.S. currency. He'd assumed Ken was Canadian and had quoted the price in Canadian dollars. His cash register had two drawers, one for U.S. funds, the other Canadian.

Ken was about to hand over the bills when he spotted the Chevy Suburban through a window. It had just pulled up to a stop sign near the store. The gas station's exterior lighting illuminated the driver's side of the SUV.

"Son of a bitch," Ken muttered.

"What?" the clerk asked.

The Suburban pulled out, heading south toward the marina.

Ken sprinted to the door and watched the taillights of the Suburban as it sped away.

Laura didn't notice her husband's sports car parked next to the fuel island. Another vehicle fueling hid it.

"They should have more than one lane open," commented Yuri as traffic came to a halt.

"That's for sure."

The lineup into Point Roberts stretched for over a quarter of mile northward along Fifty-sixth Street. It took forty-five minutes to reach the border crossing.

At the border, the CBP agent made a cursory examination of their passports but didn't bother to look in the back of the Suburban. It contained a pair of steel high-pressure gas cylinders, each about four feet long.

Yuri had a ready explanation if questioned. "Gas supplies for the workboat *Hercules*."

Laura wasn't pleased with what she and Yuri had done earlier—outright stealing.

As expected, the North Vancouver diving company's yard was locked. Yuri used the bolt cutter borrowed from the *Herc*'s tool room to sever the padlock.

They had driven into the yard, closing the chain-link gate behind. Laura parked behind a forty-foot-long shipping container, concealing the Suburban from the road and the yard's overhead lights. There were no obvious surveillance cameras. Yuri culled through the stack of high-pressure steel bottles stored next to a corner of the office building.

He remembered the collection of cylinders, hoses, control valves, and manifolds from his previous visit—the gas supply for a saturation dive system.

Yuri found most cylinders depleted or near empty. But he did find seven bottles with residual pressure. He selected the best pair, one with helium and the other oxygen. The pressures were not sufficient to recharge the rebreather fully, but they'd do.

Just before closing the yard gate, Laura walked over to the office and slipped a folded sheet of paper into the entry door's mail slot. Printed on the paper she'd written *Sorry, I hope this is enough*, and inside the folds she left five one-hundred-dollar bills.

Laura turned off the main road and entered a marina parking lot. As they headed south down the driveway Yuri asked, "Do you think they left anything for us to eat?"

"You want hamburgers, don't you?"

"Of course!"

Laura checked the dashboard clock: 7:05 P.M. "If there isn't anything aboard, I'll order cheeseburgers from Fat Billie's."

"With fries and chocolate shakes?"

She smiled. "Of course!"

After striking out at the beach house, Ken found the Suburban parked near a marina restroom building. He sat on a waterside park bench about a hundred feet from the Chevy. In front of him were hundreds of moored boats, backlit by an ocean of amber dock lights.

Where the hell did she go?

Ken was thinking about retreating to his car to find dinner, when he noticed the huge boat moored at the end of a nearby floating pier. It dominated all nearby craft. The aft deck of the massive vessel lit up, illumi-nated by a bank of overhead floodlights. Two figures walked into the light.

Ken stood up and walked closer to the shore. The male limped.

Gotcha!

CHAPTER 57

Yuri and Laura sat side-by-side on the stern deck of the *Hercules* surrounded by diving equipment. Paper wrappers from their take-out dinner lay at their feet.

Laura gestured at the diving backpack in front of Yuri. "How long will it last?"

"At least three hours."

"Are you really going to stay down that long?"

"It's all about bottom time; the longer I'm working on the bottom, the longer the decompression will be." Yuri did not volunteer that the gas supply was only partially charged.

"How do you figure out your decompression?"

"Well, at the *Neva*'s depth, and using a rebreather, it's a bit tricky. First, I have to program my dive computer to . . ."

Ken Newman was perched on the flybridge of a cabin cruiser parked four slips landward of the *Hercules*. He couldn't hear the conversation but he had a clear view of the couple.

Ken had watched as Laura and three men stood on the workboat's fantail talking. One of the guys was the bastard who'd attacked him at the beach house.

A blonde appeared carrying a bag full of takeout. She and two of the men returned to the cabin, leaving Laura and Ken's nemesis alone.

Who the hell are these people and just what are they up to?

And why is Laura with them?

"What's wrong?" asked Laura, still sitting on the *Herc*'s fantail deck.

"I don't trust these batteries." Yuri held the dive light that he'd retrieved from Viktor's corpse. He aimed the beam at a sailboat about a hundred feet across the navigation channel.

"It doesn't look very bright," Laura offered.

"I think the batteries are going." He had replaced the original spent batteries with eight D cells he found aboard the *Hercules*, most scrounged from flashlights.

"Are there any more aboard?"

"Not that I could find."

"What about the batteries in the light Nick bought?"

"They're rechargeable—not compatible with our system." Nick's light was useless for Yuri's needs, limited to a hundred meters' depth.

Laura stood up. "I'll run up to the store and get some spares. How many do you want?"

"At least ten. And I'd like fresh batteries for my dive computer."

"What kind?"

Yuri provided the specifications and added, "You know, the crew's going to be famished. Can you buy some more food for them?"

"Sure, what should I get?"

"Whatever you can find that's simple to prepare—canned food, sandwiches, fruit. Get as much as you can. I don't know how long we'll have them aboard before they go home."

"Okay." But then Laura thought about it: There were over thirty men.

"I'll need someone to help carry the groceries."

"Take Orlov. And have him pay for it."

Laura laughed. "Okay."

Yuri rested on a bunk in the darkened forward crew cabin. Captain Miller and Elena sipped coffee while watching TV in the galley. Laura and Nick had yet to return from the grocery run.

The once welcome pain in Yuri's left calf now taxed him. He'd taken a couple of ibuprofen tablets earlier, but they'd had no effect.

What would happen when he entered the water again?

Yuri would be violating a cardinal diving rule: Avoid diving while recovering from decompression sickness. It takes several months or more of recuperation before a bent diver can return to the water. Yuri's body had had just two weeks to heal itself.

The frigid bottom waters also concerned Yuri. He had used a chemical heating pack over his chest to warm his heart and lungs during the ascent but had no spares. He would have no choice but to don extra layers beyond his standard dive dress. He'd already raided Captain Miller's locker, selecting a thick sweatshirt, thermal underwear, and two pairs of socks.

If he could resist the cold for half an hour, he had a chance.

Yuri would not be returning to the surface. Without the extra heat to warm his chest cavity, he would not survive the lengthy in-water decompression even if he had enough gas, which he did not. Instead, he would reenter the *Neva* and decompress in the aft escape trunk. He and Viktor had used the system during their lock-out work.

One slipup could be his undoing.

Should the rebreather stop flowing gas, he would expire within minutes. A suicidal sprint to the surface would retrigger the bends, this time tearing his guts out. But he'd probably pass out during that ascent; an involuntary inhalation of seawater would finish him off.

Sucking on a dry tank is a diver's fundamental terror. Even if Yuri's rebreather delivered gas on demand, its mixture control must work flawlessly. If the blend of pure oxygen and diluent were off, death could be just a few breaths away. A mixture rich in oxygen would result in convulsions and an abrupt loss of consciousness. Lean oxygen levels would starve the brain, also causing unconsciousness. For both conditions, death by drowning would follow.

The debris inside the torpedo room presented another worry. *Little Mack* provided a preview of what waited ahead. Yuri would need to take special care to avoid the maze of jagged and scorched equipment scattered throughout the compartment.

The prospect of swimming with the decomposing corpses of his former shipmates horrified Yuri; he nearly gagged at the thought. He decided he would not look at their faces.

Yuri wondered about another risk. It would be noisy aboard the *Neva* tonight; he worried that underwater sensors might detect the rescue effort.

It had been almost two weeks since he'd disabled the Venus network. Yuri deployed an autonomous underwater vehicle from a torpedo tube. It crushed the fiber-optic cable that linked the bottom sensors to the shore; the damage mimicked impact from a ship's anchor.

The plan had been to shut down the Venus array for several days to allow the *Neva* to enter and depart the Strait without detection by the hydrophones. But enough time had passed for a repair. When he'd checked the Venus website earlier in the afternoon, it remained offline. That comforted Yuri; still he fretted.

Yuri considered Captain Miller. Just what would Miller do if he succeeded tonight? But that wasn't Yuri's problem; Nick and Elena would have to handle it—somehow, maybe with more cash.

And finally Laura, sweet Laura, she'd risked everything. How could he ever repay such a debt? How could he leave her?

Yuri reminded himself to focus on the mission. As he had done most of his adult life, he rehearsed critical tasks in his head, previewing events to come. He worked out potential problems before they became real ones. He would repeat the process until he had it down pat.

Yuri would need his plans to unfold without a hitch if he were to survive the next twenty-four hours.

CHAPTER 58

After following the Suburban from the marina, Ken parked his Corvette on the far side of the grocery store's parking lot, pulling into a stall next to a pickup truck. He stood in the shadows beside the tailgate of the Dodge Ram—spying.

Laura and one of her boat companions spent nearly an hour inside before wheeling out half a dozen shopping carts bulging with bags and boxes of groceries. They were currently loading the last cartful into the rear of the SUV.

Why so much food? he wondered.

"Release your line," ordered Captain Dan Miller. He stood on the port bridge wing peering downward. The workboat's diesel idled, filling the still night air with a deep-throated growl.

"Okay," Nick Orlov said. He stood on the floating pier near the center of the workboat's hull—amidships. Nick released the spring line from the dock cleat.

Standing on the side deck above, Yuri retrieved the

mooring line. The bow and stern lines had already been taken up.

Nick stepped to the far end of the float and climbed aboard.

Miller walked back into the wheelhouse. He took his customary position behind the wheel, spinning it a couple revolutions to the starboard before advancing the throttle. The *Hercules* crawled away from the pier.

Watching from the rear of the bridge, Laura admired Captain Miller's skill as he navigated his vessel southward down the center of the marina channel.

They were on schedule, the weather was favorable, and even Elena was cooperating by making a fresh pot of coffee in the galley.

Nevertheless, Laura remained antsy.

Yuri was about to risk everything.

Ken Newman sat in his Corvette, now parked in a public parking lot near the marina's entrance channel. He peered down the channel. The navigation light on the tip of the offshore breakwater blinked red. The night sky seemed as black as his heart.

Ken had just watched the *Hercules* cruise by and then pass around the breakwater. Illuminated by a barrage of overhead lights, he observed Laura as she walked out of the bridge house. She headed aft to the main deck where she joined a male working with some type of gear near the stern. He moved about with a pronounced limp.

Ken slumped into the bucket seat, disheartened. The fully provisioned vessel had just departed with his wife—and her lover—aboard, bound for parts unknown.

* * *

Laura reached forward and tugged on the left strap of Yuri's backpack harness. "How's that?" she asked.

"A little tighter."

She yanked down one more time.

"That's good."

Laura and Yuri stood on the aft main deck of the *Hercules*. The workboat had just pulled up to the *Neva*'s VLF buoy. Captain Miller, under the watchful eye of Nick and Elena, nudged his vessel into the ten-knot southerly breeze with just enough thrust to maintain thirty feet of separation. Elena helped by keeping the deckhouse spotlight zeroed in on the buoy, and Nick monitored the radar display for nearby traffic.

Laura stepped back and surveyed Yuri's attire. Clad head to toe in a black dry suit and equipped with a rebreather backpack and a buoyancy compensator, he appeared ready for outer space.

The bulges along the thighs and waist of the dry suit caught her eye. She probed the nearest one with a finger. "Are those weights?" she asked.

"Yes."

"But they're sewn inside your suit." Laura knew just enough about diving to grasp that something wasn't quite right.

"That's correct."

She frowned. "Shouldn't you be wearing a weight belt or something, you know, so that you can release it in an emergency?"

"We don't work that way."

"What do you mean?"

"We're not allowed to surface if there's a problem."

Laura put it together. "Because you're operating in enemy waters?"

"Yes."

"That's not right," Laura mumbled while shaking her head.

Yuri turned to his right, checking the nearby video monitor. The open door between the torpedo room and the second compartment filled the screen.

Before taking up station next to the VLF buoy, Yuri and Laura retrieved *Little Mack*'s tether. The cable reel was suspended ten feet below the sea surface by three of the *Herc*'s air-filled dock fenders. Yuri plucked the reel with the crane. After unsealing and drying the cable leads, Laura reconnected them to the ROV's shipboard electronics and *Little Mack* returned to life.

"Remember now," Yuri said, gesturing toward the monitor, "once I get inside I'll clear the tether and you move *Little Mack* closer. I can use all the light I can get."

"I will." Laura looked up at Yuri. "Do you know how you're going to make the vent?"

"There should be some isolation valves in the bilge that I can work with."

"That's what the wrenches are for?"

"Yes."

Laura eyed a canvas bag on the deck next to Yuri. It was full of tools from the engine room of the *Hercules*. Captain Miller would have a fit if he were aware of the pilfering.

"How long do you think it will take you?"

"Whatever it takes."

"But the cold—didn't you say that would be a limiting factor?"

"I'll manage."

Laura moved to Yuri's side. She wrapped her arms around his waist, tilting her head back at the same time. She stood on the tips of her toes and offered her lips.

He responded—vigorously.

CHAPTER 59

"It's over seven hundred feet deep here," Captain Miller said as he gawked at the Fathometer readout. "Is he really going that far down?"

Miller and the two SVR officers stood in the boat's wheelhouse. All three just returned from the starboard bridge wing after watching Yuri leap overboard. He had remained on the surface for about a minute checking his gear and then submerged.

"Don't worry about him," Nick said while he studied the radar display. "He knows what he's doing."

"My God, man, I don't know that much about diving, but that's so deep. Won't he need a decompression chamber when he comes back up?"

Elena joined in, "It's all been covered, Captain. He'll be fine."

Miller rolled his eyes.

Yuri completed a second equipment check at ten meters. While grasping the VLF cable, he looked upward wondering if he could still see the *Hercules*. He aimed his dive light downward to minimize topside interference.

A ghost shadow loomed off to the side, but something else caught his attention. The sea exploded with bioluminescence. Tiny phosphorescent creatures put on a spectacular lightshow: miniature carmine flares and dazzling turquoise sparks.

With his light switched off and his legs anchored to the cable, he waved his right hand by his face mask. The wake burst into a firestorm.

Transfixed by the spectacle, Yuri luxuriated in the presence of the light-emitting life forms until the exhibition dissolved. Whatever had been swimming with the current had moved on.

Time for Yuri to move on, too.

Yuri passed the hundred-meter mark, almost three hundred and thirty feet deep—no bio-display here, just the deepest coldest black imaginable. Propelled by the deadweight of his dive dress and with a safety line clipped to the buoy cable, he dropped fins first. He concentrated on monitoring the LED displays on his depth gauge and dive computer, both strapped to his left forearm. He paced himself at twenty meters per minute, an aggressive but tolerable descent rate.

Several minutes into the dive, the pain in his injured left leg had begun to fade; it had now disappeared.

The water temperature dropped steadily as he descended, but the ensuing cold had yet to penetrate through the extra layers he wore. What had penetrated, however, were his utter sense of aloneness and the ever-present fear of death.

God, don't let me die down here!

* * *

"Captain, I hear something," reported the *Neva*'s sonar operator as he adjusted his headphones.

"Is it Yuri?" asked Captain Borodin. He stood next to the technician. They were alone in the sonar room.

"I'm not sure—wait. Yes, there's the signal!"

Borodin didn't need headphones. The hammering on the pressure casing telegraphed the entire length of the hull.

"He made it, Captain!"

"Yes, he did!"

Borodin couldn't help but grin as he envisioned his friend. *Good going, Yuri. Now please get inside and get to work.*

After pounding his hammer on the hull from inside the VLF buoy compartment, Yuri heard three dull metallic thuds in return. Grateful for the confirmation, he swam out of the compartment and proceeded along the deck. Thanks to the near slack tidal conditions, he tolerated the crosscurrent.

Yuri aimed the dive light forward, toward the bow. A thin pale ribbon streamed in the distance. *Little Mack*'s tether arced over the *Neva*'s sail—a twelve-foot-tall raised section of the hull that housed the periscopes and other surveillance equipment.

Yuri pulled himself over the bow and peered into torpedo tube five. He used his dive light to illuminate the forty-foot-long bore. He shoved the tool bag into the tube and pulled himself inside.

The bulk of his dry suit and rebreather made a tight

fit. He could feel the backpack scraping the top of the tube while his belly pressed against the bottom. Yuri kicked but barely made any headway. Fearing he might become stuck, he stopped. Yuri wiggled out of the torpedo tube and hung on to the lip of the opening. He repositioned the dive light within the tube so that its beam aimed outward, illuminating his torso. The tool bag held the light in place.

Yuri released his hold on the torpedo tube and reached down, blindly searching for the straps that secured the rebreather backpack. He unbuckled the waist strap. He released the left shoulder and then the right. With his teeth clamped to the mouthpiece of the breathing hose, he reached over his shoulders and pulled the backpack over his head.

Yuri held the backpack with both gloved hands, pulling it tight to his chest. He worried that his unorthodox maneuver would cause the water trap in the counter-lung to flood the breathing loop. But the breathing bag continued to function. The gas flow remained steady and seawater had not contaminated the CO_2 absorbent.

He looked back toward the bow, his dive light serving as a beacon. He had sunk almost to the bottom. He kicked hard, his fins stirring the mud into chocolate slurry. A few seconds later, he returned to tube five.

Yuri pulled himself inside, pushing the rebreather ahead. He had plenty of room now. He removed a twenty-meter coil of line from the tool bag. He lashed one end of the line to the handles of the canvas bag and attached the other end to a chest harness D-ring.

With his left hand holding the light and his right anchored to the backpack, he pumped his legs and the fins propelled him into the tube.

Yuri took great care around the broken rail guide that had snagged Viktor.

He reached the end of the tube and stopped. The light beam streaked into Compartment One. His motion inside the tube had already upset the equilibrium of the flooded torpedo room. Weightless particles swirled about in the light beam.

Yuri retrieved the tool bag. He swam into the torpedo room, reminding himself not to look at the faces.

Yuri followed *Little Mack*'s tether straight to the snag. He removed the coil from the pipe stem and continued farther into the hull.

"I see something!" Laura announced.

"What?" asked Nick.

She pointed to the top right-hand corner of the video monitor. "There, see how it's getting lighter?"

Nick studied the display. "Yeah, I see it. Do you think that's—"

He stopped speaking, startled by the sudden change of *Little Mack*'s camera angle. No longer focused on the open bulkhead door between Compartments One and Two, it swept clockwise. "What are you doing?" Nick demanded, facing Laura.

"Nothing—I haven't touched the controls."

"But what's happening?"

Yuri's face mask filled half of *Little Mack*'s viewfinder. His gloved right hand with the thumb pointed up occupied the other half.

"It's Yuri—he's okay," Laura announced.

Nick muttered, *"Neverojátnyj!"* Incredible.

Yuri peered into the camera lens, holding the ROV in place. Reaching to the side and grabbing the tether, he held the cable in front of the camera and again displayed the thumbs-up signal.

The ROV's dual lights blinked off and on three times—the pre-arranged signal.

Yuri opened the bulkhead equalization valve between the torpedo room and Compartment Two.

"He's heading back to the door," Laura said.

"Okay," Nick replied.

Little Mack hovered about six feet away as Yuri swam to the bulkhead door. He released the mechanism that held the door open and swam through the circular opening into Compartment Two, carrying the tool bag. He dropped the bag onto the deck. He reached back into the torpedo room and pulled the steel door shut.

Laura and Nick watched as the door's rack-and-pinion locking ring engaged, activated by Yuri pulling a steel lever on his side of the door.

"Why did he shut the door?" Nick asked.

"It's a safety measure."

"How do you know that?"

"He told me that if something happens to him, the door will already be closed. That way the crew can pump air into it."

Nick responded, "But how will we know if he's having a problem?"

"If he doesn't come back in ten minutes that means he's . . ." Laura couldn't say it.

"Oh," Nick said.

Nick engaged the stopwatch feature of his wristwatch. He said, "What's he doing now?"

"Looking for a way to make a more efficient seawater vent."

"Can't they just pump the air into it with the door sealed?"

"That's what I thought, too. But no, it doesn't work like that."

"So how is he going to add a new vent?"

"Find a pipe that penetrates both compartments and open it up somehow."

"How big of a pipe?"

"He didn't say, but the bigger the better—the more seawater it will carry."

"Hmm. That sounds like it could take awhile."

Yuri advanced into Compartment Two, following a passageway through the crew's quarters.

The condition of the space bewildered Yuri. Unlike the torpedo room that had been peppered by shrapnel from the exploding torpedo breach door and scorched by the runaway rocket motor, this chamber showed no damage. The storage locker doors lining the passageways remained closed and the decks were clear of debris. Other than a hint of detritus in the water column, everything appeared in its place. Yet, as he swam farther into the crew's living quarters, dread chewed away at his comfort.

He had invaded a tomb.

The dead littered his route, some grounded on the deck and a few suspended at mid-depth with their heads down and arms spread eagle. Most of the corpses bobbed against the overhead, the skulls rubbing against the cable bundles, pipe chase ways and other hardware that occupied the ceiling.

As he'd rehearsed, he avoided face contact and took care to steer around bodies. Still, he couldn't help but notice as he passed by how the hair rippled against their skulls as if swept by a macabre ghost wind.

Nick checked his watch. Four minutes had elapsed since Yuri closed the hatch door. Laura remained fixated on the video display.

Yuri's head and shoulders projected above the water surface. The upper deck of Compartment Two had not completely flooded. Compressed bubbles of air and leftover toxic rocket exhaust gas matched the sea pressure. He used the dive light to scan the partially flooded space. He counted five bodies in the officer's wardroom, including Captain Tomich, all floating on the air-water interface.

Although he did not remove his face mask, Yuri sensed the stench of rotting flesh. He re-submerged to the lower level.

* * *

"How long?" asked Laura.

"Eight minutes."

"Thanks." Laura turned back to the video monitor. She unconsciously chewed the index fingernail of her left hand.

Even Nick was jittery. He paced on the deck behind Laura.

Both were oblivious to the *Herc*'s surroundings. A gigantic northbound containership passed three hundred yards to the west.

Yuri swam in the bilge space, two deck levels below the bulkhead door that isolated Compartment Two from the torpedo room. Thankfully, he had not encountered any dead here.

He followed a pipe about eight inches in diameter, looking for a valve. To eject the most seawater, he needed to vent Compartment Two low in the hull cross-section.

Halfway through the bilge space Yuri found the inspection port, part of a T assembly in the bilge pipeline. He opened the port's control valve. As he expected, nothing happened.

The bilge pump in the flooded sections never worked after the sinking. But with the inspection port open, it would drain seawater when high-pressure air flowed into the space.

Yuri and Captain Borodin's plan for de-flooding Compartment Two consisted of releasing the *Neva*'s compressed air reserves into the flooded space. With proper venting, the expanding air inside Compartment Two would force seawater through the vent into the forward compartment, and then through the still open torpedo tube. Although the calculations indicated that the *Neva*'s compressed air reserves did not have anywhere near the sufficient volume to displace all of the seawater from Compartment Two, there might be just enough to make a difference.

Unlike U.S. submarines, which operate with minimal reserve buoyancy, Russian submarines have generous reserves. The *Neva* was designed to surface should any one of its eight compartments flood. With the ballast and trim tanks already air-filled, every ton of seawater vented from Compartment Two would bring the *Neva* closer to positive buoyancy.

Should Yuri not be successful in venting Compartment Two, releasing high-pressure air into the sealed compartment could overstress the bulkhead door that separated the second compartment from the central command post. Failure at this critical juncture would be the end for the *Neva*.

That's why Yuri had already opened the equalization valve between the first and second compartments. A flow path, although considerably undersized, would remain, allowing seawater a slow escape route if compressed air were dribbled into the second compartment.

Yuri made his way back to the torpedo room. With every minute critical and the cold seeping into his bones, he kicked harder.

He had one more task to complete.

CHAPTER 60

The band hammered out a string of rock-and-roll hits with an occasional country song thrown into the mix. Few of the Saturday-night crowd cared about the music or its quality; most of the Pod Room's patrons had been drinking for the past few hours.

Ken Newman occupied a table near the back. He'd already slammed down two Crown Royals and just started on his third.

The incessant chatter of the table full of women next to Ken matched the intensity of the music; yet he ignored it all. He focused his thoughts on Laura: *If the boat belongs to the gimp, he must be loaded. That's why she's with him!*

No; Laura already had plenty of her own money.

Ken gulped another slug of whiskey and refocused on the man who had humiliated him.

I'm going to get that son of a bitch—somehow!

CHAPTER 61

"Oh my God, there he is!" Laura shouted.

"*Fantastičeskij!*" `Nick said.

They both stared at the video monitor. Yuri had just popped through the hatch, reentering the torpedo room.

He swam toward *Little Mack*'s camera and flashed the thumbs-up signal with his left hand.

Laura teared up.

Nick checked his wristwatch: Yuri was three minutes late. Knowing every minute counted at such an extreme depth, Nick's stomach tightened. *Hang in there, Yuri—you can do it!*

"What do you think he's doing, Captain?"

"I'm not sure. But from the racket he's making, he's obviously hammering on something."

Captain Borodin and the *Neva*'s senior chief petty officer stood at the bottom of the pressure casing next to the bulkhead that separated Compartments Three and Two. The noise originated from the forward compartments.

"He must be working on the bilge system," Borodin said.

"For the vent?"

"Yes."

Yuri caught his breath—not so easy to do with a rebreather, especially at his depth. He was back in the first compartment and straddled a fat bilge pipe, the same one from Compartment Two. He clamped his knees and inner thighs vise-like around its circumference.

Yuri studied the inspection port. About four inches in diameter, the port projected upward nearly two feet from the bilge pipe. Unlike the port in Compartment Two, this one had a steel cover plate secured by bolts. He had removed five of the six bolts. But the remaining bolt wouldn't budge because of corrosion. Since he'd stripped off the corners of the bolt head with the socket, he had no choice but to use brute force.

Using a cold chisel from the tool bag, he pried the head back, exposing the bolt shaft.

Partially rested, Yuri again inserted the chisel under the bolt head and swung the hammer. As in a slow motion video, the hammer landed on target and a dull "clang" rang through the compartment. He swung again, and then again.

After the eighteenth impact, the bolt head detached. He removed the cover plate, completing installation of the vent system.

The inspection port was just forward of a check valve built into the bilge discharge line that fed the defunct forward bilge pump system. With the port now uncovered, seawater displaced by high-pressure air from Compartment Two could flow into Compartment One and vent to the sea by the open torpedo tube. The check valve would be critical to the *Neva*'s rescue; it allowed one-way flow only, from Compartment Two into one. Otherwise, the second compartment could reflood after ascending and send the *Neva* back to the bottom.

Laura turned away from the television monitor to stand and stretch her back. She walked to the nearest railing and peered northward. The Point Roberts peninsula was blacked out, but in the background, a shimmering luminous glow diffused upward into the evening sky.

Vancouver, she concluded.

"He's back again!" Nick called out.

Laura raced back to the monitor.

Yuri had just swum into camera view; its lens remained aimed at the closed bulkhead door between Compartments One and Two.

"What's he doing?" Nick asked.

Laura sat back down and craned her neck for a better view. Yuri hovered next to the bulkhead, his gloved right hand turning a handle.

"He's closing the equalization valve."

"Then he must have made the new seawater vent."

"Right. He's almost done!"

"That's fantastic."

Laura was so relieved that she cried again.

* * *

After closing the valve, Yuri verified that the bulkhead door remained sealed. He turned around. The dual floodlights mounted above *Little Mack*'s camera shone into his eyes. He reached out with both arms and aimed his gloved thumbs up.

"There's the signal!" Laura said.

"Right," agreed Orlov.

Laura reached for the ROV's control panel. She flipped a switch, dimming *Little Mack*'s floodlights. She waited a second before switching the lights back on. She repeated the signal a second time, and then a third.

Yuri waved at the camera. He checked his dive computer. *Oh no!* He should leave now but needed confirmation first.

Laura lowered the makeshift loudspeaker overboard. "Okay, Nick," she said, "give the signal!"

He pressed the Transmit key on the mike. "Attention. Attention. Attention," he shouted in English. Using the code that Yuri and Captain Borodin concocted, Nick said, "Commence Alpha. Commence Alpha. Commence Alpha."

Nick repeated the signal at fifteen-second intervals for the next two minutes.

* * *

Compressed air blasted into Compartment Two.

Yuri remained inside Compartment One, half a deck level above the sealed doorway. He swung the hammer, aiming it at the bulkhead. A sharp "clang" rang out.

Yuri used the hammer's acoustic rebound as a crude measure of the dewatering progress. With his left arm still looped around the torpedo rack as an anchor, he swung the hammer again half a foot lower. A dull "thud" broadcast from the impact.

The water level inside the second compartment had already dropped a meter.

Yuri again checked his computer.

Dammit, I've got to get out of here now!

"There he is again!" Nick said.

"Oh my gosh!"

Nick and Laura stared at the video screen. Yuri's upper body was on full display. He gave the double thumbs-up again, then pointed forward and swam out of view.

"He must be heading back," Nick offered.

"I hope so."

"Do you think it worked?"

"I don't know, I think—" Laura stopped talking. She noticed that one of the digital displays in the upper right-hand corner of the video display had changed. After Yuri freed *Little Mack* and Laura parked it on the deck next to the hatchway, the depth reading hardly moved. It crept from 718 to 719 feet, the result of the now flooding tide. But in the last few minutes, the reading had changed to 702 feet.

She pointed to the screen. "Look—the depth numbers are decreasing—it must be going up!" The display changed again: 700 and a few seconds later 698.

"It's really working—it's coming up!" Nick proclaimed, grinning.

Laura remained uneasy. Yuri had told her it might take hours to break the suction. Why was it moving so quickly now?

Yuri didn't check his depth gauge or computer as he worked his way through the torpedo room debris, using *Little Mack*'s tether as a guide.

Arriving at torpedo tube five, he slipped off his backpack and held the rebreather with his right hand. With the dive light strapped to his left wrist, he swam into the opening.

He was startled at the sudden rush forward. Without thinking, he pulled his legs up, forcing his back hard against the top of the tube and knees onto the bottom. The rubberized surface of his dry suit jammed against the tube lining, stopping him cold.

What's going on?

The seawater displaced by the air rushing into Compartment Two had only one outlet. When Yuri wedged himself inside the opening of the tube, trying to figure out what had changed, his bulk dammed off the flow.

Just as Yuri made the connection, the back pressure increased and the friction bond between the cylinder and his dive suit started to erode.

No longer able to fight the flow, Yuri released his legs and dipped his head down.

The broken rail guide that had snagged Viktor was just ahead.

Watch out for that thing, he warned himself.

CHAPTER 62

Yuri squirted from the torpedo tube like a champagne cork. He tumbled head over fins, barely hanging on to the rebreather backpack.

When he stopped, his heart raced and he breathed at an accelerated, dangerous pace. Thanks to the wristband, he still had the dive light. He pulled the rebreather over his shoulders and strapped it on. He rotated in place, following the light's beam as it pierced the ink-black waters, desperate for a landmark.

The light captured the mass of the *Neva*'s bow eight meters away. He realized that he'd sunk several meters below tube five. He directed the light downward, looking for the bottom—nothing.

What's going on? He pulled up his depth gauge: two hundred and six meters. *Govnó!*

Yuri pumped his legs, sprinting upward to catch the rising hull. The *Neva* had slipped free of the bottom muck with ease.

With every ballast and trim tank empty, and with seawater discharging from Compartment Two as compressed air continued to flow into it, the submarine ascended uncontrollably toward the surface. For every ten meters of rise, the pressure inside the first and second compartments reduced by one atmosphere. The pressure reduction allowed the gas bubbles in both compartments to expand further, which expelled even more seawater through tube five.

At its current rise rate, the *Neva* would break the surface in less than ten minutes. Yuri had just three minutes to save his life.

With Nick Orlov at her side, Laura remained fixated on the video monitor. Perspiration beaded on her brow as she concentrated. Her right hand worked the joystick control.

Little Mack backtracked, following its tether. The ROV had just entered Compartment One—the torpedo room. Before making the dive, Yuri asked her to retrieve the underwater robot in case he needed it in the future.

"Reel in more of the cable," Laura ordered.

Nick reached down and rotated the cable reel, pulling in three meters of the *Little Mack*'s pencil diameter fiber-optic tether. "How's that?"

"Take in a little more—five feet."

"Okay," Nick said, mentally converting to meters.

Laura adjusted *Little Mack*'s alignment, directing its floodlight to illuminate the pathway ahead. The neutrally buoyant yellow tether snaked inside the passageway. Filled with equipment and debris, potential snags abounded.

God, don't let me screw this up!

* * *

Yuri pulled the hatch shut and locked it in place. He reached down and yanked off his fins, letting them sink. With his hands grasping the ladder rungs he worked his way down the flooded chamber into the aft escape trunk.

He located the purge controls and activated the system. High-pressure air surged into the chamber, expelling the seawater.

As the chamber evacuated, Yuri held on to a ladder rung with both hands. After being weightless, the sudden load of his dive dress caught him off guard.

He made it—barely!

While the *Neva* made its premature rise to the surface, Yuri scrambled to reach the escape trunk before the submarine ascended too far. By the time he dropped through the hatchway, the *Neva* had risen thirty-eight meters 125 feet. Because of his extended bottom time, Yuri's body only just tolerated the unplanned ascent.

Captain Miller's heart skipped a beat, startled by an obnoxious high-pitched alarm that wailed from the *Hercules*'s instrument panel. He stood at the helm.

"What's that?" asked Elena. She sat on the bench seat at the aft end of the wheelhouse.

"That can't be right," Miller muttered, staring at the indicator light.

"What's wrong?" Elena asked, now at his side.

He pointed to the depth sounder. "This thing's screwed up. It has a shallow water warning feature; I set it to ten fathoms for when we head back in, but it says we're in shallow water."

"What do you mean 'fathom'?"

He converted, "Sixty feet." He turned off the alarm and switched the sounder's scale to feet. It displayed 52.

"But it's much deeper out here than that."

"Of course—over ten times." Miller's forehead wrinkled. "It must be on the fritz."

Elena studied the digital display: it read 48 feet. She glanced at a backup depth sounder mounted adjacent to the primary unit; its digital display flashed 47 feet. "But what about this other one?" she asked, pointing.

Miller leaned forward, his eyes squinted and his brow furrowed. "That can't be right." He looked back at the primary; it now read 42 feet. "What the hell?"

Miller pressed the Reset button on the primary. The screen blinked blue and refreshed, reporting 39 feet. The backup unit read 38 feet.

Miller checked the GPS display. He glanced at the NOAA chart on the adjacent plotting table, his hands raised in frustration. "We're right where we're supposed to be—I don't understand what's wrong with these echo sounders."

Elena checked the nearest depth finder. It read 27 and switched to 26.

Elena shouted, *"Vot der'mó!"*

"What?"

"Hang on to something!" Elena yelled as she grabbed the handrail next to the helm.

Miller turned away from the chart table, puzzled at Elena's warning. Her hands were white-knuckled on the stainless steel grab bar.

"What are you doing?"

Before Elena could respond, a colossal shudder shook the *Hercules* from stem to stern and the deck flipped on its side. It took all of Elena's strength to hang on.

Captain Miller fell onto his back and slid headfirst down the fifty-degree incline toward the pilothouse's port wing door. His skull smacked the steel door frame with a sickening thud.

Just before midnight, Yuri remained standing inside the *Neva*'s dewatered aft escape trunk with the rebreather apparatus still strapped to his back. He removed his face mask but continued to breathe through his mouthpiece. Without warning, a monstrous "clang" rang out. A heartbeat later, he crashed against the steel chamber's wall. He absorbed most of the impact with his outstretched arms, but his forehead nicked a pressure gauge, ripping his eyebrow.

Stunned by the impact, he unconsciously spat out the mouthpiece. Pressurized with air, the escape trunk's nitrogen content had the equivalent of a ten-martini lunch.

Yuri picked up the mouthpiece and inhaled. To his relief, the rebreather still worked. He didn't want to think about what might have happened if it had smashed into the steel wall.

With his left palm compressing the wound, he pushed the intercom button with his right hand. He heard the buzzer as it announced his presence on the escape trunk's console three meters below his feet. No one answered his call.

Yuri had no idea what had occurred. For all he knew, the *Neva* had crashed back on the bottom, mired even deeper in the muck.

The gash bled profusely. Yuri pressed the open wound, yet blood seeped around his hand. The ring of residual seawater encircling the sealed hatch at his feet turned crimson.

CHAPTER 63

Day 14—Sunday

Laura Newman straddled the bulwark as freezing seawater rushed over her body and poured into the open aft deck. The *Hercules* lay hard over on its port, almost half-capsized.

The frigid water shocked her body and short-circuited her ability to reason. She reverted to survival mode: *Don't let go!*

Nearly submerged, Laura hung on with her hands and thighs clamped to the steel wall that rose three feet above deck level. With her neck awash, she struggled to breathe. She'd already inhaled a mouthful, gagging in the process.

Laura shut her eyes waiting to go under, sensing that she would have to abandon the vessel to save her life.

When she opened her eyes, the sea had dropped half a foot. She looked to her right, back toward the main cabin. The lights were still on.

A few more seconds went by. The water continued to retreat.

After the *Hercules* had nearly righted itself, Laura slid over the top of the sidewall and plopped onto the deck. She landed on her hands and knees, splashing through a wedge of trapped water about a foot deep.

Her teeth clattered and she took short quick breaths.

She had survived, but survived what? She wasn't sure.

The *Hercules* listed just five degrees. The scuppers at the base of the port bulwarks continued to drain.

Laura crossed her arms over her chest and shivered. She peered aft at the open deck. The ROV's control console and video monitor were jammed up against the port bulwark, both units smashed and waterlogged. The tattered end of the ROV's tether trailed from the drum reel bolted to the afterdeck of the *Hercules*. *Little Mack* remained on the bottom. Laura had guided the robot out of the torpedo tube but in the aftermath of the collision, the tether sheared.

What happened? Laura wondered. *And where's Nick?*

Laura stepped to the port and looked seaward. Nothing. She crossed the deck to the starboard side. A huge dark form lurked low in the water about a hundred feet away. Residual light from the boat's cabin and wheelhouse revealed the *Neva*'s hull—350 feet in length.

"Oh dear Lord," she said, "Yuri did it!"

Like Laura, Elena marveled at the *Neva*'s resurrection. She stood on the starboard bridge wing. Captain Miller remained inside the wheelhouse, unconscious and sprawled on the deck.

The *Neva*'s fin rose a dozen feet above the hull. The

forward end had a vertical face but the aft section sloped downward like a turtle's back.

Both vessels drifted.

While gripping the guardrail, still overcome by the magical presence of the behemoth, Elena noticed movement on top of the fin.

Captain Borodin stood alone on the bridge. The rest of the four-man observation party waited below for permission to join him.

He inhaled deeply. The salty fragrance of the evening air was a welcome respite from the manufactured environment of the pressure casing.

Anxious to be topside, he didn't bother with his sea coat. He embraced the chill.

Borodin searched the horizon for other vessels. It took just a moment to locate the *Hercules*. The work boat drifted off the port beam.

He turned away and peered aft. That's when he noticed the open VLF buoy hatch. The port door had failed to retract after reeling in the buoy. The CCP indicator panel warned of the problem; he ignored it, ordering the blow anyway.

Just aft of the open VLF hatch door he spotted the damage: several missing sound absorbing rubber tiles that exposed the bare steel of the outer hull. The *Neva* had struck something just before broaching. Everyone aboard heard the "thud."

Unable to control the submarine's ascent, Borodin and the CCP crew had eagerly counted off the rise rate. To a man, their hopes of deliverance multiplied exponentially each meter closer to the surface they came.

When the *Neva* had neared the surface, the open VLF hatch reflected sound waves from the *Hercules*'s depth sounders, announcing its pending arrival.

Borodin turned his attention back to the workboat, pulling up a night vision scope that hung from his neck. He aimed the sensor end at the vessel, targeting the wheelhouse.

With hair billowing about her face, the woman signaled with her arms.

"Yuri's friends!" he said to himself. "Thank you, whoever you are!"

The loudspeaker built into the conning tower's intercom unit activated. "Captain, permission to come to the bridge?"

Borodin reached down and pushed the Transmit button. *"Da."*

"What happened?" asked Elena. She stood on the deck next to Laura and Nick.

Laura knelt by Nick. He lay facedown on the deck, a pool of water enveloping his body. Laura looked up. "He was thrown overboard. Somehow, he managed to climb back aboard. I didn't even see him until he collapsed here."

Elena dropped to her knees, opposite Laura. She lowered her head to within inches of Nick's right cheek. "Major Orlov—Nicolai," she said in Russian, "are you all right?"

His eyelids flickered and he managed a weak smile. "Vodka, *požalujsta*!"

Relieved, Elena reached for his shoulders. "Help

me, please?" she asked Laura. "We need to warm him up."

"Okay."

"I want the compressor up and running in five minutes."

"Understood, Captain. We'll have it online in three."

"Very well."

Borodin, wearing a headset with a boom mike, remained on the bridge atop the sail.

The four men stacked around him in the observation well were silent. The watch-standers searched their designated sectors for targets, each set of eyes glued to their individual night vision devices. One of the radar domes mounted to a retractable mast in the sail extended ten feet above bridge. It, too, probed with electronic eyes, the low-pitch hum of its orbit reminding them all that the *Neva* had returned from the dead.

Captain Borodin could see his breath as he exhaled. A few minutes earlier, he'd gratefully accepted his coat, brought topside by a sailor.

Borodin keyed the microphone, connecting with the CCP. "This is the captain, put me through to Kirov."

"Yes, sir."

Thirty seconds passed and then his headphones came alive: "Stephan, Yuri here."

Borodin smiled, never quite used to how helium altered the human voice. Kirov sounded like Donald Duck.

"When are you going to start sucking on some real air?" Borodin asked, laughing.

A high-pitched chuckle. "It'll be awhile yet."

"Are you all right?"

"So far. I banged up my head a little." Yuri coughed. "What happened?"

Keeping an eye on the proximity of the nearby workboat, Borodin said, "We came up so fast. I had no control whatsoever—surfaced right under your boat. Knocked a few tiles off but we're fine."

"The *Hercules*—what happened?"

"Don't know yet for sure, it's about forty meters away. I'm looking at it right now; it appears to be structurally intact but it's dead in the water."

"What about her crew?"

"Lights are on." Borodin raised his NVD and scanned the *Hercules*. "I see movement on the aft deck, several people. I'm sending over a raft with a portable radio."

"Good, there are two SVR officers aboard. Work with the male—Major Orlov. I don't trust the other one. Her name is Krestyanova, Elena. I don't know her grade."

"I understand."

"Do me a favor?"

"Anything?"

"Talk with Laura Newman and let her know I'm okay."

"She's the American that helped you?"

"Yes, helped us all—at enormous risk to herself. She's aboard the *Hercules*."

"What does she know?"

"Everything—we'd never be where we are now without her."

"Don't worry. I'll let her know personally."

"Thank you."

* * *

Nick Orlov shivered and his teeth chattered. He sat on a chair in the galley of the *Hercules*, his naked form encased by a wool blanket. Elena and Laura flanked him, each vigorously massaging his back and shoulders, trying to revive his chilled body.

Although miserable, he relished the attention. "Elena, a little more to the right, please." She moved a few inches. He poked his left hand out of the wrap and ran it up the inside thigh of her skintight jeans.

"Nicolai, you *bábnik*!" she shouted while jerking her leg from his grip. "Watch out, Laura, he's warmed up way too much now!"

Laura smiled as she, too, stepped away, wary of another sneak attack.

Nick turned around, grinning. "Thanks, ladies, I'm feeling much better."

Elena muttered, "No kidding."

"Remember, Lieutenant," Yuri said, "the partial pressure of oxygen must remain constant."

"Yes, sir. I'll set it up as you directed."

"The instructions are in the manual. If you have any questions, I'll walk you through it."

"I understand, sir."

"Very well."

Yuri's voice remained distorted by helium yet his directions were unambiguous. He would die if misunderstood. The supply officer operating the control panel at the base of the escape trunk knew nothing about diving. But he now served as Yuri's lifeline, responsible for mixing helium and oxygen from the storage tanks in Compartment Six into a sustainable blend.

Yuri continued to rely on the rebreather, taking the mouthpiece out whenever he spoke. Its supply of heliox would soon run out and he'd need to tap the sub's onboard stock.

His split eyebrow had clotted; blood only oozed from the wound.

Yuri reached forward and turned a valve handle. The hiss of high-pressure air venting to Compartment Six reverberated inside the escape trunk. He monitored a gauge mounted to the side of the chamber. The pressure decreased. Yuri checked the dive computer strapped to the left forearm of his dry suit.

The delay in engineering the bilge vent had cost Yuri dearly. For every extra minute spent working beyond his planned bottom time, an hour of decompression added to his original schedule.

By turning the trunk's air release valve, Yuri started the decompression process. He would bleed off pressure inside the steel chamber in measured steps and hold the lower pressure at specific stop points for predetermined time intervals. This would allow the helium dissolved in Yuri's blood and tissues time to seep out without forming deadly bubbles—minuscule gas spheres that cause appalling ruin to the human body.

His first bout with decompression sickness had left him crippled. Another case of the bends would probably kill him. Yuri could not afford to cut any corners.

Using the aft escape trunk as a decompression chamber would safely return Yuri to normal pressure. But it would be an agonizingly slow process. The LED display on his dive computer broadcast the schedule. It would take fifty-eight hours before he could exit the trunk.

"Helm, engine ahead slow," ordered Captain Borodin.

"Ahead slow," replied the officer of the watch.

Borodin remained on the sail, connected via intercom to the central command post.

As the bronze propeller bit into the sea, a tremor reverberated through the *Neva*'s hull. Borodin trained a portable spotlight on the bow and waited for the boat to gain momentum.

Moving at just three knots, the bow was almost completely submerged, leaving just a meter of freeboard. "Helm, full right rudder," he said. "Make your course zero one zero."

The watch officer echoed the order.

The boat began an unhurried turn.

Over the next few minutes, Borodin ordered several additional course changes. The flooded bow compartment severely impaired performance; maneuvering underwater would be even worse. During the test maneuvering, Borodin kept a close eye out for the powerless workboat, orbiting it.

"Helm, engine all stop," ordered Borodin.

The *Neva* and the *Hercules* both drifted with the current, separated by two hundred meters of water.

Borodin keyed the microphone again and ordered the deck parties topside. The first group climbed onto the outer casing. One at a time, the lead three-man team exited through a door recessed into the port sidewall of the sail. They wore wet suits, carried canvas tool bags and flashlights. The men stepped onto the narrow deck adjacent to the sail and headed toward the bow. They stopped at the forward escape trunk hatch.

While the first team worked on opening the hatch, the next team emerged from the sail door. They struggled with a heavy bag about the size of a storage trunk. Within five minutes, the inflated eight-man rubber raft rested on the deck just forward of the sail.

The team leader, a senior warrant, looked up at Borodin. "Captain, that it?" he said while pointing toward the *Hercules*.

"Affirmative."

"Permission to depart."

"Granted."

The men lowered the raft into the water. The team leader and two sailors climbed into it and paddled toward the workboat.

Several minutes passed when a bridge lookout reported, "Sir, the forward hatch is open."

Captain Borodin stood next to the open hatch. The forty-eight-year-old chief of the boat had just climbed out of the forward escape trunk. Standing shy of six feet with a heavy build, he reeked of death; water dripped from his saturated jumpsuit.

"What's the status, Dima?"

The chief coughed, trying to clear out the residual foul air in his lugs. He'd spent ten minutes on the upper deck of the *Neva*'s torpedo room wading through waist-high water. "Bad, sir. As we expected, massive damage. Everything I could see was scorched to hell."

"The crew?"

"Body parts on the surface. It's just awful."

Borodin grimaced. "Can you get to tube five?"

"I think so, using EBAs we should be able to insert a temporary plug and then dewater."

"What about sealing off for diving. We'll need a hundred meters' depth."

The chief coughed again. "We'll have to weld a plate over the breach opening, but I don't know how we're going to do that."

Neither did Borodin. The ship's electric welder was stored in a workshop on a lower deck in Compartment Two. Submerged in seawater for over two weeks, it would never spark again.

"Thanks, Chief. Get some dry clothes on."

"Yes, sir."

After the chief departed, Borodin remained beside the hatch, staring into the opening. A whiff of rotting flesh flowed into the still night air. He stepped back, appalled at the foulness.

He would never forget the stench.

CHAPTER 64

Elena watched from the wheelhouse as the Russian sailors paddled toward the *Hercules*. She stood watch over the now idling workboat; Laura restarted the diesel. Elena turned and faced the open stairwell. "They're almost here!" she shouted.

"Okay," answered Nick. He and Laura were one deck level below, cleaning up. The *Herc*'s cabin had been in shambles after the collision—half of the galley's lockers had spilled their guts onto the deck.

Nick and Laura stood on the aft main deck. He wore a pair of dry slacks and a wool Pendleton shirt, liberated from Miller's cabin.

Nick helped the submariner climb aboard, lending the sailor a hand as he pulled himself up and over the stern railing. His companions remained in the rubber raft, which was tied to the workboat. Nick and the visitor stood on the deck. Laura and Elena stood nearby.

"Major Orlov?" asked the warrant officer in Russian.

"Da."

The sailor removed the satchel strapped across his

right shoulder. "Captain Borodin asked me to give this to you."

Nick pulled open the covering flap of the handheld Russian military radio.

"This is a secure unit?"

"Yes, sir. You can speak freely with Captain Borodin. He's on the bridge." He pointed back toward the *Neva*, still adrift a couple of hundred meters to the north.

Nick extended the built-in antenna and turned on the radio.

"Channel one?" he asked.

"Correct."

Nick pressed the microphone's Transmit switch and spoke, "Major Orlov here."

There was a slight delay before the built-in speaker activated. "Major, this is Captain Lieutenant Borodin. I'm acting commanding officer of the *Neva*."

"Greetings, Captain. Welcome back to the world!"

"Thank you. We are very happy to be off the bottom."

"We are all amazed that it worked. Are you okay?"

"Yes, but what about you—is your vessel damaged? We had no control over our ascent."

"We were knocked around but I think we'll be okay." Nick neglected to mention Captain Miller's injury. The master of the *Hercules* had fractured his skull. Earlier, Nick, Elena, and Laura moved the comatose Miller to his cabin. That's when Nick discovered the .45 in Miller's coat pocket. He confiscated the pistol.

"Major, on behalf of the surviving officers and men of the *Neva* and me, we thank you and your associates for all that you have done to help us. We are forever grateful."

"We're pleased that you're okay, Captain." Nick turned toward the two women who had just joined him and smiled.

Laura frowned, not having an inkling of what had just transpired. Elena translated for her.

"Ask him about Yuri!" Laura said.

Nick held up a hand in acknowledgment. He activated the mike. "Captain, can you tell me about Kirov—how's he doing?"

"He's fine. He's currently decompressing."

Elena again translated. Laura beamed.

Borodin asked, "Major, how are we going home?"

"We're still working on that, Captain."

"How can that be? We've been stranded for over two weeks now. A plan of action should have been in place long ago."

Nick faced Elena. She sulked.

"What's the matter?" asked Laura, observing the mutual regret.

Nick replied, "Captain, we've had some coordination problems. It's taken much longer to arrange your out than expected."

Borodin replied, "Can you at least indicate what your general plan is?"

"Stand by, Captain."

Nick again turned toward Elena. "What should I tell him?"

"Go with the original plan, we'll resurrect it—somehow."

Nick keyed the microphone. "Captain, first you and your crew will need to transfer onto our vessel. We'll transport you to shore and a holding facility near Vancouver. From there, you'll be shuttled to a private hangar at the airport. And then we'll fly you out."

"We all travel as a group?"

"Yes."

"When will this occur?"

Elena broke in, "Tell him we need at least a day to complete the flight arrangements."

"A minimum of twenty-four hours for the flight. But we're prepared to take you and your crew now."

"We can't do that."

"Why?"

"Kirov's decompression will take two and a half days to complete."

"Why so long? He didn't say anything like that before."

"It took him longer to vent Compartment Two than he'd planned. He's paying the price."

Before Nick replied, Elena preempted him, "Nick, if we have a couple of days, I'm sure we can get everything in place." It would also provide her time to smooth things over with their boss.

Nick continued, "Captain, what about the *Neva*, is she still seaworthy?"

"We're checking. We have power and helm control. We're also recharging the high-pressure flasks in preparation for diving."

"You plan to submerge again?" Nick asked, bewildered.

"Yes, during daylight hours. We'll make repairs in the dark."

"We can take some of your men now if you want."

"Thank you but no. We need everyone aboard—

we're shorthanded. What we could really use is some food; we're getting low."

"We can help with that!"

The rubber raft returned twice to the *Neva*, loaded down with dozens of grocery sacks and cardboard boxes.

Orlov and Borodin again talked over the encrypted radio circuit. Elena selectively translated, not fully trusting Laura.

"Thank you for the supplies," Borodin commented. "Once again we are in your debt."

"You're welcome, Captain," Nick said. Now ready for closure he continued. "When Kirov finishes decompressing we'll meet you here again and make the transfer."

"We can't do it here."

"Why?"

"I'm not going to scuttle the *Neva* here—offshore of Point Roberts."

"I don't understand."

"We need to find a more secure location, deeper water and not in United States territory. There's a deep hole north of here about eighty kilometers, near Nanaimo."

Borodin referred to an abandoned underwater ammunition dumpsite, marked on the Canadian charts. The shattered hull of the *Neva* would blend in with the bottom debris. When the scuttling charges detonated, the sound print from the explosions—if picked up by Canadian or U.S. underwear listening posts, would be chocked up to munitions cooking off—he hoped.

Nick faced Elena. "Where's Nanaimo?"

"On the east coast of Vancouver Island, not too far away."

"Okay, Captain. Provide us with coordinates and we'll pick you up at the new location."

"We'll do that, but before we can head north we must make repairs."

"What's the problem?"

"The first compartment is still flooded, which affects our maneuverability. I have marginal control on the surface. We can submerge if we stay shallow but she'll be a pig to steer, especially in any kind of cross-current. We must correct the problem before heading north—it's too far to go without full control."

"How can we help?" Nick asked after Borodin explained the root of the *Neva*'s dilemma.

"We need a welder and pumps. Do you have any of that equipment aboard?"

"Just a minute." Nick switched to English as he addressed Laura. "Do you know if there's a welder aboard plus some pumps?"

"I don't know, maybe. There's a lot stuff stored in the engine room."

"Can you check for me?"

"Sure."

Nick keyed the mike. "We're checking, Captain."

Captain Borodin and Nick went over other operational protocols until Laura returned.

"There's no welder that I could see," she said, "but there could be one stored someplace aboard. Only Captain Miller would know." Laura continued, "I did find an acetylene torch and a portable gas-powered pump with a bunch of hose."

Nick reported, "Captain, we couldn't find a welder but there's a torch and a pump."

"We've got to have a welder—a heavy-duty unit. That's our only hope for sealing the tube."

Elena joined in again, "Tell him we'll rent one."

"Captain, we can get you a welder and come back in the evening. Will that work?"

"It'll have to."

"Will you be okay—submerged, I mean."

"I think so—if we don't go too deep and avoid—" Borodin stopped.

Nick pressed the microphone switch. "Captain, you still there?"

Forty seconds passed and then Borodin replied, "Our radar just picked up a surface target that's moving at forty knots from the north; it's vectored straight for us. It'll be here in twelve minutes. We're diving now. Start monitoring this frequency at seventeen hundred hours your time later today and we'll rendezvous again."

"What kind of target?"

"We don't know, maybe the authorities. Regardless, the *Neva* must not be seen. Get your cover story in place in case you're boarded, and bring us a welder. I've got to go."

The radio link clicked off.

CHAPTER 65

Nick, Elena, and Laura stood on the starboard bridge wing. The *Neva* submerged, leaving a faint bubble trail. They watched the approaching craft. The flashing amber strobe light on its mast marked its high-speed advance.

"What is that thing?" Nick asked in English.

Elena had the binoculars pressed to her eyes. *"Chyort."*

"What?" Laura asked.

"It's the Canadian Coast Guard," Elena said.

"How do you know that?" asked Nick.

"They're the only ones that have hovercraft around here."

"Really?" Nick said.

"Yep, that's why it's going so fast."

"Oh no," Laura mumbled as she remembered Captain Miller. He remained below, laid out on his bunk, unconscious. "What do we do now?"

Nick took charge. "Okay, here's what we need to . . ."

* * *

The ninety-four-foot air cushion vehicle made its approach from the north at forty knots and executed a full-speed orbit around the *Hercules* before slowing. Riding on top of the water surface, it produced hardly any wake wash.

With its twin variable pitch propellers still whirling at a furious rate, the hovercraft scooted across the fifty yards of open water to the *Hercules* and stopped about ten feet away. The high-pitched whine of its engines faded and the pressurized air-filled skirt that encircled the craft deflated. The ACV's hull settled about two feet into the water. The only sound now, a muted rumble, broadcast from the *Hercules*'s idling diesel engine.

Laura and Nick waited on the stern deck. Elena remained in the cabin, cleaning up the last of the chaos from the near capsizing.

Nick still had Miller's .45, but a shoot-out would be a disaster; talk was the only way out—a skill Nick did well.

The hovercraft's front hatch opened. The silhouette of a man backlit by crimson cabin lighting appeared. "Hello there," he called out in a friendly voice.

Laura and Nick returned the greeting.

"Are you the skipper, sir?" asked the Canadian Coastguard officer.

"Yes, this is my boat," Nick said. "Is there a problem?"

"Permission to come aboard, skipper?"

"Ah, okay—sure."

He tossed Nick a mooring line. Nick pulled the ACV forward until its rubber skirt kissed the *Herc*'s hull. The officer climbed over the rail, followed by a second crew member. Neither man carried a firearm. Two other crew members remained inside the ACV; a female sat at the controls, another male stood nearby.

"What's the problem?" Nick again asked, addressing the ACV's captain.

"Sir, are you having difficulty with your vessel?"

Nick had his story ready, prompted by Laura's brainstorm. "Yes, we had a power failure. I just fixed it."

"Was your radio out of order, too?"

Laura answered, expecting the officer's question. "Yes. I was in the wheelhouse when everything shut down—nothing worked."

"So you weren't monitoring Channel sixteen?"

"Not after we lost power."

The ACV's CO turned to face his companion. "That certainly explains it."

The man nodded his agreement.

"What's going on?" Nick asked.

"Skipper, the reason we were dispatched is that Vancouver Vessel Traffic Control has been trying to contact you for the past hour. You've been slowly drifting toward the shipping lanes."

"Oh, I forgot about that."

"You're very close to the northbound lane."

"But aren't we still in U.S. waters?"

"Yes but we share responsibilities with your Coast Guard in this area of the Strait of Georgia."

"I'm sorry," Nick offered. "I wasn't thinking about the shipping lanes; we're so far offshore it just didn't register."

"That's understandable." The Canadian shifted his stance. "Were you assisted by another craft?"

"I don't understand."

"As we made our approach, our radar showed two contacts but then they faded to one blip."

"Ah, no. We're alone here."

"Must be a glitch with our system." The coast-guardsman shuffled his feet. "Well, anyway, are just the two of you aboard?"

Laura had been anticipating this question, too. Under no circumstances could they reveal the presence of Miller. If they discovered the unconscious and obviously injured man, the Coast Guard crew would mount a full investigation.

"Ah, there's one other aboard," Laura said. "She's in the galley."

"Okay. And just where are you headed?"

"Point Roberts," Nick answered. "We came up from Seattle—almost got there but lost power."

"I see." The Canadian gestured toward the bow. "If you don't mind, I'd like to make a check of your pilot-house, see if everything's in working order. That okay with you, skipper?"

"Sure."

Nick and Laura led the way, entering the main cabin, passing through the galley, and climbing the companionway to the bridge.

Elena nodded at the two visitors as they passed through the main salon. Seated at the mess table, she nursed a cup of coffee. Unlike Nick, she had prepared for trouble. Her suppressor-equipped Beretta lay on the bench seat at her right side, covered by a towel.

The inspection took five minutes. The Canadian officer requested that Nick switch on the AIS system. Laura complied, thankful that Captain Miller had briefed her on the *Herc*'s automatic identification system.

* * *

The *Hercules* had been under way for forty-five minutes. Several steel plates on the starboard hull had dents and one of the depth finder transducers no longer functioned. But that was the extent of the damage. The submarine's outer covering of rubberized anechoic tiles cushioned the impact. Had the *Neva* hit the hull farther aft, the workboat's rudder and propeller assembly would have been crushed.

The *Hercules* approached the south shore of Point Roberts. About a hundred yards ahead, a flashing red light marked the western end of the marina's breakwater. Laura stood at the helm. Elena and Nick flanked her.

"Are they still following us?" Laura asked.

Nick looked aft. The yellow strobe light marked the presence of the Canadian patrol craft. "Yeah, it's still there."

"Do you think they'll come into the marina, too?" asked Elena.

"I hope not," Laura said.

Navigating in the confined spaces of a small craft harbor strained her navigation skills.

Laura maneuvered past the breakwater and lined up with the center of the marina's entrance channel. The *Hercules* crawled forward.

"Hey, they just turned away," announced Nick.

"Captain, sonar. Target has increased speed and is heading west. Sounds like he's accelerating. Thirty-plus knots."

"Very well, keep monitoring." Captain Borodin rotated his chair to face the officer of the watch, who stood next to the central command post's helm. "Let's run another sweep."

"ESM sweep, aye, sir."

Thirty seconds later, a slender steel tube rose from the top of the sail and pierced the sea surface by two meters. The antenna sniffed for hostile electronic transmissions, radars in particular.

The *Neva*'s electronic support measures officer made his report by intercom. "Captain, I'm picking up the same transmitters from our previous sweep. No new contacts."

"Very well." Borodin then addressed the watch officer. "Up periscope."

"Up periscope, aye, sir."

Borodin peered through the eyepiece. "No close-by contacts. Get me a bearing on the target."

The watch officer relayed the command to sonar.

"Captain, sonar. Target bears two seven seven. He's really moving—forty-plus knots."

Borodin turned to the designated bearing and increased magnification. The flashing strobe caught his attention. "I have it. He's departing the area."

Smiles and grins broke out on all those assembled in the *Neva*'s CCP.

CHAPTER 66

The *Hercules* was docked. The crew reassembled in Captain Miller's stateroom.

Miller remained unconscious, sprawled out on his bunk. His right pupil did not react to light. Blood still seeped from the tear in his scalp and it had crusted inside an ear.

"We need to call for an ambulance," Laura said. She sat on the side of the bunk caressing Miller's forehead with a moist cloth. "He needs to be in a hospital."

"We can't do that," Elena countered. She stood next to the bunk with Nick at her side. "If we call for an ambulance, it'll probably come from the States, maybe even here, but not Vancouver. Remember, this is Point Roberts. Do you realize how much of a hassle that will be?"

Laura did not reply.

"I guarantee you," Elena continued, "that if you call for help we'll have the local cops here plus the entire volunteer fire department, and then all the issues of getting him across the border crossing. We'll be filling out paperwork for hours." Elena scowled. "How long do you think it will be before someone decides to check on Nick and me? Our cover legends are good but not that good. Besides, Miller knows too much. We can't let him out of our sight."

"What do you mean he knows too much?" Laura said with an acid tone. "You want to get rid of him, dump him overboard like garbage?"

"He's expendable."

Laura jumped to her feet, ready for battle. "You're not going to harm him, do you understand?"

Elena backed up a step, startled at Laura's fury.

"Hold on, both of you!" Nick said as he stepped between the women. He addressed Laura first. "Miller is not going to be harmed. I promise you that."

"But he needs help!"

"I know he does, and we're going to take care of that."

He turned to face Elena. "Where's the nearest hospital."

She told him.

"Okay, here's what we're going to do."

Yuri Kirov remained in the *Neva*'s aft escape trunk. He'd weaned himself from the rebreather and now inhaled heliox supplied from oxygen and helium flasks stored at the base of the escape trunk. The shipboard gas blend and its constant partial pressure of oxygen mimicked the rebreather's supply. The new mask he used and a spare had been stored on a shelf inside the trunk before Yuri's dive. He and Viktor used the masks during their work.

Yuri had been decompressing for about two hours. Fifty-six hours remained.

He dreaded the ordeal. The escape trunk's chilled environment hadn't yet seeped through his dry suit, but it would. For every breath inhaled through the mask, an equal amount of exhaled gas vented to the steel chamber, which increased the carbon dioxide level. Because the trunk did not have a scrubber system, CO_2 would eventually build up to a lethal concentration despite periodic decompression venting.

As long as the gas supply to Yuri's breathing mask flowed, he would be fine. If it stopped, forcing him to inhale trunk air, he would not survive.

Despite the risks, Yuri remained optimistic. Earlier he spoke with Borodin, who had reported on his plan to seal up tube five and head north to the abandoned munitions dumpsite. The crew would transfer to the *Hercules* and then Borodin and two other officers would scuttle the *Neva*. The two plus days it would take to accomplish those tasks dovetailed with Yuri's decompression schedule.

But best of all, Laura would be waiting when he reboarded the *Hercules*.

Yuri leaned back against the curved steel wall and listened. Earlier he'd asked the sailor operating the escape trunk's control panel to tie in the *Neva*'s master intercom to the chamber's loudspeaker. That way he could monitor the ship's communications. The traffic was routine, mostly status reports and change of watch matters. Nonetheless, he took comfort in listening to the familiar voices.

Yuri was home, back with his crew and fellow officers.

*   *   *

The Canadian border agent watched as the SUV pulled into her interview lane. She waited for the driver to roll down his window.

"Good morning," the man offered while handing her three passports.

"Where are you headed, sir?" she asked.

"Back to Vancouver."

She looked past the driver. The female in the passenger seat had her eyes shut and her head rested on the door column. The male in the backseat also slept; his head slumped to the side.

None of this appeared unusual to the agent. The taverns and bars had closed half an hour earlier and these were the last of the stragglers. Another Saturday party night at the Point had run its course.

The border agent glanced at the passports and addressed the driver. "Sir, how long have you been in Point Roberts?"

"Ah, we just came down this evening. We had dinner with some friends that have a beach house and then we went out for a few beers."

The driver spoke without slurring his words and no odor of alcohol escaped the vehicle. Any suspicious drivers would be ordered to pull over and the Delta District Municipality police summoned.

She handed the passports back. "Okay, sir, you're free to enter."

"Thanks."

*   *   *

Nick Orlov pulled out of the Canadian border station and turned onto Fifty-sixth Street. The Suburban headed north into Tsawwassen.

He heaved a sigh and commented, "That wasn't so bad."

"Right," Laura agreed. She sat next to Nick. "Is that Elena?" she said, peering over the hood. A Mercedes sedan had just pulled away from the curb in front of them.

"Yes."

Elena had crossed the border about ten minutes earlier.

"How long will it take to get to the hospital?" asked Laura.

"Half an hour or less."

"Good."

Laura turned around to glance at Captain Miller. He breathed shallow and perspiration had beaded on his forehead.

CHAPTER 67

Nick found the vacant wheelchair parked outside the ER next to the ambulance entrance. He rolled it two blocks back to the parked Suburban. Elena's Mercedes was just around the corner. Out of view of the hospital's security cameras and with help from Laura and Elena, Nick loaded Captain Dan Miller's inert form into the chair. To keep Miller upright, Nick removed his jacket and lashed it around Miller's chest and the chair's seatback.

Nick returned to the ER, pushing Miller through the entrance. To help conceal Nick's face from the surveillance cameras, he continued to wear a broad-brimmed hat and a pair of sunglasses, both liberated from Captain Miller's cabin. During the transit from the Suburban, Miller had slumped to the right side of the chair but remained upright for the most part.

Thankfully, the emergency room was crowded this early morning—leftovers from Saturday-night revelry in Vancouver Metro. Dozens sat in chairs and milled about the lobby waiting to see a physician.

Nick rolled Miller to a quiet corner next to an Asian woman sitting in a chair. She read a magazine.

Kneeling next to the unconscious Miller, Nick said, "Dan, I need to use the restroom. Just wait here. I'll be right back."

Two minutes later, Nick returned to the Suburban and drove off.

Ken Newman's eyes rolled open and stared into the dimness. The sun would not rise for another hour.

Ken sat slumped in the driver's seat of his parked Corvette. The crown of his skull pulsated and his mouth tasted like a two-week-old cat box. He opened the door and climbed out, leaning heavily against the car to steady himself. A few seconds later, he unzipped the fly to his jeans and relieved the pressure in his bladder.

During the long seconds of urination, Ken managed to recall fragments of the previous evening. Back at the Pod Room, he'd chatted with a thirty-something legal secretary from Vancouver. But it never went anywhere. Just before midnight, and after he bought a round of drinks, Allison and her three friends exited the bar.

Ken continued to order a succession of Crown Royals. His binge only ceased when the bar closed. Already tagged with one DUI at the Point, Ken retained enough sense not to be a repeat offender. He slept in his car, parked in the back lot away from the road, without moving it.

Ken stomped his feet on the gravel and pulled his arms close to his chest. He was cold and stiff from sleeping in the car. His head throbbed. Ken knew from experience that the hangover would get much worse before it ended. He cursed himself and climbed back into the car. It was time to find a cup of coffee.

"Do you think we can rent what they need at that place?" asked Laura.

Nick sipped from his coffee mug. "Yeah, that's what Elena said."

They were in a café on the outskirts of downtown Vancouver. Their booth was in the back, away from the crowds.

Laura checked her wristwatch: 6:57 A.M. "I wonder if they might open early?"

"I doubt it—it's Sunday. We're lucky it's open at all."

Laura finished the last slice of her toast. She'd already polished off the omelet and hash browns, her body craving nutrition. Nick pushed aside his half-empty plate of scrambled eggs and Canadian bacon. Preferring caffeine to calories, he sipped the last of his second cup of coffee.

"What's going to happen when Dan wakes up?" Laura asked. "You know the first thing he's going to want to know is where his boat is."

"Don't worry about that. We'll be done with it soon. It'll be there, waiting for him."

"I hope so."

Laura drained her mug and meeting Nick's eyes said, "He'll get the right care, won't he?"

"Absolutely, Canada has first-rate coverage."

"But he's American; won't that be an issue?"

"No, there's no ID on him. They'll treat him as a John Doe—a Canadian John Doe. He'll get the same care as any other citizen."

"Good, that makes me feel better."

A waitress refilled their coffee mugs.

Laura took a couple of sips and still at unease she said, "He must have a fractured skull—the blood coming out of his ear and that wound to his head."

"You're probably right. It looked pretty bad to me."

Laura slumped in the bench seat. "I hope he makes it."

"He's in good hands, Laura. We've done all what we could for him—like I promised you."

"I know—thank you."

Laura sat up straight, stretched her arms, and asked, "What's Elena doing this morning?"

"She's at the mission. She'll return to Point Roberts later today."

"Is she working on the escape plan for the crew?"

"Yes."

"Good." Laura exhaled. "I'll be so relieved when this is over."

Nick flashed a friendly smile. "We all will be." He leaned forward. "Yuri—he's an amazing fellow, risking his life to save his submates." He beamed again. "And you, helping Yuri and his crew, you are the truly amazing one."

Laura broke eye contact, gazing down at the table-top. *What am I doing?*

She'd just shared a meal with a foreign intelligence officer after having given away a whopping chunk of her money to help a group of strangers—spies—all because a man who had held her hostage had·asked. He would soon go away with his crew and she'd probably never see him again.

Orlov read Laura's dejection. "Do not be so hard on yourself. You and Yuri did a noble deed. If both of you had not persisted, the *Neva* would still be on the bottom and the crew close to, if not, dead."

Laura raised her head. "You and Elena would have helped them."

"We don't have your skills. Plus, Moscow has been moving slowly. The crew might have perished." He skirted the Kremlin's decision to sacrifice the crew.

"Laura, you have much to be proud of."

After driving around the commercial core of Point Roberts, trying to buy a cup of coffee, Ken gave up. Nothing had opened yet so he opted for Tsawwassen.

He was turning north onto Tyee Drive when a new thought occurred. He made a U-turn. Three minutes later, he drove past the beach house. As expected, he observed no cars in the driveway or lights on inside the house.

Ken parked his Corvette a couple of blocks to the east. He walked down the public walkway to the water's edge and made his way to the house, using the exposed beach as his cover.

Standing on the deck, he jimmied the frame of the locked sliding glass door and yanked open the slider. The sun was just peeking above the Cascades when Ken slipped inside Laura's rental.

Ken searched the house, concentrating on the up-stairs. When he opened the closet door in the master bedroom, he found a collection of Laura's garments hanging on the rack: a couple of dresses, her favorite skirt—it showed off her shapely legs—and several blouses.

He opened the chest of drawers and discovered more of her clothing: rows of panties and bras neatly folded and stacked—again, just like at home.

She must be coming back!

Maybe he would wait right here.

Too tired to bother with coffee, Ken commandeered the bed.

As he sank into the mattress, welcoming sleep, a new suspicion materialized.

He screwed her in this very bed!

Just before succumbing to fatigue—and the residual alcohol in his blood, he knew what he had to do.

I'll get even when they come back.

CHAPTER 68

"Captain, sonar. Contact change."

Captain Borodin grabbed a microphone from an overhead panel. "Sonar, report."

"Captain, target eight has deployed some type of underwater instrumentation. High-frequency modulations, narrow band spread."

"What is it?"

"Not sure, but it may be surveying equipment. The signal strength is weak. It bears one seven two degrees relative; range is ten point five kilometers."

"Let me know when you've identified the signal."

"Aye, Captain."

Borodin returned the microphone to its receptacle and leaned back in his chair. Eight men in the CCP sat at consoles and control stations. It was late morning.

The *Neva* navigated five kilometers southwest of Point Roberts, forty meters below the surface. It orbited in a two-kilometer radius at four knots.

The flooded torpedo room continued to vex Borodin and his crew. The *Neva* made wild swings in depth. During one maneuver, the sail came within ten meters of the surface. However, by running in a tight circle at minimal speed and adjusting the blow planes, the diving officer compensated for the sub's bizarre handling.

Optimistic for the first time in days, Borodin planned to jog offshore of Point Roberts until dark. He would then surface and make repairs.

Crew morale soared. No longer mired on the bottom was the bell-ringer event. But full bellies came in a close second. The food transferred from the *Hercules* the previous night was a blessing.

"Captain, sonar. I have an update on target eight."

"Report."

"Target eight is streaming side scan sonar. It appears to be conducting a survey."

"Survey of what?"

"I don't know, sir."

"Keep monitoring. Update in ten minutes."

"Yes, sir."

Ken might not have heard the vehicle if he hadn't been in the bathroom. It was 11:20 A.M. The headache that had been hounding him for hours had reached migraine status. He opened the medicine cabinet in the ground-floor bathroom but found nothing helpful. What he really needed was a drink—hair of the dog as the saying goes.

When the automobile turned off the road and drove onto the driveway, the engine noise put Ken on alert. The engine switched off and a set of doors opened.

*   *   *

"It won't take me long to pack," Laura Newman said. "Help yourself to what's in the kitchen if you're hungry."

Nick Orlov stood next to Laura. They were in the foyer of the rental house.

Laura sprinted up the stairway to the master bedroom.

Nick walked into the living room.

Ken hid in the closet under the stairway. He squatted behind a vacuum cleaner and a cardboard box of cleaning supplies.

With the door shut, he couldn't see much but he could hear muffled talk—a familiar female voice. And he'd armed himself with a butcher knife snatched from the kitchen counter.

She's with that bastard!

He wanted to burst through the closet door.

Not yet!

Ken cringed when Laura stepped on the carpeted stairway treads over his head. He heard the man walk into the living room, his sneakers squeaking on the hardwood floor.

Just enough light diffracted from under the closet door to allow Ken to step over the box. With the knife cocked in his right hand, he used his left to crack open the door.

The target stood about twenty-five feet away with his back to Ken.

Wound coil tight, Ken prepared to strike.

* * *

Orlov peered through the living room window. On the distant horizon, he noticed a powerboat tracking westward. He hoped the waters would remain smooth for tonight's mission.

Nick settled into a sofa, removed his phone from a coat pocket, and pressed a speed dial number—Elena's cell.

"Allo, Yelenu," he said.

Ken was ready to pounce when the male took a couple steps and sat on a sofa. That's when Ken realized something was wrong.

He's not limping.

Still peeking around the edge of the closet door, the eight-inch blade in hand, Ken studied the man's profile.

It's not him.

Ken retreated, closing the closet door.

After finishing the call, Nick wandered into the kitchen. He opened the refrigerator and removed a can of Coca-Cola.

The can was half-empty when Laura walked down the stairway, carrying her suitcase.

"Would you like a Coke?" he asked. "There's another in the refrigerator."

"Sure, that sounds good."

Laura joined Nick at the kitchen table. She asked about Elena.

"She's coming down late in the afternoon."

"What else did she have to say?"

"She's still working on the passports. That's the hang-up."

"Do you really need passports—I mean if you get them on the charter flight in Vancouver and it's your own people flying the plane, who would know?"

"That's not the problem. We can probably pull that off without IDs. But when the plane lands in Finland, that's where the passport check will come in—no way around that."

"Hmm, I see your point." Laura ran a hand through her hair. "Why can't you fly them directly to Russia?"

"If we filed a flight plan like that there'd be a record of it. If the story about the *Neva* leaked, someone might make the connection and then trace it back to here."

"I see, by flying to Helsinki and then crossing the border by bus and driving to Saint Petersburg there's some insulation against a direct link."

"Yes."

Laura said, "Keeping this whole situation secret might be hard. I could see something leaking all right."

"We can't let that happen. Everything we do from now on must be absolute low profile. We can't leave one loose end. If Ottawa or Washington has even a tiny inkling that we left a submarine up here, they'll never stop looking for it."

"Yeah, you're probably right."

"Moscow just wants this debacle to go away, regardless of what the Ministry of Defense and the Navy might think. And believe me, if ordered, the SVR will sacrifice the *Neva*'s entire crew in a heartbeat to keep the Americans from finding out." He met Laura's eyes. "So, from here on out, we can't afford one mistake."

"I get it, Nick."

* * *

Ken could barely contain himself, stunned at his wife's bizarre conduct. He stood by the front door. He opened it a smidgen to verify that Laura and the male had left in the Suburban.

Ken had just run through a gauntlet of emotions: rage, jealousy, curiosity, and finally revulsion. He tried to make sense of what he'd heard.

When the stranger began speaking in Russian, Ken listened to the one-sided telephone conversation but he learned nothing. It wasn't until Laura trotted down the stairs and sat at the kitchen table with the mystery man that Ken put it together.

Passports, Helsinki, Moscow—a submarine!

There was only one explanation.

My wife is a spy!

CHAPTER 69

Ken watched the *Hercules* from the edge of the boat basin. He sat inside the Corvette, parked half a dozen stalls away from the Suburban. The workboat occupied the same berth from the day before.

Ken didn't dare venture onto the floating pier—not in broad daylight. Instead, he spied from shore. Laura and the same male he'd almost gutted earlier attended to equipment scattered on the workboat's stern deck.

What are they doing?

And where's the gimp?

After collecting her clothing from the beach house, Laura and Nick drove back to the marina. They removed the hefty electric arc welder and two pumps from the Suburban's cargo bay, transferring the gear to dock carts. Laura and Nick wheeled the rental equipment to the *Hercules* where Nick employed the hydraulic crane to transfer the apparatus aboard.

There was a glitch at the Point Roberts border crossing with the rented welder and pumps. The U.S. Customs and Border Patrol officer hassled Laura and Nick about the foreign imports. Laura resolved the dispute by paying the full import duty on the retail value of the equipment.

For the next half hour, the pair assembled and tested the gear. There was one item left.

"I can't get this thing started," Nick said. He was on his knees next to the rented welder on the workboat's main deck.

Laura squatted beside Nick. She studied the control panel.

Nick said, "I keep pressing the Start switch but nothing happens."

Laura stood and reached forward, pulling open an access panel. She peered into the guts of the machine. "One of the battery cables came off," she said.

"No wonder it wouldn't start."

Laura again dropped to her knees and searched through a toolbox that she'd removed from the engine room earlier. She found the right size socket and snapped it onto the wrench.

She reached inside the welder and reattached the cable, tightening the terminal clamp with the socket.

"Try it now."

Nick pressed the Start button with his right thumb. The gas engine exploded to life.

"Wow, what would I do without you?" he said with a broad grin.

Laura returned the smile.

Surveying the equipment they had assembled and tested, Laura announced, "Everything works."

"Time for a coffee break."

"Sounds good."

* * *

Elena sat alone at the conference table in the Trade Mission's code room. She held a telephone handset. The directors of the SVR and FSB were on the other end of the encrypted satellite telephone circuit, each at their residence. Neither man was happy about the *Neva*'s miraculous resurrection.

"I know, sir," Elena said. "There wasn't anything we could do about it. By the time we were ready to deal with him, Kirov had already implemented his rescue plan. Major Orlov and I were not in a position to stop him."

"You and Orlov were ordered to terminate Kirov if he did not cooperate. Explain yourself," ordered SVR chief Smirnov.

Elena glanced down at her notes on the tabletop. "Sir, Kirov's American friend engineered the operation. She used a remote-controlled underwater device to enter one of the *Neva*'s torpedo tubes. It had a television camera that Kirov was able to use to figure out a repair."

"You knew nothing of that?"

"That's correct. Apparently, they'd been working on this plan from the beginning. Major Orlov and I only found out about it when we followed them out of the marina last night."

FSB General Golitsin responded next. "That's when you saw the *Neva* on the surface?"

"Yes, sir. When we arrived on scene, the submarine had already surfaced."

Elena lied. If she revealed the truth, both she and Nick would be banished from the service, or worse.

They could have halted the operation with a bullet to Kirov's temple and another to his female partner.

"Where is this woman now?" asked Smirnov.

"In Point Roberts with Major Orlov. I spoke with him half an hour ago."

"What about the Operation Eagle team—what are they doing?" asked Golitsin.

"As ordered, I set them up in Bellingham yesterday, unaware that the *Neva* was about to be rescued. They were supposed to search for the hulk today. I have not yet heard back from them."

"And the *Neva* has moved out of the area?" her boss said.

"I don't know where it went—only that Major Orlov and I are supposed to rendezvous with them tonight to work out the transfer details, and then they're supposed to scuttle the sub."

"Where?" asked the FSB general.

"North of Vancouver, at an abandoned underwater ordnance disposal site."

"And Kirov—he's back aboard the submarine?"

"Yes, General. After diving down and implementing the repairs, he remained aboard, decompressing."

Ignoring Elena, the military counterintelligence chief addressed his counterpart, "Borya, this news is incredible. Kirov has pulled off the rescue despite the odds. How do you recommend we bring them home?"

The SVR director did not share his colleague's enthusiasm. Spiriting out three dozen men without detection would be a monumental undertaking. If the effort failed, it would be his head mounted atop a pike pole on a Kremlin wall.

"What do you propose?" the SVR chief asked, redirecting his colleague's question to Elena. If the rescue mission turned sour, he would have some insulation from the aftereffects by blaming a subordinate.

"Well, sir, if we can charter an aircraft that has . . ."

Kirov remained inside the escape trunk. He'd been decompressing for about fifteen hours yet he didn't dare leave the steel cylinder. His body tissues and blood remained partially saturated with helium. Exposure to surface conditions for even a few minutes would be lethal. Expanding helium bubbles would turn blood into froth and vital organs into slush.

The cold hadn't been a problem, as he'd feared. An external heater warmed the gas feed line to his breathing mask, which maintained his core temperature.

Yuri continued to inhale a mixture of oxygen and helium with the blend periodically adjusted to compensate for the reduction in the trunk's pressure. But he had no control over that process. A nineteen-year-old sailor monitoring the gas panel had that duty, which troubled Yuri.

Yuri's greatest concern, however, was thirst. With no freshwater in the escape trunk he could no longer salivate.

He had another critical decision to make. His original plan called for him to remain in the escape trunk for the entire fifty-eight-hour decompression process. But he toyed with an alternative.

The *Neva* was equipped with a recompression chamber. Located at the base of the aft escape trunk, the 1.5-meter-diameter by 3-meter-long steel cylinder might be his lifeboat. Although not an option when Yuri first entered the escape trunk, he'd decompressed enough that it might be possible, albeit risky, to make a swift surface ascent. That would allow Yuri to climb out of the escape trunk, transfer to the chamber, and recompress.

The lure of the *Neva*'s recompression chamber tempted Yuri. He would be able to lie down on a bunk, read a book, and eat a meal. Most important, he would have water.

There would be a price for this luxury. If Yuri made the transfer now, he would have nearly sixty hours of *additional* decompression to endure—the consequence of subjecting his body to ultra fast decompression. However, should he elect to continue his current decompression schedule, he would be free of the escape trunk in about forty-three hours.

With the *Neva*'s precarious operational characteristics, the pending crew transfers to shore, and Captain Borodin's decision to deep six the *Neva* in an underwater junkyard, Yuri's decompression had become a burden to everyone aboard.

He decided to stick with the original plan.

The prospect of another day and a half plus of thirst troubled Yuri. It would be especially tough when he started breathing pure oxygen. Hydration would be essential at that time.

Without water, he might not survive.

The afternoon sun started its retreat over the peaks of Vancouver Island. The trawler yacht *Explorer* lumbered along at five knots about four nautical miles south of Point Roberts. Both crew members were in the main cabin. The female stood behind the helm; the male sat at the galley table.

Captain Duscha Dubova turned away from the steering wheel and eyed her charge. He stared at his laptop screen. "What is it?" she asked.

Lieutenant Grigori Karpekov looked up. "Looks like boulders to me."

"Are you sure?"

"They're strung out over the bottom for a hundred meters. I increased the resolution on the second pass. You can see some of them—stacked a couple of meters high."

"Chërt voz'mí!"

After spending most of the day in a fruitless search, the side scan sonar revealed one tantalizing reflection. The gray-black smudge on the screen indicated a potential bottom target in the range of the *Neva*'s length: 110 meters. They continued mowing the lawn via a GPS navigation system, towing the sonar-emitting fish over the bottom in overlaying transects until mapping the entire area. Only then did they return to the one promising target of the day.

But now, after lowering the fish for a close look, the results were in—*rocks*.

Dubova had been certain they'd found the derelict submarine. She next said, "Why would there be boulders out here? There's nothing geologically around here to account for them."

"They were probably dumped. We're in the northbound shipping lane. A barge could have turned turtle, dumping its cargo."

She conceded defeat.

For most of the early morning, the FSB special operators searched for the *Hercules*, expecting to transfer the underwater surveillance gear to the larger work-boat. Dubova repeatedly called and texted Elena's cell but received no response. Finally, after waiting at the rendezvous point just north of Lummi Island for ninety minutes, they reverted to the original work plan.

Karpekov faced his boss. "So what do we do now?"

"It's time to head back to Bellingham."

"Fine with me."

"Reel in the fish."

"Okay."

It would take only forty-five minutes for the Russians to motor north to Point Roberts where they could rent an overnight berth at the marina. But the mission orders were explicit: Conduct all search operations from Bellingham. They had at least a two-hour voyage ahead of them.

Ken Newman's headache was replaced by a tepid, all-too-friendly buzz. So far, he'd downed three double whiskeys and had just poured his fourth. Ken's current slide started after he'd spied on Laura and her new companion while they tinkered with gear on the work-boat.

After the pair retreated to the cabin, Ken moved on. Still hungover, he drove to a local store where he purchased a fifth of bourbon. He next returned to the beach house, confident that he'd be alone for a while. Laura had cleaned out the drawers and closets of the bedroom and bathroom. That's when he started self-medicating.

Ken slouched on the living room sofa, his feet propped

on the coffee table and glass in hand. He'd been hashing it out, running from one scenario to the next. The advancing alcohol in his bloodstream fueled his rising bitterness.

No matter how he cut it, Laura's filing for divorce offended the most. He no longer had any hope that she'd take him back.

He considered Laura's admirer—the gimp bastard who had ambushed him. It wasn't as if Ken had caught them naked in bed together, but he sure had imagined it.

Laura's stock awards were another worry. She would be due another colossal payout in the form of company ownership. Laura's divorce attorney would certainly try to screw Ken out of his share.

And what about the Russian connection? Ken had eavesdropped on Laura and the other man. But with his brain now awash in booze, none of what they said made any sense to him. He was confident, however, about one underlying fact: No one was going to steal his wife.

Ken slugged down the whiskey. He sat up, reached down, and removed the bludgeon from the bag at his feet. He brought it from Bellevue. He used it to bash salmon after reeling them into a boat; it also made an ideal billy club.

Ken tapped the working end of the fourteen-inch-long oak baton against one of the glass panels in the coffee table. He once again pictured Laura in bed with her lover; his blood pressure spiked. He raised the billy above his head and slammed it down onto the table, smashing the panel into shards.

"You two-timing bitch!" he roared.

CHAPTER 70

After testing the rental equipment, Laura and Nick returned to the galley for coffee. While sitting with Nick at the mess table, Laura dozed off. Nick shook her awake, led her to Captain Miller's cabin, and ordered her to rest, promising that he'd wake her at five o'clock—a couple of hours away.

She lay on the bunk, fully clothed and covered with a blanket from the locker. After an hour's sleep, a wave of nausea woke her; then the queasiness passed. Although partially refreshed, Laura remained antsy, especially over Captain Miller's injury.

Laura turned on her side and focused on Yuri's decompression—another worry. She pulled the blanket over her shoulders but was not ready to sleep again.

Her ordeal would soon be over and she'd be able to rest. Once Yuri and his crewmates were safely ashore, Laura would arrange for both Captain Miller and the *Hercules* to return to Seattle. She planned to return to her Redmond home and collapse.

Laura smiled as she recalled the news about the singular uncertainty that had consumed her for the past day.

While in Vancouver, she'd asked Nick to stop at a pharmacy. She needed a few personal items. He waited in the Suburban; she purchased three different brands.

Before napping, she'd tested herself in the privacy of a shipboard lavatory.

Laura closed her eyes. She caressed her abdomen with a hand and whispered, "Are you a boy or a girl?"

Nick Orlov stepped into the head located off the main cabin. About the size of a phone booth, it contained a toilet, a miniature sink, and storage lockers. After three cups of coffee, he needed to relieve himself.

Finished, he zipped up and faced the sink.

Nick washed his hands and looked at the mirror mounted above the sink. He rubbed his right hand across the two-day-old chin stubble. He needed a shave.

Nick turned his torso to open the door when Captain Miller's .45, stuffed in the small of his back, snagged a locker handle. He sucked in his belly to clear the obstruction. He turned the knob and stepped out.

In the passageway next to the head he noticed movement to his right side.

A blinding flash seared his eyes and everything went black.

CHAPTER 71

Laura hovered on that fine line between awareness and apparition. The dream had faded and with it, any memory of that seemingly real-life encounter. For eight minutes, but what seemed like hours, she'd been back in a Caltech classroom agonizing over a physics examination she hadn't prepared for.

Laura turned over in the bunk and faced the cabin's interior. Now that the sun had set, the stateroom was dark.

Laura settled into her new body position, not yet asleep, when she sensed an environmental shift. Her nostrils twitched, detecting the alien odor.

Her eyes opened. She stared into the blackness.

What is that? It took a few seconds. *Booze!*

She sat up. That's when she heard it: a telltale creak in the mahogany deck boards.

"Who's there?" she called out, her voice quavering.

No response.

Her heart rate spiked; her arm and leg muscles contracted.

She fumbled for the bunk-side light.

She flipped it on.

"No!"

Ken Newman stood three feet from the bunk. He gripped the fish billy with his right hand, smacking its kill end into his left palm.

His eyes focused onto Laura's; he fed on the terror she radiated.

"You two-timing bitch, I'm going to beat the crap out of you!"

He stepped forward, the oak club cocked and ready.

The first swing whacked Laura's right forearm; she'd managed to lift her hands in defense.

Ken raised the club for another swing, but Laura initiated a preemptive strike of her own. She pulled her knees to her chest, and then thrust her legs outward. The heels of her stocking feet slammed into Ken's belly.

He reeled backward, crashing into a locker.

Laura sprang out of the bunk and rushed for the door. She almost made it through when Ken counterattacked. He lunged forward and his left hand snagged an ankle.

She smashed onto the deck.

CHAPTER 72

His head throbbed, the coppery bite of blood flooded his mouth, and his right eyebrow was swollen to twice its normal size. Nick Orlov lay facedown on the hardwood deck in Captain Miller's cabin. He smelled the polish. His hands, bound behind his back, were knotted to his ankles and cinched up into a hog-tie position. His joints screamed.

Voices broadcast somewhere to his left. He turned his head toward the closed cabin door. Its louvered vents still transmitted.

He concentrated on the male voice.

"What a crock, Laura. Do you think I'm gullible enough to believe a fairy tale like that?"

"But it's true."

Ken Newman towered over his wife. The fish billy remained in his right hand.

Laura cowered at the base of the galley table, her lower legs tucked under her buttocks and her bound wrists resting in her lap. Blood stained her blouse, spillage from a lip tear. Besides the deep ache inside the arm walloped by the billy, Laura's right knee throbbed; she'd slammed it on the deck when Ken tripped her. Her hands and outstrctched arms absorbed much of the impact, but not all.

Ken set the bludgeon on the table and grabbed a bottle of Redhook from the refrigerator. After removing the cap, he took a healthy swig and turned back toward Laura. "Who is this other jerk, the gimp?"

"His name is Yuri. He's the one who jumped overboard from the freighter."

"So how many times has he screwed you?"

"It's not like that!"

"Oh, sure. What was that little love nest down at the beach all about?"

My God, that must be her husband, thought Nick.

He knew bits and pieces of Laura's past; Yuri had told him about the beatings.

He strained to pick up Laura's voice.

"I rented the house—to get away from you!"

"Is that what your shyster lawyer told you to do—so she could serve the divorce papers on me?"

"Yes."

"So this Russian guy washes up on the beach and you take him in like a stray dog!"

"Not exactly."

"Well, be exact."

"He broke into the house, thinking it was vacant. He took me prisoner."

"Oh, come on, Laura, that's pure bullshit. I saw you with him."

"No, just wait. He was hurt and didn't know what to do. After he'd recovered some, he asked for my help—to defect."

"Why didn't you just call the cops?"

"That's what I wanted to do—call the FBI. He insisted on contacting the State Department. He wanted nothing to do with the FBI or the police. He thinks they're all thugs."

Orlov was dazzled with Laura's seamless mix of fact and fiction. If he weren't already part of the story-line, he'd believe her, too.

Ken said, "The Russian wants to defect to the good old U S of A, and the bozo hog-tied in the cabin is a CIA agent who is supposed to help him?"

"Yes, except he said he's with the State Department, but that might be just a cover—I'm not sure who he works for."

"I see," Ken said. He dropped his nuke. "So what's this stuff about chartering a plane to Finland?"

"What?"

"I heard you talking with your so-called State Department guy—back at that beach house."

"You were there?"

"That's right. I heard everything. You were talking about planning a charter flight from Vancouver to Finland. Now that doesn't fit very well with your defector bullshit, does it?

"Oh," he continued, "I almost forgot, what's the story about the sub?"

"Súka,"—bastard—mumbled Nick, now horrified at Ken Newman's disclosure about the *Neva.*

He strained to move his bound hands around the small of his back. Captain Miller's .45 wasn't there.

Nick worked at the bindings.

Laura stared at the deck, devastated by Ken's revelation. Near panic, she tried to recall what she and Nick had discussed: *Flying from Vancouver to Finland— Passports—the* Neva. *Oh no! What else?*

"Come on, Laura, no more BS. What are you really doing with these people up here?"

He leaned against one of the galley counters a couple of steps away, beer in hand.

"What do you want, Ken?"

"Just the truth, babe, just the truth."

"I can't tell you."

"Sure you can. But if you don't I'm sure there's a couple of guys up at the Point Roberts border station that would really like to have a little chat with you and your friend." He gestured toward Miller's stateroom and grinned. "He's not with the State Department—I heard him speaking Russian. He's from Russia!"

Laura bowed her head and closed her eyes.

"Come on, Laura, what's the real story here?" He took another swig.

She looked up. "I'll sign over half my stock—right

now, if you'll just get out of my life and forget about all of this."

Ken said, "I don't care about the damn stock. Now, what's really going on up here?"

Laura's trump card had failed. She turned away, devastated.

"Come on, Laura, fess up."

Desperate, she again faced her husband. "Ken, I'm preg—" But she stopped in mid word, instantly sensing it would be a horrible mistake to reveal her secret. Ken would never believe the child was his—it would be an excuse to beat her again.

"What was that?" he asked.

Laura changed tactics, now in pure survival mode. "I'm a Russian agent, Ken. I've been passing secrets from the company to Russia for a year."

"Wa—what?"

"I'm helping the Russians."

"You really are a Russian spy!"

"I work for them."

"They're paying you?"

"No, of course not. I volunteered."

Ken's eyes ballooned. *"You what?"*

"I can't stand our government. It's going to drag us into a war for sure. Russia needs all the help it can get, so I decided to . . ."

Laura delivered her punch line. "Ken. If you turn me in, the government will confiscate everything I own. That means all of the stock will go away. You'll get nothing."

CHAPTER 73

The *Neva* surfaced inside Canadian waters. Captain Borodin and his observation team climbed to the bridge atop the sail.

Borodin raised his night vision scope and peered northeastward. The beacon at Lighthouse Point, Point Roberts, flashed every quarter minute.

Borodin set his NVD aside and picked up the portable radio set. He keyed the microphone and began transmitting. The encrypted UHF signal had an effective range of about twenty kilometers—deliberately limited to minimize detection.

"Tiger, this is Lion. Come in, over." Borodin spoke in Russian, using the pre-arranged code names that he and Orlov had agreed on the previous night.

No response.

Borodin repeated the call.

No response again.

He waited thirty seconds and tried again, "Tiger, this is Lion, acknowledge, over."

* * *

"What the hell is that about?" Ken Newman said as he eyed the portable radio on the galley table. Orlov had set the Russian military radio on standby mode after checking the unit earlier. A tinny voice had just broadcast foreign call signs through its speaker.

"Don't answer it," warned Laura.

"Why not?"

"You say the wrong thing, and they'll come and kill us all."

"Is that your spymaster calling?"

"Worse—it's a detachment of Russian commandos. They're waiting offshore on a boat to rendezvous with us."

"Dammit, Laura! What are you mixed up in?"

"Walk away from this—you'll live. Keep poking around and you won't."

Borodin prepared to make another transmission when his radio speaker burst to life: "Whoever is out there jabbering on this channel, speak English."

"What's this?" Borodin muttered, baffled at the response.

The two portable radios and their encryption software were unique to each other; the chances of a third party picking up the initial transmission, decoding it, and resending on the same frequency were out of this world.

Borodin had limited English-speaking skills. "I talk with Orlov," he said. "Put on frequency, please."

"He's not available. You're going to have to deal with me."

Something's wrong here, Borodin thought. "Stand

by," he replied in English, and set the portable radio aside. He called the *Neva*'s electronic countermeasures officer over the main intercom: "Fyodor, I need a fix on the next transmission from the portable unit. Can you do it?"

"Affirmative, Captain. Give me thirty seconds to set up an intercept."

Borodin activated the portable radio. "Tiger, Lion. Who is speaking, please?"

"A concerned citizen. Now, who are you and what do you want?"

Borodin waited for his ECM officer. It took just ten seconds.

"Captain, the signal originates from the northeast—in line with Point Roberts."

Borodin activated the transmitter. "Put Orlov on frequency now!"

Twenty seconds passed and no response.

Borodin repeated the call.

Ken was about to respond when a voice from behind called out a warning: "Step away from that radio or I'll shoot you!"

Elena Krestyanova stood in the open aft doorway to the main cabin. She held a pistol with both hands, aiming at Ken's chest.

Ken dropped the microphone and raised his hands in stunned surrender.

"Where's Nicolai?" Elena demanded as she stepped farther into the cabin.

"Who?" Ken asked.

Laura answered, "He's in Captain Miller's cabin,

tied up." With her bound wrists, she pointed to the closed door ahead of Elena.

As Elena walked forward, Laura noticed that Ken was staring at the bulkhead to his left. Mounted to the wall just a step away was a red-handled fire ax with a wicked pick end and a fire extinguisher. *Oh no!*

Elena stood next to Miller's cabin door. With her left hand still gripping the Beretta, she released her right hand from the grip; the pistol remained targeted on Ken. She reached for the door. As soon as she turned the knob, Ken made his move.

With common sense and ordinary fear muted by alcohol, Ken yanked the twenty-pound fire extinguisher from its wall mount and hurled it at Elena. The steel cylinder smacked her rib cage under her extended left arm. The Beretta spilled onto the deck and she dropped to her knees.

As Elena scurried to retrieve her pistol, Ken fished for something inside his coat pocket. Laura watched horrified as he pulled out Miller's .45. Before Laura could yell, he pulled the trigger. The slug plowed into a mahogany deck plank six inches from Elena's left thigh. The report rang. The stink of gunpowder flooded the cabin.

Elena froze in place.

"All right, blondie," Ken said with the smoking Colt still pointed her way. "You just sit tight right there or I might have to punch a few holes in those lovely tits of yours."

Elena, on her knees, remained motionless.

The portable radio broadcast in English: "Tiger, Lion. Come in."

Ken faced Laura. "Tell your Russian buds that we're going off the air for a while."

Captain Borodin was about to repeat his call, when an English-speaking female voice broadcast from the speaker: "Lion, this is Tiger. We have a situation here. We'll get back to you later. Out."

What are they doing over there?

CHAPTER 74

Laura was in the galley, ordered by Ken to make him a sandwich. He and Elena were in the wheelhouse. Laura could have made a run for it, but Ken threatened to shoot both Elena and Nick if she bolted. Nick remained tied up in Miller's cabin and Ken had locked the door.

As plastered as Ken was, Laura heeded his warning—almost.

She knelt next to the cabin door and whispered through the louvered vents, "Nick, are you all right?"

"Get me a knife."

Ken, Laura, and Elena occupied the *Herc*'s wheelhouse. Elena sat on the deck cross-legged, her hands bound behind her back. Laura stood on Elena's right; she leaned against the chart table. Her wrists remained bound in front. That way she could function as Ken's gopher.

After wolfing down the ham and cheese and guzzling through another bottle, Ken reached for a fresh

Redhook. Half a dozen bobbed in an ice-filled container on the deck at his feet. Laura hauled it up the companionway stairs when the trio relocated to the bridge.

Nick was on his right side, his ankles and wrists lashed together at the base of his spine. He gripped the four-inch paring knife with his left hand. Unable to see, he'd already sliced his right wrist. Blood dripped onto the deck. He ignored the sting as he continued to attack the rope.

Ken sat on the edge of the captain's chair and rotated it so he could face the women. He held the .45 in his right hand; a fresh Redhook, his fifth, filled his left palm.

He took a swig and belched.

"All right, blondie"—his words slurred—"let's try this again. I want to know who you really are and what you're doing with my wife."

Elena stared at the deck. She offered nothing, not even her name.

Frustrated, Ken faced Laura. "Who is this bitch?"

"She works at the Russian Trade Mission in Vancouver."

"She KGB?"

"I don't know—probably, but they don't call it that anymore."

Ken took another gulp. "So what are you supposed to be doing—the three of you here on this boat?"

Laura did not respond.

"Laura, answer me—*Now!*"

"We're supposed to meet up with a ship that's coming into Vancouver tonight. Transfer some operatives off it and then bring them down to the Seattle area."

"Are these the commandos you were talking about?"

"Yes."

"So what are they up to?"

"I don't know, they didn't tell me. I just follow orders."

"What about the submarine they left here—where's it at?"

"It's gone."

"Gone where?"

"I don't know, back to the ocean I guess."

Ken teetered on the chair. "What are you doing? You give away software secrets and now you're helping Russians infiltrate our country."

"I'm in over my head, Ken. I can't get out. If you persist with this, you won't get out, either."

"Well, screw that. I'm going to put an end to this."

Ken turned and set the half-full beer bottle onto the nearby chart table. With his gun hand still aimed at the women, he fumbled with the controls to the VHF radio. Although his brain remained alcohol fogged, he knew that the Coast Guard monitored Channel 16.

"What are you doing?" Laura asked, alarmed.

"I'm going to have a little chat with the good old U S of A Coast Guard."

"No, don't do that!"

He ignored Laura as he flipped on the Power switch; the radio had been pre-set to Channel 16. He picked up the coiled microphone and leaned toward Elena. "You're going to rot in a prison for a million years."

Ken eyed Laura. "And you, you keep your mouth shut, and just maybe I can keep you out of the can. But it's going to cost you. You drop the divorce and sign over control of all your stock to me. If you don't, I'll turn you in and then you'll join your two Russki friends in Leavenworth."

Ken keyed the mike. "Calling U.S. Coast Guard, calling U.S. Coast Guard, over."

The reply was immediate. "Channel sixteen traffic, this is Coast Guard Group Port Angeles, identify yourself."

Ken again activated the microphone. "Never mind that. You just need to know that something's going down in the Strait of Georgia, offshore of Point Roberts. There's some Russian spies that are coming in tonight on a ship plus there's a sub running around somewhere up here, too. You should send—"

Ken never finished. Electrical power to the *Hercules* clicked off in an eye blink. The wheelhouse blacked out and the VHF radio died.

"What the hell?" Ken bellowed. Residual illumination from a pole-mounted pier light allowed him to see Laura's and Elena's faces.

"We were on shore power—the dock breaker must have tripped," Laura offered.

Ken noted that the marina's dock lights remained lit. "So how do you turn the lights back on in this thing?"

"I'll have to start the generator; it's in the engine room."

"Get going."

"I'll need a flashlight. There's one up here some-place."

Laura was opening a nearby drawer when a shadowy form charged from the companionway.

Nick crashed into Ken, knocking him to the deck.

CHAPTER 75

The workboat exited the marina and ran on a south-westerly course at ten knots. With the running lights just extinguished and the AIS switched off at the dock, only radar could track the vessel as it faded into the dark.

Laura had the helm; Nick stood at her side. Elena was below in the galley making sandwiches.

Ken Newman occupied the deck inside Captain Miller's cabin, still drunk and banged up from Nick's sneak attack. Nick took pleasure in cinching up the rope.

"How long do you think it will take to get there?" Nick asked.

"About an hour."

"Good."

Laura leaned to her right to check the radar display. She noted the faint return a couple miles offshore of an island inside Canadian waters. The track line matched the heading of the *Hercules*.

Nick stepped up the radar unit. "Still there?"

"Yep."

* * *

The six-man detail descended into the torpedo room. Clad in coveralls with wet suits underneath, each man wore a full-face fire response respirator and lugged a portable air tank on his back. They also carried half a dozen plastic body bags.

After assembling on the partially flooded upper deck, the men surveyed the carnage. Three intact corpses along with a horrific blend of scorched body parts bobbed in the waist-deep water.

"Okay, guys," the leader shouted through his face mask, "you know what needs to be done, so let's do it."

In silence, the men set about the grizzly task. They collected the remains of their submates with reverence, placing them inside the bags.

Laura guided the *Hercules* alongside the *Neva*'s starboard hull. The workboat's three-foot-diameter rubber fenders cushioned the impact. She cut the power and walked onto the port bridge wing.

Standing below on the side deck at amidships, Nick tossed the spring line to one of the sailors standing on the *Neva*'s deck. The crewman secured the line to a retractable cleat on the sub's outer skin.

Nick scurried forward and repeated the same arrangement with the bowline.

As Nick headed aft to secure the stern line, Laura finally noticed the heavyset man standing on top of the *Neva*'s sail. He wore a gray sea coat, and an officer's cap covered his head.

At eye level with Laura and just thirty feet away, he raised his right hand to his brow and saluted.

Laura waved back in response.

Captain Borodin watched as the woman stepped back into the pilothouse. *Thank you, kind lady, whoever you are.*

He had yet to speak directly with anyone aboard the *Hercules*, but already his crew busied themselves with preparing to transfer its cargo. The man who had just handled the mooring lines assisted them.

Borodin noted the three portable pumps with their coils of suction and discharge hoses laid out on the aft deck. Also stored nearby were four plastic five-gallon containers that he assumed contained gasoline. But what peaked Borodin's interest the most was the portable welder. A heavy-duty unit, it was exactly what they needed. Because of its bulk, the welder would have been a struggle to haul aboard by hand. However, the workboat's deck-mounted crane could handle it.

Captain Borodin looked away from the *Hercules*, peering westward. Thankfully, the sea remained calm and the skies were clear. He could see lights on the nearest shore—Mayne Island, one of the hundreds that made up Canada's Gulf Island archipelago.

Behind and above Borodin's perch, he heard the muted whine of the dual search radars as they probed the darkness. Other than a freighter steaming southward in the main shipping lanes four miles to the east, the *Neva* and *Hercules* remained alone in this section of the Southern Strait of Georgia.

So far, so good.

* * *

Laura and Elena stepped out of the cabin onto the workboat's main deck. Nick sat at the control station for the crane. He lifted one of the gas-powered pumps and transferred it to the *Neva*.

Elena said, "This is surreal; I still can't believe we're doing this."

"No kidding," Laura said as she watched the Russian sailors guide the pump onto the deck of the submarine.

"Chief, how long?" asked Captain Borodin. It was a quarter to midnight. He stood on the *Neva*'s outer skin next to the forward escape trunk. The head and shoulders of a chief petty officer projected from the hatch opening.

"We should be complete in half an hour."

"How's the patch holding?"

"Ivan did a superb job. We'll need to run some live tests but I think it'll hold just fine."

"And the flooding?"

"We should have it pumped out soon."

"That's good news, Chief. Well done."

"Thanks, sir. I better get below."

"Go ahead."

Captain Borodin watched as the sailor descended into the torpedo room. He looked back across the deck toward the sail. The pumps and welder covered the foredeck. The drone of multiple gas-powered engines filled the otherwise tranquil night.

Borodin took one last look downward into the open hatchway, holding his nose. An awful concoction of electric arc exhaust gases, chlorine, and putrid flesh flowed out of the opening. Portable lighting inside revealed the metal grating of the torpedo room's upper level.

What a hellhole.

After storing the body bags inside an empty and dry upper level torpedo tube and installing a pumped fresh air hose system, the six-man detail continued its work. Their first order of business called for temporarily plugging tube five. The detail used an inflatable life raft, stuffing it inside the open breach and then triggering the compressed air bottle.

The next phase involved dewatering Compartment One. The repair team employed the portable pumps transferred from the *Hercules*. With a combined capacity of nearly two hundred gallons per minute, the two rental pumps and the *Herc*'s emergency unit expeditiously drew down the water level in the torpedo room. The *Neva*'s bow gained over six feet of freeboard after pumping, leaving tube five almost dry. The temporary plug dammed off most of the flow, but seawater still trickled through the tube into the compartment.

Although the two-hundred-pound steel breach door was blown off its hinges during the accident, the repair team manhandled it back onto torpedo tube five. A wet-suited welder spent over an hour welding the entire circumference of the door onto the rim of the tube and its deformed locking ring.

Diagonal steel braces welded to the breach door and to the deck and overhead reinforced the plug. Captain

Borodin instructed the crew chief to make certain that door would not blow off under one hundred meters of seawater.

With the torpedo room no longer open to the sea, the crew began pumping out the remainder of Compartment One. When the water reached the lowest level of the torpedo storage space, the men again donned their emergency breathing apparatus. Borodin wasn't sure what would happen when the main battery compartment was dewatered.

The worry was a release of chlorine gas—deadly stuff for sure. Fortunately, nothing dire happened when the batteries were exposed, just whiffs of the gas—like at a public swimming pool.

Captain Borodin turned from the hatch and walked back to the sail.

He thought of the weld.

God, please make it hold.

CHAPTER 76

Laura and Nick arrived in the *Neva*'s central command post at half past midnight. Elena remained aboard the *Hercules*, guarding Ken.

The control room's tight quarters bewildered Laura. The compartment overflowed with mechanical equipment, electrical gear, and electronic consoles. The men stared at her.

Laura was positive that she looked ghastly: wrinkled blouse, no makeup, and her hair limp and stringy. But maybe it was the dark color of her skin.

The senior warrant officer stood. He smiled and in practiced English said, "Miss Laura, Captain Borodin tell us you help Yuri save *Neva*." His posture stiffened. "On behalf of crew, thank you for our lives." He barked an order in Russian. The central post staffers stood up, snapped to attention, and in unison saluted Laura.

She almost cried.

Captain Borodin escorted Laura and Nick to his compact cabin. Sitting on the edge of the bunk, Laura listened as Orlov and Borodin conversed in their native tongue. More annoyingly, she'd yet to speak with Yuri.

"So far, our radars haven't picked up any threat," offered Borodin. He sat behind his desk. A Canadian chart of the Strait of Georgia covered its surface.

"That's encouraging," Nick said. "Maybe they think it was a hoax." He occupied the lone guest chair.

"Let's hope so. We need a break for once."

"Yes, we certainly do."

Nick and Borodin remained leery of Ken Newman's aborted warning to the U.S. Coast Guard—hoping they really had evaded catastrophe. If Nick hadn't shut down the *Hercules*'s power, Newman could have stirred up the proverbial hornets' nest: sub tracking and electronic attack aircraft from NAS Whidbey plus more Canadian air assets from CFB Comox. Borodin employed the *Neva*'s electronic sensors to sniff out any hint of increased air or sea surveillance in the Southern Strait of Georgia. English-speaking crew monitored all U.S. and Canadian Coast Guard and military frequencies. At the first sign of trouble, the boat would submerge.

"Will the repairs allow you to head north now?" asked Nick as he shifted position in the chair.

"They should make a huge difference. But first we'll need to test the patch on the torpedo tube to make sure it'll hold."

"How will you do that?"

"Take the boat down in stages—twenty meters at a time. I need a hundred meters capability for operational purposes."

"Then we head up to that underwater explosives

dump area?" Nick said, pointing to a chart on Borodin's desk.

"Yes, we'll follow submerged, tracking the workboat's propeller."

"The underwater racket it makes?" Nick said.

"That's right, but you'll need to keep your speed down. Five knots max. At that rate we should be able to control the *Neva* without too much trouble."

"When do you plan to get under way?"

"We should have everything wrapped up in a couple of hours."

"Good, that should work." Nick turned toward Laura. "Captain, can you please arrange for Laura to speak with Yuri?"

"Of course."

Laura sat at a vacant console near the aft end of the central post. Assorted gauges and displays, all with Cyrillic markings, made up the bulk of the instrument panel. The built-in vertical computer monitor mounted above the console base displayed a gray screen.

Laura wore a headset with a voice-activated lip mike. Yuri remained in Compartment Six, still sealed up inside the escape trunk. For the last few minutes, they caught up.

When Yuri first spoke, his cartoon accent startled Laura. He remained on helium.

"How's your leg?" Laura asked.

"About the same."

Even with his squeaky voice, Laura noticed something upsetting but she'd held off until now.

"You're coughing a lot. What's wrong?"

"I'm a bit parched."

"Are you ill?"

"No, I just need some water."

"Why don't you have water?"

"There's no way to open up the trunk until decompression is complete."

"How long will that be?"

"About a day and a half to go."

"Another day and a half—without water—and you've already been in there a day. That's awful. There has to be a way to get water inside that chamber."

"It's okay. I'll be fine."

"But you'll become seriously dehydrated—especially when you start breathing pure oxygen, and that's not okay."

"I can make it."

"Tell me how that escape trunk is constructed."

Knowing Laura would not drop the subject, Yuri described the basic layout. Laura asked, "Those gas supply lines, you have both air and oxygen, is that right?"

"Yes, plus diluent—a blend of oxygen and helium."

"But right now you're just using one line, right?"

"Yes, the diluent. Just what do you have in mind?"

CHAPTER 77

"What's the schedule?" Elena asked.
"They're going to make the first test dive in half an hour."

Nick and Elena sat at the mess table in the galley.

"When's she coming back?" Elena inquired.

"Soon. Captain Borodin said he'd make sure she departs before they submerge."

"What's she doing?"

"Trying to get freshwater to Kirov. He's still locked up inside the escape chamber."

Elena processed the news. "They have to be lovers."

"I guess, but who knows? They're both a bit odd if you ask me."

"The odd couple—yes, I do agree with that."

She broached a subject that both had avoided until now.

"How do you want to take care of them?"

"What do you mean?"

Elena removed a newspaper from the tabletop, exposing the Beretta.

Nick cringed. "We can't do that."

"They're security risks."

"Her husband—yes, I agree. But not Laura."

"She knows too much—the chief said she has to go."

"She's off limits, Elena."

"It's a mistake."

"I don't care. She walks—you got that?"

Elena said, "All right, we'll do it your way. But she'll be here soon. How do we get rid of him with her aboard? Even though she's divorcing him, she'll never stand for that."

"I'll take care of it—you just back me up."

The left side of Ken Newman's head throbbed. He couldn't remember much of the evening. He'd been talking with the Coast Guard and then nothing. Hogtied and dumped onto the deck in Captain Miller's cabin, Ken had unwillingly exchanged positions with Nick Orlov but with a twist. The rank sock stuffed in his mouth and secured with duct tape would gag a rat.

"Yuri, we're ready to try it now. Are you set?"

"Yes, go ahead."

Laura turned to the sailor at her side and motioned with her right wrist. They both stood at the base of the aft escape trunk in Compartment Six.

The rating turned the valve handle mounted on top of a compressed air tank. The valve connected to a high-pressure rubber hose coiled in multiple loops at the base of the tank. The opposite end of the approximate one-inch-diameter hose snaked up the side of the escape trunk ladder and ran along the exterior surface of the trunk, where it terminated at another valve. The ball valve connected to a pipe stub that penetrated the chamber's steel sidewall. The stub coupled with another valve inside the chamber.

Laura heard a hiss as air surged into the hose. The hose stiffened under the strain.

Laura pressed the intercom mike. "Yuri, the line is charged. Try the valve now."

"Okay."

Yuri kneeled next to the compressed air port. He held one of his rubber boots in his right hand. He cut it away from the ankle of his dive suit. He poised the boot opening next to the valve discharge and cranked the handle with his left hand.

Nothing.

He turned the valve farther and compressed air bled into the chamber. He turned it again; more hissing followed by a gurgling for just a second or two. Water spurted from the valve opening and flowed into the boot.

Yuri couldn't wait. He dropped to his knees and slurped like a dog.

"Captain, I'm picking up military air communications now," said the technician sitting at the central post's communications console.

"From where?" asked Captain Borodin.

"From the Whidbey Island naval base—two aircraft. They've just gone airborne."

"Orions?"

"Unknown. I heard the controller clear a flight of two for a runway launch."

"Training mission, patrol, what?"

"Unknown, sir. They're climbing to altitude. The controller vectored them on a northerly heading. Radar should pick 'em up soon if they're coming our way."

Borodin grabbed a microphone from the overhead and activated the Talk switch. "Bridge, command."

"Command, bridge," replied the watch officer from the observation well on top of the sail.

"Sasha, the Americans may be sending aircraft. Get the deck crew below, close the forward hatch, and clear the bridge for immediate dive."

"What about the equipment on deck?"

"Isn't it clear yet?"

"There's one pump left plus hoses. Everything else has been transferred to the workboat."

"Dump it all overboard—but be careful. I don't want that *govnó* banging into my hull."

"I understand, sir."

"Release the moorings to the workboat and radio Orlov that he should head north according to the plan."

"What about that woman? She's still aboard, isn't she?"

"Chyort!"

Borodin forgot about Yuri's accomplice in Compartment Six.

A radar watcher at a nearby console called out, "Captain, I'm picking up something."

Like most submarines, the *Neva* was equipped with surface search radar. Because it conducted espionage operations, it also had been fitted with aircraft search radar.

The air watch technician continued, "I'm tracking a pair of possible hostiles on a heading of three five five degrees, four hundred knots, sixty-three kilometers out."

Borodin keyed the microphone. "Bridge, stand by." He turned to face the radar tech. "What's the projected course?"

"Straight for Point Roberts!"

"Chërt voz'mi!"

The *Hercules* plodded northward at four knots on autopilot. Nick Orlov and Elena Krestyanova stood outside the wheelhouse on the starboard bridge wing. Ken remained locked up below.

Nick and Elena peered eastward into the pre-dawn sky, tracking the running lights of two jet aircraft patrolling offshore of Point Roberts.

Although miles away, the deep-throated roar of the low-flying EA-18G Growlers resonated across the waterway with the intensity of a summer thunderstorm.

"They're sure noisy," commented Elena.

"Yeah," agreed Nick as he peered through binoculars.

"What do you think they're doing?"

"Waking up everyone on Point Roberts—that's for sure."

Elena laughed and asked, "Can you see anything?"

"Just the nav lights."

"That must be why the *Neva* submerged so quickly."

"No doubt."

Orlov had been astounded at how rapidly the *Neva* submerged. He'd received an abrupt radio message ordering him to retrieve the fenders and mooring lines, and head northward—nothing more.

Several minutes after the *Neva* disappeared, the electronic attack jets from NAS Whidbey roared across the Southern Strait of Georgia at a thousand feet.

"Do you think they spotted it?" Elena asked.

"I don't think so. Otherwise they'd be all over us."

"Yeah."

Elena watched the distant flashing lights. "It must have been Newman's radio call."

"Probably."

Like a shark tracking its prey, the *Neva* followed two hundred meters behind the *Hercules*. It cruised silently some seventy meters below the sea surface.

Captain Borodin plopped into his leather-lined chair in the central command post. He retrieved his mug from the gimbaled holder. While he sipped the lukewarm tea, he glanced at an overhead computer monitor displaying the *Neva*'s position on a digital chart.

Borodin expected a cascade of calamities: leaks, erratic helm and depth control, and a deaf sonar system. But so far, the repairs held.

The welded breach door on tube five remained watertight. And although 60 percent of the passive sonar sensors had died, the remaining hydrophones heard just fine now that the hull was off the bottom.

Borodin settled farther into the chair. He returned the mug to its holder. Although thankful that the starboard reactor continued to function without a glitch, he still worried.

Should the reactor falter from the fouled seawater cooling system, the *Neva* would not be able to maintain powered flight for long. The backup batteries would provide about an hour of propulsion. But when they petered out, Captain Borodin would be faced with the ultimate dilemma—should that event transpire during daylight hours. Surfacing deep inside hostile waters to transfer the crew to the *Hercules* would place the *Neva* on full view to whoever might be nearby.

Alternatively, Borodin could allow the *Neva* to settle back onto the seabed in shallow water and wait for nightfall. The ballast tanks would then be charged with compressed air from the full storage flasks and the submarine would pop to the surface—maybe.

Captain Borodin planned for both prospects, knowing that each was fraught with its own unique set of hazards.

He considered Yuri. What would happen to his friend—the *Neva*'s redeemer—if the crew were forced to abandon ship before he completed his decompression?

Borodin closed his eyes, not by choice but by need. In just five minutes, he was snoring.

CHAPTER 78

The *Hercules* crept northward for several hours, the autopilot in command. The tedious drone of the diesel seeped through the deck boards, numbing Ken Newman.

The cabin remained blacked out when the pair entered. Lying facedown, all Ken could see in the diffuse light were shoes—a pair of men's sneakers and sleek women's running shoes.

Ken was now up and moving. The two Russians herded him aft through the main cabin.

His wrists remained bound behind his back, the sock still crammed inside his mouth. And they'd just blindfolded him. The male gripped Ken's left bicep. The female followed; perfume marked her.

Neither of his captors spoke.

Outside on the main deck, the night air chilled Ken. They steered him to an exterior stairway adjacent to the portside cabin superstructure, where the male ordered him to step up.

Ken stood on a grated metal landing, still sightless.

The male released his grip and stepped away. The female's scent told him she remained nearby.

Now what?

Ken heard a metallic scraping sound behind his back.

What's that?

He felt something at his feet.

Horror struck in a lightning flash.

No, this can't be happening!

Ken raised his right foot and blasted it backward.

Nick squatted behind Ken to lash a line from the anchor chain to Ken's ankles, when the boot heel slammed into his crotch. The jolt to his testicles sent him reeling.

Ken rushed blindly forward, homing in on the scent. He pinned Elena against a bulkhead and head-butted her, inflicting a nasty whack to her forehead.

The blow partially dislodged Ken's blindfold, allowing a quick look with his right eye. Elena collapsed to her hands and knees. Nick lay on his side groaning.

Ken looked for something to sever his bindings.

Shit!

He ran into the cabin.

Elena got back on her feet; blood dribbled from a tear to her left brow. She eyed Nick. Still on his right side, he had pulled his legs into the fetal position.

He's useless!

Elena reached into her coat pocket and pulled out the suppressed Beretta.

In the galley, with his hands still bound behind his back, Ken grabbed the carving knife from a countertop receptacle. He shoved his spine against the mess table and sawed the rope. Finally, the rope parted. Ken reached up, pulled down the rest of the blindfold, and then yanked out the gag.

A nine-millimeter round passed an inch from his head; it splattered into a locker door. Ken dove to the deck as another bullet followed. As he slithered around a corner, he caught a glimpse of the blonde advancing across the cabin. He scrambled into the companionway and charged up the stairs to the pilothouse.

Elena entered the companionway and looked upward. Amber radiance from wheelhouse lighting diffused into the passage.

Ken surveyed the wheelhouse, searching for anything to use as a weapon.

Shit!

He heard the telltale creaking of deck boards as the executioner crept up the stairs.

With no options left, Ken grabbed a pair of lifejackets from a nearby rack. He rushed through the doorway of the starboard bridge wing and leaped overboard.

CHAPTER 79

"You sound better," Laura said. She sat at the escape trunk's control panel, watching Yuri. A closed circuit television camera inside the chamber broadcast his image to a monitor.

"I feel much better now . . . how did you think of that?"

"Piece of cake."

"What?"

"Sorry. It was easy. I just used differential pressure to push water into the chamber."

"No one else thought of that. You're a genius."

Although just over an inch of steel separated them, they were a world apart. His body remained highly pressurized.

"Would you like more water? I'll recharge the hose again."

"I'm good."

Yuri stored the last discharge in the rubber booties he'd cut from his dry suit, both cradled in his crotch. He sat cross-legged next to the hatch.

He still used the face mask to breath heliox, removing it only to use the intercom. Once he dropped below the equivalent pressure of fifty feet of seawater, he'd switch to pure oxygen.

The real danger, however, resided in the escape trunk's carbon dioxide–rich environment. Without an efficient way to flush out his exhaled breath, other than partial releases during stage changes, the CO_2 had risen to a lethal level. As long as Yuri remembered not to inhale too deeply when using the intercom, he'd be okay.

"How much decompression time do you have left?" Laura asked.

Yuri checked his dive computer, removed the mask, and depressed the intercom switch. "About thirty hours."

"And then what?"

"I must stay with the crew to help make sure they return home safely."

"But I don't want you to leave."

"I know. We'll find a way—somehow."

Laura left the control panel and was directed to Yuri's bunk, in need of a nap. Unlike the other built-in accommodations aboard the submarine, Yuri and Viktor's quarters were an afterthought. Instead of vertical stacked bunks, the sides of both freestanding beds butted against the pressure casing. Sound-absorbing insulation with a fiberglass coversheet isolated the beds from direct contact with the inner hull's steel ribs and plates. That section of the casing was cut open to install the recompression chamber and then welded shut.

A metal locker separated the two beds. It had two hinged doors, one on top of the other. Laura couldn't resist investigating. She opened the top unit first. Taped to the inside of the locker door was a color photograph of a cute twenty-something redhead holding a toddler in her arms.

Her heart sank. *He has a family!*

Laura raced through the locker's contents. It contained assorted clothing, including a military uniform, two pairs of shoes, one pair of polished leather boots, and an electric shaver along with other toiletry items. Finally, at the base of the locker, she found a cardboard box filled with photos of Viktor Skirski and his family.

Yuri's half of the locker contained similar items as Viktor's but no photographs of loved ones on the door. Laura did find a leather packet containing official documents with a photo of Yuri in uniform, part of his credentials as a Russian Naval officer. That's when Laura discovered he was two years younger than she was.

The only obvious personal item was a leather-bound Bible in Russian. Stored inside the back cover she came across a faded black-and-white photograph of a young couple in full wedding apparel—the groom in a Soviet Army uniform, standing arm-in-arm at a garden setting.

Yuri's parents, she'd guessed.

Behind the wedding photo, Laura discovered a color snapshot of sixteen-year-old Yuri and a distinguished elderly man. They sat in the cockpit of a small sailboat, both grinning.

The only family Yuri ever mentioned was his grandfather, Semyon.

Laura returned to the bed and lay on her side, nauseous again; it came in boiling waves radiating upward from her belly. She placed a wastebasket next to the bunk, just in case.

She wanted to tell Yuri about the pregnancy but decided to wait. Right now, it would just complicate matters.

Laura shifted her head, burrowing into the pillow. She turned a bit more and sniffed the pillowcase, savoring Yuri's scent. She smiled and shut her eyes.

Stay awake! Ken Newman ordered himself as he fought to remain conscious.

He would have drowned by now without the lifejackets, and his dormant U.S. Navy training.

After he jumped overboard, the ebbing tide carried him southward while the *Hercules* continued to motor north. He watched in alarm as his would-be killers turned the workboat around and backtracked. It took them several more minutes to figure out how to operate the spotlight. They gave up thirty minutes later.

Don't fall asleep! Ken commanded while pumping his inert legs. For over two hours, he had tracked diagonally with the current. The nearest shore was somewhere to the west.

As he had done during BUD/S Hell Week, Ken struggled to keep his eyes open, not wanting to fail yet again. But his senses were numbed. The chilled seawater had transcended into a gentle caress, lulling him into a stupor—hypothermia's delicious delusion. Falling asleep would end his life.

His eyelids fluttered before rolling shut. His head slumped to the side. Supported by two bulky lifejackets, his immobile body now hung vertically as it drifted with the current.

A dagger-like pain exploded in Ken's right shin-bone. It instantly woke him. Another searing flash erupted from his left knee.

What's happening?

Still buoyed by the lifejackets, he reached into the predawn blackness probing with both hands.

Rocks!

CHAPTER 80

The leak started with a trickle. The background racket from the engine and turbo generator masked the tiny hiss. Six minutes later, the pinhole fissure in the hatch seal eroded exponentially. The high-pitched screech jolted Yuri awake.

He checked the pressure gauge: the escape trunk was losing pressure at a prodigious rate. He'd just passed his next decompression stage change—two hours ahead of schedule.

Yuri kneeled over the lower hatch. The residual ring of bloodstained seawater encircling the hatch had disappeared. He cranked on the hatch-locking mechanism, hoping to squeeze the rubber gasket farther. But the outflow continued unabated. The seal had been scheduled for replacement during the *Neva*'s last inspection, but that task along with countless other maintenance work had been canceled due to the submarine's pending retirement.

Yuri activated the intercom mike. "There's a leak in here. Add more pressure!"

He repeated his call twice but received no response.

The conscript assigned to monitor Yuri was taking an unauthorized break in an adjacent compartment.

Yuri used his dive knife to cut away one of the lead weights from his dry suit. He slammed it against the escape trunk's steel casing.

Clang! Clang! Clang!

"Kakógo chërta!"—What the hell—roared Captain Borodin.

The CCP watch officer responded, "Sir, it's coming from aft."

Clang! Clang! Clang!

Borodin grabbed a microphone to call the sonar room, when a female voice speaking English blasted from an overhead speaker, "We need help back here. Yuri's going to die if we don't do something now!"

It took Captain Borodin seventy-two seconds to reach Compartment Six. He stood at the base of the escape trunk, his heart galloping. Laura handed him the microphone. A cluster of crew, including the derelict sailor, milled about at the base of the trunk, unsure what to do.

Borodin activated the mike. "Yuri, what's going on?" He spoke in Russian.

"The seal on the hatch is blown. It's venting."

"Stand by, I'm going to check it out."

Borodin handed the intercom mike back to Laura and clambered up a ladder to the base of the hatch. He grabbed the lower locking wheel with both hands and applied everything he had. The wheel rotated a few degrees. No change. High-pressure air continued to vent.

He dropped back down and faced the conscript assigned to watch Kirov: "How long ago did this happen?"

The young man stared at the deck in shame.

Borodin reached for the microphone. "Yuri. We can try adding pressure to the trunk, but that leak isn't going away."

"I don't have a choice, do I?"

"No, I'm afraid not. What's your pressure?"

"I'm down to two point one bars."

"You feel anything yet?"

"No."

"That's good." Borodin's forehead wrinkled. "What pressure were you at when this started?"

"About four bars."

"Okay, start venting the trunk. We'll get the chamber prepped for you."

"Stephan, I want you to do it!"

"Don't worry, I'm not going anywhere."

On his knees, Yuri unlocked and pulled open the inner hatch. Captain Borodin looked up from below; Laura stood at his side, her face lined in worry.

"Come on, Yuri!" commanded Borodin. "The chamber's ready."

Yuri made it down the ladder before he collapsed, his injured left leg buckling. As Borodin and two sailors lifted Yuri, his head spun. He vomited.

CHAPTER 81

"Is he going to be okay?" asked Laura as she huddled with Captain Borodin next to the recompression chamber. She could see Yuri through a viewport.

He lay on a mattress on his left side with eyes closed; sweat pooled on his forehead. The *Neva*'s medic knelt next to Yuri, taking his blood pressure.

"Yuri okay," Borodin replied with his limited English. "I think we get him recompressed in time."

It had been a chancy six minutes in all—the time it took to pick Yuri up from the deck, manhandle his near deadweight bulk through the narrow hatch of the recompression chamber, seal the hatch, and then charge the chamber with compressed air. During that entire process, the medic remained at Yuri's side, to keep him from aspirating vomit.

The three minutes that elapsed from closing the chamber hatch to pressurization were an agony for Laura. Yuri shrieked as the expanding helium bubbles circulating in his bloodstream and tissues wreaked havoc. The mini-mines targeted his joints.

Once the chamber reached four atmospheres—equivalent to about one hundred feet of seawater—the attacks subsided. Exhausted, Yuri lost consciousness.

"How long will he have to stay in there?" Laura asked Borodin.

The captain picked up a clipboard and consulted a Deep Blowup nomogram. He ran his finger across the chart. "Yuri has about fifty-six hours ahead of him in chamber."

"But he'd already spent over thirty hours in decompression."

"When hatch seal fail, we must throw out original schedule. Yuri start over."

Laura said, "Can I go inside and help? I've had first aid training." She'd already observed how the chamber's airlock worked, allowing the transfer of personnel and supplies into and out of the chamber.

"Maybe later. Yuri in good hands." He gestured to the porthole and the medic inside. "Dimitry know how to care."

An overhead speaker blared out a message in Russian.

Borodin retrieved a nearby intercom mike and exchanged words with the caller.

Laura watched as Borodin's brow wrinkled and the inflection of his voice altered.

He hung up the microphone. "I return to command center. Stay here, please."

He sprinted up a stairwell.

"What's it doing?" asked Elena.

"It's still hovering. But it just dropped something into the water. I can see a cable hanging down." Nick stood next to Elena with a pair of binoculars held to his eyes.

They were in the *Herc*'s wheelhouse; it was late morning. The workboat lumbered northward six miles from shore; it just passed Nanaimo, one of Vancouver Island's largest cities.

The Canadian military helicopter hovered just above the water surface about half a mile west of the *Hercules*.

"What do you think they're doing?"

"I have no idea."

Although Nick did not recognize the threat, the *Neva*'s chief sonar operator did. He called the captain.

"Where is it now?" asked Captain Borodin. He stood next to the senior technician, out of breath from his dash from the recompression chamber. The boat was at ultra quiet mode with the power to the propeller cut. The *Neva* drifted ninety meters below the surface. Four hundred meters ahead, the *Hercules* pulled away.

"Still a kilometer out, Captain." The sonar operator concentrated on the tones broadcasting from his headphones. He also studied the graphical display on his console. "Still no pinging. They must be listening."

The heavy beat of rotors on the sea surface altered the *Neva*'s sonar tech to the helicopter's presence. The technician also heard the splash of the helo's dipping sensor unit when it entered the water.

It was unlikely the helicopter's passive sonar would hear the *Neva*'s minuscule sound output. On the other hand, should the sonar unit's active mode be triggered, all bets would be off.

"Captain, he's retracted the probe and is moving off."

Borodin sighed but his blood pressure continued to spike. The *Neva* had become prey.

Another helicopter patrolled the Strait of Georgia thirty kilometers farther south, near the City of Vancouver. Configured for antisubmarine warfare, both rotor aircraft operated from a Canadian Forces Base at Comox on Vancouver Island.

A cutting edge U.S. Navy P-8A Poseidon antisubmarine jet from NAS Whidbey also prowled the southern end of the Strait of Georgia. Two additional patrol craft, soon to be mothballed propeller-driven P-3C Orions, traversed the Strait of Juan de Fuca from Whidbey Island to the Pacific Ocean.

It took several hours for the impact of Ken Newman's aborted radio call to make its way up the military chain of command. A staff analyst on watch at the National Military Command Center in the Pentagon took the call. The Navy lieutenant commander had already read the sighting report of the *Barrakuda*. It didn't take her long to piece together the possibility. She reported her findings to the officer in charge of the NMCC, suggesting that the rogue sub had not returned to the Pacific after all. The U.S. Army major general concurred.

Ordered to investigate, NAS Whidbey dispatched a pair of EA-18G Growlers to Point Roberts, but the jets reported nothing suspicious. Later in the morning, antisubmarine warfare patrol aircraft from NAS Whidbey started patrolling the Strait of Juan de Fuca and the

Southern Strait of Georgia. About the same time, Canadian forces began to deploy.

To defuse public reaction to the flurry of military activity, NAS Whidbey prepared a press release announcing a joint U.S. and Canadian naval training exercise and then e-mailed it to local media outlets throughout western Washington and southern British Columbia.

To protect killer whales that also hunted in the same waters, the allied forces had orders to limit the use of active sonar. High-powered sonar pulses could only be used after a suspected target was identified by passive measures.

Unaware of the *Neva*'s resurrection, the FSB team continued to survey the Southern Strait of Georgia. This afternoon they worked the southern approaches to the passage, north of Sucia Island. With no further contact from their local coordinator—Elena Krestyanova—or any sign of the *Hercules*, Captain Dubova carried out her orders. But everything was about to change.

The Russian special operators watched the P-8A Poseidon eject another cylinder from its belly. A tiny parachute deployed, retarding its descent. It splashed into the water.

Lieutenant Karpekov turned to face his boss. "That's the third one so far. I don't think it's on a training mission."

"They're obviously looking for something," Captain Dubova replied.

"Maybe they know about the *Neva*."

"Maybe."

Based on the Boeing 737 airframe, the brand-new U.S. Navy patrol plane dropped sonobuoys throughout Dubova's search area. Designed to detect sounds generated from submerged submarines with passive sonar, the sonobuoys radioed their findings back to the P-8A for analysis. The stinger at the tail end of the aircraft also housed sensitive magnetic anomaly detection equipment. The MAD gear could sniff out ferrous-based hulls under hundreds of feet of seawater.

Captain Dubova and her assistant watched as the jet climbed in the distance and took another wide turn to the right.

"Looks like it's getting ready for another run," commented Karpekov.

Dubova agreed. The Poseidon was about to commence a new survey track that would be even closer to their current position.

"We're done here, Grigori. Reel in the fish."

"We heading back to Bellingham?"

"Yes, we need to get out of here before we attract interest."

"Yes, ma'am."

Dubova's orders were explicit: Avoid detection at all cost.

CHAPTER 82

The *Neva* surfaced. Only the sail and the upper half of the rudder assembly protruded above the water.

Although the sun had set twenty minutes earlier, the partial surfaced condition represented a precautionary measure. The reduced radar cross-section disguised the hull's true length.

The ESM mast detected three distant radars, each probing the tranquil waters north of Vancouver. It also picked up several encrypted military radio frequencies.

Captain Borodin stood in the bridge well on top of the sail. The usual compliment of watch-standers occupied their stations. The *Hercules* drifted about a hundred meters off the starboard bow, its silhouette barely visible.

Borodin held the microphone to the portable radio set. The twin remained aboard the *Hercules*. He triggered the Transmit switch. "I know this is supposed to be a secure circuit but just the same, I'd like you to come to me. I can't leave for obvious reasons."

"All right, Captain," Nick Orlov replied, "send your raft over."

* * *

Orlov and Borodin were alone in Captain Tomich's cabin. Borodin summarized Yuri Kirov's predicament.

"Fifty more hours!" Nick exclaimed, flustered. "I don't know if we can wait that long."

"We have no choice. Yuri will die if we deviate from the new decompression schedule. It may even take longer than planned."

"We'll just have to wait and then make the transfer."

"I'm not comfortable waiting here that long."

"Why?"

"The Americans and Canadians are obviously looking for us. We've been lucky so far. I don't want to push it."

Nick's brow wrinkled. "What are you getting at?"

"It's time for us to leave."

"What do you mean, leave?"

"Now that the flooded compartments have been pumped out, the *Neva* is functioning tolerably. As long as we don't dive too deep we should be okay."

"Are you suggesting that you might be able to return home on your own power?"

"Maybe not all the way, but enough to get into international waters—very deep waters where we can be picked up by our own forces. Then the *Neva* can be scuttled."

"But I thought that's what you were going to do here—we're over that dumpsite right now."

"That's still an option—after Yuri completes decompressing, but it's by no means ideal."

Nick raised his hands, signaling his confusion.

"The bottom here is only four hundred meters deep.

The Americans and Canadians—if they were to discover the hulk, even after setting off the charges—could still salvage the fragments."

Borodin continued, "Believe me, Major, they have the technical capability to recover everything. If we can get offshore in water twenty times as deep, and have enough time to remove all critical electronics, code equipment, and other gear, the shattered hulk won't be as interesting. Besides, we'll be able to watch the area in case the Americans start sniffing around."

"What about all the activity to the south?" Nick argued. "They're still looking for you there. Besides the helicopter, we spotted one of those sub hunter planes today."

"I expect there's more than just one patrolling. The U.S. Navy has a large air base on Whidbey Island. They probably realize that we were spying on the Nanoose torpedo test area and are trying to escape to the Pacific."

Nick rubbed the stubble on his chin. "That means they'll be waiting to ambush you."

"Yes, but I have an alternative."

"What do you mean?"

Captain Borodin unrolled a navigation chart and placed it on the table in front of Nick. He pointed with his right index finger. "This is what I have in mind."

Nick and Laura were in the captain's cabin, seated at the desk.

"Laura," Nick said, "before we return to the *Hercules*, there's something you need to know."

"Yes?"

"It's about your husband."

"What about him?"

"He's escaped."

"What?"

"I don't know how he did it, but last night after you boarded the *Neva* he managed to untie himself and then slip overboard, probably with a lifejacket."

"How can that be?"

"The last time we checked him was around one in the morning. An hour later, he was gone."

"Where could he have gone?"

"We were close to the shore at the time, several kilometers—about two miles. You could see the lights."

"Two miles! That's a long way."

"It is and the water's very cold. We're certain he wore only street clothes."

"He's a strong swimmer, but with the cold water—"

"I'd say there's a small chance he made it ashore."

Laura fidgeted in her chair. "He's crazy, Nick. I don't know what he'll do." She threw her hands into the air. "I fed him a lot of BS about what was going on. If he gets someone to listen to him . . ."

"Did you mention the *Neva*?"

"No, other than what he overheard when we—" Laura stopped. "But if he was free at that time he had to have seen the *Neva*. It was moored next to the *Hercules*."

"I know. Both Elena and I are convinced that he saw it. That's why we think he risked swimming to shore."

"Then he knows everything."

"I'm afraid so."

"We need to get back to the *Hercules* and get moving."

"Yes, let's go."

As they exited the cabin, Nick's anxiety eased a bit. He had motivated Laura as planned albeit with a twisted recount of Ken Newman's escape.

Surely, Newman had drowned—the water nearly freezing and so far away from land.

That expectation further appeased Nick's angst.

Nick and Laura returned to the *Hercules*. The *Neva* remained nearby, still semi-submerged. Both vessels drifted northward with the current.

Nick, Laura, and Elena huddled around the wheelhouse chart table. A Canadian chart covered its top. Nick summarized Captain Borodin's new plan. A lead pencil line drawn onto the chart outlined the proposed route.

"This is madness!" protested Elena. "How can he ever think they'll make it through there?"

Nick answered, "With some luck and our help, Captain Borodin is confident it can be done."

"It's really not a bad plan," Laura added. "It's very deep most of the way, but there are several shallow or narrow spots that will require operating near or at the surface." She pointed to the chart, tapping a fingertip at the locations. "Seymour Narrows, here at Current Passage, and then up around Alert Bay."

"It's a clever plan," Nick offered. "The Canadians won't be expecting it."

Elena did not buy it. She stared at the chart, studying the sinuous pathway that separated the north end of Vancouver Island from the British Columbia mainland—part of the Inside Passage to Alaska. A multitude of islands, fiords, shoals, and channels lined the route.

Elena looked up. "These channels are narrow. How will it fit through them?"

"That's where we come in," Nick said.

"Right," agreed Laura. "Timing will be critical. We'll be running ahead and . . ."

Nick and Laura spent the next several minutes completing the briefing. Elena let out an obvious groan of irritation. "This plan of Borodin's is too risky. Moscow will never approve it."

"That doesn't matter," countered Nick.

"What do you mean?"

"Captain Borodin's not going to contact Moscow."

"Why not? Now that he's on the surface, he can use all of that fancy radio gear he has on board. I bet he can even talk with Moscow direct."

"True, but he's not going to risk it, even with encryption and burst transmissions. If the Americans or Canadians pick it up, which they very likely will with all of the activity up here, it will confirm to them that hostile forces are in their backyard."

"I still don't like it. We have no authorization for any of this." Elena switched to Russian. "Borodin should scuttle the *Neva* right now and we'll take them all ashore tonight."

"What did she say?" Laura demanded.

"In a moment." Nick then directed his attention back to Elena, answering in their native dialect, "That's not going to happen. Kirov has two days of decompression to go. He can't leave the *Neva* until then."

"What about Yuri?" asked Laura, having heard Nick use his surname.

Nick ignored Laura. "Borodin is not going to sacrifice Kirov after what he's done for the crew, so just forget about that stuff. It's not going to happen."

"Then we'll wait."

"Borodin's not going to wait. If the Canadians get wind of what he has planned, they'll block the escape route." Nick checked his watch. "In less than ten minutes he's expecting us to begin heading north. The *Neva* is going to submerge and follow us."

Elena turned away, conceding defeat.

"What was all that about?" Laura said, addressing Nick.

"Everything's okay."

"Then we should get going."

"Right."

Elena retreated to the galley as Nick and Laura prepared the *Hercules* for getting under way. Elena busied herself by making a fresh pot of coffee. But she seethed, convinced that Nick had stabbed her in the back.

CHAPTER 83

DAY 16—TUESDAY

The *Hercules* approached the Seymour Narrows. The one-half-mile-wide waterway separated Vancouver Island from the considerably smaller Quadra Island. It was slack tide. With currents up to ten knots or more, passage at any other time would be tricky for the plodding *Herc* and the crippled *Neva*.

Nick had the helm and handled the portable Russian radio; Laura monitored the radar display. Elena observed from the rear of the pilothouse.

Laura studied the radar image of the waterway. Trouble was half a mile ahead, heading toward the *Hercules* at eight knots. The orange icon blinked onto the scope just as the *Herc* completed a right turn, passing the red navigation light that marked the south end of Maud Island and the southern entrance to the Seymour Narrows. Land formations had blocked the radar signal until the *Herc* aligned itself with the Narrows. The southbound fishing boat, the northbound *Her-*

cules, and the semi-submerged *Neva* were the only traffic in this stretch of Discovery Passage.

The *Hercules* and *Neva* ran tandem, averaging six knots over the bottom. Separated by just seventy feet of open water, the *Herc*'s wheelhouse ran even with the *Neva*'s sail. Captain Borodin commanded from the sail with his team of observers, all on the lookout for trouble.

To help conceal its presence, the submarine ran semi-submerged, with just the upper half of sail and the massive towed array sonar pod on top of the rudder assembly awash. On radar, the *Herc* and the *Neva* appeared as two vessels running parallel with a smaller boat trailing the pair.

The approaching fishing vessel compromised the *Neva*'s stealth. The partial moon in the sparkling clear night sky created the worry—the *Neva* did not belong in these waters. Nick radioed the threat to Borodin.

Laura turned to the starboard. The *Neva*'s sail appeared black as the night. The phosphorescent wake of both the sail and rudder assembly contrasted with the ink-black waters. She peered ahead. The rack of overhead floodlights on the approaching fifty-eight-foot purse seiner lit up its decks like a Broadway musical. It would pass a hundred yards to the *Herc*'s port.

"What should I do?" asked Nick.

"Stay on course. There's no time for anything else."

"But they might actually see it—for sure their radar does."

"I know."

* * *

Borodin addressed the four watch-standers that surrounded him. "Men," he said in a hushed voice, "remain silent and no moving about for the next few minutes."

Laura stood on the port wheelhouse wing. She peered aft with binoculars. The southbound fishing boat turned to the port, following the reverse of the *Herc*'s course. She did not observe any movement on the decks.

Laura returned to the bridge. "Anything?" she asked Nick.

"All quiet." He monitored the VHF marine radio as well as the secure radio link to the *Neva*.

She checked the radar screen: no new targets.

"Do you think they saw it?" Nick asked.

"I don't know. I didn't see anyone come out on deck. I think that's a good sign."

"And there was no call to the Coast Guard," he added.

Laura stared through the windshield into the blackness of the channel. She hoped the next passage would not be as hair-raising.

CHAPTER 84

DAY 17—WEDNESDAY

All day Tuesday, a steady procession of military aircraft and warships operated in the Southern Strait of Georgia. The FSB team observed from the *Explorer* without deploying the side scan sonar. Later that afternoon when they returned to the marina, a messenger from the Trade Mission met them. Dubova returned to Vancouver. An encrypted message from Moscow waited for her in the mission's code room: *Terminate Operation Eagle and return home immediately.* Russian military reconnaissance satellites had detected the joint U.S. and Canadian ASW search.

"They must be searching for the *Neva*," offered Karpekov as he flopped into a chair by the cabin door and picked up a magazine. The yacht remained inside its Squalicum Harbor boathouse.

"Probably."

Dubova expected the Americans would eventually discover the hulk, employing their vast arsenal of ASW gear. But it no longer concerned her. She focused on executing the exit plan.

Ken Newman struggled to stand, wobbly on his legs. He took a couple steps from the bed to the kitchen. At the counter, he worked the manual can opener, removing the lid from a tin of peaches. He gulped down half of the contents. Juice dribbled down his chin.

Too weak to continue standing, Ken sat in one of the two wood chairs at the tiny kitchen table, placing the can on the tabletop. The one-room shack was about twenty feet square. It was his home for the past two days. He gazed out the single window. The Strait of Georgia was about one hundred yards way. How he made it up the embankment to the vacant cabin continued to amaze Ken.

The swift ebb tide current swept him into a cluster of rock outcrops off the eastern shore of Valdes Island, part of the Gulf Island chain. Just after sunrise, he dragged his frigid and waterlogged body across the rocky shoreline onto dry land.

About a mile wide and ten miles long, Valdes Island was located north of Galiano and Mayne Islands. Sparsely populated with much of the island held in reserve for Canadian First Nations, the island had no water, electrical power, or telephone services.

Ken slurped down the rest of the peaches, draining the syrup to the last drop. He shuffled back to the bed and collapsed.

*   *   *

He sat behind the wheel, monitoring the autopilot. The Herc *surged forward into the oncoming seas as it navigated the Inside Passage. Whitecaps dotted the mid-morning seascape.*

Elena entered the wheelhouse. She sat on the bench seat behind the helm. "Well, it's done," she said.

"What's done?" he asked without looking her way.

"She's no longer a threat to any of us."

"He swiveled the captain's chair toward Elena. "What do you mean?"

"Neither you or Nick would do anything, so I took care of it."

"What have you done?" he yelled.

Yuri raced down the stairwell into the galley and sprinted to Captain Miller's quarters. He ripped open the door. "Oh my God!"

Yuri's heart sprinted as he struggled to pull himself up, horrified by the nightmare. In his dream, he'd discovered Laura's bullet-riddled and blood-soaked body sprawled on the bunk where she'd been sleeping.

Yuri had just enough room inside the recompression chamber to sit upright. Fresh sweat oozed from his brow and both hands trembled. He jerked the oxygen mask off. A bout of coughing doubled him over.

He reached for the intercom handset and triggered the pager.

Yuri heard the buzzer's tone outside of the steel cylinder, his home for the past two days. He had about half a day of decompression to go.

Yuri's watcher sat on a portable chair next to the recompression chamber, dozing. He picked up the handset after the third buzz. "Yes, sir."

"I need to talk with Captain Borodin."

"I'll patch you through to the central post on the intercom."

"No. I need him here—now. Go get him. Tell him it's urgent."

"Yes, sir."

CHAPTER 85

DAY 18—THURSDAY

Captain Borodin stood in the sail with his team of observers. The sun rose an hour earlier but you'd hardly notice. The mile-thick mat of vapor-rich clouds hung just a hundred meters above the sea surface. A chilled drizzle soaked everything, and one-meter-high swells rolled in from the northwest.

The *Neva* was at the very northern tip of Vancouver Island with the Pacific Ocean just ahead.

By following the acoustic trail blazed by the throttled-back *Hercules*, surfacing only in darkness to maneuver the most demanding passages, the crippled submarine completed the transit from the Seymour Narrows to Queen Charlotte Sound in two days.

A hundred meters to the starboard, the *Hercules* bucked into the oncoming seas.

Captain Borodin and Nick Orlov were speaking over the encrypted portable radios.

"He's in really bad shape," reported Borodin.

"What's wrong?"

"While he was decompressing, he came down with

a chest infection. Our medic is certain it's pneumonia—in both lungs."

"That sounds bad."

"It is. He needs to be in a hospital. We don't have the right antibiotics."

"What do you want to do?"

"I think we should transfer him to your vessel. Now that you don't have to babysit us, you can speed back to Vancouver and get him the care he needs."

"Okay, we can do that."

Borodin shifted position inside the bridge well. "Yuri told me that your partner is with the Trade Mission, correct?"

"Yes."

"I think it would make sense for her to contact the mission and let them know Yuri's on his way. They can make arrangements to get him treated and then flown back home."

"Okay, I'll have her phone the mission."

"Do you have encrypted communications aboard?"

"Only what we are using now, but they're short range only so we'll have to use a cell."

"Nothing can be transmitted in the open without encryption. The Americans and Canadians are monitoring everything in the region—land lines, cell phones, texts, e-mails, marine bands."

"Looking for us."

"Yes."

"What can we do then?"

Borodin waited to respond. "After we transfer Yuri, send your partner over. She can use our encrypted radio to contact mission."

"Great, I'll let her know."

A short time later, as the *Hercules* wallowed in *Neva*'s lee, Borodin maneuvered the bow, quartering the oncoming waves. The mass of the submarine's hull partially attenuated the waves, making the transfer possible.

Yuri Kirov was first. Barely able to stand, Borodin watched as two sailors helped him into the raft. Just before shoving off, Yuri raised his right hand and saluted the bridge. Borodin returned the gesture.

With Yuri aboard the *Hercules*, it was Elena's turn. Borodin observed as she lowered herself into the bobbing raft. After she took the center seat position, the two sailors began paddling.

When the raft docked with the *Neva*, Borodin keyed his intercom microphone. "Control, bridge. What's the ETA on that contact now?"

"Sir, target five one remains on the same heading and speed. Estimated time of arrival at our coordinates is forty-six minutes."

"Very well, stand by."

Borodin turned toward the north and pulled up his binoculars. Visibility remained less than two kilometers—about a mile.

This is perfect.

Laura hugged Yuri, pulling him tight with her arms. She looked up, still in shock.

"I thought I'd never see you again," she said.

Yuri smiled and said, "I love you—with all my heart."

They were in the salon alone. Nick just woke Laura.

She'd had the mid-watch and was sleeping in Dan Miller's cabin when Borodin proposed the transfers.

Laura was about to respond to Yuri's tender words when he started coughing. That's when she noticed his pale skin.

"What's wrong, honey?" Laura said, breaking her bond.

He continued coughing, almost doubling over.

"Do you need water?"

He looked up and was about to answer when his eyelids fluttered. An instant later, he collapsed onto the deck with a colossal thud.

"Yuri!" Laura screamed.

Elena Krestyanova entered the central command post. The men sitting at their consoles couldn't help but stare. Elena's skintight jeans, long blond hair, and lovely face were impossible to ignore.

"Dobro požalovat'!"—Welcome—Borodin announced. He offered his hand.

"Spasibo"—Thank you—Elena said, shaking his hand. She looked around. Crowded with equipment and men, the CCP reminded her of a Moscow subway car at rush hour. The ripe odor emanating from the crew didn't dispel the comparison.

Borodin glanced at his wristwatch and said, "We should make the call. I do not like being exposed on the surface for so long."

"I agree, Captain."

He smiled. "Please, follow me to the radio room."

Elena and Captain Borodin relocated to the radio

compartment, a minuscule space located just off the CCP. She sat at a compact table with a telephone-like device mounted on one corner. Borodin stood at her right side.

"Is it ready?" Elena asked.

"Yes. Just dial direct, like a regular telephone."

But there was nothing regular about this phone.

Elena picked up the handset to the encrypted satellite link and dialed. Long ago, she'd memorized the number to the secure phone at the Vancouver Trade Mission.

She held the handset to her right ear. After half a minute, she looked up. "I don't hear anything—no ringing, no dial tone, nothing."

"Hang up and try it again."

She did and while still holding the phone to her ear she frowned. An intercom speaker in the radio room activated. "Captain, control. Radar reports an approaching vessel seven kilometers to the north. It's heading directly for us at seven knots."

Borodin raced back into the CCP. He retrieved a microphone and called the watch officer on the sail. "Bridge, Captain. Can they see us?"

"Not yet, Captain. The visibility remains at about two kilometers."

"Signal *Hercules* that we're diving. Tell them we'll rendezvous at these coordinates when the traffic has departed to transfer the passenger back."

"Aye, aye, Captain."

Borodin turned to face the diving officer. "Ivan, make ready to dive the boat!"

* * *

"What do you mean, it isn't there?" asked Elena.

"They must have departed. See for yourself." Captain Borodin switched on an overhead monitor. Linked to the search periscope, a DVD drive in the CCP recorded all surface observations.

"This is a recording of what I just observed," continued Borodin. He'd already retracted the periscope.

The flat panel screen blinked on revealing gray seas and bleak skies.

Elena stepped closer to the screen. The image slowly tracked to the right. Projecting two meters above the sea surface, the video camera at the top of the search periscope mast came within a foot of inundation as ocean swells rolled in from the northwest.

"It's much rougher now than when submerged." The *Neva* crawled near the bottom for over an hour as the tugboat and its football field–long barge stacked sky high with logs passed overhead. Only when it transited through the area did Borodin risk the observation.

"The *Hercules* must be out there waiting for me," Elena said.

"No, I'm afraid not. We would hear its engine on our sonar. There's no vessel traffic in this area at present."

The color in Elena's face paled as she began to put it together. She ignored the stares from the other nine men that staffed the CCP with Borodin. "So where is it?" she asked.

"The weather's turning and your colleague needs immediate help, so I expect they're headed back to Vancouver."

"So what do I do?"

"You're coming with us."

*   *   *

After running four hours westward, well beyond Canadian territorial waters, Borodin ordered the *Neva* to ascend to periscope depth. Then for the first time in almost four weeks, the submarine's UHF radio mast rose above the surface and beamed an encrypted microburst transmission heavenward to a Russian military satellite. Borodin expected that the Americans might detect the broadcast, but he no longer cared. He reported that the *Neva* was on its way home.

CHAPTER 86

DAY 19—FRIDAY

Ken Newman sat in a chair by the fireplace bathing in the warmth of the blazing Douglas fir. The sun descended behind the coastal mountains of Vancouver Island, casting a chilled shadow over the Valdes Island cabin.

Ken remained dog-tired and sore. Maybe tomorrow, he would feel strong enough to explore his surroundings. He had no idea where he'd landed or how to return home. He was just thankful to be alive.

It had been nearly five days since Ken had a drink. Recovering from his hypothermia-induced near-death overshadowed the alcohol withdrawal symptoms. For the time being, the craving remained muted.

Ken found himself thinking often about what had happened aboard the *Hercules*. The Russian killers had come within a whisker of sending him on a one-way express trip to Davy Jones's locker.

But what rattled him the most was Laura.

She's a damn spy!

* * *

Captain Dubova and Lieutenant Karpekov almost made it home. After the ten-hour flight from Vancouver to Amsterdam, they sat in a packed bar inside the international terminal waiting for their connecting flight to Moscow. Dubova was knocking back her second Stoli when the Samsung came to life. She reached down to her waist and extracted the device from her belt case.

Karpekov could not help but notice. "You have a call?"

"Text."

Dubova opened the messaging box and scanned the communiqué. She then turned the glass display toward Karpekov. He read the one word message:

RIAN.

"Govnó," he muttered.

Dubova surveyed the terminal. She spotted a cluster of pay phones near the next gate. The code word from Moscow required Dubova to use a landline to call a special number that she had memorized.

Karpekov drained his shot glass. After signaling the bartender for a refill he said, "I bet they're sending us out on another mission. Dammit, I wanted some time off."

Duscha Dubova walked toward the phone kiosk. Her colossal frame towered over lesser passengers that milled about. With no strong ties to anyone or any place, starting another mission was fine with her.

CHAPTER 87

DAY 20—SATURDAY

"How much farther?" asked Nick. He sat in the captain's chair behind the helm.

"About sixty-five nautical miles," answered Laura. She leaned over the chart table as she plotted a course.

"So we should be back to Point Roberts around six o'clock tonight."

"Yeah, counting tides that's about right."

The *Hercules* cruised at eight knots as it headed southbound in the sloppy seas of the Strait of Georgia. Massive Vancouver Island loomed toward the west, Lasqueti Island to the east.

Earlier in the morning, they navigated through the Seymour Narrows, this time southbound, without incident. The remaining voyage would be a cakewalk.

"Do you think we'll have to deal with U.S. Customs?" Nick asked.

"I don't know. Other than the place we bought fuel, how would they know we stopped in Canada."

"You're right. Maybe we'll be okay."

"Yeah, let's just keep going. If we get stopped we'll deal with it."

"Fine."

"You'll deal with what?" asked a new voice.

Laura turned around.

Yuri Kirov stood near the top of the companionway that connected the galley and the wheelhouse. He hugged the portside handrail with both hands and dragged himself into the wheelhouse. He then slumped onto the bench seat behind the helm.

"Yuri, dear, why are you out of bed?" Laura asked, hurrying to his side.

Sweat poured from his brow and his face blushed. He'd been coughing a tempest for the past two days, but his breathing, like the rest of him, was improving.

"I was tired of lying on the bunk. Besides, I need to keep working my leg."

The numbness was back.

Laura placed her wrist on his forehead. "You're burning up."

"I'm all right."

Besides suffering from the lingering effects of decompression sickness, Yuri had actually contracted bronchitis instead of the more severe pneumonia. His extended confinement in the recompression chamber and his weakened condition led to the illness. Yuri's sickness mimicked pneumonia, which left him depleted. As part of his pact with Captain Borodin, he had planned to embellish the condition when transferring from the *Neva* to the *Hercules*. But it wasn't needed; Yuri was critically sick. None of the *Neva*'s crew could suspect that Yuri had left for any other reason than medical. The storyline Borodin fed to the crew emphasized that Captain Lieutenant Kirov, their savior and hero, had become so impaired that he might die if not hospitalized soon.

The second part of the deal concerned Elena Krestyanova.

When Elena had placed the call on the *Neva*'s satphone, the transmitter never broadcast a signal. Borodin had disconnected the cable to the antenna port.

And then, just as Captain Borodin had ordered, the watch officer reported the approaching vessel. Borodin already spotted the tug and log barge with the submarine's radar.

After submerging and waiting for the all clear, Borodin made his bogus periscope observation, reporting to Elena that the *Hercules* had already departed.

Elena went ballistic, convinced that Nick left her behind.

"So, what were you talking about?" Yuri asked. "You know, 'we'll deal with it later.'"

"When we return to Point Roberts," Laura said. "Nick and I were discussing whether we need to check in with U.S. Customs when we return—we're not."

Yuri turned toward Nick. "I wonder how Elena is doing?"

Nick just grinned.

Yuri also smiled when he thought about Elena. She no longer represented a threat to Laura or him. It would take her several weeks to return to Vancouver.

Yuri would be gone by then and with Nick's help, there would be no need for her or anyone else to initiate a manhunt.

Nick and Yuri now discussed Yuri's future. Laura listened, feigning intense interest in cloud formations.

"What will you do for work?" Nick asked, still using English.

"I'm not sure . . ." Yuri's voice trailed off as he thought further about the question. "Maybe I will open a hamburger place, like Fat Billie's!"

That drew a chuckle from both Nick and Laura.

Nick continued, "I don't know if that's such a good idea, Yuri. The way you love cheeseburgers—you just might turn into a Fat Billie yourself."

Yuri laughed.

"You could work for me!" Laura volunteered.

Yuri cocked his head to the side. "Doing what?"

"With a little bit of studying and my mentoring you'll be writing code in no time. You already have the basic skills."

"But how will I be permitted to work in America? There are immigration laws, no?"

"I'll figure something out."

Laura stepped down the companionway to the galley. Nick and Yuri remained in the wheelhouse. Nick stood at the helm. Yuri used the opportunity to close a loose end.

"Major," he said in Russian, "will your SVR or the FSB come looking for me?"

Nick shifted his stance. "I don't know why we would. You died on the trip back to Point Roberts and we buried you at sea. End of story."

"Thank you, my friend."

CHAPTER 88

Ken Newman stood on the rocky shore of Starvation Bay at the north end of Valdes Island. Tied up to a nearby floating pier was a sleek twenty-three-foot Grady White. Two elderly men were at the stern, working on something.

Ken walked down the gangway and stepped onto the wood float. One of the men noticed his approach.

"Sorry to be using your dock, mister, but something fouled the propeller. We'll be out of here in a minute."

"That's okay. Take your time," Ken said, masquerading as the owner. He'd already checked the adjacent cabin. Locked up tight, no one was home.

Ken was impressed as he examined the boat, which was tricked out for serious recreational fishing. He walked to its stern and observed the problem. The outboard motor was elevated, exposing the propeller. A basketball-size clump of bull kelp encased the prop.

"Wow, you guys really got into it."

"We sure did," said the taller of the pair. Both men were in their early seventies and appeared overwhelmed with the fouled prop."

"Let me give you a hand with that," Ken said.

Fifty minutes later, Ken sat in a quiet corner of the restaurant sipping coffee, thankful for his good fortune.

After Ken cut away the kelp that strangled the propeller, the two fishers were more than pleased to ferry him to a marina in Ladysmith where he found the restaurant.

Lucky for Ken, his wallet had survived the ordeal, stuffed in the back pocket of his jeans. He devoured the hotcakes, scrambled eggs, and sausages. Finally rested and with his aches and pains mitigated, his body had craved calories.

While he sipped his third cup of coffee, Ken briefly considered contacting the local police. But he soon dismissed the thought. Who would ever believe him? Russian spies, secret operations, his near execution.

Other than his bruised body, Ken had no evidence to back up his astonishing tale.

What had happened to Laura—and her lover? If the Russian assassins were willing to murder him, maybe she had suffered the same fate.

What if she were dead? Maybe she never changed her will. If so, he'd inherit everything.

It was too much for Ken to process. All he wanted now was to hitch a ride to Sidney—near Victoria, catch the ferry to Tsawwassen, and then retrieve his Corvette in Point Roberts.

His most urgent desire was to sleep in his own bed tonight.

CHAPTER 89

For over a week, the *Barrakuda* loitered off the northern California coast until it received new orders. Two days later, Captain Second Rank Oleg Antipov and his crew of sixty-two had arrived at the coordinates provided by Russian Naval Supreme Command.

The submarine maneuvered 320 nautical miles west of Prince Rupert, British Columbia. Antipov ordered the *Barrakuda* to ascend to one hundred meters. As the submarine rose, the inner hull reacted to the reduced pressure by expanding. Mini pops and snaps broadcast into the water column as the steel hull plates shifted. The nominal noise would not trigger any of the U.S. Navy's acoustic bottom sensors. In order to detect such sounds, another submarine would have to be very close by.

And that happened next.

"Captain, sonar. I have a close submerged contact—it just started up. Bearing zero five five. Single screw. Blade count for five knots."

"What is it?" Antipov asked, using a microphone to call the sonar room.

"Working on it, sir. I should have an answer momentarily."

Ten seconds passed. "Captain, I have a positive ID; it's the *Neva*!"

Captains Antipov and Borodin were now connected. Russian submarines come equipped with standard underwater radios, which allows for secure voice-to-voice contact while at close range.

Antipov devoured Borodin's details of the *Neva*'s miraculous resurrection. "This is just incredible, Captain. I've never heard of anything like this."

"We were lucky. The Americans think we're still trying to sneak out through the southern route."

"How can we help?"

"I think we have a good chance of making it across but . . ."

Borodin spent the next few minutes revealing his operation plan.

Although severely damaged, the *Neva* remained seaworthy. Borodin cautiously predicted that his boat could make it back to Petropavlovsk if they took it slow and stayed shallow.

The *Barrakuda* would follow and serve as a lifeboat. At the first sign of trouble, the *Neva* would surface. The crew would transfer to the *Barrakuda* and Borodin would scuttle the boat, allowing it to sink to the bottom—two to three miles down.

"Okay, Captain," Antipov said, "you can count us. We'll support you the whole way."

"Thank you." Borodin said next, "Before departing, we could use some replenishment."

"Absolutely, what do you need?"

"We're low on food and need numerous equipment repairs and . . ."

The *Neva*'s crew had devoured the foodstuffs from the *Hercules* and Borodin had a list of spare parts needed for critical repairs.

The *Barrakuda* had plenty of extra food and many of the requested parts.

Borodin also requested help. His shorthanded crew could barely manage the crippled submarine's systems.

Antipov asked for volunteers and nearly every man aboard responded. The captain selected two officers, five warrants, and three sailors.

The *Barrakuda* rode with the low swells that swept in from the northwest. The late-afternoon cloud ceiling hung low to the horizon. A steady rain obscured Captain Antipov's view from the sail but he could see enough. Riding high in the water, the *Neva* drifted about fifty meters to the east.

Captain Antipov towered over the other watch-standers. He raised his binoculars and focused on the *Neva*'s sail. He counted six men. He then pressed the handheld Transmit switch, activating the boom microphone of his headset. "Lion, this is Lighthouse, come in please."

"Lighthouse, this is Lion, over."

Both short-range radios had built-in encryption systems.

Antipov observed one man raise an arm and wave. "Good to see you, Captain," he said, raising his own arm.

"You too, sir."

"Are you ready to make the transfers?"

"Yes, sir. If you could have your men come along our starboard side that should provide the most protection."

"I'll let them know."

An inflatable raft made it to the *Neva*, and its cargo of food and spare parts was transferred. The raft and its three-man crew remained moored to the *Neva*, ready to return for crew transfers and additional supplies.

Captain Antipov was monitoring the raft when a new individual exited a side door in the *Neva*'s sail and stepped onto the deck. The blond hair marked the woman's presence. He pulled up his binoculars. *"Klássnyy"*—Nice—he whispered as her face and slim torso came into detail.

Borodin had been vague on how the SVR officer ended up on his boat. He wanted her off. With just one toilet that barely functioned, no real privacy, and her constant complaining, she'd become a complete pain in his backside. Even the crew who hadn't been around women for months wanted Elena off the boat.

Antipov agreed to take her. By relocating a couple of his officers, he could give Elena a cabin to herself.

As Elena climbed into the raft, he smiled. It would certainly be an interesting trip home.

*   *   *

Ken Newman made the border just after sunset. He took a cab from the Tsawwassen ferry terminal. Instead of proceeding to the U.S. border station, the cabbie dropped him off a couple of blocks away. He walked westward along a residential street that paralleled the borderline. High-end Canadian homes lined the roadway.

Ken's passport remained in the Corvette. He could not reenter the United States without it.

It took Ken twenty minutes to reach the westerly limits of the 49th parallel. In darkness, he walked over the open border and entered the United States.

CHAPTER 90

With Laura at the helm and Yuri and Nick tending the lines, the *Hercules* docked at Point Roberts an hour after sunset. The workboat moored at the marina's guest dock next to the fuel dock. An eighty-foot yacht occupied the end-tie that the *Hercules* had previously rented. Exhausted, the crew decided to spend one last night aboard. Nick made a quick run to the local grocery store for steaks and wine. Laura prepared dinner.

Nick enjoyed the meal, especially the Merlot. After Laura and Yuri had retired to their cabin, he stood on the port bridge wing, smoking.

Nick took a final drag and flipped the butt; it arced over the floating pier and plopped into the water next to shore. He yawned and stepped back into wheelhouse, ready to hit the sack.

Ken Newman stood onshore in the shadows—spying. Watching one of his almost-killers aboard the workboat was bad enough. Seeing Laura and her lover drove him crazy.

Ken weighed his options. A call to the U.S. border station would do it. Or would it? He still had no concrete proof, just his word against theirs. He'd have to contend with the court order forbidding Ken to be anywhere near Laura.

With Ken's luck, he'd end up in the Point Roberts jail tonight—again.

No, that would not work.

Laura's cheating still infuriated him. He imagined her in bed with the stranger. The vision sent his pulse soaring.

Ken's wrath surged even higher when he again thought of the bastard who had tried to drown him. And then he considered the killer's accomplice who came within a hair of blasting a hole in his skull. Ken had yet to ID the sexy Russian assassin but he expected she was aboard, too.

Ken scanned the boat basin. That's when he spotted the fuel dock. The scheme crystallized.

Laura stood in front of the mirror combing her hair. She wore pink pajamas. Thick white athletic socks covered her feet.

Yuri admired the view from the bunk, his spine propped against the headboard. He'd shed his day clothes for a two-piece set of gray long johns that were six inches too wide in the waist and four inches too short in leg length. He liberated the underwear from the dresser draw next to Laura. They had commandeered Captain Miller's stateroom.

Laura spun around and walked to the opposite side of the bed where she laid down on top of the covers. She turned on her side to face Yuri. "That was a fun dinner with Nick. I really like him. He's funny."

"He's a good man all right. I think he likes living in America."

"I'll say. A Forty-niners fan and he lives on a houseboat. I don't think you have those back in Moscow."

Yuri chuckled. "No, we don't."

They chatted for several minutes, Laura asking about his family.

"Sounds like your grandfather Semyon was a wonderful man," she said with her head propped up by a pillow.

"He was. He really looked out for me. I still miss him."

"Do you have other family members there?"

"No one close."

They next talked about Elena, both relieved that she was out of their lives.

The discussion shifted to tomorrow's activities.

"I think it's best if Nick goes alone," Yuri said.

"Why? I'd like to see him, too."

"I know but in case there's a problem, Nick has the skills to protect himself. You don't."

"Oh yeah, I see what you mean."

Before heading back to Redmond, Laura insisted on checking up on Captain Miller and arranging for the *Hercules*'s return to Seattle. That required a visit to the hospital where Nick had dropped Miller off the week before. All three assumed the critically injured mariner remained at the hospital. Nick continued to insist it was too risky to make inquiries over the phone; the authorities were likely trying to identify the John Doe.

"After Nick visits Miller and finds out what he wants done with the boat, we'll drive to your place."

"Okay, sounds good."

Nick offered to drive to Redmond. Elena's Mercedes remained parked in a marina lot. He had the keys, discovered inside Elena's purse that she'd inadvertently left aboard the *Hercules*.

Finally, after alleviating Yuri's worries about his fake passport and the border crossing at Blaine they would make tomorrow, Laura changed subjects.

She sat up, crossing her ankles. "There's something I need to tell you." She looked away from Yuri.

He noticed how she'd clasped her hands, as if to suppress a tremble.

She turned back. The neutral expression on her face confused Yuri.

"What's the matter?" he asked.

"I'm pregnant—by Ken."

Taken aback, Yuri took an instant to process the news. He broke into a broad grin and said, "That's wonderful. I'm really happy for you."

He slid over to her side and hugged her. "I love you. I'll always be there for you."

"Thank you," Laura said as a solitary tear cascaded down her right cheek.

And then he kissed her.

CHAPTER 91

DAY 21—SUNDAY

Yuri awoke to the pain in his left leg. It was a quarter past midnight. Laura lay beside him asleep.

Will this miserable thing ever heal? he wondered.

Yuri's ailments plagued him but Laura's welfare came first. At dinner, he had wondered why she'd declined the wine.

A baby, he thought. *She'll be a wonderful mother!*

Guilt soon gripped Yuri. Because of his actions—abducting Laura and then seeking her help—the baby would not have a father. All aboard were convinced Ken had drowned.

That would not have happened if I hadn't interfered with her life.

Yuri next thought about his future. No way would he return to Russia. During the southbound voyage, he pried the whole story out of Nick. Their government had abandoned the *Neva* and its marooned crew.

But just what can I do to earn a living here?

Laura wanted Yuri to work for her company, but software development didn't rouse him.

He then considered another idea. *Geophysical surveys use underwater instrumentation. Maybe I could adapt . . .*

Yuri's brainstorm evaporated when a dull thump reverberated through the workboat's hull.

What's that?

"Dammit," muttered Ken Newman as he tripped on an unseen stern mooring line and fell onto the *Herc*'s deck. The plastic tank clutched in his right hand slammed onto the steel plating. The thud echoed across the marina basin.

Ken knelt next to the five-gallon container and checked for damage. Filled to the brim with gasoline, the tank remained intact.

Although the fuel dock had closed hours earlier, one of the Point's gas stations remained open. Ken drove to the mini-mart where he purchased the container and fuel. He also picked up a six-pack of Coors and bought a pocketknife.

Ken remained hunched down on the deck. No lights were on inside the cabin.

He waited another minute and crept forward.

Yuri listened for follow-up noise but heard nothing. Too wired to sleep, he decided to brew a cup of tea in the galley. With considerable exertion, he extracted himself from the bed, using both hands to pull his near lifeless lower left leg over the edge without disturbing Laura. He headed toward the door.

* * *

Ken entered the main cabin and fumbled with the tank's spigot. He tipped the tank and poured gasoline onto the deck.

Yuri stood at the cabin doorway. He could make out a shadowy mass a few steps away in the galley.

What's he doing?

Yuri was about to call out, believing that Nick might be impaired from drinking. But then the stench hit.

Ken tilted the tank forward while stepping aft. Gasoline streamed across the hardwood deck. The fumes stung his eyes. The tank was nearly emptied when a nearby cabin door burst open and a blur rushed toward him.

Supercharged with adrenaline, Yuri rammed Ken with the force of a mini-locomotive. They both crumpled to the deck, Yuri on top.

The gas tank slipped from Ken's grip; it crashed to the deck on its side. Gasoline surged out.

Ken jabbed his left thumb into an eye socket of his adversary and rolled away.

Yuri howled. Blood spurted from the laceration, clouding his vision. But he could see with the other eye. His opponent slithered along the deck through a pool of gasoline, making his escape.

On his knees now, Ken reached into the right rear pocket of his jeans. He removed the knife and pulled out the three-inch blade.

Yuri retackled Ken, pulling him down onto the deck and straddling him. He slammed his right fist into Ken's face. Yuri struck again, and then out of the corner of his good eye he detected a flash of silver.

Ken aimed for the torso just below the rib cage.

Yuri blocked the knife thrust. The blade slashed deep into his left forearm, nicking an artery. He groaned while grabbing Ken's wrist to prevent another strike.

Ken clasped Yuri's other arm.

Ken's breath reeked of beer; sweat flowed from his pores. Yuri summoned a new burst of strength and pressed harder on Ken's knife hand, twisting the wrist. "Drop it," he yelled.

Ken almost complied, the fire in his wrist unbearable, when the pain began to abate. Yuri's strength eroded as blood gushed from the tear in his forearm.

Yuri's shriek woke Laura. She bolted from the bed and rushed to the door. Although the main cabin remained blacked out, she saw Yuri thrashing on the deck with an intruder—a bulky form that appeared to be gaining the upper hand. Both wallowed in the blood from Yuri's wounds; the stink of gasoline permeated everything.

And then the real horror hit Laura.

Oh my God, it's Ken!

Ken rolled back on top of Yuri and straddled his chest. Yuri's left hand still clasped Ken's knife hand, keeping it at bay. But the power in Yuri's wounded arm was ebbing as his body reacted to shock.

Sensing the weakness, Ken aimed for the base of Yuri's neck. He smiled, knowing that he'd won.

"You're dead now, prick!"

"Leave him alone, you bastard!" screamed Laura as she ran forward. She jumped onto Ken's back and lashed at his face with her fingernails.

Ken reared back and bucked Laura off. She toppled onto her side, landing next to a bulkhead. That's when she saw the fire ax, mounted to the wall just a few feet above her head.

Laura reached upward when a phantom figure pushed her aside.

Yuri hung on to Ken's knife arm as both rose. Ken body-slammed Yuri; the back of Yuri's skull smacked the hardwood deck.

Ken again rose, yanking his knife hand free. Yuri could no longer protect himself.

Just as Ken raised the knife over his head for the kill strike, Nick Orlov swung the ax like a Louisville Slugger. The pick end smacked Ken's temple with a gushy thud.

Ken collapsed onto Yuri; the knife spilled onto the deck.

Laura rushed to Yuri's side. She grabbed Ken's shoulders and rolled him off Yuri. Blood oozed from Yuri's right eye and surged from the deep tear in his forearm.

She cradled his head with her hands and said, "Yuri, Yuri, can you hear me?!"

Nothing. He'd lost consciousness.

She checked his body, looking for other wounds.

"Yuri, wake up!"

No response.

She placed her right check next to his nostrils. "Oh, thank you, Jesus!"

Laura turned around to check her husband. Ken's lifeless eyes stared at the overhead. She then stood and surveyed the cabin. It remained blacked out and Nick had disappeared.

"Nick!" she screamed, "I need your help. *Right. Now!*"

She grabbed a towel from a galley drawer and then flipped the main cabin light switch. Nothing happened.

Laura returned to Yuri's side and wrapped the towel tightly around his bleeding arm. She used the flap of her pajama top to swab blood from around his right eye while pleading, "Yuri, wake up! Come on, honey, wake up, please!"

Nick sprinted aft to the main deck and onto the floating pier, where he tripped the shore power circuit breaker and unplugged the power cord.

The fume-rich environment inside the *Hercules* had the equivalent explosive yield of a stick of dynamite. A light switch thrown, a water pump starting, the heater cycling on, anyone of the myriad electrical systems aboard could trigger apocalypse.

Nick ran back and dropped to his knees next to Laura.

"Yuri, please wake up!" Laura pleaded. She faced Nick. "What's wrong with him, why won't he wake up?"

"I'll be right back." He raced up the companionway to the pilothouse two steps at a time.

A minute later, he returned carrying a first aid kit and squatted beside Laura. "Let me try this," he said.

"What is it?"

"Smelling salts."

The pungent odor of ammonium carbonate revived Yuri, but it took a couple of minutes before he became lucid.

"Am I still alive?" he asked, looking up at Laura's beaming face with his surviving eye. Nick flanked her.

"Yes, honey. And thanks to you we're alive, too."

CHAPTER 92

Aftermath

Laura drove Yuri to the same hospital ER where Nick Orlov had dropped off Dan Miller. Yuri was admitted as a U.S. citizen—John Kirkwood—who'd injured himself from a fall aboard his yacht moored at a Vancouver marina. Laura explained that her husband had inadvertently left his ID on the boat in their rush for medical help. Without proof of medical insurance, Laura signed a hospital form guaranteeing payment and used her Visa card to pay the admitting charge.

An ER doc used a local painkiller to numb Yuri's arm and then she stitched the nicked artery. The on-call ophthalmologist treated Yuri's lacerated eye and placed a patch over it. Yuri promised to have the eye checked by his doctor in Seattle.

Finally, just after eight o'clock in the morning, Yuri was discharged from the ER.

On their way to the Suburban, Laura and Yuri walked through the hospital's main lobby.

"Just a second," Laura said. "I want to check something."

She stepped to the counter desk that lined a nearby wall. Yuri hobbled behind.

"Excuse me," Laura said, addressing the receptionist, "but I wonder if you can help me."

"Yes, ma'am. What can I do?"

"I'd like to visit a patient here but I don't know his room number."

"Certainly. What's his name?"

"Ah, Dan Miller, from Seattle."

The young woman checked her computer screen. "Sorry, ma'am but there's nobody by that name here."

"Hmm, we were told he was in an automobile accident a week ago and was brought here. Do you have any John Does? Dan may have not had any ID on him."

"Let me do some checking."

It took several minutes of keyboard inquiries and finally two phone calls before the hospital receptionist made her report.

"We did have a John Doe that was admitted a week ago with a severe head injury." She broke eye contact. "I'm sorry but he passed away three days ago."

Laura stood rigid, bracing her hands on the counter. She felt faint.

Yuri took over. "No, that's not Dan," he said, moving next to the counter. "He had a broken leg, no head injury. And we know he's okay. Another friend of ours told us he talked with Dan by phone yesterday."

"Then he must be at another hospital," the receptionist said, relieved.

"That's probably it."

"Would you like me to check for you?"

"No, that's okay." Yuri pointed to the patch over his eye. "I had a little accident myself. That's why we're here. When we get home we'll call our friend and find out which hospital Dan is at. Thanks for your help."

"You're welcome."

Laura and Yuri walked to the Suburban. It was just ahead. Yuri had his right arm around her waist. He worried that she would collapse. He helped her into the passenger seat and then hauled his battered and bruised body behind the wheel.

"I'm sorry, honey," he said.

"It was my fault."

"No, it was just bad luck."

CHAPTER 93

"How's he feeling?" Nick asked as Laura entered the pilothouse.

"He's resting. The meds finally kicked in."

"Good. He needs to take it easy."

It was early afternoon at Point Roberts. The serene cloudless sky extended to the southern horizon. A slight tremor pulsed in the deck boards; the mammoth diesel deep inside the steel hull idled. A trace tang of gasoline loitered inside the bridge.

"What's the weather report?" Laura asked.

"Light winds from the north, minimal swell. No rain."

"We should make it back to Seattle tomorrow morning."

"Right."

Laura scanned the surrounding marina—wall-to-wall boats. The workboat had relocated from the guest dock to a side tie near the head of the basin.

"You want to take her out again?" she asked.

"*Xorošó* —OK."

Earlier in the predawn morning, while Laura had

rushed Yuri to an emergency room, Nick piloted the *Hercules* solo. After opening every hatchway, door, and porthole and venting the hull for nearly an hour he started the diesel. He then headed into the Strait of Georgia. The stench of gasoline had permeated almost everything. Airing out the cabin was his excuse; Laura didn't question him. She knew what he was up to—disposing of evidence.

Just before sunrise and about two miles north of Sucia Island, Nick deep-sixed Ken's corpse. He used sixty feet of anchor chain and assorted scrap metal looted from the engine room.

Nick then motored back to Point Roberts; he avoided the guest dock when returning to the marina. U.S. Customs and Border Protection officers were busy checking in a Canadian mega yacht that had just arrived. The marina manager assigned Nick a temporary slip for the day.

"I'll release the lines," Laura announced as she started to head below.

"I'm sorry about Miller," Nick said.

She stopped and turned. "So am I."

"We did everything we could for him," Nick said. "It was an accident."

"I know."

Nick smiled. "Remember, you have much to be proud of. You and Yuri saved all of those men who faced certain death."

"Thank you."

Laura again turned and headed down the companionway. The least she could do was return the *Hercules* to its homeport and hope that the heirs to Dan Miller's estate would benefit from it.

* * *

Two people watched as the nearly one-hundred-foot long vessel crept southward in the marina's navigation channel. They stood on a public shoreline walkway south of the guest dock. Both were severely jet-lagged, having arrived at Point Roberts just ten minutes earlier. Unable to book a direct flight from Amsterdam, they had been delayed in Montreal due to aircraft equipment problems. It then took forever to rent a car at Vancouver International this morning.

The exceptionally robust woman held a pair of compact binoculars to her eyes.

"Is that her?" asked the male, a bantamweight compared to his boss.

Captain Duscha Dubova focused on the female standing on the boat's port bridge wing; it was just forty meters away. When they drove past the marina, Lieutenant Grigori Karpekov had spotted the workboat as it pulled away from the dock.

Dubova lowered the glasses, using the strap around her neck for support. She then removed her cell phone from a coat pocket and opened an e-mail file. The Samsung's screen displayed a color photograph of Laura Newman captured over a week earlier.

"Yes, it's the subject."

As part of her report on Yuri Kirov, Elena Krestyanova had photographed Laura and then e-mailed the digital image to the SVR director.

"Who do you think she is?"

"I don't know. Moscow provided no details." The senior FSB officer held up her cell and snapped half a dozen photos of Laura and the workboat.

"That boat looks well equipped."

"It was the one we were supposed to use." Dubova turned to face her charge, holding up the cell phone with a magnified image of the vessel's stern nameplate—HERCULES filled the display.

Karpekov smirked. "I wonder what happened to Elena."

Dubova muttered a curse. She remained peeved that their SVR liaison had left them high and dry.

"What do we do now?" Karpekov asked as the *Hercules* passed around the breakwater. "That boat could be going just about anywhere."

"We're in no position to follow it," Dubova said. "We return to the Trade Mission. I need to use the secure phone to report to headquarters."

"Maybe they'll let us go home now."

"Maybe."

CHAPTER 94

The *Hercules* cruised southward at eight knots with Nicolai Orlov at the helm. Laura Newman and Yuri Kirov walked out of the cabin onto the main deck. Standing near the stern, they watched a lone seagull patrol above the workboat's churning wake, on the lookout for an easy meal.

Laura and Yuri wore parkas to ward off the afternoon chill. His left forearm was in a sling, covered by the jacket. A patch of white gauze covered his right eye; the limp still dogged him.

Yuri glanced forward at the wheelhouse. "Nicolai's turning out to be quite a skipper," he said.

"He's a fast learner, plus I think he enjoys piloting the boat," Laura replied.

Yuri turned back. "What about when it gets dark tonight?"

"I'll help him. With GPS and radar, it shouldn't be a problem."

"Ah, a piece of cake."

"That's right," Laura said, impressed that Yuri had mastered a new American colloquialism.

Laura rubbed her hands together to warm them and said, "Have you given any more thought to what you want to do?"

Not cold, Yuri yawned instead. "Right now, I just want to rest and try to get my health back."

Laura, too, craved physical recuperation. Her body felt depleted. She also was in desperate need of emotional curing.

"You'll find my home quite comfortable," Laura said. "It has a sauna and a hot tub, and a lovely view of the lake."

"Sounds like heaven."

What Laura really wanted to know was Yuri's long-term plan. She worried that he'd have to return to Russia. Despite what had happened, Yuri remained a commissioned officer in the Russian Navy with a brilliant career ahead.

But that could wait.

Later, Laura and Yuri, still on the stern deck, gazed north at the retreating Point Roberts peninsula. From their vantage, it appeared as a jade-capped isle immersed in a placid gray sea.

Laura gestured with her right hand. "It all happened out here."

"Indeed," Yuri said. The dread and repulsion came roaring back in a torrent: the *Shkval* sending the *Neva* to the bottom, his escape, suffering from the bends—twice, his colleagues marooned and he their only hope, the betrayal of his own country, the submarine's resurrection, the death melee with Ken Newman.

Laura said, "You know, Yuri, what happened was truly a miracle."

"I do know. I am blessed, and I thank you and God for it."

Yuri turned to face Laura, leaned forward, and kissed her—a lingering delicious kiss.

ACKNOWLEDGMENTS

Thanks to my sister Julie Urban for her critical review of the manuscript. Her observations and advice were invaluable to me.

I wish to thank Todd Wyatt of Carson Noel for his assistance with negotiating the contract with Kensington Books.

I'd like to thank my editor at Kensington, Michaela Hamilton, for her enthusiasm for the book. Michaela is a terrific editor who took time to work with me to refine and improve the story. It is deeply gratifying that Michaela and her talented team at Kensington really care about my work.

Finally, I'd like to thank my wife, Meta, and my daughters, Kerry and Kim, for encouraging me with my writing career and helping me to make this book possible.

Special bonus for fans of fast-paced espionage
fiction—
Keep reading to enjoy a preview of Jeffrey Layton's
next exciting thriller
starring Yuri Kirov and Laura Newman

THE FOREVER SPY

Coming from Kensington Publishing Corp. in 2017!

CHAPTER 1

It was an ideal time to work on the ice—no wind, clear skies—and a balmy 20 degrees F. The helicopter deposited the two researchers from the University of Alaska onto the frozen sea. Alaska's Point Hope was twenty-eight nautical miles to the east. The international boundary with the Russian Federation lay twenty miles to the west.

The sheer white veneer the men stood on appeared to extend to infinity in all directions. To the north, the Chukchi Sea stretched to the Arctic Ocean and its polar cap. To the south, the Bering Strait connected to the Bering Sea, which abutted the immense North Pacific Ocean.

The technicians from the School of Fisheries and Ocean Sciences had just over two hours to install the equipment before the helicopter would return. Although it was 1:20 P.M., the February sun barely rose above the southern horizon. In about three hours, it would disappear entirely. The chopper pilot refused to fly during Arctic dark.

Designed to measure and record current speed and

direction under the ice-sheet at five depth levels, the array when deployed would extend 170 feet to the bottom. Real-time data from the current meters would be transmitted to a satellite and then relayed to the chief scientist's office at the Fairbanks campus.

Although not expected to survive more than a week or so due to shifting ice floes, the data from the instruments would be used to help verify a mathematical model of late winter water exchange between the Pacific and Arctic oceans. The study was part of a larger effort to document climate change. The polar ice cap was in an unprecedented retreat. By the end of the coming summer, sea-ice extent would likely again shrink to a new record minimum.

It took the technicians an hour to assemble the current meter array, laying it out in a straight line along the ice. Their next task called for boring an eighteen-inch-diameter hole through the seven-foot-thick ice sheet.

The senior tech fired up the gasoline-powered auger, referred to as the "ball buster" for its affinity to toss operators pell-mell when concrete-hard ice jammed the bit. The racket of the auger's top-mounted engine polluted the otherwise tranquil environment.

Finally ready, the senior tech shouted, "Let's go, Bill."

"Okay, boss."

The assistant grabbed the handle on the opposite side of the auger, and the senior tech goosed the throttle. The bit tore into the first-year ice, advancing three feet in about half a minute. A cone of splintered ice mounded around the borehole.

As the auger continued to penetrate the ice, the operator backed off the throttle, expecting the bit to break through any moment. That's when the assistant spotted the change.

"What the hell is that?" he said, gesturing at the black material spewing from the auger hole.

Just then, the bit pierced the ice keel and a torrent of blackish seawater erupted from the hole, pumped onto the ice surface by the still spinning auger. The boss tech switched the engine off and both men extracted the auger from the borehole. More black fluid surged inside the puncture.

"What is that stuff?" asked the assistant.

"I don't know—this has never happened before."

The senior technician dropped to his knees. He reached into the hole with his right arm. A moment later, he pulled up his gloved hand with the tips of the fingers blackened. He raised them to his nose.

"Son of a bitch!"

"What?"

"It's oil!"

"How can that be—we're out in the middle of frigging nowhere."

"I don't know—something's not right."

The senior tech stood. Dismayed, he wiped the soiled glove on the side of his coveralls and said, "I've got to report this right now."

He reached into his parka and removed a portable satellite phone. Forty seconds later, he connected with the chief scientist in Fairbanks.

Within an hour, a transcript of the technician's report would reach the desk of the President of the United States.

CHAPTER 2

DAY 1—MONDAY

Laura Newman cradled the coffee mug, embracing the warmth radiating from the porcelain. She stood on the spacious deck of her home, overlooking the tranquil lake waters. It was half past seven in the morning. Up a few minutes before six o'clock, she'd already run forty minutes, following her usual route of narrow lanes and streets that snaked up and down and across the hillside of her neighborhood.

A snow-white terrycloth robe concealed her lanky frame from neck to ankles; she'd just showered and shampooed. Her damp auburn hair remained bundled in a towel, turban-style. Clogs housed her petite feet.

In her early thirties, there was little need for makeup. Nevertheless, she would complete the ritual before heading to work, touching up her chocolate complexion.

Always a morning person, Laura cherished the solitude of the early hours. She used the quiet time to think and plan.

Once she stepped into her office building, it would be a whirlwind for the next eight to ten hours.

Laura sipped from the mug, savoring the opulence of the gourmet blend. Yuri ground the premium beans and then brewed a pot, something he did every morning.

They had been together for over a year—lovers, best friends, and recently business partners.

Leaning against the guardrail, Laura spent the next few minutes strategizing, preparing for a teleconference she would chair at 10 A.M. With at least a dozen participants from Los Angeles, Denver, and Houston, she would serve as ringmaster for the launch of a new project that would hopefully further enrich her company.

Laura drained the mug—she limited herself to just half a cup a day. She turned and walked back into the living room. A few steps away she entered the nursery; it was just off the master bedroom. Madelyn remained fast asleep in her crib.

Laura beamed as she gazed at her darling daughter. Born eight months earlier, she was finally sleeping through the night. Laura reached down and gently stroked Maddy's angel soft chestnut hair. She stirred but did not wake.

"See you in a little while, sweetie," Laura whispered. Before driving to work, she would nurse Madelyn.

Laura walked into the kitchen.

Yuri stood at the island, his lean six-foot-plus frame propped against the granite countertop and his arms crossed across his chest. A couple of years younger than Laura, the trim beard he wore complimented his slate-gray eyes and jet-black hair. While staring at a nearby wall-mounted television, his forehead contorted unnaturally. Laura had observed that look before and was instantly on alert.

"What's going on, honey?" she asked.

Yuri pointed to the TV; a Fox News Channel logo hovered in the lower left corner of the screen. "Oil spill in Alaska. A big one."

"Where?"

"Chukchi Sea."

"Oh no—isn't that near where you're supposed to work?"

He nodded, his lips pursed.

Laura focused on the television screen. A ringed seal encased in thick gooey oil lay lifeless on a sheet of ice.

"Do they know what happened?"

"No, just that some researchers found the first oil far offshore over the weekend. Then someone else found the seal near Barrow."

"This is going to change everything."

"Yes, it is."